# THE EMPRESS OF FIRE

## THE ZEMIRAN CHRONICLES
### 3

# D.L. BLADE

*To my book besties: Valerie, Kaeli, Rachel, and Danni.*
*Our passion for books was the ribbon that tied our lives together, and that blossoming friendship quickly became a sisterhood. Every time I doubted myself, when I struggled, you all held faith in my strength to overcome and supported me in ways I couldn't be more grateful for.*
*Thank you for being more than my friends.... You four are my anchor when the storms grow fierce.*

# SOCIAL MEDIA

**Goodreads:**
@D_L_Blade
**TikTok:**
@authordlblade
**Facebook:**
@dlblade
**Instagram:**
@booksbydlblade
**Pinterest:**
@DLBlade
**YouTube:**
@DLBlade
**Newsletter:**
www.linktr.ee/dlblade

# AUTHOR'S NOTE

*For book one and two recaps, see the beginning of the ePub edition.*

The third book will bring together the couples from books one and two while introducing new characters and a new love story.

It will be told from multiple points of view from different parts of the realm.

All three books must be read in order.

The last book in the series contains **several graphic and disturbing situations, including sexual assault.** I trust my readers to know their triggers. To read full content warnings, please visit my website, www.dlblade.com

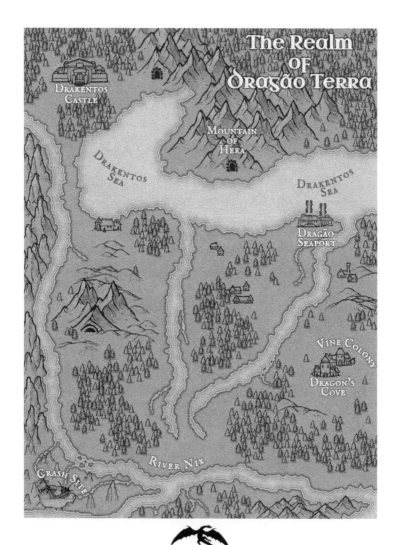

# PROLOGUE

## ANARU

TWENTY-EIGHT YEARS IN THE PAST

DRAGÃO TERRA

As Dragão Terra's sun set over the mountain peaks, the scent of imminent death lingered in the air, tainting its beauty. With smoke overwhelming her, Anaru struggled to breathe. It was much easier to handle the thickness in the air while in her dragon form, but she couldn't transition. They needed to get out of Chaetei as fast as possible.

The sound of dragon wings cutting through the air told her they were close.

Kade had found them.

Her gaze swept across the village, taking in the ash-covered roads and the haunting aftermath of destruction.

Lord Dorion Amulius, leader of the Brotherhood, and his two brothers, Kade and Merrick, had already razed several cities to locate her; Anaru had been on the run with Julian for the last two years. Now her future had changed, nearing a fate worse than death—her captivity within the walls of the Red Dragon Brotherhood.

*Every loss of life is because of me*, she thought.

They moved from one home to another, never finding refuge, even within the sanctuary of the mages' sacred temples.

Now the Red Dragon Brotherhood had found her, and running was tantamount to a death sentence. By defying the gods and choosing another as her mate, she had sealed her fate—an irreversible judgment dooming your path forever. You could find another love—maybe even happiness—but never *truly* find peace.

Anaru didn't want to believe that, though, because what she felt for Julian was real. Pure.

*We must survive*, she thought, holding tightly to Julian's hand as they hurried through the forest, wincing as her bare feet took the brunt of each rock and fallen branch along the way.

Anaru and Julian soon came upon an old, wooden cottage in a clearing. They barreled through the door, rushing to the back of the living room before collapsing to the floor, their heads pressed against the wall.

Her ears rang with the screams of the slain villagers from just outside the forest. Once again, her presence had put an innocent town in harm's way, and its people paid a bloody price.

Two years before, she'd found safety in Graeten, the city of the Ember Guild. That was where she met Julian and fell in love—a love destined to end.

*Because nothing this beautiful can last*, she mourned in her thoughts.

When Graeten no longer felt safe, Anaru and Julian fled, moving from place to place until they came to the quaint town of Chaetei. It was so far from the palace that Anaru believed they would be protected.

She was wrong because nowhere is safe.

The people of Chaetei were their last line of defense, but now those lives were being slaughtered outside of the cottage doors. Mangled bodies littered the village, and burnt flesh was torn from bones lying in smoking heaps. Men, women, and children were all destroyed because of *her*.

Anaru turned as Julian placed a gentle hand on her cheek. He tenderly caressed her light-brown skin with the tip of his thumb while his other hand slipped through her thick, straight, obsidian hair. With a gentle pull, their foreheads touched. "You have to kill me, Anaru," he implored soothingly, his breath skating across her skin while her pulse raced in her throat.

She shook her head, tears streaming down her cheeks. "No," she said, attempting to create space between them, but he pressed his hand firmly to the back of her head, keeping her close. "How could you ask this of me? I can't, Julian."

"If they capture us, they'll know my true nature. They will discover what she is. But if I'm dead, our world will absorb my power, and her secret will be *safe*," he told her.

Anaru placed her hand on his chest. "What if you send us to another realm?" she asked. "I know you've told me countless times that it would be dangerous, but it may be our only hope of escape."

Julian shook his head. "We cannot risk her life. When you enter another land, there's no guarantee that you'll be able to maintain your human form. Your shifting abilities are tied to Dragão Terra."

Anaru placed her hand on her belly, feeling the tiny beating heart through her skin, and the rest of the world fell silent. "I can't leave you," she said. "I won't."

Julian rested his hand on her belly with her. "They will kill her," he said. "We don't have a choice."

He leaned forward, pressing his lips gently to hers. As they kissed, Anaru's hands tenderly held his face, tracing her thumbs delicately along his ivory skin. She wanted to memorize every detail about Julian's face. She tried to carve his image in her mind, to never forget his beautiful, shining white hair, sky-colored eyes, and the sound of his brave heart.

They had to protect their child.

"Someday, Julian," Anaru said in a mere whisper as they broke their kiss, "I will share stories about you with our daughter. She'll know who you are. She will know without a doubt that you love her. More than anything. More than your own life." A rush of wind blew through the open window while tears poured down her golden cheeks. "I'll never love another man as I have loved you." Her voice trembled when she spoke, and she parted her full lips for one last kiss. Anaru hesitated, feeling his heart pound beneath her palm, tears now streaming down his face as she summoned fire, and then magic burned deep into his flesh. "I'm sorry." She closed her eyes tightly. "I'm so sorry."

"I love you, Anaru," he choked out, "from this world into the next."

As Julian slumped over, Anaru rose to her feet, keeping her eyes averted from him. She couldn't bear to carry that final image in her mind.

She gently placed her hand on a nearby chair, feeling the warmth from her fire magic flow through her fingertips. The flickering flames cast crimson sparks that danced gracefully in the air. The magic spread across the floor like a stream of lava, swiftly engulfing every corner of the room.

With the flames rising higher, Anaru hurried out the cottage's back door before she became trapped in the inferno. She tightened her thick cloak, running deeper into the forest and leaving the burning cabin and her beloved behind.

The moment Anaru entered the woods, a wave of grief gripped her heart, mourning the senseless death she was leaving behind. Chaetei had become more than just a place to lay her head down at night; it was her sanctuary in all the turmoil and tragedy. She felt a true belonging amongst the people who accepted her and Julian.

However, death continued its relentless pursuit, leaving those Anaru considered family strewn lifeless on the streets—a massacre orchestrated by the Red Dragon Brotherhood, all in their quest to find her.

Though there was the risk of being caught, by setting that cottage ablaze, she held onto the hope they'd never find Julian's body, and with that, her child would have a chance at survival.

Above the canopy of trees, Anaru heard dragon wings flapping again. She came into another clearing, and her eyes fell upon the Gallow Tree, an oak tree that the villagers would use to administer justice to their criminals. There, Kade landed gracefully beside it, his red wings tucking back into his light bronze skin. Kade

Amulius was Dorion's youngest brother, the most dangerous and unpredictable of the three men.

Kade's self-assured smile caused her to scowl as he strutted toward her. "Quit these childish games, Anaru. Dorion is waiting for you," Kade said as he steadily picked up his pace. He was all sinew and muscle, not having dressed once he transitioned to his human form.

As handsome and powerful as Kade was, she regarded him with disgust. "Fuck you, Kade," she said, holding back tears. "You and both your brothers. Dorion may say he has a claim over me, but I'll never accept him as my mate. You're all traitors and murderers."

Beneath her skin, she felt the presence of her dragon, desperately wanting to unleash its wrath upon Kade. But with the growing child inside her, she couldn't risk it. Exhaustion had taken Anaru, and she sank to the ground, trying to catch her breath.

Kade raised his hand and signaled with his fingers for her to stand. However, Anaru refused to move, not because of the horror that awaited her, but because the pain of losing Julian had stunned her body into complete stillness. The weight of his death by her actions weighed so heavily on her heart, and she would have to keep that secret until she took her last breath. Anaru couldn't even process what had just happened and grieve properly. She couldn't even shed a single tear.

Kade rolled his eyes and then grabbed her at the elbow to pull her with him. She used her other hand to tighten the cloak around her body, concealing her belly.

"Keep your claws sheathed on our journey," he said. "It's time to come home."

They traveled for several hours, and for the first time in two years, the stark reality of her captivity set in. With each thump of her heart racing against her ribcage, an overwhelming fear surged through her body. She would no longer taste freedom nor feel the wind against her wings as she glided through the beautiful amber skies.

In one last desperate attempt to escape Kade's powerful hold, she dug her nails into his skin. All he did was squeeze tighter, and she winced in pain.

"That's enough, Anaru. I'm twice your size, so I suggest you quit trying to fight me before I break your arm."

He shoved her forward through the doorway of the house—a cave—deep in the forest beside the sea. It wasn't too far from the palace, a quick journey through the woods before reaching the field that led to the gates.

Gas lamps lit each wall, and small amounts of sunlight trickled in from the skyline through the mountaintop, lighting up the more open community spaces.

As they approached Dorion's bedroom, Anaru planted her feet, trying to stop herself from crossing through the threshold. Ignoring her fight, Kade threw her forward inside. This caused her stomach to hit the floor, and she winced, feeling the intense burn inside her belly.

*Shit*, Anaru cursed in her thoughts, knowing she had hit the floor too hard.

When she looked up, Dorion had appeared at the door, watching her.

His shoulder-length, wavy brown hair touched his shoulders—it was longer than she remembered. His yellow-brown eyes glowed brighter, and his tanned, muscular torso had new, black, branch-like markings along the chest and to his neck. He breathed power and strength as he stalked forward, his eyes never leaving hers.

She cut him with a sharp look as he approached, kneeling beside her and stroking her long, dark hair. He looked over her body, noting the soot staining her arms and the tattered state of her feet.

*He hasn't noticed yet,* she thought. *But the moment this cloak is gone...*

"Welcome home, Anaru," he said. But as he gave her a smug smile, Anaru slapped him hard across the cheek.

"You're a monster! A traitor! *Where* are my parents, Dorion? Are they still alive?" she asked, ignoring the venomous, stone-cold glare he gave her. The grim look on his face answered her question. "You bastard!" She spat in his face, a new wave of pain seizing her heart. "The throne to rule this land will never be yours. I'll not stand by and watch you destroy everything my bloodline has built. All this death and destruction just because your ego got hurt after I left you and that a *woman* would be your ruler someday. Rejecting you was the greatest experience of my life because I knew any other path was better than the one in your arms. I saw the real *you*, Dorion, and it was despicable."

Dorion reached out and caught her throat, pulling her to her feet at arm's length. Anaru froze, knowing there was no way to fight a dragon as strong as him. He adjusted his grip on the back of her neck and shoved her toward the bed.

As she turned to run for the door, she saw her cousin, Dergis, step into the bedroom, and relief swept over her.

"Lord Dorion," Dergis said, clearing his throat. "May I please speak with her?"

Hesitantly, Dorion nodded and stepped back, allowing Dergis to come further into the room.

His amber eyes looked as pained as she felt inside, and a heavy sob escaped as she desperately clung to her cousin, burying her head in the crease of his neck. Anaru's tears soaked his tunic and trickled down his olive-toned skin.

"Dergis, what are you doing here?" Anaru asked, pulling back. "Are you okay?"

"Surviving," Dergis said, tilting his head to the right. "As much as anyone else here. They've destroyed the palace, killed your parents, and I..." His voice trailed off, and he looked out the window behind her instead of her eyes as if ashamed. "Anaru, if we don't pick sides, my baby and wife will fall with them."

She shook her head. "It didn't have to be like this, Dergis. You could have run with me."

Dergis gave her a slight grimace. "Running is not a life, cousin."

"And living under the Brotherhood's claw is?" she said. "Where is the freedom in that? They killed *both* of our parents. They attacked our home."

"I know. But we either join the Brotherhood or we die. At least we have a new home *here*. Those loyal to Dorion will have food, water, and a place to fly. Besides, this place is where your mother was born and grew up. You know the colony better than anyone else. The people here will respect us."

Anaru stepped back from her cousin. "With exceptions, Dergis," she said, glaring at Dorion. "I'll not change who I am. If that means that I die, then I die."

"You best abide by the new law, Anaru," Dorion interrupted. "The people will soon elect Dragão Terra's new emperor."

"Have you forgotten the order of law?!" she shouted. "You don't carry Rylanthion blood, which means the Council of Drakentos must be the ones to elect the next ruler or select someone else from *my* bloodline." She snuck a glance at Dergis. Her cousin would have to agree to the role of being the new emperor, but she knew he wouldn't. To challenge the Amulius brothers would be certain death, and his loyalty was to his wife and child. It wasn't to her. "They would never elect you to govern our world."

Dorion smiled and folded his arms, as if her words amused him.

There was no denying Dorion's beauty. Any woman would have dreamed of being marked as his mate, but she had seen the monster he'd become since his father died and he became the leader of the Red Dragon Brotherhood. Their protection was not worth being chosen by someone who would kill anyone who stood in his way in the most brutal, vile fashion.

"The Council will hear my words, and when I share with them that the stars chose you as my mate, they'll realize you and I were made to rule this world together," Dorion said. "I *own* you, Anaru. I always have. Do you realize what kind of embarrassment I've endured after the woman I claimed ran from me and hid for the last two years? Choosing another life other than what I could have given you here? Power. Wealth. Love."

He closed the gap between them and grabbed her arm, but she refused to back down.

"My parents gave me a choice," she said, trying not to show how painful his grip was. "I was next to rule this land, Dorion. Not you. Not a *man*. For the first time in history, the royal family gave their female child a choice. I took it. I chose to leave and deny you what you thought was yours." A defiant smirk touched her lips. "I would sooner die than give you my heart."

Dorion released her arm and lifted his hand to strike, but when she covered her belly instead of her face, he stilled. Her gaze slowly returned to his.

Pulling back her cloak, Dorion revealed her stomach. The yellow in his irises dimmed, almost black. "You're fucking *pregnant*?" he fumed, stepping forward, forcing her to move back and hit the bedpost behind her.

Anaru kept her lips shut. They couldn't know what Julian was. She had to come up with a lie, something to placate Dorion. "I met a dragon, fucked him, then went on my way," she said. "He meant nothing." Though she hated the lie, his wrath would be worse if he knew how much she loved Julian.

Dorion's smug look caused a primal urge in her to attack, but he'd overpower her within seconds. Male shifters were stronger than females, and Anaru wouldn't risk her baby by fighting a man twice her size.

"Of course, he meant nothing. You're *my* mate after all. The only one your heart will ever go to is me. But that *thing* inside you..."

As fear clutched her chest, agonizing pressure grew between her legs, and water dripped down her thigh.

"Oh, my Gods," she cried, falling forward into Dorion's arms. She hated his touch, but the strength in her legs failed as the pain ripped through her.

"Fuck!" Dorion cursed. "Dergis, get Borenna. Now!"

Dergis, who had been standing silently behind him, nodded quickly and ran from the bedroom while Dorion helped her onto the mattress. The pain was immense, and she knew the baby would arrive any second. Anaru spread her thighs and took slow, deep breaths. She was prepared to deliver her child alone if she had to.

Her hands rested on her round belly. She could feel her child move, ready to emerge from her womb and spread her wings for the first time. Anaru checked to see if her baby was crowning yet, and as she pulled her hand away, she noticed it was coated with blood. Panic trickled like ice down her spine. Another tearing pain wracked her body, and Anaru screamed.

When Dergis returned, he brushed Dorion aside with his shoulder to stand beside her. She knew she couldn't communicate aloud with Dorion standing there, hovering over her, but she had to reach him.

"*Dergis, I need your help,*" Anaru said through her thoughts, projecting to him and only him through their familial dragon bond. "*Please. He's going to kill her. You have to help me.*"

Dergis shook his head but kept his features neutral. "*I won't let that happen, cousin. If it comes to that, Luna and I will take and raise your child as our own. I will make Dorion listen. You can be with Dorion as his queen and still—*"

"*No!*" she shouted down the bond, watching Dergis flinch slightly. She could barely breathe or think. "*You don't understand. They'll kill her because she isn't fully dragon.*"

The faint glimmer of hope Anaru had during the journey to the cave had clouded her reason. But now, in immense pain, she was thinking clearly. There was no negotiating with Dorion.

Anaru's eyes flickered toward the hallway as Merrick and Kade rushed through the door and inside the cell. Borenna, the colony's oracle, pushed past them to reach her.

Dergis gave her a quick nod and stepped back.

Borenna was a tree dryad, a revered entity in Dragão Terra. She possessed the power of foresight and counseled many rulers in Anaru's family. Borenna had the body of a human woman, but her skin was covered in dark brown bark and thick green leaves, and her limbs resembled branches. She had helped deliver generations of Rylanthion children, including Dergis and Anaru.

"Easy, Anaru," she said, climbing onto the mattress and settling between her legs. "You did well, princess. I want you to take slow and steady breaths. Stay with me. Okay?" Borenna's vine tendrils extended out, reaching between her legs. She positioned herself carefully, ready to catch the child when she pushed.

"Borenna, something's wrong. I'm bleeding too much. The baby—" Anaru panted, sweat beading her forehead. Her words grew thick on her tongue, and her vision darkened.

Anaru's head spun as the blood gushed between her legs. Dergis rushed forward and grabbed his cousin's shoulder, resting his hand on her back to help her sit straight. "What's wrong with her?" he said, reaching out his other hand to grip hers. "What's happening?"

The tree-like woman closed her eyes, tilting her head to the side. "I...I see something," the oracle said. When she opened her eyes, they were milky white. "Anaru, you're going to bring Death into our world—a darkness that will plague your people."

Anaru shook her head while Borenna moved her branches, and the leaves fell around her as Anaru pushed.

"Not yet," the oracle said, snapping out of the vision. "Don't push yet."

"She's coming," Anaru cried, unable to comprehend the reading Borenna forced upon her. "I can't—"

After one more push, Anaru's child's head pressed through her opening, followed by her shoulders and body. The oracle gently cradled the newborn in a small blanket, her branches delicately securing the baby's head from falling back.

After she eased off the mattress, she turned to Dorion. "She's healthy and beautiful."

Anaru let out an exhausted cry, tears running down her cheeks.

Dergis wrapped his arm around Anaru, giving her a comforting squeeze. "You did it, cousin," he said to her, but all Anaru could focus on was watching Borenna hand her daughter to Merrick and not being allowed to cradle her in her arms. Not only pain but fury burned inside her.

Anaru hauled herself up and off the bed, reaching for her and gripping Merrick's elbow. "Give her back!"

"Release Merrick's arm, Anaru," Dorion said from the doorway, his icy demeanor sending numbing fear through her. "That child should never have been born. Let go of my brother and be done with this!"

Anaru ignored the steady flow of blood trickling down her thighs and onto the wooden floor. She dug her nails deeper into Merrick's flesh. "She deserves to live, Merrick. Please, I will—"

As Anaru studied Merrick's hesitant look, she heard the walls crack above her, causing her to look up. The cave's stone walls violently split into two, and debris rained from above. The world seemed to shatter, and a blinding light burned into her vision.

While Merrick looked up with her, Anaru seized an opportunity to rescue her infant daughter once more. She yanked on his arm, but her grip slipped when he pulled back, causing her to lose her balance and send Dergis and Borenna crashing to the floor with her. Merrick spun on his heel and bolted out of the collapsing bedroom, taking Anaru's baby with him.

Anaru screamed for her child while the floor broke open beneath her.

A tremendous pulling sensation seized Anaru, Dergis, and Borenna, and they fell through the crack, zipping through time and space.

Suddenly, everything became eerily dark. When Anaru opened her eyes, there was nothing but water, the feeling of algae and rock below her feet, and the salt stinging her eyes as the sea enveloped her.

Long fingers gripped her arm as she sank, bringing her to the surface.

It was Dergis.

The delicate sand stuck to her skin as he pulled her onto a small island's shore. Anaru cast her eyes around, desperately searching for the dryad—the oracle—but she wasn't there.

"Borenna! Borenna, where are you?!" she shouted.

When Anaru glanced down, she saw splashes of blood in the sand. She was still bleeding; the pain from her torn skin caused her to almost faint. Anaru groaned and doubled over, drawing shallow breaths into her lungs.

"Dergis, I'm still bleeding pretty badly. I need something to staunch the flow, or I'm going to die."

Dergis glanced around frantically, trying to find something to stop the hemorrhaging, but the land was barren. He removed his shirt, handing it off to her, so she could place it between her legs.

"What is this place?" Dergis asked. "Where did the portal send us?"

Anaru bent down and moved her hand through the sand, taking a handful in her palm and feeling the grains against her skin. "I...I don't know," she said. "But if we are in another realm, you know what that means for our dragon forms."

Dergis lowered his gaze as he watched more blood trickle down Anaru's leg. "Fuck." He pointed to a stream. "Come on. We need to clean you in fresh water. I can see a stream just up ahead." He wrapped an arm around Anaru's shoulder and slowly guided her further into the island.

The crystalline stream shone radiantly, as if the magic of the stars had created it. Before reaching the sea, the stream formed a small pool where the water was collected. Dergis cautiously guided Anaru into the water, which appeared deep enough for wading.

She felt euphoric as the water lapped over her legs and torso. When she looked down, the blood flow had stopped. "How is this possible?" she asked, feeling between her legs. Her wounds had knitted together, and her strength gradually returned.

Anaru blinked, her brows pulling together.

"Dergis?" she said. "The water...it's *healing* me."

Dergis groaned, falling to his knees, and slowly looked up at her. His skin turned to scales, and his wings flapped out. "I'm shifting," Dergis said. "Fuck! I can't control the change, Anaru. I'm trying." Anaru hurried out of the water toward Dergis, but before she reached him, her wings ripped free from her back, knocking her to the ground, and her body began to take on her dragon form. Anaru had no power to stop it, just as Julian had predicted would happen if they left Dragão Terra.

Once the transition was complete, Anaru willed herself to shift back, but nothing happened. Her claws dug deep into the sand, and she looked up at her cousin.

Together, they turned their attention to the sky, but at that moment, it wasn't the foreign world the portal had thrown them into that she feared; it was her child's life. Would she ever see her again, and would Dorion kill her as he promised?

As fury thickened her veins, she turned to Dergis, projecting her voice to his mind. *"I'll not stop trying to find a way for us to get out of this world, cousin, and I will make sure every last member of the Red Dragon Brotherhood pays for what they've done."*

# I

## MAZIE

### PRESENT DAY

### MOMENTS AFTER THE CRASH IN DRAGÃO TERRA

As Lincoln wrapped his arm under Anaru's armpits and lifted her up, her legs buckled beneath her, causing her to slip from his grasp and fall back onto the ground.

Lincoln leaned down and placed his hand on her back, just beneath the ribcage. "Fuck," he cursed as his eyes slid over a wound, his hand coated in blood. A four-inch shard of plank wood from the boat was lodged deep into her side, which they hadn't noticed while she was lying down. Anaru pushed herself onto her knees, reaching around and pressing her hand on the jagged wood. Blood oozed from the wound between her fingers, and she winced when she shifted on the rock, leaning her body into Lincoln's chest for comfort.

"We can't remove it. Anaru will bleed out," Mazie cautioned, watching Anaru look up, the embers of her irises burning as tears glistened in her eyes. "Tegan, can you help her?"

Tegan rushed over and knelt beside Anaru, placing her hands over the wound. "My magic doesn't heal, Mazie, but I can try. Elf magic is better for this."

They all turned to Aiden, but Mazie shook her head. "Elven light is something else," Mazie said. "She'll have to anchor Aiden's magic, but I don't want him touching her. We need Janelle."

"We don't even know where Janelle and Elijah landed," Tegan reminded her.

Mazie stared blankly at the Kroneon, now smashed beyond recognition, the shattered pieces slipping between her fingers and falling to the ground. She opened her hand and let the remaining shards of metal fall. "Well, shit," she cursed silently.

Choosing to enter that world was one thing, but being unable to head back to Earth was entirely another. Without the Kroneon, they were fucked.

The plan was as simple as they all had thought it would be when they discussed it earlier that day. They were to stab the Shadow Creature and force it into another world. If they had failed, at least Myloria would have been safe. The ship and the Kroneon shattering into pieces wasn't part of that plan.

They were now stuck, and the only person who knew the realm better than anyone else was too injured to move.

"What now?" Nola asked, worry shining in her amber eyes.

Mazie glanced over her shoulder at Tegan and then looked back at Nola. "Ask Tegan. I sure as fuck didn't send us here," she said, exasperated.

Tegan looked up. "From what we know, the Newick witches created the Kroneon and their gems by elemental magic tied to Earth, and though a dragon holds some power, it may not work in Dragão Terra. Even if I could figure out how to piece it back together."

She held her hand out. "Mazie, give me the Kroneon's key." Mazie walked over and placed the ruby in her palm. "See?" Tegan said sadly. "Even the key has cracked at the center. I can't feel any trace of its power." She rose to her feet, collected the broken compass pieces from the ground, and placed them in the pouch around her waist. "We may be stuck here until we get the Kroneon fixed. *If* we get it fixed."

Mazie noticed Tegan had dropped Aiden's sword on the ground when she went to tend to Anaru. She hurried over, watching the elf to gauge what he would do. She carefully picked it up and gripped the hilt tightly, stepping back.

Aiden didn't even attempt to lunge for it; he only observed her, which made her more uneasy. Aiden claimed that the dark force inside of him had subsided with Kieran's death, but Mazie felt differently. She sensed that power was merely biding its time, waiting to strike when they were most vulnerable.

The last thing they needed was an Elven warrior possessed by powerful dark magic to have the one weapon they knew could defeat any evil in their world. Mazie walked back to the group, giving Aiden a wide berth. "What should we do now?" she asked her captain.

Lincoln, who now had his hand on Anaru's wound, lifted his gaze to the sky, as if taking in this new world all over again. "We'll have to find out everything we can about this place," he said as Anaru leaned into him. He wrapped a wool blanket Nola had salvaged from the wreckage around her shivering body. "This is not a world we've visited before. I didn't even know—" He paused, looking down at Anaru, who hadn't spoken since the crash. Instead, she seemed lost in a daze, staring at the tiny river flowing through the sandy terrain.

"Didn't know this realm existed?" Mazie asked. "Or didn't know your dragon was a shifter?"

Lincoln met Mazie's eyes. "Both."

The little voice in the back of Mazie's mind reminded her that venturing into another world had risks, but they didn't have a choice when the entire country of Myloria and all those who lived there were at stake.

Mazie placed Aiden's sword by her feet and unzipped the bag she'd brought, filled with supplies to aid them if something had gone wrong. "It doesn't matter now," Mazie said, pulling out her pistol. "The only thing I care about is getting the fuck out of this place once we find Janelle and Elijah. Bay and I will stay on the ship. Before we fought that creature, I had stocked the Sybil Curse with food, water, and weapons. We can't just abandon the ship, Captain."

They weren't near the ocean anymore, but they landed in the middle of a burned forest surrounded by rock and a tiny stream of water to their right. The ship had landed at the edge of a short, muddy hill—as if it had just rained—tilting itself into a tree. Upon impact, the Sybil Curse had been torn in half and smashed into splinters of wood and rope.

"Mazie," Lincoln called. "It's not safe to stay here alone. That pistol won't do shit against a dragon. Aiden's sword might be our only hope, but even then...We don't even know what exactly this place is or what to expect."

"No," Mazie retorted. "We don't." She gestured with her pistol toward Anaru. "But *she* does. Perhaps Anaru can stop staring at that damn river and speak to us."

Mazie looked down at the dragon shifter, whose slender body slowly curled into a ball, knees tightly pressed to her chest despite the dreadful wound on her back.

Mazie threw up her hands, shifting her attention from Anaru to Aiden again.

She didn't trust the elf after what Kieran did to him. The darkness within Aiden was his new comfort, much like a warm, soft blanket lulling him to sleep. The responsibility to the warrior was now Tegan's problem. Mazie was the only one who protested when they suggested Aiden help them pull the ship through the portal.

*No one fucking listened!* she screamed in her thoughts.

Now they were stuck with an unpredictable Elven man with Newick magic coursing through him—the kind that fed on power and malice.

"Alright," Tegan said, drawing Mazie's attention back to her. "This is what I think we should do, at least." Tegan walked up to the dragon and met her eyes briefly before her gaze turned to Lincoln. "We need to get that sliver of wood out of her and then use fire to cauterize the wound. There's no other choice. We can't leave her bleeding out on this rock." She turned to Anaru. "Use your human voice, Anaru. What dangers are we to expect here?"

Anaru lifted her head to look at her, moving her thick, black hair away from her eyes. "We're near the River Nix," she said in a soft, feminine tone. Her accent didn't match theirs; it had a melodic cadence that danced like flames. "The palace is a day's journey on foot, but shifters destroyed it two years before I departed from this world. My enemies hunted me down and attacked us twenty-eight years ago in a remote village—almost everyone I loved died that day." She paused, looking over until she made eye contact with the captain. "The last time I was here, rebel dragon shifters kidnapped me and took me to their den. I was only there for minutes before I gave birth. The moment my child took her first breath, they snatched her away from me. They stole her, Lincoln." She looked down at her feet, and a hard sob escaped her. "For the last three decades, I've believed they had killed her. I never even tried to come back once I gave up hope."

"And why is that?" Lincoln asked. "Why come here now?"

"The oracle on Kieran's land told me to. Her name is Borenna, and she's from Dragão Terra as well. Borenna once lived with my parents and me in my home before the Lord of the Red Dragon Brotherhood, who started the rebellion, abducted her, forcing the dryad to work for him and his two despicable brothers. She shared a vision with me before we fought the Shadow Creature. I saw that my captors had taken over the castle, rebuilt it, and are now ruling this land. I then saw my daughter standing in a field right outside its gates. She was afraid, Lincoln. My Gods, she was so afraid of...something."

Anaru winced as she clambered to her feet, pressing her wound tightly with one hand.

"Anaru, you need to sit," Lincoln said, catching her slightly on her hip as she fell forward.

"I'm fine," she said, balancing herself on the rock as she attempted to walk on her own. "I sensed Borenna's presence inside Kieran's mansion when I landed in Myloria for the first time. When we fought Kieran, she had made her way onto the field, reaching out to me and connecting our minds." A lone tear fell down Anaru's cheek. "My daughter is alive, Lincoln, but she's in grave danger."

As Anaru stepped forward, she paused and looked over her shoulder at Nola and the others. "I'm sorry I brought you to this place, knowing the dangers ahead." She winced, pressing down on the wound again. "But I didn't know any other way."

"How did you even get into our world to begin with?" Nola asked.

Anaru opened her mouth, but Mazie scoffed. "We're going to get ourselves killed!" the pirate said, scowling at the captain. "Anaru, I have grown to love you as much as the captain has these last two years. Believe me when I say we'd risk our lives to protect you. But we're not from this world. We don't have a fucking clue how to fight your people. If there were even a chance we could win, then I'd say fuck yeah...let's go. But even I'm afraid, and that doesn't ever fucking happen."

"So, what is the alternative, Mazie?" Lincoln asked. "Leave Anaru, who has saved our lives more than once, might I add? We owe it to her to try, at least."

Mazie glanced at Anaru. She knew the captain was right. Although she never had children of her own, a part of her empathized with Anaru for the lengths she'd gone to protect her family. Mazie would do the same for the captain, the crew, and Bay.

"Oh shit, where's Bay?" Mazie asked, a sudden panic hitting her in the chest as she looked around frantically, only to spot the pixie sitting quietly on a broken plank by the ship, watching them. She gave Bay a small wave, and her friend waved back while avoiding the banter.

*This wasn't her problem,* Mazie thought.

Nola smiled at Mazie. "You know what we must do," Nola said. "Right now, Anaru is asking us to put her first, for once."

Mazie gripped the Elven sword, nervously biting her cheek. After a few hesitant moments, she gave Nola a subtle nod while keeping her expression neutral.

In their world, Anaru was a fierce dragon who risked her own life in each realm the Kroneon sent them to. She'd position herself between the crew and any creature who tried to attack them until they ran to safety. Mazie reminded herself that Anaru wasn't just a dragon who bonded with her captain...she had become their family.

Anaru looked up at Lincoln until their eyes met. "Lincoln, I chose you to be my rider because I saw deep within your heart. Dragons can see what a human cannot. You were the first human I trusted completely. I told myself that even though you had the Kroneon in your hands, I couldn't bring you here, but the more we used it, the more I thought of my child and wondered if she was still alive. Once I learned the truth through that vision, I had to return, no matter the cost. For that, I'm deeply sorry."

Mazie stepped forward, her features softening. "What did your enemy want with you?" she asked.

Anaru looked away. "He marked me," she explained.

"Marked?" Nola asked. "Like, claimed you as his mate?"

Anaru nodded. "This world bears many resemblances to Earth. One of them being the destiny of fated mates. Although people can choose their mates in your world, our gods determine our relationships here. Once you're marked and chosen, that's it. You must marry and become theirs. But—"

"You fell in love with another," Mazie finished for her.

True love was a fairytale in Mazie's mind. Her father had a deep love for her mother before he passed away. He was as caring a father as he was a husband, and after he died, Mazie cursed the gods for taking such a decent man from the world. Mazie's mother never loved another, and Mazie never wanted to experience the pain she had witnessed in her mother's eyes.

Of course, she and Veronika shared a love when they were younger, and Mazie believed it was real...but it sputtered and died. Veronika didn't fight for her when the rest of Mazie's family blamed her for her sister's death.

She was alone.

Unlike Anaru, Mazie had the freedom to decide who she loved. It was her decision alone to choose whom she would spend the rest of her life with.

"The moment she was born," Anaru began again, "they ripped her right from my arms before I even had a chance to memorize her face."

Nola's eyes were filled with pain as she took a step forward and held Anaru's hands. "I'm so sorry, Anaru," she said. "I cannot imagine what that was like, watching them take her from you."

"Nola, I never even got to hold her to my chest," Anaru said. "Seconds after giving birth, they took her from Borenna, who attended me, and then something else happened. The ground shook beneath us, creating a portal from the elements of our world. I teleported through it, taking my cousin, Dergis, and the oracle with me."

Lincoln held up his hand. "Wait...Anaru, are you telling us you moved through a portal with nothing?" he asked. "Without a Kroneon?"

She nodded. "Upon landing in your world, we came upon the Eastland Forest. There, we found that the island's water had magical healing properties, which healed my wounds from childbirth. However, your land suppressed our magic to shift freely and turned us into our dragon forms. Our ability to become human again had become lost. It all happened a few years before Cassia, Argon, and their people were exiled from Zemira. Once they arrived, they discovered us and declared us *their* dragons. We had been the only ones on that island for so long that we embraced a new family. The Fae didn't even know where we came from, all while Borenna ended up in a different land far from us."

"Myloria," Nola said. "Right into the hands of the Newick witches. Enslaving her to their power."

Anaru shook her head. "Not at first. Borenna told me she traveled the lands for almost twenty years, desperately searching for me and Dergis. When she met Kieran, he took her in and made her feel safe. Once she had settled with the Newick coven, she realized she could no longer leave. They had trapped her."

As Anaru wiped tears from her eyes, Mazie saw the pain etched on her face—the events from her past had traumatized her.

"I've been in your world for almost three decades, but I have not aged," Anaru continued. "Once we reach adulthood, dragon shifters don't age like humans. My enemies will know it's me the moment I'm spotted. We need a hiding place until I figure out exactly where my daughter is."

"Was it your power that opened the portal, then?" Tegan asked. "If the Kroneon can't be fixed, then perhaps we might have some hope of getting home."

"I'm sorry, Tegan," Anaru said, shaking her head. "Portals and other realms are no secret to our people, but the power that took us there was not mine. I wish I had more answers for you, but I don't. Right now, we need to search for my child."

Tegan nodded and looked back to Lincoln.

"And my sister," Aiden said from a distance, speaking for the first time. His malicious eyes made Mazie's jaw tighten and caused her to step back instinctively, gripping the sword.

Nola looked at him. "We would never leave Janelle and Elijah, but this isn't the first time portals have separated us upon landing in another realm. Sometimes, we would be miles apart from each other. Too many times, the portals would dump us into entirely different cities. Reuniting could take days, so we may be in that same predicament here. We'll have to split up to find them."

"Split up?" Mazie said, looking over her shoulder at Bay. "I get Bay and me staying behind to watch our things, but shouldn't the rest of you stick together?"

Lincoln nodded. "I understand, Mazie, but I think it might be safer to split up. You know that. We can meet back here in the morning and then search again."

Anaru stepped forward. "You can search for your friends; I must go, Lincoln. The vision I received showed her at the palace in Drakentos. At least, in that moment, she was. I don't know if it's something that has happened already or will happen. But I have to search the land until I find out."

Lincoln looked up, eyeing the blood oozing through Anaru's fingers. "First things first," he said. "Mazie, we have some torches on the main—"

"On it, Lincoln," she said. "You pull it out, and I'll do the rest."

Lincoln nodded, helping Anaru sit back on the rock before placing one hand behind her on the wound. "Can we give her something to bite down on, please?"

Nola searched through the wreckage, found another broken wooden piece, and placed it in Anaru's mouth. "Here."

Lincoln then cautiously removed the piece of the plank from her side, blood trickling down her skin and onto the stone. She winced briefly, biting down hard on the wood.

"Lincoln, keep your hand pressed on the wound, and don't lift it," Nola said as Mazie joined them.

"There's not enough fuel to light the torches," Mazie said.

Anaru spat the piece of wood out of her mouth. "We won't need fuel. I've got this."

Lincoln kept his hand on the open wound, putting as much pressure as possible until she replaced his hand with hers, and fire ignited from her palm. Anaru screamed as the wound cauterized.

"Fuck!" Anaru cried out, but she shook her head when Nola moved closer. "I'm fine. It's only fire."

Once Anaru finished sealing the wound, Nola made a makeshift bandage and wrapped it around her upper torso. She then wiped away as much blood as she could, and Lincoln helped Anaru to her feet again, holding her steady as the shifter panted.

Mazie placed the sword in the sheath where she usually kept her cutlass and said, "Alright, let's clean off that blood and get her dressed." Then she turned to her pixie as she flew beside her, tapping Mazie on her shoulder. "Let's get on the ship, Bay."

"Wait," Tegan called. "Aiden and I will stay with you. Lincoln, you, Nola, and Anaru can search northwest. We'll look around the area near the ship first."

As the clouds moved, Mazie's eyes quickly scanned the surroundings. The land came into view with a bright sun shining above, encompassing trees, water, and vegetation for miles. Though splitting up was riskier, they would find Elijah and Janelle much faster that way. There were too many places to cover.

Tegan and Mazie turned to Aiden, who gripped the bottom of his shirt and closed his eyes.

"Aiden?" Tegan called. "What's wrong?" When his eyes opened, they were so dark they looked hollow, with only a hint of blue behind them.

"I don't know what's happening," he said. "I can feel this darkness move through me like icy liquid on the surface of my skin." He closed his eyes and let out a shaky breath. "It's so cold it stings."

The darkness behaved differently with Aiden. Mazie was afraid to say it aloud, especially now that they'd be traveling with him. If he attacked her or Tegan while the others went their separate ways, she would take him down and deal with the aftermath from the others later.

Tegan cleared her throat. "Aiden, I believe the darkness in you is behaving like an entity. It's different from what Elijah and I have attached with our magic," she said. "It seems to be alive within you. Essentially, it is eating at your power and soul, leaving nothing but a monster in its wake and you as its vessel. I've seen it before when I lived with Kieran. It changed him."

As Aiden walked across the rocks toward Tegan, Mazie brandished the sword again and pressed the sharp tip against his throat. "Back away, elf boy," Mazie said, her quickening breath catching in her lungs. She'd fight the bastard if she had to, but that fear simmering on the surface of her body felt paralyzing. It wasn't his threat alone but who *gave* that threat.

It wasn't Aiden, that was certain.

"Your eyes look dimmer than they were ten minutes ago," Mazie added. "You heard what Tegan said. The power is changing you."

Aiden slowly turned his head, and his lip curled. "Do you think I'm going to kill you, Mazie?" he asked, his voice taking on a sudden shift. It sounded menacing. It was so eerie that the hairs on Mazie's arms stood straight. "Afraid I'll overpower you, get my sword back, and drive it through your thin chest?"

Mazie twisted the sword, digging it lightly into his pasty skin. She remained unbothered, watching him wince.

"Mazie," Tegan said. "It's okay. He won't hurt me."

Tegan stepped in front of Aiden, and he looked down into her eyes. Mazie saw the conflict drumming through him. Despite the entity's attempts to manipulate him, the elf still cared for Tegan.

It shocked Mazie to discover that the darkness inside of Aiden hadn't vanished after Kieran's death. Instead, it now thrived in Aiden's magic, picking away at the energy. Eventually, he would lose his light and Elven power, wholly consumed by evil. But Tegan had previously dealt with the art of dark magic, and she was the only one out of everyone there who could help him. So, Mazie stepped back, placing the sword back in the sheath.

"Tread lightly, mate," she warned, glaring at Aiden. "Harm one hair on Tegan's head, and I'll sever yours from your shoulders." Aiden merely nodded and walked away, Tegan on his heels.

Once the crew had planned their next steps, they gathered their supplies. Mazie would stay by the ship with Tegan and Aiden, standing guard during the first shift, while the others would spread out in the nearby areas to search for Elijah and Janelle.

"We're ready," Lincoln said, picking up his bag and slinging it over his shoulder. He looked up and noted the sun burning high in the orange-tinged sky. "We have plenty of daylight to cover some ground."

Mazie nodded as Nola said, "We'll head toward those mountains. Search around what looks like a valley from here." She turned to Tegan. "Make sure you cover the river and over by that sea. If you come upon a town, gather whatever supplies you can find. Let's meet back at the ship by tomorrow morning." Her eyes then met Anaru's. "We will help you find your child. But we aren't leaving this world until Elijah and Janelle are safe with us. Do you understand?"

Anaru nodded. "I understand, Nola. Of course."

"Don't die, Captain!" Mazie shouted as Lincoln, Nola, and Anaru headed north. "Seriously. Don't die. I..." Mazie turned and attempted to shield her face as a tear fell down her cheek.

"I love you too, Mazie," Lincoln yelled back, his wink carrying a message meant only for her.

Tegan turned to Aiden, gesturing for him to follow Mazie onto the ship. As Aiden stepped forward, a slight smile tugged at his lips.

It was as if his true essence shone through the darkness, and there was hope that his light would be enough to keep them safe from the dark monster dwelling within.

# 2

## ELIJAH

"Greetings," Elijah heard a feminine voice say. "Are you waking up now?" With his eyes closed, a warm breath touched his cheeks. But that sensation was replaced with the scrape of a stick along his scalp. He winced and opened his eyes, trying to regain his bearings. His attention focused on the sky above him, a bright hue of orange with a smattering of black clouds floating by. He slowly turned his head, taking in the landscape. It was foreign, with colors Elijah had never seen before—colors he'd never be able to describe if someone asked him to. The black clouds moved quickly, shading out the sun hanging low in the sky.

Elijah found his surroundings interesting, but he closed his eyes tightly as a buzzing sound echoed in his ears. It caused pain to shoot through his head, threatening to drag his consciousness back down into the murky darkness. The atmosphere became silent except for the heavy breathing behind him, which snapped him back to reality.

He shifted his gaze toward the right, only to be met with towering brick buildings lining an alleyway. Each brick was a different shade of gray, a gloom of black casting shadows on the solid concrete below.

Elijah's jet-black hair swayed to one side as he turned his head, and the grinding sound started again. It was excruciating, like needles pricking at his skin. Thankfully, the sound faded away after a couple of seconds. And Elijah blew out a sigh of relief. Right then, the stick returned, poking the top of his head this time.

He swiftly extended his hand, gripping the end of the stick and twisting his wrist until it snapped in half. He rolled onto his stomach and looked at who held it. A woman dropped her broken half of the stick, retreating backward while assuming a warrior-like stance. Despite her petite and lean frame, she maintained her pose skillfully, occasionally readjusting her feet. Her narrow brown eyes peeked out from behind her black pencil-straight hair as it fell forward, her chest heaving in and out as if attempting to control her fear.

When Elijah remained still, she tucked a few strands behind her ear, revealing more of her face. A four-inch scar ran from her eyebrow straight down to the tip of her pointed nose, and sweat rolled down her sandy-beige skin and into her left eye. She didn't wipe it away.

As her lips parted, her thin cheeks curved into a slight smile. "You're alive," the woman said in a gravelly voice, as if she had not sipped water in days. Her warm, gentle smile grew until it met her eyes. "I think."

Elijah blinked. "Where the hell am I?" he asked, looking around frantically. Under normal circumstances, he wouldn't feel so afraid, given that he had powerful magic running through his blood, but Elijah hadn't a clue where he was or where any of the others had landed after the crash. "Fuck!" He attempted to stand, but the woman quickly stepped forward, gripped his shoulders, and helped sit him back on the ground.

"I'm Arabella, and you need to relax. Now," she said hastily, looking around like they were being watched.

"Oh, Gods," he blurted out. "Um...a woman, blonde hair, pale-white skin, pointy ears..." His voice trailed off as he searched the alley where he had lain. "Where is she?" Elijah's rage flared. "Is she—"

Arabella held up her hand, gesturing to his forehead. "You're bleeding from your skull, my friend. Lie down; you seem to have hit your head pretty hard."

Elijah raised his hand and felt around his head. The sticky substance was at his fingertips, and a sharp sensation burned on his hairline. The cut didn't appear to be deep enough to worry about.

She cleared her throat. "I need to get you inside my place," she said. "It's on the other side of that alley. The Raiders will be out soon. We aren't safe."

Raiders? Elijah repeated the name in his mind.

"What's your name?" Arabella asked.

Elijah looked around again. "Elijah," he said, watching the woman cock her head to the right.

"Hmm, my assumption was right," she said. "You're most certainly a human and not from around here." She held out her hand, but he didn't take it. "I can see you're worried about your friend, so let's get you inside my place, and we can talk about it, yeah?" She gestured to a building behind them with red brick and silver metal pillars framing the sides. "I've been out here for the last hour before finding you. There's no blonde woman, I swear it. But the Raiders will be out soon, so we best hurry."

Elijah held out his hand, and black smoke hovered lightly over his fingertips. "I can defend myself."

Arabella's dark brows rose before saying, "Oooh, look at you." She bit back a laugh. "The Raiders will burn those little fingers off, possibly taking your entire hand with it if you try that with them. Magic won't save you," she said, her umber eyes looking sullener than before. "Your magic will do nothing to them. We no longer have law, governing power, or security on our streets. They will kill you without remorse or consequences. Trust me, whoever or whatever you are, little magic tricks won't keep you alive out there."

Elijah lowered his power but remained wary, clinging to his magic to stay alert.

"Is this place..."—he stopped, glancing around at the dirty alley—"This isn't Earth?"

Arabella's age became apparent in the crinkles around her eyes as her grin stretched outward. "Earth?" she repeated with a tiny giggle. "That place really exists, doesn't it?"

Elijah shook his head in disbelief. "You know about Earth?"

"Stories from our world. Some folks claim they're from there. Others, it's a myth."

"But," Elijah started again, "you speak one of the languages of Earth."

"I speak in everyone's tongue, Elijah," she said. "Don't you?"

Elijah stood and pressed his back against the brick wall beside him. "What is this place?"

"Well, the planet is called Dragão Terra—it comprises colonies, villages, and provinces, covering most of the land," Arabella explained. "This place here, though," Arabella gestured to the city, "is the Ruins, formerly named Gallic. It was once a prosperous city, with thriving businesses and multiple educational institutions, until the Raiders took over. Since then, the guards have stopped patrolling the streets. No one protects us anymore, as our world has become utter mayhem. The Raiders are the predators, and those fighting for our lives have become their prey. So, I suggest we get moving."

She began walking past him, but Elijah stepped in front of her. "I need to find my friends first," he said.

"Oooor I can get us inside and lock us in," Arabella said. "The Raiders leave us alone during daylight but not when the sun sets. They'll sniff us out here soon, scale the walls, and try to break through the window if they see us running inside." She gestured to the building behind her.

"Well," Elijah said carefully before moving to the side, "I guess you might be right. I'd rather not be their next victim."

"I have some food and water inside, but it's scarce," Arabella said, ushering him with her hand to follow. "Take it easy when you walk. I also have some healing medicine that I can mix with some coffee back at my home. Do they have coffee where you're from?"

For the first time since he woke up, Elijah's face broke into a wide smile, taking comfort in the commonalities of their worlds.

"I'll take that smile as a yes," Arabella said. "I've got an entire year's worth. Sometimes, we're trapped inside for weeks when the Raiders decide they haven't had enough fun. So, we must stock up on what we need if we can't reach the marketplace. Well, what's left of it, anyway. Nowadays, everyone's hurting for business."

Elijah followed her in silence as she led him through the alley and to a tall, steel ladder. He thought they would climb up and enter through a window or balcony, but instead, Arabella revealed a hidden door behind the brick. It became visible when the cracks in the wall split open, creating an entryway. They slipped inside, and Elijah hesitated for a split second as the sound of screams and cries filled the streets—women, men, and children.

Once inside, Elijah headed to her open window facing the city, looking out while she ran into her kitchen to brew some coffee.

Elijah narrowed his dark brows. "You still go about your day in your city with those creatures out there?"

He turned as Arabella shrugged. "They only come out at night and sleep during the day."

"What are they?" he asked.

"Dragon shifters, just like me. To them, they're surviving like we are but having fun while doing it. They steal our food and take what they want. If the Raiders become bored enough, they'll kill a few locals while they can, eating us to satisfy their hunger."

*Like a cannibal*, he thought.

Elijah looked back through the window as a man's cry echoed through the streets. Whatever happened to their land was dark and ominous, and it wasn't only the marauding dragon shifters that stalked the streets.

"Tell me about this place," he said, turning from the window and facing her again. "How did it become like this?"

Arabella sat down, placing the mug of coffee on the small table. "Vipers—snake-like creatures, killing anyone they could sink their fangs into, draining them until they withered away. They fed on blood, and they craved it the more they consumed," she said. "They've been dead for ten years now. But for eighteen years, they roamed our land, killing anyone they came across. The empire collapsed, leaving us without a ruler for almost two decades, and it wasn't until ten years ago that everyone decided it was best to fight together instead of against each other. Sure, we killed them all, leading to a new emperor taking over the palace. We finally had a ruler." She looked over Elijah's shoulder and to the window facing the city.

"It doesn't look like that ruler cared much about your lives out here," he said.

"He doesn't," she replied. "The emperor seems to have forgotten about us. Ten years ago was the last time we as a people stood together and fought as one. I guess it doesn't matter, anyway. The Vipers caused so much destruction when they were alive that I can't imagine our world ever returning to how it was. Since the emperor abandoned the outer colonies and cities, the Raiders had free rein to pillage as they pleased. So, they've forced us into hiding once again."

"Where did the Vipers come from?" Elijah asked.

Arabella shrugged. "Another world, I guess."

Elijah sat beside her and reached over, picking up his coffee. The warmth from the mug soaked into his skin.

"A portal opened, and a world split," she explained.

Elijah's stomach twisted. *A portal?*

"Just like the one I saw you fall through," she added.

Elijah studied her as she shared her stories, nodding and acting indifferently. "So, you just live in fear every day?" he asked. "No laws to protect you?"

"Not everyone wants to be locked behind closed doors, Elijah. We have to find a way to survive it. We have no other choice. There are very few of us left out here."

Arabella stood and walked to the window, looking out for a second before she reached out and grabbed the window frame, pulling it down and locking it at the bottom. "This world used to be so beautiful, Elijah. The infestation of the Vipers even destroyed our crops, creating a disease that caused some women to lose their ability to procreate. We've barely gotten by. This right here is one of the few places that still have buildings standing. It's also the place the Raiders can do whatever the fuck they want; steal, murder, torture...rape." She turned to him. "There are few places we can go to be safe."

Elijah placed his coffee down and stood, walking back to the window facing the city with her and resting his hands on the windowsill. "Life is still beautiful, Arabella," he said, turning to her. "Hold on to that. Even in the bleakest circumstances, hope will persist."

# 3

## MAZIE

Mazie had greatly underestimated the damage the Sybil Curse had taken after the crash. The impact had split the cannon room in half, leaving one end partially collapsed and forming a slide-like structure to the other side. Jagged pieces of wood and iron cannonballs littered the floor, making it a hazard to walk through. To prevent injuries, they had to climb the wall to avoid falling through the cracked center.

"Bay. Please, don't fly too low," Mazie said. "This is a mess. You'll cut yourself."

"I'll grab the water," Tegan said, moving past her toward the barrels and mug. She kept her hands out to maintain her balance across the broken floor. "Aiden, please pull some blankets from the chest over there."

Bay perched herself on a barrel at the corner, and her wings fell, curling into her body. "Too broken," Bay said, her voice tiny and quiet.

"It's beyond repair, Bay," Mazie agreed. "Once we find a way out of here, we'll need to bring something from this land to keep us afloat if we're to hit the water on the other side."

Mazie hunted for the weapons secured inside the open chests. She grabbed several daggers and placed them in her bag while keeping a rifle gripped in one hand. "Grab those swords," she said to Tegan, still not trusting Aiden with any weapons.

She unlatched the bag's metal clasp and sifted through the contents. Mazie located her headwrap and twisted her thick, long braids into a high bun and away from her neck. After wrapping her hair in the cloth, she tied it off at the front, securing the knot.

Next, she strapped the rifle around one shoulder and her bag over the other. "Alright, let me gather what we need and put them all in one location, along with the water, food, and supplies. It might take me a bit before I can—"

Deep, masculine voices from outside stopped Mazie from stepping forward, causing her blood to run cold. "Fuck," she whispered, turning to her mates. She raised her finger to her lips and pointed outside with the other. It had to be at least two to three men talking.

The hairs on the back of her neck stood straight. She had been worried someone would find the ship before they were ready. The noise from the crash would have alerted all the nearby village folk to come running.

Mazie and Tegan crept slowly to a porthole, looking through the glass.

After ensuring it was loaded, Mazie held the rifle close to her chest and secured it next to Aiden's sword at her hip.

"I need a weapon. Now!" Aiden ordered, but Mazie rolled her eyes. "Give me my sword, Mazie, before I take it from you."

"Use your fucking magic, Aiden," she said. When she looked over her shoulder, Aiden was standing still with a worried look in his eyes. "What's wrong with you?"

"Aiden, what is it?" Tegan said, looking down at Aiden's hand, his fingers out and his palm forward.

"My power has shifted," he said. "I can't tap into my Elven magic...not anymore. The thing inside me is smothering it. It's speaking to me now, ordering me *not* to attack whoever is out there."

"Cut the bullshit, Aiden," Mazie cursed.

She felt the soft touch of Tegan's hand on her shoulder. "I think he's telling the truth. Look at his eyes, Mazie."

It was difficult to tell from the dimly lit cannon room, but the blue light she'd once seen in Aiden's eyes was replaced by something sinister...something that made her skin crawl. It was as if someone else was looking back at them.

Some*thing* else.

"Alright, fight with your hands if you must," Mazie said, slightly relieved that Aiden was at least recognizing that something was wrong instead of embracing the intruder that was taking over his mind. "We all need to be ready." With one quick nod, Mazie signaled to Bay to climb back onto her shoulder.

On the other side of the cannon room's entryway was a ladder leading back up to the deck. The men's feet shuffled loudly over the dry grass a few yards from the Jacob's ladder—they hadn't boarded the ship yet.

*Thank the Gods*, Mazie thought, instinctively placing her hand on the hilt.

There was a small, subtle moment where Mazie's body felt like it had fallen into a frozen lake. Bay's tiny toes pressed down on her shoulder, and she reassured her friend that everything would be okay. But she didn't believe it. Though Bay could always defend herself, Mazie still felt obligated to protect her.

*I'd die for Bay*, she thought to herself.

The pixie nodded as Mazie jumped down through the crack. However, before she landed, her belt snagged on a jagged piece of wood sticking out, ripping her sheath's strap and causing Aiden's sword to hit the bottom deck. She watched as it slid across the wood, rolling down to the ship's stern.

"Fuck me," she cursed as her boots hit the grass. Mazie attempted to climb back up, but it was too high. She glanced around and then honed her ears to the sound of the men drawing closer.

Mazie would have to leave it for now and return for it once they left.

Without the sword, she had to rely on the weapons inside the bag strapped to her back if they attacked, hoping it was enough to protect themselves from whoever was out there.

Aiden and Tegan followed behind her, all three sneaking out around one side of the ship. Mazie's shoulders tensed as the men rounded the corner. She ducked behind a broken plank with Tegan, watching them stare at the ship, probably wondering how a massive boat ended up in the middle of a deserted landscape.

Aiden quietly cleared his throat from behind them, gesturing to the other window to their right.

"At least we found the ship that brought the woman over," one man said, coming into view. "Let's raid it and get the fuck out of here."

Mazie counted two men. The closest one to the ship had peachy skin, a bald head, and a long blond goatee. The other had skin the color of ochre, short black hair, and a sharply cut jaw. With their massive builds and black vine-shaped tattoos climbing up their arms, both men stood like trees.

Shifters, Mazie assumed, as their eyes glowed a yellowish gold, the same as Anaru's.

Mazie was a skilled fighter, but those men towered over even Aiden. They'd crush her with a single blow. A small hope lingered in Mazie's thoughts that Tegan could use her powers to fend them off.

"I'll climb back up to get my sword," Aiden said, turning from them and heading back to the center of the ship to climb up.

"We don't have time, Aiden," Tegan whispered. "We'll come back for it. Use the damn darkness if you must."

Mazie turned back to the crack in the ship, looking out. Her heartbeat thumped loudly in her ears as she waited for the men to round the corner, so the three could run north for the woods.

The only thought crossing her mind was what they had said, the ship that brought the woman over. She wondered if they were speaking about Janelle. And if so, was Elijah with her?

When the men latched their fingers over the steps on the ladder, Mazie turned to look at Bay, giving her one nod. With a sudden shift on her heel, she sprinted outside, Bay flying into the air while sprinkling pixie dust along Mazie's forehead.

The two men shouted, and their voices quickly changed into growls. They both let out a boisterous roar behind her. Mazie intended to divert the shifters' attention to only her, allowing Tegan and Aiden to escape unnoticed.

Mazie continued to bolt toward the trees, dropping her bag to the grass as her feet lifted off the ground. Aiming her rifle, she turned and fired two shots, narrowly missing them by an inch.

From below, the dragons turned their massive heads toward the source of the gunshots, their fiery breath scorching the ship's deck. The wood instantly exploded, fire erupting all around them.

"Fuck!" she cursed, looking around to see if Tegan and Aiden had made it out before the attack. She spotted Tegan behind an outcrop of rocks nearby, closing her eyes and calling up her magic. Aiden had taken shelter behind a large fallen tree several feet from the dragons.

The dragons were now facing her, their wings flapping loudly while heavy smoke from the scorched ship deck billowed between them. Tegan stepped out from the rocks and knelt, placing her hands on the ground. She remained steadfast in her power as she released her white smoke-like magic along the grass. The magic smoke seized the larger of the two dragons, and she dragged him away from where Mazie floated.

The dragon roared angrily and whipped his head toward Tegan, red flames flickering from his mouth. Suddenly, Aiden shouted at the top of his lungs, throwing his hands out, while Newick magic created a force field, pushing the dragons away from Mazie and Tegan.

As the power knocked the dragons off-balance, Mazie shot two more bullets, striking between their eyes. Blood sprayed out from the back of their skulls. Their bodies fell to the ground, blood dripping onto the grass below.

Mazie floated down toward the fallen dragons to ensure they were dead after being shot. However, as she bent forward to watch their chests, the beasts wriggled and growled. Their colossal heads lifted from the grass, and their eyes burned with red fire moments before they lunged at her.

"Mazie!" Tegan shouted as a fireball flew over Mazie's head from behind, the blaze hitting both shifters and knocking them back against the ship. The ship immediately caught fire, going up in an inferno within seconds.

"Shit!" Mazie shouted. *And there goes Aiden's sword.*

Both dragons screamed, attempting to fend off the flames and latch their nails into the wooded side of the Sybil Curse. It surprised Mazie that they couldn't move much further, coiling themselves up in a ball as the fire scorched their bodies and devoured the ship. Though the bullets weren't enough to take them down, the power of fire was. She remained still, unable to look away as the two dragon-shifters took their final breaths, their bodies now completely charred, with black ash raining down.

Mazie was so immersed in the scene that it hadn't even registered yet that the flames had come from somewhere else.

A crack of the dried leaves behind her caused goosebumps to stand straight. She was out of bullets, and someone was behind her.

"Mazie, don't move," Tegan said to her right.

Mazie stilled, lifting her hands in surrender, and slowly turned around. A stunning woman with lightly tanned skin and long white hair captivated Mazie. The hints of blue in her white hair resembled a frozen lake in the heart of winter. The woman's posture was perfectly straight, her diamond-shaped face staring back at Mazie with silvery-blue eyes locking onto hers. Remnants of gray smoke floated over her body, as if she were fire itself.

Someone else cleared their throat, and when Mazie turned, her eyes glued to Tegan and Aiden standing by the burning ship with a massively tall man holding an arrow to her friends' heads. The man's warm russet-brown complexion complemented his eyes, which gleamed like liquid gold. When they both smiled and lowered their weapons, Mazie breathed a sigh of relief.

"Whew," the white-haired woman said. "I've wanted to do that to them for over a decade." Her smile grew. "You're welcome, by the way...stranger."

"What the hell do you mean, 'you're welcome?'" Mazie scoffed. "I fucking had them!"

"Did you, now?" the woman said, stepping toward her.

Mazie raised her gun and pointed it straight between the woman's eyes, but she remained unfazed. Instead, she stepped closer until the barrel pressed against her forehead. "I can match this energy all day long, stranger. Put down your weapon, so my cousin, Xander, and I can help you."

Mazie looked over at Xander and raised a brow. "Cousin?"

The woman smiled. "We have the same chin...I think."

"And temperament," Xander added, chuckling to himself.

Mazie hesitated momentarily before slowly lowering the rifle and relaxing her shoulders, giving Tegan a nod. "I'm Mazie, and that's Tegan and Aiden. We're not here to hurt you. I swear it."

The woman brushed her hands against her clothes, dusting off the lingering smoke from her powers. "Well, I sure hope not after saving your life, stranger." She gave Mazie a wink. "I'm Kaeli," she said before looking at her cousin. "Alright, Xander. Let's get them out of here, shall we? Where there are two, there are more. And they'll come looking for their comrades."

# 4

## NOLA

The crystalline seawater along the banks flowed gently against the rocks. Nola watched curiously as tiny seashells shifted beneath the waves. The elements were like those of Earth—seas, streams, and mountains—except the colors were unlike anything she had ever seen, even in her wildest dreams.

"We've searched all day," Nola said, "and we haven't found any clues as to where Janelle and Elijah are, Lincoln. We need to rest."

"The first city I escaped to was Chaetei," Anaru started. "There's a temple there that can offer protection for a few nights—"

"We don't have a few nights, Anaru," Nola said. "We need to get back to the ship by morning."

Lincoln gripped Nola's hand. "It's almost nightfall, love, and Anaru is in no condition to travel further. We'll have to sleep here for the night inside that cave." He pointed toward a rocky hillside along the shoreline.

Anaru placed her hand on her wound—purple bruising spreading around the burnt skin. "It hurts," she said. "Lincoln, the damage may have already been done, despite my efforts to cauterize the wound. I need a healer."

Lincoln removed his bag from over his shoulder, beads of sweat dripping down his forehead. "Where would the nearest town be to find a doctor?" he asked.

She turned to meet his eyes. "In Chaetei. There are healers within the temple. The Ember Guild was my family."

"Guild?" Lincoln said. "What is the Ember Guild?"

"It's a sacred family of mages. For the longest time, the mages protected me and kept me safe. That was where I met Julian. We fell in love, and during my time there, I met the healers, who used our world's elements to create spells for the sick or injured. Julian's family may still be alive, Lincoln, but I can't be certain. We left that place to protect them, but I fear it may have been destroyed years ago."

"Alright," Lincoln said, the weight of the mission hanging heavily in the air. Nola felt it. Lincoln had to have felt it, too.

"How far is that city?" Nola asked.

Anaru let out a breath. "A half a day, at least."

Lincoln nodded and turned his gaze to Nola's. "I don't believe we have a choice, Nola. The crew will have to search without us." Lincoln rested his hand on Anaru's shoulder. "I'll need you to rest. I'll keep watch outside the cave until morning."

Lincoln turned to Nola, exchanging a meaningful look. Deep down, they knew Anaru's desperation to search for her child would outweigh any logical thinking, risking the safety of all three of them. Their priority was finding a healer for now, so she'd have the strength to keep going. "I'll stay with Anaru and check on her throughout the night," Nola said. "Wake me if you need to sleep, and I'll keep watch."

Lincoln's love for Anaru had steadily grown stronger over the past two years. Nola never felt jealous or insecure about their bond because it was ingrained in them, like an unbreakable thread weaving through their souls.

She saw it in Lincoln's eyes, that pain of the possibility of losing her and not being able to stop it from happening.

Anaru let out a quiet laugh. "I know seeing me in my human form is different, Lincoln, especially injured like this. You see me now as a fragile human woman, not the fierce beast you once knew. Trust me, the wings on my back do not define my strength or the bravery behind the fire I breathe."

Nola placed her hand on Lincoln's shoulder. She knew he saw Anaru as his child when he became her rider. Losing his family so many years ago pushed them to create an unparalleled bond that even Nola couldn't compete with.

"Let's get inside, Lincoln," Nola said. "I know you're worried about Elijah, too, but if anyone could handle a place like this, it's him." She paused, watching Lincoln's shoulders slump. "And Mazie. You know damn well she can take care of herself. Everyone will be okay. I know it."

Lincoln gently rested his hand on Nola's cheek, meeting her amber eyes. His lips pressed against hers before slowly releasing their kiss a moment later. "We can only hope," he said. "Time to sleep, my love."

Come morning, their journey would continue, and every decision they made from then on would be a matter of life and death.

# 5

## JANELLE

Strong hands stroked Janelle's long white hair, making tension creep into her shoulders, and she pulled back. She slowly opened her eyes and saw a man staring back at her. Looking deeper into the stranger's gaze, she tried to make out the color—a deep brown with hints of yellow. The colors within the man's irises seemed to change, swirling like a coiled snake. Janelle shifted and realized she was lying on a plush mattress covered by a cozy wool blanket.

She sat up with a start.

"You're awake," the man said. He smiled slightly, his hand slowly sliding down his neatly trimmed beard. "You've been asleep for half the day." He moved away from her and took a seat in a tall leather chair in the corner of the room. Once settled, he leaned back casually, idly drumming his fingers over the armrest.

Her eyes followed him as he shifted to get comfortable, his partially open shirt showing off each crease of his smooth, tatted, muscular chest.

*Well, he's beautiful,* she thought, noting that he held himself like a god. The man's dark hair wasn't as black as Elijah's, but he somewhat reminded her of him—the way he carried himself, calm and collected. It made her stomach flip with anticipation. What was he going to do with her?

He slid his arms forward across the armrest, his elbows resting on his knees. "It seems you've made a rather exciting journey into our world. My men spotted your ship from the skies before it slammed into *my* land."

*His land,* she repeated the words in her head. *He talks as if he's the king.*

"So, this world is *yours?*" she asked. "Are you a king?"

Of course, she was unsure where she was and who governed it. The thought of trespassing on the property of such an intimidating man made her uncomfortable.

"Kind of like a king," he replied, his voice now eerily calm. "I'm Lord Dorion Amulius. But you'll call me Dorion." He shifted in his seat. "This is the part where you tell me who the fuck you are and where you came from."

She stubbornly pressed her lips together and averted her gaze, but he lunged from the chair, gripped her jaw, and forced her to look at him.

"Your silence will only get you killed, little intruder," he warned. This time, his words lacked the gentleness from before, and the level of intensity shook her.

None of that mattered, though, because she sure as fuck wasn't going to give the man what he wanted. "Go fuck yourself, Dorion."

A smile curved at the side of his lips, and he dropped his hand, leaning back. "Fine," he said. "Should you continue withholding information from me, then I'll refer to you as"—his grin grew so broad that it touched his eyes—"my pet."

*No fucking way,* she cursed in her mind. "My name is Laila."

"Laila," he repeated, and his smile dropped. "I'm exceptionally good at knowing when someone is lying to me, my pet. But in time, you'll grow to trust me enough to share with me your *real* name."

*In time?* she thought. *Oh, Gods.*

She cleared her throat. "What are you, exactly?" she asked, watching the yellow glow in his eyes intensify.

"I was going to ask you the same question. You look like a fairy, but your ears are a bit sharper at the point." He gestured to her as she pulled her hair forward to shield her ears.

*At least that answered one thing,* she thought. *He's aware of other realms and species.*

"What are *you*?" she asked again.

Dorion moved forward and sat on the mattress beside her. "A dragon," he said. "Most of us are shifters in *this* world."

She lowered her brow. "Shifters?"

He nodded. "We can control the change from human to dragon as easily as we can breathe." Another side smirk touched his lips. "But you, little intruder, you're quite a phenomenon, I must say."

"Ever hear of an elf?" she asked, immediately regretting giving away that detail about herself.

"Hmm," he hummed. "I've heard the name, but they've not crossed over here yet...until now, of course." He let out a slight sigh. "Most are stories we've not heard since the war. Twenty-eight years ago, the veil between our world and another cracked open. We lost a few of our own that day, and many creatures from your world or wherever spilled into ours. Unfortunately for them, they've been kept prisoner here or killed." His smile slipped. "Well, most of them. A few might have slipped through our prisons and made a home for themselves in Dragão Terra, adapting to our law."

Her expression fell. The thought of the Fae and other creatures from her world being kept as a prisoner in another realm made her hot with rage. Would that happen to her? Was she doomed to be subjected to torture as they figured out exactly what she was and what she could do?

"Others, though,"—the dragon stopped, but he didn't smile that time, he only looked weary—"others have helped us."

Her brows pulled together. "Helped you...*how* exactly?"

Dorion smirked. "Well, my pet. If you want answers, provide me with more information about *yourself* and the location of your companions. Because you'll not convince me you traveled through a portal on a ship that size all by your lonesome."

She scowled, tilting her chin up. "I enjoy traveling alone, asshole," she said. "And stop calling me 'my pet.' I'm not a fucking dog."

Janelle shrugged off the blankets he had her wrapped in and looked around. It wasn't a dungeon or cave, but it was a room that reminded her of where she slept in Elijah's castle. It was odd to see a different world, so foreign to their dimension, yet there were similarities. The colors of the walls and tapestry were unlike those in Janelle's world. The clothing Dorion wore was dull compared to what Janelle was used to. Although they spoke the same language, his dialect differed from any country she had visited on Earth.

"Aren't you afraid I'll use magic against you?" she asked, raising her brow.

Dorion flashed his white teeth and let out a hearty laugh. "I'm afraid of *nothing*, my pet."

"Stop calling me that!"

"No," he said sharply, his tone cutting through the room. "It'll be *my pet* until you tell me what your name really is."

The shifter stood, and Janelle scurried back until her head hit the headboard, watching him tower above her while he tightened his jaw. She breathed in his earthy scent as he leaned forward. "Are you going to kill me?" she asked, pushing her chin up.

He tilted his head to the right, keeping a smile plastered on his full lips. "No, my pet," he said. "Killing you will serve no purpose. But mark my words. I can do whatever the fuck I want with you...*Laila*." Yet another smug grin. "I can torture you painfully and keep you locked up in this room, tied to that bed for the rest of your existence."

He closed the gap between them and placed his large hand on her cheek. Then he caressed her skin with his thumb gingerly until he reached her chin and squeezed.

*This cannot be happening*, she thought, screaming in her thoughts for him to stop touching her.

"I can even fuck you and make you mine." The hairs on Janelle's arms stood straight, and terror seized her breath. "It's all contingent on you and how much you're willing to divulge. So, hear me now. You are *mine* and my brothers' until we decide your fate, whether that be walking out that door with your heart still beating or being thrown into the pit."

# 6

## ELIJAH

For several hours, Elijah remained with Arabella, learning all he could about her world and how to protect himself from the dangers that lurked outside her home.

Arabella picked at her nails while Elijah stirred the sugar into his third mug of coffee before she looked up, giving him a warm smile. It was as if she was waiting for him to say something. Elijah didn't like to make small talk, but the silence made him uncomfortable.

"Anaru would have been a fine leader," Arabella said suddenly, and Elijah looked up, his eyes growing wide.

"Who?"

"Anaru," she said. "The true empress."

Elijah hadn't seen that coming.

"Her bloodline governed Dragão Terra for thousands of years. The day the Vipers entered our world, Anaru and her cousin, Dergis, fell into a portal. No one ever saw them again."

Elijah shifted uncomfortably.

Despite this new information about his brother's dragon, Elijah kept his mouth shut; he didn't know Arabella well enough to share information that could hurt his friends. She was a stranger to him, and even though she was friendly and offered him shelter, keeping the details of his arrival a secret was for the best.

"I'm sorry to hear that," Elijah said, clearing his throat. "Uh, what do you eat around here?" His head buzzed as Arabella poured him another drink.

*More coffee*, he thought.

Elijah looked down at his drink. "I think I've had enough," he said, carefully placing it back on the table to prevent the hot liquid from spilling. "Thank you, though."

He pressed his hand against his head, suddenly feeling disoriented. The room started to spin, and bile rose in his throat.

"Are you okay?" Arabella asked, leaning forward to look into his eyes.

Elijah cleared his throat. "I don't feel well," he said.

"You hit the ground really hard." She sat her mug down on the table beside her. "I watched it happen. You fell straight from the sky through a portal floating near the top of a building. It's a miracle you survived the impact. You ought to lie down."

Elijah shook his head. "I can't. I have to find my friend," he said. "One minute, I held onto her for dear life, and the next, the portal ripped her from me. I don't have a clue how far she is from here. But if she's out there, she'll be in harm's way from those Raiders..."

It wasn't that he didn't fear where Lincoln and the others landed, but they had been traveling through other worlds for the last two years. A small part of him believed they'd be fine.

*Who am I kidding?* Elijah thought. *Janelle can damn well take care of herself, too.*

"If you go out there to find her, you're dead," she said. "Spend the night here, and when morning comes, I'll help you look for her."

Elijah's eyes widened, his head suddenly clearing. His hand immediately came to his cloak pocket, feeling around. When he found nothing, he stilled.

*It's gone,* he thought. *The Voleric pendant is gone.*

"I dropped something," Elijah said frantically. "I need to go back to that alley and check the area."

Arabella shook her head and placed her hand on Elijah's chest when he jumped up, attempting to pass her. "Not a chance. You'll die before you reach the streets. You're being a fool, Elijah. I'll help you look for whatever you dropped when we search for your friend in the morning."

"You don't understand. What I'm looking for will *help* me find her." Elijah pushed forward, causing Arabella to step back. "I'm leaving this house."

"Excuse me, asshole," Arabella said, standing a little taller than she had moments ago. "You'll not speak to me like that in my own damn home, especially after I just saved your life. So, go on. Get out there and see exactly what you're up against. I don't give a fuck anymore." She nodded toward the door.

Elijah stepped back, adjusted his shirt, and maneuvered past her to get out the door. As soon as he stepped onto the balcony next to the secret staircase, the scorching heat of dragon fire brushed against his face. He couldn't see where the Raiders were, but they weren't far, given how close the harrowing cries from their victims were.

He climbed down the stairs and made his way to the door, carefully opening it and looking around the corner. Several buildings were on fire, and bodies lay in the street.

*Does she hide like this every night?* Elijah wondered.

An ear-splitting explosion came from just beyond Arabella's apartment, and Elijah had to cover his ears to alleviate the painful ringing left by the noise.

*Fuck me,* he cursed in his thoughts, casting his eyes toward the explosion before spinning back to the alley where Arabella had found him. Time was running out.

Elijah hurried through the doorway and into the streets. As he headed down the darkened alley, a shiver ran down his spine, and the hair on his arms rose, causing goosebumps.

There was something there, watching him.

A low, guttural growl echoed against the brick walls, drawing closer to him from the deepening shadows. Elijah instinctively stepped backward when two yellow eyes looked back at him under a flickering street lamp.

The dragon crouched low, as if ready to attack. Rough-looking scales turned up, resembling sharp thorns growing out of his back. The dragon dashed to the right, and Elijah stiffened. He thought the Shadow Creature was terrifying, but a dragon with fire and murderous eyes drew a numbing fear out of him he didn't realize was possible.

The dragon hissed, its jaws opening to reveal a gaping maw of razor-sharp teeth and red flames flickering from its throat. Suddenly, a stream of fire shot from the dragon's mouth, hitting the sleeve of Elijah's tunic and setting it ablaze. Elijah quickly ripped his shirt off, tossing it to the ground. The flames had burnt the flesh of his right arm, angry red blisters forming quickly. The pain was blinding, almost bringing him to his knees.

"Fuck!"

Elijah turned to run back toward Arabella's home, but the dragon charged forward, wrapping its massive tail around his waist. As it yanked him back, the tail squeezed, and the pain became unbearable. It wasn't only from the dragon's pressure on his ribs that made him wince, but also from the burns covering his arm. Elijah tried to conjure his magic to fight back, but he was met with only silence. It was as if the flames that burned him had smothered his power.

As his vision faded, a red dragon leapt over his head. It slammed its body into the attacking dragon, freeing Elijah from its tail and causing him to collapse to the ground, unable to move.

He attempted to summon his magic again but was too stunned to do so. Even if Elijah could gather enough strength, his body refused to obey him. Instead, he slid away from the two battling dragons until his back pressed against a brick wall, holding his hand over his injured arm. He could only sit there and watch as the dragons attacked each other, tearing into the other's scales and flesh.

As the Raider attempted to fly up toward the sky, the red dragon snapped its teeth around its throat and tore it out in one swift motion.

The Raider coiled its body into a ball before it shifted into a human man. The red dragon folded its wings back into its skin, replacing its scales with smooth, beige skin, before she lay on the street, exhausted.

*Arabella.*

"Shit, Elijah," Arabella cried out, jumping up and rushing toward him, stark naked.

His skin still burned like a hot stove, but it almost felt numb at that point. "Well, this is my first time getting burned by dragon fire," he said shakily. "This ranks up on the pain scale."

"I have medicine to help heal you, but, Gods, that looks awful."

Elijah turned slowly to his side to rest against the wall, feeling his power dwindling beneath the surface. His heart slowed down to a steady beat, and he forced himself to shut his eyes, allowing his darkness to diminish into nothing. His powers were giving up, and he felt like dying.

Perhaps he was.

# 7

## MAZIE

Mazie, Tegan, and Aiden traveled with the strangers for three hours before they reached a city. Mazie knew it would have been wiser to venture there as a group, but Nola, Lincoln, and Anaru had traveled so far in the other direction that they would never make it back before dark.

"A pirate," Kaeli started, tapping her fingers on the table between them. "An elf, a pixie, and a witch-elf hybrid?" She turned to her cousin, Xander. "This isn't how I thought our day was going to go. But I'll admit, it's quite enthralling."

"Sounds like the beginning of a joke, doesn't it?" Xander teased.

"Retired pirate now," Mazie corrected her, a humorous smile playing at the corner of her lips. "I can't sail without a ship."

Bay perched on her shoulder, digging her tiny fingers into Mazie's skin to assure her she felt safe.

Mazie may have been one to crack jokes in the face of danger, but Bay saw through her facade. When it came to strangers, Bay had a unique sense of intuition none of them possessed.

Although Mazie sensed that Kaeli and Xander weren't dangerous, the world around them gave her pause. She wouldn't admit it aloud, but Mazie was terrified of what they were up against.

She cleared her throat. "Kaeli, we still need to know where we are exactly," Mazie said. Before they had gone their separate ways, Anaru had given them little information about where they were. There was still so much she didn't know.

Mazie was just like her captain. Everything was always in order on the Sybil Curse, even when they traveled to different worlds with the Kroneon. If the crew needed to escape from danger, they had to press down on the ruby, and they would be home safe and sound. However, in Dragão Terra, there was no way home.

"This is the Vine Colony, which is a part of Dragon's Cove. It provides safety to my people and to you, as well," Kaeli explained.

Mazie and Tegan exchanged glances, while Aiden stayed silent in the corner, watching them.

*Always fucking watching*, Mazie observed. It made her feel more uneasy around him.

"Safe from what?" Tegan asked.

"Most dragon shifters in our world cannot openly fly anymore; the empire won't allow it unless you're a part of the Brotherhood," Kaeli said. "When our planet was on the brink of destruction almost thirty years ago, this town became a refuge for our people, offering solace within our walls. We govern ourselves outside of the empire's laws because the only leaders we can trust are ourselves. The lord and his brothers don their golden crowns, spewing lies about their benevolence while ruthlessly oppressing us into poverty. Meanwhile, they bask in riches on their thrones. They deny equality and rule over all with an iron fist." Kaeli leaned back in her chair. "My commitment to the people is to teach them, especially the younger generation, that they do not have to submit to the Brotherhood. Yes, the Brotherhood will eventually come for those living within our walls, recruiting them young to shape their minds to their ideology. Hopefully, by then, they'll be able to fight back."

"And until then, you hide and do nothing?" Mazie asked, unsure if her question would offend them.

"It may seem like we've given up," Kaeli said. "Most of us are too afraid to fight back. But someday, we *will* overthrow the self-righteous bastards that have made Dragão Terra a living nightmare. We're just not ready."

Mazie's heart ached for them. She never had that life. Her parents loved her, and she had a safe home, free from the rule of a king or queen. Until Matthias killed her people, that is. But before then, she lived under the guidance of the elements of Earth, *not* man.

"Behind these walls are only whispers of our plans," Xander said. "As Kaeli mentioned, just because we're not currently storming the palace doesn't mean we won't. I believe that day is soon, as long as we do it together without acting on our emotions." He turned to Kaeli, as if he were reminding her. Perhaps she was ready to do something about it, but he wanted to protect her and keep her from acting rashly. "We're watching, though."

Kaeli gave him a hint of a smile. "And when we do, we'll destroy everything they've built."

Xander acknowledged her with a nod, his muscular arms crossing over his broad chest as he leaned back in his chair.

"Those in power are nothing more than arrogant fucks who would rather degrade me just for being a woman than recognize my true strength," Kaeli added.

Mazie's lip curved into a smile. She was already liking that one.

"And we're safe here?" Tegan asked. "Away from those men in power that you speak of?"

Kaeli nodded. "As I said, I don't share the same ideologies as the Brotherhood. Xander is the only dragon in our country, besides myself, whom I trust completely. Should the opportunity arise, I will bring those three brothers to their knees."

"Secretly, of course," Xander added, leaning against the wall. "Even you are not exempt from those laws. You face off with the leaders of the Brotherhood, and you might as well dig yourself a grave—not unless you have an army behind you."

"Fuck the laws, Xander. Today was the most exhilarating experience we've had in a while," she said, turning to Mazie and flashing her a smile.

The two shifters seemed oddly unbothered after burning two men alive who, by the looks of it, seemed to be essential commanders to their ruler.

"How can you even keep us safe here?" Tegan asked. "Won't someone report their men having gone missing?"

"Well," Xander started. "We scattered the ash and buried their bones. So, unless someone from the empire witnessed what we did, it will be a few days before they begin their search."

"But they'll see the ship," Mazie reminded them. "I think it's quite obvious we'll be to blame."

"Yes. A ship that suddenly landed on dry land in the middle of nowhere will spark some talk around town, but it's nothing we can't handle," Kaeli said.

"And who exactly were those men you killed?" Tegan asked. "Were they the emperor's guards?"

Kaeli stole another glimpse at Xander and then met Tegan's soft green eyes. "They're part of the Red Dragon Brotherhood," she said. "There are hundreds of loyal servants to the empire's lord, and if I hadn't done what I did, you'd be dead—if not by their hand, then the fighters who would follow their trail to avenge them if you had managed to kill them yourselves."

"But wouldn't they trace the killings back to you and come here, then? To kill you?" Mazie asked, and Aiden snickered under his breath. "What the fuck is your problem, Aiden?"

Aiden let out a deep sigh, clearly annoyed. "Oh, I don't know, Mazie," he said in a snarky tone. "We're stranded, the ship and my sword burned up, and you're worried about the lives of strangers?"

"Do we have to worry about that one, Mazie?" Xander asked, gesturing to Aiden as if the elf were some disobedient pet.

"Yes," Mazie responded simultaneously as Tegan said, "No." Mazie rolled her eyes. "Don't be a fool, Tegan. Look at him."

When Tegan shifted her gaze to Aiden, she immediately noticed the same thing Mazie did. The darkness was taking over his features—he barely resembled the Elven warrior he had been just days earlier. Under his tired eyes, his pale skin bore the marks of dark circles, while his irises were almost deep, jet black. Above all that, he emitted an unsettling energy that made Mazie's neck hairs stand on end.

The longer they stared at Aiden, the fiercer and more twisted his expression became. Mazie quickly stood up and placed her hand on the cutlass that rested on her hip, sensing a sudden change in the atmosphere.

Slowly, Aiden placed his hand into his bag and searched through it. He let out a low growl that rumbled deep in his chest. "What the fuck, Tegan? You didn't pack me any weapons?" he asked, his lips pressed together in a tight line. "If it wasn't already tragic that Mazie dropped my father's sword and sent it up in flames, you sent me out here without even a fucking pocket knife?"

"Sorry about the damn sword, Aiden," Mazie intercepted, "but if your first instinct is to search for a weapon from simply placing my hand on the hilt of my cutlass, then there's a reason Tegan didn't pack you anything." Mazie tightened her fist on the hilt. "And don't blame her. I was the one who told her not to. So, if you try anything, *elf boy*, I'll end you faster than you can blink."

"Ooh, I like you, stranger," Kaeli said to Mazie, leaning back in her chair. "You've only been here an hour, and you're willing to kill one of your friends."

"He's not what I would consider a friend, per se," Mazie stated, a subtle grin adorning her lips. "However, there's a dark entity possessing him at the moment, and no matter how hard he's fighting it, I don't think we'll last through the night unless we tie him up."

"Tie him up?" Tegan shook her head. "Mazie, I don't think that's the way to treat—"

Mazie gently grabbed her upper arm, turning away from the rest of the group. "Tegan, I know this isn't what you want, but it's what's right. Something's wrong. I know it, and you do, too."

"Mazie," Tegan tried to interrupt her, but Mazie didn't allow it. She settled for a harsher approach now.

"Even if you don't fully want to acknowledge it, these people have taken us in. I don't think it's right to jeopardize our safety—or theirs. He's getting worse, Tegan."

Tegan looked back, first at Aiden and then at Kaeli and Xander.

"Fine. Mazie's right," Tegan said quickly, finally acknowledging the obvious. There was an apologetic look in her eyes as she looked at Aiden. "Do you have any rope?"

"I'm right here, Tegan!" Aiden snarled, but all eyes left him when they heard a roar echoing over the house that was so loud that it shook the walls.

"Oh, shit," Kaeli said. "Xander, hide them in the library and crack the door. I'll handle this."

All three rushed to follow Xander inside a barely furnished room, where three shelves lined the far back wall, filled with disorganized stacks of books.

Xander slightly cracked the door while the three of them slid down to the floor. They were now in perfect view of the main room, but no one could see them.

Aiden's breath warmed the back of Mazie's neck as they crouched together, making her skin crawl.

"Be ready to use your magic in case that thing attacks," Mazie warned, looking over at Tegan and Aiden, who were already poised with their magic hovering slightly at their fingertips.

"What do you want?" Kaeli asked a man with a sun-kissed complexion who had burst through the door and brushed past her.

"Kaeli, let's not pretend you don't know," the man said, looking around the room. "Where are they?"

"Being a little aggressive within the first ten seconds of coming into my home, don't you think?" Kaeli asked, crossing her arms.

The warning tone in the man's voice deepened. "Don't play coy with me, girl. I won't ask you again."

"Oh, are you talking about the travelers?" she asked, and Mazie bit the inside of her cheek. She didn't want to kill the woman, but she wouldn't have a choice if she gave up their location.

"Kaeli!" the man growled.

"They're not here," she said. "Gods, give it a rest."

"It's true, Lord Dorion," Xander said. "They came through needing water and food. We aren't monsters. Of course, we helped them, and then they went on their way."

The man he called Lord Dorion folded his arms. "You're going to tell me if they return. Do you understand?"

After exchanging a glance, Xander and Kaeli both nodded.

Dorion looked around once more, and then his eyes turned to Kaeli before he reached out and gently brushed his thumb over her cheek. "I think it's time you tell us where you've hidden the Ember Guild, Kaeli. I protected you once. If you had anything to do with this," he said in a soft, gentler tone that surprised Mazie, "I won't be able to protect you again."

Kaeli's beautiful features twisted in a mix of disgust and horror. She pushed his hand away, stepping back to put some distance between them. "You know they didn't do this...and neither did I. Please leave...*Father!*" Venom laced the last word as it rolled off her tongue.

Mazie's eyes widened, and she whispered to the others, "Oh shit."

Dorion's nostrils flared. "Alright, fine. Hate me as much as you want, but our people would have killed you years ago if it weren't for me. Your uncles and I were the only witnesses to what happened, and we will continue to share our truth—"

"A truth that gets innocent lives killed!" she shouted, stepping forward as if she didn't fear him at all. "Leaving Xander and me responsible for protecting them. It was so easy for the Brotherhood to blame the mages for something I did. Me! Not them." She pounded against her chest with her fist. "I was a baby, Dorion. They would have understood."

"No, Kaeli, they would have told me to kill you so that your uncontrolled power would no longer touch our land. You and I both know it was better this way. The Ember Guild had a dark history with our kind for centuries. They were much easier to blame, especially after it resulted in your mother's death...their future empress. We had to blame them."

Kaeli stilled and stepped back, tears streaming down her cheeks.

"I remember the horror on your face the night I sat down with you," Dorion continued. "You were barely ten when I shared the truth. My Gods, Kaeli, I didn't want you to know. I wanted that secret to die with us, but one day, you'd realize you had magic to open portals and that I wasn't your birth father. That truth I couldn't escape from. I'd much rather you hear it from me than learn from someone else. It was my way of showing you how much I loved you, regardless of the truth. I've always wanted to be honest with you. I never blamed you for killing your mother, never blamed you for letting those Vipers into our world, but *they* would. Your people would, and the Council of Drakentos will drag you in the streets and kill you themselves." He stepped forward and reached out, but she flinched. "You can deny me the title of 'father' all you want, but I will never stop being one for you."

Kaeli's features turned venomous. "You'll never be my father. Get the fuck out of my house!"

The man clenched his fist, his knuckles turning white, and even from a distance, Mazie saw his jaw tighten and his lips twitch. "I also cannot promise this will not spark a war. A portal opening is a clear violation of our agreement with the mages. You can protect the Ember Guild all you want, but the Council of Drakentos has written the law in stone. Whoever did it must be brought to trial and executed. I'll ask you once more. Was it you?"

"It wasn't me!" she shouted before leaning in and whispering so softly that Mazie could barely hear. "I swear it."

"Alright," he continued. "At this very moment, the Council of Drakentos is gathering in the court, preparing a plan to uncover the identity of those responsible for letting in a massive ship and a group of creatures from another world. At the moment, we have only retrieved one who came through, an elf woman."

Mazie's stomach dropped.

"As far as the mages go, no amount of protection from you will stop them from searching for the guild. We only stopped searching years ago because they were no longer a threat. But today, with the realms opening again, it changes everything."

"Well," Kaeli said with a smile, "it's a good thing you don't have a clue where I've hidden them. You're too much of a coward to tell your people that you've known this entire time that it was *me* twenty-eight years ago that let those Vipers in, not the mages. Your own daughter, a tiny baby who crumbled the walls of your cave, crushed my mother, and then let in monsters that wreaked havoc on our planet. They would strip you of your title and drag you in the streets themselves if they knew the truth."

Dorion slammed his fist on the table beside him. "As the ruler of this land, I am obligated to bring someone to justice. Do not force my hand."

Kaeli smirked. "To be honest, I would rather the people know the truth. They should know it was me. You've been too afraid to lose everything since the moment you realized my birth father was a mage, and that same power sparks within me, too. The only reason I've never come forward to the Council is because of Xander. If I tell them the truth, they'll kill him, too, for protecting me."

Dorion clenched his jaw.

"Don't you dare, Mazie," Tegan whispered, gripping the back of her collar when Mazie slightly moved forward. "Stay out of it."

"I can protect you both," Dorion said, drawing Mazie to look back at them while her temper simmered down.

"You only wish to protect yourself, Dorion. Do not place your hands on me again," Kaeli seethed through her teeth.

Mazie's hand went to her pistol at her hip, hovering there. Waiting.

The dragon shifter shook his head. "Fine. I'll go. But you are to let me know if they return. We need to be prepared for another war if any dangerous creature comes through that portal. We'll have to defend ourselves, not just against those invaders, but against those accountable for allowing it to come through in the first place. And remember, my sweet child, that it is my love for you that keeps me from destroying this colony and the others you've built."

Kaeli's shoulders stiffened as her father moved past her and left the house.

Mazie turned to Tegan and Aiden, and her jaw dropped. "Well," Mazie said. "I think we just met Anaru's daughter."

Once Dorion shut the door behind him, they watched through the window as the dragon soared back into the darkening sky, filling the air with the sound of his mighty wings.

They quietly left the back room and returned to the kitchen, with Kaeli glancing back at them, but only her lips parted, unable to speak.

"Well, isn't that interesting," Aiden said.

Mazie scowled at him and snapped, "Not now, Aiden!" Everything about the elf irritated her at this point. As if Tegan could sense it, she tried to put some space between them, moving in front of Aiden and placing her hand on his arm.

"Aiden, we need you to stand on guard," Tegan said. "Warn us if Dorion or anyone who serves him comes back."

Aiden nodded and left through the front door, entering the courtyard outside.

Mazie needed to address the more critical matter now—the one that would change Kaeli's life. She took a deep breath and said, "Kaeli, did I understand correctly that sorcerer magic opened the portal that slipped Anaru into the Earth world?"

Kaeli blinked and let out the air in her lungs. "What? How..." Xander and Kaeli shared a quick look. "How do you know about Anaru? What do you mean 'slipped her into the Earth world?'"

Mazie looked at Tegan briefly before her eyes locked back on Kaeli's. "Kaeli...your mother is alive."

# 8

## MAZIE

Over the next hour, Mazie explained how Anaru came into their world and how Lord Dorion kidnapped her in the months before Dragão Terra fell into destruction. She told the story about Anaru's journey with the crew and how important she was to all of them.

Mazie revealed Dergis's story, Xander's father, who fell for Queen Cassia's deception and ultimately perished by Aiden's arrow, so he could save the crew. But most importantly, she made it clear to Kaeli that Anaru was alive and searching for her at that very moment.

Kaeli looked like the air had been sucked out of her lungs, pale and drinking in every word that left Mazie's lips.

"Anaru believed Dorion killed you, Kaeli. She made Earth her home for years because she thought she had no one to return to. That was until she found the oracle that once lived within the home that fell with her, and she showed Anaru a vision that you were alive."

Kaeli was still silent, like she couldn't fully process what she was saying. Mazie couldn't blame her. In the blink of an eye, her entire life changed. Everything she'd ever thought was true....wasn't.

Tegan placed a small piece of the compass on the counter. "This is how we got here, but the crash destroyed it. Perhaps you or this Ember Guild can help us return home, if possible."

Mazie turned to Tegan. "We'll have to find Anaru first." They owed that much, not just to Anaru but also to Kaeli, considering all she had done for them.

Kaeli shut her eyes and dug her fingers into the wooden table. For the first time in nearly an hour, she spoke. "He lied to me, Xander. Dorion and my uncles made me believe that as a baby, my magic got my mother killed," she said. "Why would they do that?"

Xander reached out and gripped her hand to comfort her, but she pulled away.

"I know little about this world and your relationship with your father," Mazie said, "but from what I've seen...he hardly seems like the kind of man you can trust, Kaeli. With anything."

Xander nodded. "You're not wrong. Who knows what else he's been lying about? I wouldn't put anything past him."

"What if we don't find her in time?" Kaeli asked him. "If my father discovers she's alive, he'll kill her to keep her silent over what happened. He told the Council of Drakentos that she was dead. Her death sealed his place on the throne when it was finally time to elect the next ruler of Dragão Terra. He won't give up his crown and will kill anyone who knows the truth."

Xander's eyes filled with determination. "We'll do what we had always planned if war became inevitable," he said. "Cousin, we've strategized to wage war against your father and the Brotherhood for years. This might be the final push we've been waiting for."

Tegan reached into her bag and then stepped forward. "Kaeli, have you ever seen something like this?" she said, holding out more of the broken Kroneon pieces and the cracked key. "This ruby used to sit at the center of this compass. Do mages use gems as power?"

Kaeli shook her head. "No, I'm sorry. I've never seen anything like that. The source of a mage's power comes from within, not from a relic."

Tegan's face scrunched up, as if she was thinking the same thing Mazie was—to some extent. Tegan thought she was onto something with the Kroneon's gem, but Kaeli's words left them with nothing again.

Kaeli turned back to Xander. "Then we do something."

He nodded. "Starting where?"

"One of their friends is being held captive by Dorion," she said. "We plan to save them first, locate my mother, and then I'll personally be the one to drive a sword through my so-called father's heart."

Mazie stood up and rested her hand on the sword hanging from her sheath. "While you may not be familiar with pirates, trust me when I say we are loyal to those with honor. If you help us rescue our friend, Janelle, and find the others, we will help you fight."

"Thank you, Mazie," Kaeli said, placing her hand on Mazie's shoulder.

Sincerity shone in her eyes, but it wasn't what struck Mazie then. No, it was the beautiful swirl of silver and blue that intertwined in her irises.

Kaeli continued, "My father, he's been this way for as long as I can remember. He despises disorder, and there are countless things more important to him than me in his world. After the Vipers died and the Council of Drakentos elected my father to rule, Xander and I realized it was better to fight against them than to become something we weren't. We had to save ourselves and restore the planet's beauty, as the corruption severely distorted my father's desire for peace." She shook her head. "When we're two steps ahead, he pushes us back. Because he fears the unknown, he confines creatures like you within his palace walls. Your friend, Janelle, isn't safe. So, not only will we take down those prisons, but I will dismantle everything he's ever built. If there's ever been a moment to fight back"—she raised her eyes to meet Mazie's, a look of cold determination in them—"it's right now."

Mazie thought about the Shadow Creature and what it had done to Myloria. She understood the destruction caused by something so evil, the sounds of chaos and death echoing through abandoned streets. The people of this land were experiencing the same fear as they had.

Aiden yanked open the door and re-entered the room. Mazie and Tegan both turned to him. "Weren't you meant to stand guard and warn us if anyone came back?" Mazie snapped.

*What is it with him? He can't take a simple order and help us out?* she thought.

"Tell us more about this place," Aiden asked, ignoring Mazie's question. "From what I could see here, everyone hides in their homes. It's a ghost town out there."

"We always have to lock up after dark," Kaeli explained. "It isn't safe when you can't see within or beyond the forest."

"The more you tell us about what is out there, the easier it will be to find the rest of our crew," Tegan said. "What will happen if the Red Dragon Brotherhood catches the others?"

Kaeli blinked. "Well, they'll probably kill them or experiment on them, to be honest. They only care about themselves. Everyone else is expendable. Lord Dorion isn't too fond of unknown species coming into our land from other realms. It isn't the first time, and he'll want to know what he's up against. So, the fate that awaits your friends isn't a bright one. Which is why we need to devise a plan of attack."

"Great," Mazie said. "Well, we know he has Janelle. Let's hope the others found a safe place to hide."

"You can stay here for as long as the three of you need," Kaeli said.

Xander's eyes turned to Aiden. "We might need to keep you on lockdown, though," he said.

"What the fuck does that mean?" Aiden snarled, towering over Xander, but the dragon seemed unfazed.

Xander smirked. "I'm a full-blooded dragon shifter," he said. "I can sense your heart and desire, and you want to rip us to pieces."

Aiden snickered. "Well, if I were going to kill you, dragon, I'd have done it by now."

"He's right, Aiden," Tegan said, moving in between the two of them. Mazie stepped forward, too, clutching the sword hanging from her sheath. Tegan was softer in her approach with Aiden, but Mazie was ready for violence if needed. "I know you don't want to hurt anyone, but that darkness inside you is gaining control over your inner light. For now, we need you to be honest with us. If you feel like that thing inside you is taking over, you *must* let them secure you."

Aiden remained silent, his face cold and emotionless as he reached out and gripped Tegan's arm, digging his nails into her skin until she winced.

*That's my cue,* Mazie thought to herself before she quickly pulled out her cutlass and slammed the back of the hilt against Aiden's head, knocking him out cold. The four of them surrounded him as Bay frantically flew around, all staring at the sight of Aiden on the floor.

Mazie looked up at Kaeli, smiling wickedly. "Alright, do you have some chains or something?"

# 9

## NOLA

The sun from Dragão Terra felt different on Nola's cheeks. She sat for a moment, watching it rise above the horizon. The light touched her skin but didn't warm it. It created a tingly sensation, as if someone were whisking the tips of their fingers along her cheeks. Nola rose, brushing the sand from her palms, and went back into the cave.

"We can't abandon her here, Lincoln," Nola said, her eyes filled with concern, as they looked at Anaru leaning against the wall with her knees curled up to her chest. Her breathing seemed normal while she slept, but her skin looked ashen, sweat beading down her forehead. "But if we force her to keep going, she won't make it."

Lincoln nodded. "Perhaps you can stay here with her, and I can look for a mage and bring them back." Suddenly, his steps faltered, and Lincoln placed a hand on his chest. His breath caught in his throat.

"What is it?" Nola asked, watching Lincoln's features change.

He shook his head. "Our bond," he started. "Anaru released our bond."

In the silence that followed, Nola processed what that meant. Was Lincoln feeling empty without that connection? Sad or perhaps relieved? The truth was, she didn't want to know.

"I'm sorry, Lincoln," she said. "I don't know how that feels." She reached out and placed her hand on his cheek. "But you need to bury whatever pain you feel because we *must* keep moving. Our friends are still out there."

Lincoln nodded, stepped forward, and cradled her cheek in his hands. "We have to assume they've taken them. But before we can continue searching, we need to get Anaru to a healer as soon as possible."

Nola nodded but froze when she heard a noise outside the cave—a roar that sent chills down her spine.

They exchanged a look, and Lincoln took her hand as they hurried to the entrance. Lincoln attempted to pull her back, but she stuck her head out, and her heart raced as a dragon slowly moved through the trees. The dragon appeared to be searching for something or someone. The dragon sniffed the air, its wings unfurling as it readied to take flight, but instead, it moved toward their cave.

*It caught our scent,* Nola thought.

"We need to run to distract it from here. They can't find Anaru," Nola said. She took a step back into the cave, taking slow breaths to summon her siren form.

Lincoln placed his hand on his cutlass and slowly unsheathed it, his other hand resting steadily on the bridge of Nola's back. Her eyes changed from amber to white, the roughness of her scales prickling along her spine. When Nola was ready, she walked out of the cave and toward the dragon.

With a gentle, melodic song, Nola gradually lured the dragon closer to a flowing river near the cave. As she sang, the massive creature swayed and closed its eyes, slowly descending to the ground. With a heavy thud, it fell on its side, leaves and sticks crackling beneath it as it slipped into a dreamless slumber.

"Now," Lincoln said, intertwining his fingers in hers and hurrying to the dragon.

When they reached the creature, Lincoln placed his hand on its head and ran his fingers down its rough scales.

The dragon's chest rose and fell, and its steady breaths told them they had time to escape.

"I saw lights last night, northeast of the forest. Perhaps there's a city there," Lincoln said. "That's where we'll go."

The crack of a branch pulled their attention to look right. Five men, clad in armor with swords out front, stood along the forest pathway, glaring at them.

"We were right. There are others from the crash," said a man with ashy blond hair, addressing the others.

"We were right about her being a siren, too," another man with a smooth, bald head replied, his lip turning up. "Lay down any weapons you have. Let's make this go as smoothly as we can."

"Lincoln," Nola said, stepping back into his chest. He wrapped one arm around her waist, pulling her back, before positioning her behind him for protection. He raised his sword in front of himself.

"Sing again, Nola. Subdue them," he said.

Nola let her siren call echo through the forest, but the men responded with laughter and mockery.

"That pretty tune doesn't work on us, siren," the blond man said. "My name is Merrick Amulius of the Red Dragon Brotherhood. We charge you with trespassing on our land." His lips turned up again. "Come on, Gavin. Quit playing and get up."

Nola swallowed, and terror wrapped around her lungs. She and Lincoln quickly moved away from the now awakened beast.

The dragon she thought she had subdued let out a gentle moan before reverting to his human form.

"Fuck," Lincoln cursed, watching the bare-naked man walk past them to join the others.

"Any ideas?" Nola asked, looking up to meet Lincoln's eyes.

"Only one," he whispered. "We fight."

Nola's eyes turned almost pearly white as she experienced the enchanting swirl of magic. Her skin returned to scales, and her nails elongated, resembling a cluster of razor-sharp knives.

"Are you ready, love?" Lincoln asked, looking down at her hands. "I've only got the cutlass on me."

Nola had left her sword in the cave.

"I don't need my sword," she said confidently, stretching out her hands.

"We respectfully decline to be arrested," Lincoln said to the men. "You'll have to kill us first."

Merrick grinned. "That won't be a problem."

The six men stretched out, forming a circle before collectively shifting into their dragon forms within seconds. Fire blazed from their mouths, their lips turning up to show their sharp, jagged teeth.

Nola swiftly moved around Lincoln, charging toward a dragon with light-gray scales, her claws slashing at it. The gray dragon released a ball of fire, but Nola managed to dodge it. She then jumped into the air and attacked the dragon's wing, shredding his flesh with her claws.

After destroying the dragon's wing, Nola flipped back, landing on her feet. She lunged forward again, this time latching onto his neck and ripping out scales and pieces of flesh, her mouth and hands now drenched with blood.

Nola couldn't see where Lincoln was amidst the fighting. Her peripheral vision darkened as she focused on the creature she was ripping to pieces. She thrashed her arms repeatedly, the dragon roaring and bucking its neck back to throw her off, but she clung to him. Skillfully, she dodged the dragon's attempt to bite down into her flesh, the creature missing her each time.

When Nola loosened her grip, she pushed off the dragon's body and landed on the rocks. She looked up to see the dragon throwing its head toward her to knock her off her feet. Her fist came out and slammed into the dragon's throat, knocking his head up. Her fingers then dug into exposed, tender flesh. With a sickening tear, Nola pulled back, ripping his throat wide open with her claws.

As it hit the ground, the dragon's lifeless body transformed into a human. Nola looked for Lincoln and saw him surrounded by three men, with one holding a cutlass to his throat.

"Impressive," Merrick said. "Dorion isn't going to be too keen on the fact that you killed one of his strongest men. But perhaps I can convince him to go easy on your punishment."

"Run, Nola!" Lincoln said, but she already knew what she had to do.

Her nails pulled back into her skin, no longer sharp and jagged, and her skin smoothed over. She had to compose herself before she attacked them; she'd risk Lincoln's life if she did.

"I'm sorry," Nola said to Lincoln, watching his eyes grow in fear as he staggered to stand straight, blood oozing from a wound on his forehead.

The man holding Lincoln's cutlass raised the weapon high above his head before slamming the hilt hard against the back of Lincoln's head, knocking him out.

They wouldn't kill them; Nola was sure they needed them for something, or they would both be dead by now.

"Fine," Nola said, knowing that she had to do whatever it took to get them away from the cave, so they wouldn't find Anaru asleep in there. She would find a way to deal with the men when they weren't expecting it. "I surrender."

# 10

## JANELLE

The light of dawn had broken over the horizon. However, despite the sun rising, Janelle was unable to see much through the window from the bed, peering out through the thick fog covering the landscape. For the first time since they brought her to the palace, her captors opened the windows for her. They told her she could survey their lands from the confinement of the bed, but it didn't matter. When Janelle looked out, all she saw were thick white clouds in the sky and gray wisps of fog covering the land.

The dense fog enveloping the castle was broken by the enormous trees beneath it, giving her the only sense of nature in their world.

Dorion and the others told her it was a privilege to breathe fresh air. Soon, they would shut the windows all over again, sealing her back into a prison of confinement.

Janelle turned her gaze from the window, laid her head back down, and looked up, focusing on the carved details of the ceiling within the gloom of the room.

The bedroom had two light sources: a table lamp and a concealed light on the washroom ceiling. The lighting was dim, but it provided Janelle with some comfort. Everything she had seen in the castle so far was nothing more than dark shadows in every chamber.

There was no warmth. No peace.

She rested her eyes, once again waiting for someone to come and feeling her body ache from a restless night.

As her mind drifted off, the creak of the door abruptly brought her back to reality. Lord Dorion smiled as he entered the room. He stood shirtless, with only black trousers loosely hanging on his hips. Janelle's eyes involuntarily wandered to every curve and dip of his muscles, creating an uncomfortable tension in the air. She blinked away, not wanting to stare, but it was clear that every man she'd met since she arrived radiated an aura of power.

"You're up early, my pet," he said calmly, setting down a tray of food on the table in the corner of the room.

He continued closer to her and stood by the edge of the mattress, still as stone.

Dorion's smile broadened as he produced a key from his pants pocket. He reached down and grabbed the cuffs binding Janelle's wrists. She flinched away from his touch, eyeing him suspiciously as he turned the key. Once the lock disengaged, the cuffs and chains fell to the mattress with a cold rattle against the headboard behind it. Janelle rubbed her wrists while simultaneously trying to ignore the rumble in her belly. She wanted to eat but was afraid they'd poison her if she did.

"You're joining me for a meal this time," he ordered.

She didn't move, only watching as he sat at the table and removed the silver lid from the plate. Instantly, the scent of freshly baked food hit her nose, causing her stomach to rumble again.

Janelle had refused food since she awoke in that room more than a day ago and was unsure if she could resist any longer. She had to eat to keep her strength to fight back when the opportunity arose.

After sliding off the bed, she carefully crept toward him, his unwavering gaze on her the entire time. Dorion had pulled his long brown hair back in a low bun, with a tiny strand falling over his right cheek, barely concealing the small scar she had seen earlier.

Once she sat, he took a bite of his food. "It's called a casserole," he said, swallowing a bite.

"I know what a fucking casserole is, you idiot," she said, watching him smirk at her remark before dabbing his cheek with a napkin.

"Well, I don't know. You seem a little lost here, as if the world you came from was so different—"

"It *is* different," she said, looking around the room. "I mean, we have light, but not like that." She pointed to the lamp. "Some places have running water, like yours, but all this seems so strange to me, and I don't understand it."

"I know the unknown can seem a bit scary, my pet," he said while she scowled back at him. It was as if he couldn't help but find her amusing, letting out a chuckle. "But I can help you feel more at home. Let me unravel your little secrets and answer my questions."

She huffed, reaching for a dinner roll. The warmth of the bread spread in her hands, and she bit down, savoring the buttery taste. Once she swallowed, she looked back up. "What are you going to do with me?" she asked.

He set his fork down and smirked once more. That time, the smile reached his eyes.

"Why is that question so funny?" she asked. "I'm a prisoner to dragon shifters. You may want to put in a little more effort to convince me I'm safe."

"Oh, my pet, you're anything but safe with me. But I can assure you I have no plans to kill you...not yet, anyway. We're going to have a *lot* of fun together first. I can promise you that."

"Fucking fantastic," she said, using a spoon to scoop out the casserole onto her plate. She waited a few seconds, taking a moment before placing her fork down and adding, "Please make it quick when you do. I won't be cooperative, so if you expect that from me..."

Her time with Elijah came to mind. During the days he'd held her captive, she remained incredibly stubborn and refused to disclose any information regarding Kieran or his intentions. But he had eventually managed to find a way to get her to open up and reveal what he needed to know. Would Dorion be the same? Or this time, would she fight until they killed her?

*I'd rather be killed fighting back against him*, she thought. *It's better than being locked behind a door again and fed by monsters.*

Just as she was about to make another snarky comment, the dragon shifter flung the table across the room, his skin glowing red and eyes gleaming like gold. Heat radiated from his body as he stomped forward, his hand lashing out and seizing her throat.

The situation had escalated dangerously in the blink of an eye. Janelle's heart hammered so wildly that she could barely breathe. As Dorion's hand tightened, he cut off her breath completely. She struggled against his grip, trying to wrench his hand from her throat. But her strength was no match for his, and her body went limp. Dorion lifted her off the floor, her feet kicking weakly in the air, and slammed her against the wall.

He eased his grip, giving her a moment to breathe. "Is this really what you want?" he asked, his breath brushing softly against her pale cheek. "For me to crush the life out of you with the strength of my hand? Make no mistake, my pet. I *will* do it if you force me to."

Janelle closed her eyes, her powers stirring within her. With all her strength, she unleashed her light magic, a blast of white crashing through the room. She braced herself to fall to the ground, but when her eyes opened, he was still standing there, his hand wrapped around her neck, seemingly unfazed by the impact of magic.

Her magic had done nothing.

Janelle's heart hammered, her hands shaking uncontrollably as she realized the mistake of revealing her power to him.

Suddenly, a wicked smile spread across his face, and the brute power seemed to subside. "Well, my pet, you continue to surprise me. All the other magical creatures who made their way into our world lacked the ability to harness that kind of power. Fascinating, honestly. Don't get me wrong, that felt like little needles against my skin, but it was *something* at least."

Frustration bubbled in her chest. Aside from the force of her powers, her magic was supposed to change someone's heart and sway them to her light. But they were useless against a dragon, and fighting back now would be too dangerous.

*Great*, she thought.

Dorion released her throat, her knees hitting hard against the marble tiles when she fell. She drew a deep breath and immediately coughed, rubbing the bruised flesh of her throat.

"I'll send a servant up to clean the mess in here. But for now, I want you to change out of those hideous clothes."

Janelle looked up right as Dorion reached down and tore away her shirt. She slowly rose, watching the fire and smoke curl from his fingers. The magic didn't leave his mouth like she had expected from a dragon, but rather from his hand. He sent an ember from his fingertips to burn away her remaining garments until she stood stark naked, the heat of the flames warming her bare legs.

He turned back to her, looking up and down at her exposed body with a lascivious grin on his handsome face.

"I would much prefer you like *this* while you stay here, but you might get a little chilly." He backed away from her and continued to stare. She wrapped her arms around her body, trying to cover up what dignity she had left, and sneered at him.

*Fucking bastard,* she thought.

"You'll wear that outfit hanging by the wall, and I'll have my people fill that closet with more clothes of my liking."

She swallowed as she looked down at the ash but stilled when the glint of pearl caught her eye; the Voleric was buried within the mess.

*It must have been in my pocket,* she thought.

Janelle looked up quickly, not wanting to draw attention to the gem at her feet. Dorion's eyes turned dark as he pointed toward the closet door.

"Get dressed, and I'll be back this afternoon. A few of my men are scoping the area where they found you. Where there is one, there are more. Whoever you came with through that portal, we'll find them."

Janelle tried not to show panic on her face. She didn't want that bastard or his cohorts to find her companions. It was better that she was the only captive rather than all of them being tortured by the sick monster in front of her.

Her mind went back to the gem hidden in the ash. Janelle had never used the Voleric on her own, but Elijah taught her exactly what he did to harness the magic.

So, she had to try.

Dorion stepped back, giving her one more look before turning on his heel and heading out of the room. Janelle gave his back a filthy gesture, turned, and looked at a silky nightgown hanging by a clip under the closet's mirror.

*Fucker*, she thought. But it was better than being naked.

She slipped on the gown, the silk soft against her skin. It was sleeveless, loose-fitting, and had a lace trim reaching to her knees. Janelle turned, eyeing herself in the mirror.

These bedroom garments were vastly different than the fashion of her home. Instead of comfort and warmth, this gown made her feel exposed.

She balled her fists, her fingernails digging into the silk, and stared at her reflection in the mirror, making a silent promise. *I'm going to kill them all.*

Janelle examined the dark circles forming under her eyes and her disheveled white hair hanging in her face. She could only imagine how awful she smelt, too, and hoped she'd be able to bathe soon. But until then, she had to hurry and use the Voleric before Dorion returned.

She sifted through the ash, picked up the Voleric, and wiped it clean. Clenching it in her hands, she closed her eyes and focused on Elijah, just like he had shown her before. She tapped into her light magic to help form the connection she needed to make the Voleric work.

The room spun a little, making her feel dizzy and unsteady on her feet. She fought against it, determined to harness its power until she found Elijah and spoke to him within his dream state.

What happened next was not what she expected.

Elijah rested on a plush, black sofa inside someone's home, and a woman knelt beside him, with thick black hair covering most of her face. Her stomach jumped as the woman looked at her through the veil, connecting through the link meant for Elijah...*not* her.

*Well, that's interesting*, she thought. *She can see me.*

Janelle could read the woman's thoughts in a strange, cosmic way. Words came through as if she were projecting them to her.

*You'll be okay, Elijah.* The woman's thoughts seemed to pass through Janelle and into Elijah's mind. *It's not as bad as it might look. Let me gather the medicine that will help you.*

She tried to reach Elijah's mind again, but whoever that woman was had somehow breached their link, intentionally or not. Janelle tried to clear her mind again, returning her attention to him. From what the vision revealed, he looked deathly pale, and his right arm had been severely burned. Janelle's lips parted, and her entire body went numb.

*Elijah, I'm here*, she said in her thoughts, projecting to him.

"Come on, you idiot," Janelle said aloud. *Look at me.*

The woman broke their gaze and looked down at Elijah again, placing her hand on his chest, and said, "There's a power here. I can feel it." She reached out, removing his hand from his wounded arm.

*Elijah*, Janelle projected, feeling the link between them falter, and tried to re-connect. *Elijah, I love you. Listen to me. I love you.* She believed it in her bones as she looked at him. The fated connection that bound their hearts in their realm was starting to break. She wasn't sure why, but she knew something was causing it to slip away.

As if he could sense the Voleric's power fading, Elijah suddenly opened his eyes and turned his head to look at Janelle. The sofa he laid on shifted into a grassy meadow.

"My love," Elijah said, speaking aloud inside her mind. Relief washed over her body instantly. She finally felt like she could breathe again. Janelle's heart pounded as she hurried toward him, embracing his body and wrapping her arms around his neck. Elijah was there to catch her, securing her in the familiar embrace. She let out a small sob, drawing in a shaky breath before she leaned up, kissing him so passionately that it had to be real. It was too impossible to be only a dream.

They lost themselves in their aching kiss for a moment longer before Elijah finally pulled back.

"I don't feel pain here," he told her, brushing a stray strand of her hair out of her face. "Let's stay here forever."

She shook her head. "I don't know how long I can hold on to the Voleric's power, Elijah."

He nodded and released their embrace but kept his hands linked with hers. His thumb circled over her palm, while warm tears formed in the corners of her eyes. Janelle realized she needed to see him more than she needed air after her encounter with Dorion.

"Tell me where you are, love," he said.

She looked around the meadow as it slowly started to crumble, the brick walls inside the home blending with the open field like colors from a painting melting down a canvas.

"I'm inside a castle run by dragon shifters. Their ruler calls himself Lord Dorion. I don't know where anyone else is." She closed her eyes and rested her forehead against his. The tears she had been holding in streamed down her face for the first time since she arrived. "They're going to kill me, Elijah. They're going to kill me before I can breathe in your scent again."

Elijah placed his hand on her cheek but looked around. "I'll find you," he promised. Determination was clear in his voice; it was a promise he was making to both of them. His other hand found her cheek, too, cupping her face and forcing her to look at him. His eyes locked on hers, as if he were memorizing the beautiful sapphire color. "Don't get yourself killed. Do whatever they ask, and I *will* find you."

As the space fell apart, more tears poured down her cheeks, and she let out a harrowing cry, watching Elijah slip away in a wisp of smoke, the Voleric pendant falling at her feet and back into the ash.

# II

## ELIJAH

E lijah's eyes opened gradually. He caught only a glimpse of the ceiling before his head spun, forcing him to close his eyes to prevent him from being sick.

"Don't move," Arabella said, placing a wet rag over his head and running it across his forehead. "Holy shit. You almost died, Elijah."

Elijah placed his hand on his arm, but the searing pain was no longer there. He ran his fingers over the skin and realized that the wounds from the flames were nearly gone.

"Your body healed itself. At least it looked that way. Magic dwindled on the surface, repairing the injured flesh. I don't understand it. It's as if your magic made you *whole* again."

"I—" he started, sitting up from the pillow. "My magic doesn't heal, Arabella." He had no idea what the hell was happening. From the moment he set foot in Dragão Terra, nothing made sense.

"Except it did," she said, and an unsettling feeling pulled in his belly. "It healed you; I watched it happen. You were speaking with someone the entire time, too. I couldn't distinguish the words, but your mind was elsewhere."

Elijah blinked, looking back at Arabella. It was daylight now, a small amount of sunlight coming through the window. "You saw her?" he whispered, memories suddenly flooding his mind. "But she was inside *my* mind."

Arabella smiled softly. "Is that the woman you search for?"

He sat up, and his head throbbed with intense pain. Elijah managed to give her a brief nod before leaning forward, resting his head in his hands.

"Relax, Elijah. You might have healed, but your body still needs rest. You're not out of the woods yet."

Elijah moved his legs over the side of the sofa and sat up straight. Arabella tried to push him back down, but he slapped her hand away. "Enough, Arabella. I'm fine." The surface he was lying on was hard as a rock, causing more pain in his body. Elijah couldn't be still any longer; he needed to heal entirely and find Janelle before it was too late.

"I think a bit of magic happened back there," Arabella said. "It wasn't me who healed you, but I sensed her power coming through the vision. There's no way to explain it. One moment, she was there, and the next, you were screaming for dear life, clutching your arm."

Elijah blinked, his brows pulling together. "That isn't possible, Arabella. Whoever uses the Voleric can only connect themselves to one person at a time."

Arabella let out a heavy sigh. "I know what I saw."

Elijah pressed his hand against his head as it ached again. Alarm rose within him that the Voleric was behaving differently now, and he wasn't sure what to make of it.

"What's a Voleric, Elijah?"

"Magic," he explained. "Magic that can reach your dreams or subconscious." Elijah cleared his throat. "My friend told me where she was taken," he added. "She claims to have been kidnapped by dragon shifters and a man who goes by Dorion."

Arabella leaned back and pressed her lips together. Her eyes were filled with pain and sorrow. "That's *Lord* Dorion, the emperor of our planet—the eldest of the Amulius brothers. We have little freedom out here, Elijah. I don't know what kind of world you're from, but here, if the Lord takes you...you're never getting out. I'm sorry, but—"

Elijah's stomach twisted painfully, causing him to stand up, clutching his hand against it. Just the thought of her in another man's control made him sick with rage.

"Don't be sorry. I'm not giving up. I *will* save her," he said firmly. Again, Arabella shook her head.

"I don't think you under—"

"No, I understand," Elijah interrupted her. "I understand that's what you believe, but I'll be damned if I stay here doing nothing, as that man puts his hands on her." He paused, fury twisting in his stomach. "Arabella, if I don't get her back, I will raise hell until those responsible for taking her bleed from every one of their pores while I slowly rip them apart."

Arabella's brown eyes opened wide, and her body went still. For a moment there, he thought he may have gotten through to her. "That sounds heroic and all, Elijah. I can see that you care deeply about this woman, but if Lord Dorion or any of his brothers have her, then I'm sorry for your loss."

# 12

## JANELLE

K ade escorted Janelle into the main chamber of the castle. She noticed the building bore a similar resemblance to the palace in Zemira. However, unlike the thick gray stones in Elijah's home, the material used to build the place was translucent minerals. It reminded Janelle of glass. Every surface gleamed with sparkling silver, with colorful embellishments adorning the walls. This was so unlike her home world that Janelle couldn't help but stare as if in a trance.

"Dorion will be right with you," Kade said, removing a sword from his sheath and placing it on a wooden table at the center of the room. Janelle didn't bother responding. A servant rushed into the room and picked the sword up from the table. Kade instructed the timid man to polish and sharpen the blade within the hour. For an added measure, Kade growled, baring wickedly sharp teeth. The servant nodded and fled out the door.

Janelle studied Kade as he rolled his sleeves and put his hands on the table's edge. As he leaned, she saw his muscular arms adorned with markings similar to Dorion's that traveled up high on his neck.

He picked up a piece of fruit from a basket on the table and took a bite. "All *four* of us will eat dinner here shortly," he said after swallowing. His tone was playful, as if Janelle's presence amused him. "Would you like some fruit before then?"

She shook her head. "Who's the fourth?"

He smiled wryly before walking toward her across the room, still holding the fruit. "Eat."

She narrowed her eyes at the half-eaten fruit, and her nostrils flared. Her heated stare should have told Kade her answer, but he brought it to her lips anyway, and his grin grew so wide it reached his eyes. "Such a stubborn girl you are. I just showed you it's not poisoned by eating it. It's a hashmond pear. Bite it." She stepped back, but he reached out and gripped the back of her neck. "We can do this all day," he said. "Eat the fucking pear."

Her eyes narrowed on the fruit before she bit down on the opposite side, where he took a bite. The juice from the fruit instantly hit her senses, and she moaned out loud. It was exquisite.

While she chewed, he smiled and stepped back to give them space. "That wasn't so hard," he said.

Irritated that he had gotten his way, Janelle considered spitting the fruit back into his face. But she was starving and needed something to replenish her strength, so she swallowed the delicious fruit. Crossing her arms over her chest, Janelle tapped her foot, waiting for Kade to elaborate on their mystery guest.

"You've already met Lord Dorion, but you haven't met our *other* brother, Merrick," he said. "I suggest you quit your sour attitude before you do. He isn't as pleasant as I am and won't put up with your shit."

Janelle's stomach tightened. The mere thought of more men around her made her skin crawl. As if sensing her discomfort, Kade reached out and cupped her cheek. Rather than soothing her, his warm hand only intensified the pounding in her chest. It took all her willpower not to slap it away.

"Spin around," he demanded, his gaze still roaming over her body. Lust radiated from him, so tangible Janelle could practically taste it.

"Wh...what?" she stammered as Kade dragged his gaze from her body back to her eyes.

"Spin. Around," Kade repeated. Something about his tone told her he wouldn't ask again. In fact, his smile shifted into something much more menacing.

Janelle glared at Kade before spinning on the tips of her toes. Fury burned her skin as she acted the part of a doll Kade wanted to examine. When she turned to face him, Kade stepped closer and put his hand on her cheek again, rubbing his thumb playfully over her skin while his other hand slid down between her breasts. Janelle bit her lip to keep from cursing at him. She needed to stay calm if she wanted to survive. The dragon shifter bit his bottom lip as he said, "Such an interesting little creature you are." His voice was smooth like velvet. "And so incredibly beautiful."

Janelle's stomach flipped again, and her face scowled, instantly repulsed by his touch.

As she watched his hand drop from her chest, she defiantly stepped back and lifted her chin. "Instead of harassing me, why not share more about this place? If you expect my cooperation, I want to know who lives here and who you've sent in and out of the room you've held me in for the past few days. Is everyone here a dragon shifter? Are you all family?"

"So demanding, aren't you?" he said. "Three of us are brothers, some are friends..." The side of his lips turned up into a smile. "And others serve our needs." Kade glanced down at her chest suggestively, running his tongue over his upper lip. "Every single one of them."

The three men who ruled this place were dangerous; that was clear. Whatever they had planned for her was anything but hospitable. Despite the food and warm bed, Janelle knew malice when it reared its ugly head.

Kade was evil.

Janelle tried to create more space between them by stepping back, but he reached out again and grabbed the front of her nightgown, keeping her still. The color drained from her face right before she heard a familiar voice.

"Let her go, Kade," Dorion ordered, stepping into the room. "We can at least let her relax for a day."

Janelle swiped Kade's hand away from her nightgown and turned away from him. Dorion picked up a bottle of wine hanging from a slot on the wall and brought it over, sticking a device inside the cork and pulling it off.

After he sat it down at the table, the back door swung open, and a handful of servants rushed in with trays and silverware, bringing it to the table.

"Where's Merrick?" Dorion asked Kade, taking a seat.

"He's taking care of a situation a few miles from where the ship landed. He'll be back shortly. We know there's more who came through that portal with her, and we think they killed some of our men. He and Rhashan are searching near the caves."

Janelle's body stiffened, and her face went pale. She knew for certain that Elijah was in another city and hoped it was far enough away from where the ship had crashed.

*But where are the others?* she wondered. Did they even make it through the portal? Were she and Elijah alone?

A side smirk pulled at Kade's lips. "We can always torture her for answers." He gave her a wink. "We can make it a little fun for us. The men and I have been feeling a profound sense of boredom lately." He bit his bottom lip again.

"My pet," Dorion said suddenly, his hand outstretched beside her. "Come with me."

*That stupid fucking name,* she thought, wishing her powers were strong enough to disfigure Dorion's handsome face.

When Janelle refused to move, Dorion grabbed her elbow, pulling her forward to walk. As his large hand wrapped around her arm, she closed her eyes, imagining Elijah touching her with the warmth of his palms. She longed for his touch instead.

A stabbing feeling hit her gut again—*Elijah.* Seeing him in the Voleric's vision felt real, yet when they met on the plane of that magic, she couldn't fully touch him. Their connection had become strained, and she didn't know if he was okay beyond what the vision showed her.

The door swung open, and she looked over, seeing another male shifter enter the room, but this one wasn't bare-chested as the others. Though the man's tunic covered his torso, the tattoo markings up his neck on his creamy-beige skin were still visible and identical to Dorion and Kade's. His long blond hair fell past his shoulders, its waves brushing against his cheeks, and his piercing brown-yellow eyes pinned hers with a stare.

When he looked at Janelle, though, his face grew stern. Unlike Kade's perverse nature, his demeanor seemed cold and hostile.

"You haven't killed her yet?" he asked, his lips pressed together as he joined Kade at the table. Annoyance lingered on his features.

Dorion ushered Janelle over to the empty chair. "Sit." He released her arm and handed Merrick the bottle of wine.

"Not yet, Merrick," Kade said, eyeing Dorion, who sat beside him. "Dorion seems convinced he might be able to break her."

"To tell us what, exactly?" Merrick said distastefully, filling up his glass and taking his first sip. "If she doesn't speak, we may have found a few others who will. They're being brought down to the dungeon now."

*Shit*, Janelle cursed, fighting to keep her expression neutral. She wondered who else they'd captured, but it was clear Merrick wouldn't provide more details.

Dorion didn't look at his brothers, only keeping his eyes on hers. "Drink," he ordered, gesturing to the red liquid in the glass a servant placed in front of her. "We'll find out soon enough what she's hiding."

As Janelle looked down at the red liquid, she realized it wasn't as bright as the others' glasses. It was a different wine than what the men had. Janelle pushed the glass away from her, which earned her a scathing glare from Dorion.

"My patience is running thin, my pet. I suggest you do as you're told," he said, oddly calm. Somehow, that was even more frightening than rage. "Or you won't be the only one to taste my fury. I promise you, your friends will, too."

Janelle fought the urge to curse at him as she reached for the glass, bringing it to her lips. The earthy aroma was pleasant, though, like strawberries and hibiscus.

She slowly took a sip, a slight burn in her throat as it went down. As she drank, her body warmed and became weightless, flooding her mind with complete ecstasy.

When Janelle looked up, Dorion stood. She held his gaze as he moved behind her, resting his hands on her shoulders.

"What the fuck is this?" she asked, feeling her head spin. She sunk back against her chair as the world began to blur. "So, you did drug me, didn't you?"

He leaned forward, the scruff on his cheek rubbing against her neck as his lips touched her ear.

She knew she didn't have a choice but to drink it. Whether they forced the liquid down her throat or threatened her friends if she didn't, the results were the same.

"I wouldn't call it that. It's just an elixir of compliance," Dorion said, his palms running down her bare arms while the other brothers laughed. "Sweet and utter compliance." Goosebumps prickled her skin, and a wave of relaxation washed over her body. She didn't want that reaction from his touch, but it was beyond her control. Arousal sparked between her legs as his hands cupped below her breasts, but he didn't squeeze, only rested them there.

That was worse.

So, so much worse.

"We gave you a small amount earlier to you in your food. It appears it wasn't enough, so we had to give you more. I'm sure your reaction to us may differ from how you usually behave, and that's fine with us as long as you relax. You're going to tell me your name and who came through that portal with you, or I'll keep you in this state until you die."

Janelle let out a sob as the glass fell, shattering at her feet and causing her to stumble out of her chair and onto the floor. She crawled desperately on her stomach, trying to reach the door, but she didn't get far before a hand gripped the back of her hair, stopping her. A second hand gripped her shoulder and flipped her onto her back. Janelle tried to pull free, but her mind and body were no longer connected, her hands unable to move.

Climbing on top of her, Dorion straddled her hips and held her between his knees like a caged animal. "Let the elixir do its job, my pet." One of his hands rested around her throat, while the other ran down her shoulder, causing an involuntary shudder through her body. His gaze was firm, making one thing clear: *Dorion was in control.*

He caressed her cheek with the hand that didn't hold her throat before looking at his brothers. They both turned on their heels and left the room without a single word, leaving them alone.

"What is your name?" he asked.

She shook her head. "I..." Her voice faded away as her mind entered a state of pure bliss.

"It's okay," he said. His hand dipped lower, now sliding up her thigh. She arched her back helplessly, grinding into him. "This can all feel like a delicious dream if you allow it. The more pleasure you feel, the more compliant you'll become."

She felt the poison slowly spreading through her veins, causing her muscles to weaken and her body to respond to his. A tingling sensation consumed her as he ground his erection between her legs.

Tears filled her eyes, and she closed them, not allowing him to see the effect he had on her.

"Janelle." The name she swore never to utter slipped from her tongue with ease.

"Beautiful," he said, running his fingers down her cheek. "Now, tell me, Janelle, who all came with you through that portal?"

Everything inside of her screamed not to utter another word. She strained against the desire to open her secrets, to tell Dorion what he wanted. "Fuck. You!" she managed to curse.

His hand rose from her throat to her chin as she attempted to turn her head away.

"Look at me, *Janelle*," he demanded, his voice low. "Now."

Fear mixed with involuntary arousal as she opened her eyes. His hold on her chin grew stronger as he dug his fingers into her flesh and forced her to look at him.

Dorion bore a smile of amusement. He was enjoying her struggle and the power he had over her.

"I want their names, Janelle," he repeated himself warningly. She pressed her lips together and shook her head. But he reached out suddenly and gripped her throat again. Tighter this time, squeezing just enough to threaten her but not enough to cut off her air.

He leaned down and kissed her gently on the lips. The sudden change in his demeanor, from hostility to gentleness, caused her body to become rigid. Dorion was unpredictable, and she couldn't fight someone she couldn't read.

After he released the kiss, he leaned closer to her, pressing his mouth to her ear. "Stop resisting," he whispered in a soothing tone, his voice as gentle as a cat's purr. His hand caressed her stomach before moving to her clothing, lifting her nightgown to reveal her bare thighs. Dorion's fingers moved between her legs, stroking her skin. As much as she wanted to fight it, she found herself aroused by his touch, wanting him to place his hands on her. She knew it was just the elixir.

*The more pleasure you feel, the more compliant you'll become,* she repeated his words in her mind.

Janelle didn't want this. She *couldn't* want this. Not now. Not ever.

She arched her back and let out a moan as he found her opening. He teased her with the light motion that remained on the surface and then slowly dipped his finger into the depths of her throbbing core.

"This isn't real," she said aloud. "I would never want this from you."

Dorion smiled while slowly moving his finger in and out of her pussy. "Dragons can sense someone's heart. We can feel their pain, courage, fear...and arousal." He gave her another wicked smirk. "We can also read minds if we imprint on someone." He pulled his finger out, the touch of his hand still lingering between her thighs. "Perhaps that is precisely what we do with you. My brothers haven't found their mates yet. It's the one guarantee we have to delve into the depths of your subconscious mind, revealing your innermost thoughts and secrets until there's nothing left."

Janelle closed her eyes, tears pouring down her cheeks, but she wouldn't sob. She held back her tears despite the overwhelming pain. As her mind drifted away, she recalled Lincoln's story about Anaru and the extraordinary bond he had formed with his dragon. They could link their thoughts to each other. If that were true, her secrets wouldn't stay hidden much longer.

"Fuck you," she said again. "My mind and body will never be yours. Get off me, you sick bastard."

Dorion removed his hand from between her legs and sat up, giving her a subtle smile, before leaving her on the floor with a burning sense of humiliation and shame.

*I must fight harder,* she thought. She had to be stronger, so she could escape.

"Why are you doing this?" she asked. "Why are you punishing me?"

Kade and Merrick entered the room, all three men looking down at her. She sat up, cursing herself as she struggled to resist the lingering effects of the elixir. Janelle brushed the dust off her arms and tried to ignore the men staring at her.

"Punishing you?" Dorion said. "What I just did to you, did that feel like a punishment? For a moment, you forgot you were a prisoner, soaking in a state of bliss and need." He took a step closer to her. "My fingers may have stopped before you came, but that wet pussy was screaming for me to keep going."

She'd not entertain his crude suggestion. "Are you three little boys so bored with your pathetic lives that you have to resort to kidnapping and coercing a woman into submission? Assaulting me, nonetheless. How disgusting!"

Dorion knelt beside her and reached out, running the back of his fingers against her cheek. She still felt her wetness on his fingertips from when he invaded her. "My brothers and I have been trying to help our world return to its original state for the last ten years. Just outside those gates is a community that was once broken because creatures slipped into our world. For all I know, when you came through, more of *something* else did, too. We built this empire to stand on its own since I took the crown, trying to repair the destruction that occurred in the eighteen years that came before. We want to protect, not harm, our people. When something like you comes into our territory, we will do whatever it takes to break it until we have our answers. So, Janelle, tell me who came with you and how you did it, or believe me, you'll wish we killed you on that field where we found you!"

Janelle slowly shook her head. "We have a weapon." The words slipped from her lips.

*Fuck!* she cursed in her thoughts.

"What do you mean by weapon? It wasn't a mage who helped you?"

"What the hell is a mage?" she asked, watching all three brothers exchange glances.

"What kind of weapon, Janelle?" Dorion continued, his tone more controlled. "Who are the 'we' you speak of?"

The poison still lingered, gaining strength through her body. "My brother, a sorcerer, pirates, and a dragon."

*No, no, no.*

Dorion stilled. "A dragon?"

*Fuck. Fuck. Fuck*, Janelle cursed again.

"What the fuck is a pirate?" Kade said, but she squeezed her eyes closed, the room tilting beneath her.

She pressed her lips together and shook her head. "Just kill me," she said. "Please, kill me." The bile climbed to her throat, and she clutched her stomach.

Kade rushed beside her as she doubled over and pulled her hair back. "You seem to be having an adverse reaction to the potion," he said. "Don't die on us now."

She pushed him away with her hip, a feeble attempt, as he didn't budge. "Why the hell do you care? Get the fuck away from me."

"Easy, Janelle," Kade said, keeping his hand poised on her back.

"We're not done with her," Dorion said. "The poison will wear off soon. Just answer the questions, and we'll let you rest."

"Why does it hurt so much?" she groaned as more bile rose in her throat. Janelle slumped to the floor, curling into herself.

"We might have given you too much this time," Kade said.

"Alright," Dorion said. "Kade, take her back to her room."

Kade wrapped his muscular arms around her, lifted her, and then cradled her to his chest as he took her out of the dining room.

Once inside the bedroom, he gently laid her on the mattress and covered her with a blanket. However, Janelle immediately threw back the covers, pushed past Kade, and sprinted into the washroom. She fell to her knees in front of the toilet as another ripping pain tore through her stomach.

Kade was already beside her, pulling her hair back as she vomited.

Once Janelle was sure she had purged everything they had fed her, she looked up as Kade let go of her hair and moved away. "What do you want?" she asked, feeling her head spin.

Kade's smile was barely noticeable. "If it were up to me, you'd be dead, but my brother is convinced there was someone with you when you came here. He'll not stop what he's doing until he has his answer."

"Who?" she asked.

"The shifter."

Her brows pulled together. "The dragon?"

Kade nodded. "Every dragon from our world is a shifter," he said. "I'm going to need her name."

"But...but the crew's dragon isn't. She's *just* a dragon—"

"'She?'" he asked. "What's her name?"

Janelle leaned up from the toilet and pressed her back against the cool bathroom wall. The poison's magic surged within her once again, reclaiming its hold on her mind and making it difficult to lie. It was as though she was compelled to give him what he asked for. "Anaru," she said. "Her name is Anaru."

Kade's eyes widened, his lips pressing hard into a thin line. "Just one dragon?" he asked. "Was there a dragon named Dergis with you, too? And an oracle in the form of a dryad?"

Janelle's stomach tightened in another knot.

*Cassia's dragon?* she wondered. *Wait, he and the oracle were from this world, as well? No, I can't tell him anything else. Keep your mouth shut, Janelle!*

She gave too much away. She was putting her friends at risk.

"No," she sighed, finally gaining some control. "It was *only* her who came through with us."

And that was the truth.

Kade nodded before reaching out and scooping her off the floor, bringing her back to the bed. Once he tucked her under the covers, he said, "Give your body about thirty minutes, and you'll feel like yourself again. I'll come to check on you shortly."

With those last words, he left her alone in the dark room. The heaviness of her betrayal came down on her, not just with Anaru, but because of Elijah, too.

# 13

## MAZIE

The following two days flitted by quickly. Although Mazie wanted to leave the Vine Colony in search of her friends, they had no choice but to stay hidden for a few more days until it was safe. They explored the city, dined, and made small talk with several of the shifters within the colony. However, Mazie worried that she and Tegan were becoming a little too *comfortable*, knowing their friends were still out there and in danger, while they chained Aiden to a bedpost in one of their rooms.

Mazie stepped to the edge of the bridge overlooking the lake. The size of the city Kaeli and Xander had built surprised her. Wooden and brick homes stretched for miles, and she became captivated by every place they explored. The main road was lined with several marketplaces and parks. The lakes encircled the open fields, reflecting the vibrant orange sky and creating a tranquil atmosphere.

A sense of peace at that moment made her realize she had forgotten what that was like.

Mazie imagined herself on the lush grass with her eyes closed. She saw herself basking in the sun's warmth against her skin while observing birds enjoying breakfast by the lake as they dipped their beaks under the water.

It wasn't so different from Earth after all, but it did separate itself from the life Mazie had built since she was a teen.

For some reason, the colony made her feel safe despite the looming threat of the Red Dragon Brotherhood. Looking out at the water, she felt a sense of calm, far from the chaos of battle or the uncertainty of life beyond the realms with the Kroneon. Instead, she embraced a fleeting moment that she knew would be lost again once they left, yet she wished for its memory to last.

It was a comforting yet scary thought.

Mazie was reminded of the moments she spent with her father during her childhood before his passing. She also thought about all her little adventures with her sister before her death. That was when the relationship with her mother turned cold.

It wasn't until Lincoln found her that she felt a family bond again. Mazie craved it deep within her, but she was too afraid to show it because she feared losing it all over again.

Now that the light had touched the city, Mazie didn't feel so lonely. She now saw the bustle of people walking through the streets and children playing and running in the park on the eastern side of the houses. The sound of footsteps alerted her, and she turned around.

"Tegan just brought Aiden food and water and used her power to direct him to the washroom, so he couldn't fight back," Xander said, holding out a key for Mazie to take. "We've chained him back up."

"You'll trust me with that?" Mazie asked, raising a brow.

Xander's dark eyes looked at her and nodded. "Please understand that Kaeli is the only family I have left. I'll fight to protect her if I must. We need to keep him locked up until she and I both feel it's safe. Understand?"

Mazie had only a few encounters with his father, Dergis, when they'd visited the Eastland Forest. In Dergis's last hours, he had protected an evil Fae queen, Cassia, instead of standing by Anaru. Despite what Dergis had done, she trusted Xander wasn't like him. She sensed he would be loyal to his cousin until the end, and for that, she would grant him the same respect.

"I wanted to say that I'm sorry about your father, Xander," she said sincerely, watching his features soften.

"Can you tell me about him?" he asked.

Mazie shrugged. "I honestly didn't know him." She proceeded to share more details about what she remembered. Two years ago, Aiden shot Dergis himself during the battle. It was to protect their world, though, from the wicked Fae queen who had been controlling the dragon. Mazie wanted Xander to understand the queen's influence on Dergis—it wasn't his father's fault.

It was the queen's.

"My mother is still alive, you know?" Xander said, and a flicker of surprise erupted in her stomach that Xander hadn't mentioned her until now.

Xander gestured with his head for Mazie to follow as he led her further into the city.

"More than half of our world fell twenty-eight years ago. We were without a ruler for eighteen years, watching it fall apart before a new leader was crowned emperor," he said. "We were just babies then. I had to learn the history from Dorion once I was old enough, telling us that my father had died with Anaru. My mother, Luna, did everything she could to keep me away from the Brotherhood after that. She didn't want me to become like them. Once Kaeli turned eighteen, we escaped from Dorion's colony. My mother ended up being claimed by another shifter a few years later. I had to sit back and let it happen."

"Seems you have more family than just Kaeli," Mazie said. "What your mother did was a sacrifice. She was protecting you."

Xander nodded. "It was hard to see it that way when I was young," he said. "After we realized what was happening and the corruption within the new empire, we fled, relying on each other to survive. And we became close. She became my best friend. Kaeli still blamed herself for what she believed was killing her mother, and I saw an opportunity to do something right."

Mazie thought about Luna again. "Do you ever think your mother will try to escape herself?" she asked. "I can't imagine she isn't thinking about you every day."

"She wanted to when we ran. But she knew that if she did, her mate would track her down and punish her. It was better this way, Mazie."

"Like I said, she sacrificed her own happiness to keep you safe," Mazie said.

Xander smiled and rested his arms on the railing, turning back to her. "You remind me of her, you know?" he said. "Exquisite, deep brown complexion, dark eyes filled with curiosity and wonder. Your determination to survive and compassionate heart is just like hers, too. The story your heart tells is about a woman who will stop at nothing to protect her loved ones and put herself in harm's way if anyone so much as touches them."

A tear burned in Mazie's eyes, and she looked away.

*Curse those dragon intuitive senses,* she thought.

"Stop reading my heart, Xander. It's a bit of a violation."

Xander barked out a laugh. "Oh, Mazie, you're a rare gem, I must say. Never change for anyone."

"Of course, I'm not going to fucking change for anyone," she snapped back, feeling her walls go back up, right as Kaeli stepped onto the bridge.

"Fighting like siblings already?" she said with a bright smile, carrying a basket with a lid and a small towel draped through the handle. "Xander, I haven't finished packing yet if you want to help a bit. We should leave by tomorrow night or the morning after when the sun rises."

Xander gave her a nod and placed his hand on Mazie's shoulder. "Perhaps we'll let you sail the ship when we take off, then...pirate."

As he walked off the bridge, Kaeli hesitated for a moment before turning back to Mazie. "Do you want to walk with me?" she asked.

Mazie frowned. "Shouldn't Tegan and I be hiding inside a building in case your father returns?" she asked. "We've been exposed for the last two days, trying to blend in with your people to stay unnoticed. I can't relax."

"Don't you worry; we've taken extra precautions since that night and sent a few of our people to look out at first watch beyond the wall. We'll have plenty of time to hide you if he decides to return. I promise," Kaeli said. "Come on, go for a walk with me. You haven't been to the sea yet, and I'd like to show it to you before we leave this place."

———◦———

For as long as Mazie could remember, the sea had been her home. It was where she belonged and felt most at peace alongside her crew.

That was likely why the sight before her left her in awe.

The red sand stretched for miles, glistening under the orange and red hues swirling across the sky. The rhythmic sound of crashing waves soothed Mazie's senses, wrapping her in a sense of familiarity, even now that she was on another planet in a different realm. As she stood there, the endless sea seemed to sway toward her, softly illuminated by a bright sun rising above them.

Kaeli spread a worn-out blanket over the sand, putting down a basket she carried with her filled with fresh fruits Mazie was unfamiliar with. Noticing the way she stared, Kaeli smiled at her. "I'm guessing you don't have these?" she asked softly, holding up a fruit that Mazie would describe as an apple—if it weren't for its nearly glowing purple hues.

"Definitely not," Mazie confirmed, settling down next to her. Amusement sparked in Kaeli's eyes as she handed the fruit over to her. Mazie took it, only staring at the strange colors instead of eating it.

"It won't bite you, Mazie," Kaeli teased. "But I might if you don't try it. Seriously, it's the best food around here."

Mazie had to fight a smile of her own before she finally sunk her teeth into the fruit. Instantly, a mixture of flavors hit her tongue, and she let out a soft moan.

It was sweet and sour at the same time, with a crispy texture that Mazie didn't expect. Kaeli's gaze remained locked on hers as she watched her chew, waiting for Mazie's critique.

"Delicious," Mazie confirmed, taking another big bite.

"It's called an aticuri," Kaeli explained. "The fruit is native to this land. It is one of the rare things we managed to keep after the Brotherhood seized power. The people weren't the only ones who suffered; it was the land, too." She pressed her lips together, propping herself back on her elbows as she finally looked at the sea. "You'd never guess it, but this sea used to be crowded with ships."

Mazie's gaze followed her own. It was hard to decipher where the sea ended and the sky started with how they blended so seamlessly.

"What happened?"

"It's hard to say. Something just *changed*. Few shifters use ships anymore, only if they have cargo they can't put on their backs when they fly."

"Well, luckily for you, if you ever find yourself in need of a ship and a pirate..." Mazie's words trailed off with a smirk.

Kaeli bit her lower lip, her mouth curving upwards. "I know just the woman who can help me."

A weird sensation spread through Mazie's stomach. Now that she sat so close to Kaeli, she could make out every little detail on her face, from the barely noticeable freckle under her right eye to the almost invisible scar near her eyebrow and the icy blue hues in her eyes. It was mesmerizing.

*She was beautiful*, Mazie thought.

Realizing she was staring, Mazie quickly cleared her throat and looked away. "Tell me more about your powers," she asked Kaeli.

"I can imagine that being a mage in this place comes with its fair share of challenges."

"It does. For most of my life, I've had to hide the magic. At least I didn't have to hide the fire I inherited from my mother—the only thing I had left from her," Kaeli said. The pain in her tone was so tangible that Mazie could almost taste it.

Slowly, she reached for Kaeli's hand, allowing her fingers to sink in between the dragon's. Kaeli radiated an intense heat that instantly warmed Mazie's skin, threatening to burn her if she lingered there any longer. Kaeli allowed her fingers to remain there for a moment—if that—and then she promptly pulled away.

"I don't want to hurt you," she said, looking at the sea again. "I've burned people before, Mazie."

"You don't need to hide your powers from me, Kaeli," Mazie responded. Her stomach still felt odd, but the need to comfort Kaeli—for whatever reason—came before anything else. "I see so much of your mother in you. She's as fierce as you are. The Kroneon would open portals; we never knew where it would take us until we landed there, and Anaru would protect us. Of course, we only knew her as a dragon, throwing flames at our enemy or knocking them out with the force of her wings. She even saved my life a handful of times, stepping between me and those I fought. Her bond with my captain was unlike anything I had ever seen. They were connected in such a spiritual and cosmic way that even when the weight of the world slammed down on us, they were the last ones standing."

"She sounds incredible," Kaeli said. "It hurts me that I had to miss it all."

"You'll find your mother and get the opportunity to spend time together. Make memories with her. I promise you that."

Kaeli's expression was unreadable. Mazie couldn't figure out if she was upset over her mother or if she had said something wrong. Kaeli stood, giving her a small smile that held a hint of sadness. "I need to head back home," she said. When Mazie tried to stand up, too, she gestured toward her. "Please. Stay. Enjoy the beach a little longer. And help yourself to the fruits. I picked them just for you."

If there had ever been mixed signals in Mazie's life, it was right then as she watched Kaeli head back to her home. She listened to what Kaeli told her, deciding to stay at the beach for a little longer. It was the closest to a sense of normality she could get at the moment.

As Mazie lay down, she felt the gentle touch of the sun's rays embracing her body. Her mind drifted to how soft and warm Kaeli was underneath her fingers.

It had been a while since she felt comfortable with another person's touch.

As Mazie's imagination wandered, she blinked away the thought of how it made her feel.

She was there for only one reason, and it wasn't to play make-believe in the Vine Colony or open her heart to anyone. She was there to save her family and leave Dragão Terra behind.

# 14

## ELIJAH

Arabella had packed so many bags for their journey that Elijah knew he couldn't bring them all. He sifted through each bag, sorting through the essential items like water, food, a wool blanket, and a tarp to sleep on at night.

"Why are you helping me?" Elijah asked her, tying off the largest of the four bags. He couldn't stop thinking about why a stranger would go to such lengths to help him, especially after he had treated her so poorly in her own home just days before.

With the dangers lurking in their world, he saw that life was already challenging for Arabella, and he didn't want to burden her further by asking for help in finding Janelle. He had already slept on her spare bed and eaten her food. She'd done enough.

"Because," she started, "this is honestly the first time I've interacted with someone other than a Raider trying to kill me over the last year. The Raiders slaughtered my mate, Elijah. I'll never get him back, but..." Her voice trailed off, and she looked up with compassionate eyes. "...But you can survive, and if I can do one more thing in this life, it would be to help someone like you find safety outside the Ruins, so you could find the woman you love."

The mere thought of finding and rescuing Janelle filled his heart with hope—that eagerness to escape Dragão Terra and build a life together.

Elijah placed his hand on her shoulder and gently squeezed it. "Thank you, Arabella. Please be safe. There aren't many decent people out there anymore. Your world would suffer an incredible loss if someone like you were to disappear from it."

Arabella pressed her lips together, giving him a nod before saying, "Well, that was very kind of you to say, Elijah. We can talk more about how great I am on the way."

Elijah blinked, giving her a pointed look. "Wait, what? Wait..." He held up his hand, stepping between her and the road behind him. "You're coming?"

Arabella picked up two of the four bags and slung them over her shoulders. "Of course. You don't know where you're going. You're likely not going to make it out of the city without getting yourself killed, and this place has served me nothing but loneliness and pain these last few years. I want a friend. I want to...*do* something with my life. There isn't much left for me here, Elijah, and this is my one chance to...I don't know, find something worth living for again."

It was true that Elijah would be lost without her, and the Raiders had been wreaking havoc in their city for years.

He shook his head. "No. I can't allow it. I won't let you put yourself in danger to help me."

Arabella arched her eyebrow, a stubborn expression on her face. "I don't remember asking for your permission. I was merely informing you I'm coming along." She gestured to him to get out of the way. He didn't budge.

"Arabella..."

"I'll not bicker about this with you, Elijah. I've made up my mind. You're my friend, and you need help if you want to *actually* make it to your girl."

"Janelle," he said, feeling a bit more comfortable with Arabella to share her name. He was afraid to before, as he hadn't learned to trust her yet. The more he shared, the more exposed he felt to a stranger in a new land.

But right then, as her innocent eyes brightened, he felt she might be the only one in that land he could trust.

Arabella smiled. "She has a nice name," she said. "And she's lucky to have a good friend like you."

Elijah slowly shook his head. "I'm not a good friend," he said. "Some people in my world would call me a villain or monster, but *never* a good friend."

Arabella folded her arms and gave him a quizzical look. "Are you going to kill me?" she asked. "Villain?"

Elijah fought back a smile and shook his head. "Never."

"That's all I need to hear." She pressed her lips together and reached out, taking his hand in hers. "Well, *good friend*, let's keep going. After me."

And a decision had been made.

As Arabella stepped onto the main road, he called to her, "Wouldn't it be faster if we flew?"

She shook her head. "I think it's best we go on foot. Should the Brotherhood catch me flying above the trees with a man on my back, they'd shoot us down faster than I could breathe fire to defend us. Dragon riders seem to be something that happened in *your* world, not ours."

"I see," he said. "Alright, then."

"Alright, then, indeed," she said. "Come on."

After several hours of traveling through the dense forest and dusty dirt roads, Elijah's body ached with exhaustion, and he needed a moment to rest. The road heading east led them to a breathtaking ocean view, with waves crashing against the rugged cliffs.

According to Arabella, the journey to Drakentos, the new empire where she believed Janelle was being held, was a five-day walk. They still had miles to go.

Elijah stopped at the bottom of the cliff to rest, but he wasn't close enough. After dropping his bags and removing his shoes, he walked until the water touched his knees, the chilly temperature biting his skin.

Arabella didn't follow, choosing to stay on the shore.

Digging his feet into the sand below the sea, he relished the feeling of it between his toes. The coldness of the water, the smell, all of it reminded him of Earth. Land and sea were the one constant between his world and theirs. They were the same.

*It is no wonder Lincoln craves it so much,* Elijah said in his thoughts as tiny flying insects began eddying around his head and his body. They broke off, spreading out over the salty sea.

As another wave broke against the rocks, Elijah wondered what was beyond the sea in this world. And how many planets were like Earth?

While he knew that Dragão Terra was perilous, he couldn't help but admire its beauty and even felt the excitement of experiencing a new realm.

But none of that mattered at that moment. Not until Elijah rescued Janelle, the one person who gave him a sense of purpose for the first time in his entire life. The one person who revealed his worth to him and taught him how to love—how to truly, truly love.

*Like wearing the crown for the last two years,* he thought. *And never knowing someone out there believed I was more than riches and power.*

Janelle saw him for the man he was, not the king he pretended to be.

"I'll find you," he said to himself, looking out to the sea. "I'll find you and destroy anyone who stands in my way."

# 15

## JANELLE

Janelle tried to shift the shackles on her wrists, but they held fast to her skin, each painful twist biting deeper into her flesh. She worked tirelessly to slip free, but it was no use.

A wicked smile played on Merrick's lips as he casually walked into the room, watching her squirm uncomfortably on the bed. Each step was deliberate and calculating, as if he were silently stalking his prey before the final strike.

The bed dipped as he sat beside her, but as she looked away, he reached out and gripped her chin, moving her face back to meet his. "If you haven't picked up by now, when we make eye contact with you, we expect the same in return."

"I'd rather stare at the filthy floor," she bit back. "Or the inside of a toilet."

"Cute," he retorted, releasing her chin. "You know why Dorion's keeping you here, right?" Merrick asked. "Trapped in this room for days instead of simply killing you, as I would prefer."

Janelle pressed her lips together and shook her head.

"He believes you can help us," he said.

She lowered her brow. "Help you how?" she asked. "You already poisoned me and got me to talk about Anaru. What else could you possibly want from me?"

"Well, we still don't know *where* she is."

"Neither do I."

"Well, you say that. Twenty-eight years ago, Anaru teleported out of this world in front of our eyes and into yours. For the first time since then, the same thing happened, except instead of sucking out parts of our world, another world expelled into ours. It's clear you hold magic. How about you share more with us than what you keep inside your head?"

Janelle scoffed. "I don't hold magic that can open portals," she said. "If I could, do you honestly believe I'd allow myself to stay in this room with monsters like you?"

Merrick appeared unfazed by everything, including a woman disrespecting him, and his smile showed he found her resistance more amusing than anything.

"If you say so," he said casually. "However, I know you hold the truth about exactly how it happened, and until you open that little mouth of yours, it's going to get extremely uncomfortable living here." He stood straight, no longer crouching over her. "Dorion said you mentioned a weapon. What did you mean by that?"

Janelle shrugged. "I don't remember saying anything about a weapon," she lied, realizing right away that Merrick wasn't buying it.

"Hmm," he hummed, giving her a pointed look. "You know, our empire believes Anaru died. We even buried a servant wrapped in a cloth to convince the public. The information you gave us was quite useful. The sooner we find her, the sooner we can secure that little secret, so we can continue to rule this empire instead of letting it fall."

Janelle raised a brow. The more she witnessed their actions over the last few days, the more she understood their empire was not under their complete control.

*And I may be able to use that*, she thought.

"What will you do to Anaru when you find her?" she asked, but it was clear she knew the answer.

"I don't foresee my brother killing her; he loved her too much." He wore an expression of disgust. "Anaru grew up with us. We've known her since we were children. But he *will* most likely keep her locked up in our cell and use her when he needs." He paused briefly. "Personally, I think he should kill her and then live with the pain of losing her all over again."

"That doesn't sound like someone who loved his mate. It appears he wants power more than love."

Merrick gave her a subtle nod, which surprised Janelle. "Come," he said. "I'd like to show you around."

Janelle blinked. "Is this one of your tricks to get me into another room so that you animals can assault me again?"

Merrick rolled his eyes. "Stop pretending to be repulsed by us. At least you're still alive...for now."

She gnashed her teeth. The audacity to believe death would have been worse than what they had done to her since she arrived.

Janelle's plans were still in motion. The moment the opportunity arose, she was going to kill each one of them and make it as painful as possible.

Merrick reached into his pocket, pulled out a key, and then un-locked the chains. Once Janelle was free, she rubbed her wrists. Her skin felt raw, and she knew she'd likely see bruises in the morning.

As Janelle rose from the bed and passed Merrick, he reached out and gripped her wrist, causing her to wince in pain as his fingers dug into her chafed skin. She looked away as his lips got so close to her ear that his mouth slightly brushed against her skin. "We're about to step outside. If you run, Janelle, I'll hunt you down in my dragon form and drag you back by my teeth, then I'll leave you to rot inside this dank room."

Janelle's eyes burned with fury as she turned to look at him. She was wrong to believe Kade was the most violent of the three. It was clear what kind of man Merrick was. However, being thrown back into that room, deprived of sunlight and fresh air, was the last thing she wanted. So, she'd play the part of the obedient prisoner if it meant getting even the slightest taste of freedom. "I won't run," she said. "I swear it."

"Don't test us. We still don't know *where* Anaru is. In due time, we'll get it out of your head. Unfortunately, your body didn't respond well to the elixir. The small amounts we put in your food did nothing, and for you to open up to us, we had to give you ten times what we'd have to give a dragon. No one has ever reacted to the point of regurgitating into a toilet like you did. It could kill you, and right now, the information you have in your head is too valuable. So, we'll find another way."

"Torture?" she said. "I've experienced torture before, Merrick. That won't work either."

"Torture is child's play. Maybe you'll beg for it once we're fin-ished with you."

Janelle swallowed and pressed her lips together in a firm line, refusing to speak.

"That's a good girl," he said, releasing her wrists, and she followed closely behind him, keeping her arms wrapped around her midsection and her eyes downcast.

*Keep playing the docile elf,* she thought. *They don't know you have claws yet.*

"Where are you taking me, dragon?" she asked, looking up as she entered a long hallway leading to the outside.

"If you spend any more time in that room, you'll lose your mind," he warned. She rolled her eyes. "Just remember that it was me who let you breathe in the outside air. You can thank me later."

Merrick ignored Janelle's mumbling obscenities as she followed him. All she thought about was Elijah, lying injured in someone's home, with only that stranger to help him. While she complained about being locked up in a royal castle, he was alone, and she didn't know how much longer it would be before he ended up dead.

She had to bury that fear, though, or she'd never have the strength to escape.

When they stepped outside, Janelle took a long, heavy breath of fresh air. It was daybreak, with only the slight hint of the sun peeking through the clouds.

"Enjoy this moment while you can," Merrick said, leading her to a bench. "Sit."

After she sat, she cast her eyes around the courtyard. Along the castle's perimeter, an arrangement of trimmed bushes, sculpted into various animal shapes, intermingled with vibrant, blossoming bushes and trees.

"It took us time to get this palace the way Dorion wanted," he started, sitting beside her. "We had just killed Anaru's parents, who had turned against us and destroyed the original structure of the castle." He turned, and their eyes met. "And the great empire fell."

Janelle looked away, staring back at the garden.

"When Anaru got sucked out of this world, she let in creatures we called the Vipers," he continued. "For eighteen years, we fought the beasts while it stood in shambles without an emperor. Once we killed every last one of them, finally bringing peace to the land, we proved to the people we were the best option to take over this empire to protect them. And we have for the last ten years. Our world needed a new leader after two decades without one."

"So, the people simply gave Dorion a crown?" Janelle asked.

"It took some convincing. With Anaru next in line and her mate taking her place, he became the ideal choice for restoring our world."

Janelle felt that anger boiling inside. That was Anaru's family they had killed, and he casually told the story as if he were simply describing what he had for breakfast. The Brotherhood didn't care who died, suffered, and was left without a home as long as they got what they wanted: power.

"Janelle, as a dragon, I feel something from you right now," he added, leaning back against the bench. "Sure, I can't read your thoughts...yet. But I feel an overwhelming surge of anger from you when I speak of this. So, let me be clear about one thing. Just because you don't understand it doesn't mean it's wrong. We didn't find joy in burning them alive and dismantling their order of things, but when we created this palace to reflect a better society run by a family that put others before the crown, things got better."

"Better?" she repeated. "How is your society's governing law better when women are nothing but property to you?"

Merrick shook his head and scoffed. "Anaru's family, the Rylanthions, belonged to a long bloodline of ancient royalty. Every male born into their family took the crown after their fathers. For the first time in thousands of years, no male heir was born. The empress, Inaya, tried again and again for a male heir. Nothing. Each time she became pregnant with a male, that child died the moment they were born. For that, Emperor Remus would hand his crown down to his daughter, Anaru, upon his death. Anaru would have been the first female to rule our land in thousands of years."

Janelle lowered her brow. "Oh no," she said in a monotone, sarcastic voice, "not a woman running things. Can't have that."

Merrick's lips pulled into a wide grin. "Women are not made to rule, Janelle. It angers our gods."

"Yes, because murdering innocents is so much better?"

She turned her head as he laughed. "I understand it may appear uncivilized to you. When Dorion approached the emperor with the proposition of *electing* the next to rule, instead of succession, he suggested taking Anaru as his mate while still granting her the ability to govern, albeit under Dorion's authority as ruler."

"But she still wouldn't be the ruler of the land?"

"Of course, she would be. Just under Lord Dorion."

"That's not—" She pinched the bridge of her nose. "That's not how ruling works." The conversation irritated her, and he was too blind to see the reality of things. "If she's ruling *under* someone, she's not *truly* ruling. Anaru would have still been denied her birthright."

Merrick remained silent, but his expression hardened. There was no point in bickering with him about this.

"You're all disgusting," she added, turning away again.

Merrick reached out and placed his thumb under Janelle's chin, jerking her to look at him in a sharp motion. "And you're just ignorant. Men can only run a controlled society. Our economic structure has only been maintained when women are subservient. We don't run off emotions like women do."

"Oh, sure." Janelle snorted. "How is that working out for you? You boys seem pretty damn emotional."

"It's not *just* about our worldly ways. The gods never elected a woman to choose her mate; the men do. Anaru's parents wanted to change all that by giving her the crown and rejecting Dorion as her true mate. Remus wanted Anaru to have a choice and defy our gods. We had to enact strict pair-bonding laws to ensure that only the strongest dragons prevailed. When the females rejected their mates, even after the Vipers killed off most of our species, we had to put a stop to it. Bonded mates who couldn't have children had an obligation to raise the orphaned children left behind. They would grow to obey the written law. Those who could produce a child were legally obligated to accept their fate with whoever claimed them and bear children when they were ordered to."

"Ah," she said bitterly. "It all makes sense now, coming together like a perfect puzzle. Lord Dorion got his little feelings hurt when Anaru rejected him, so he went on a murderous rampage until he got what he wanted. Then, when she left for Earth, he used her demise to warp a society into exactly how he imagined it to be. She became a martyr, and he became a king."

Janelle understood that her world held similar values when it came to the patriarchal order, but she had never witnessed such widespread violence because of it. The men honestly believed they were superior, and unless she found a way out, they'd subject her to their rule until she died.

"I understand that, as a woman, you're struggling with this. The scars of losing over half our population to the Vipers pushed us to work harder to rebuild a society that should have remained unchanged. It allowed us to empower women to accept the inevitable future of their chosen mate. Anaru was their one guide to stand up. When she died, or at least when they believed she died, women rioted in the streets. They protested that men shouldn't remain in charge and started rejecting their mates. Now everything has fallen back into place."

Janelle let out a quiet huff. "So, they stood up for nothing. They only wanted their freedom, and you stole it from them."

He turned away from her and looked back at the garden. "That's a bit dramatic. It's back to the way it was," he said stubbornly. "The fact that the Vipers entered through the portal and eliminated so many of us came to our benefit. We convinced the people more easily by proving that our way was the only system that worked. Women are incapable of providing and protecting as we can. If Anaru's parents had their way, we would have all ceased to exist years ago."

Janelle let out a sigh. There it was. All this talk about how strong and able they were, but all she saw was fear that their empire would collapse. "You little men fear more than a child does."

"The only thing we fear is the unknown. The more we understand your people and Earth, the more we can protect ourselves from you and anything that may have come through the realm with you. You said it wasn't a mage who opened the portal but a weapon. Are there still similar weapons in your world that have the power to do it again?"

"No," Janelle said, realizing she had already said too much before. They'd find out soon enough, and it wasn't as if she had the Kroneon for them to take. "The compass we used is the only one I'm aware of."

"Compass?" Merrick said. "The weapon is a compass?"

As she watched Merrick's eyes grow wide, her stomach pulled into a tight knot, and she reminded herself to stop fucking talking.

"Just a rusty ole' compass," she said. "We didn't know it would send us here."

"And where is it now?" he said.

"I don't know," she said sharply. It was the truth. Tegan was the only one holding that weapon when they fell through the portal. She didn't know where it was now or even if it made it to the other side with them.

Merrick's features turned dark right as laughter echoed off the courtyard walls. Kade came around the corner, slinging his arm over Merrick's shoulder when Merrick stood. "Have you shown her yet?" he asked with a playful smile, and Janelle furrowed a brow. "Come on, let's get some food and a drink, and then we have a nice little surprise for you."

She narrowed her eyes. "What surprise?"

He gave a sideways smirk. "Well, if I tell you now, then it won't be much of a surprise, will it?" he said, followed by a wink.

Janelle rolled her eyes. "Is this where I learn to trust you little boys and discover you're not as monstrous as I thought? Where you make me feel at home by giving me fresh air and a tour of your palace to meet all your people?"

Kade cocked a brow. "Oh, we're monsters, but no one here gives a fuck when it's us who protect them from the outside world. Just like you. You can hate us all you want for keeping you here, but the moment you see that most people in our world would rather kill than protect you, you'll be begging us to lock you back up. Right now, you're protected by the ruler of our entire *planet*. You either deal with it or spend the rest of your life in that room."

Janelle swallowed and stepped back instinctively, her powers suddenly surging at her hands. "Well, go on then...*monster*," she bit out. "Show me."

Nerves seized her stomach as they walked back toward the palace. The building may have looked beautiful, but there was something dark and menacing about it. Some evil aura she couldn't put her finger on.

A child was curled up in a ball, leaning against a young tree barely thick enough to stand straight. His eyes looked up as Janelle passed by him. His jet-black hair fell slightly over his eyes when he met her gaze. She noted his eye color was like Elijah's—bright, blue...but empty. An icy shiver ran through Janelle's heart.

Merrick stayed behind in the courtyard as Kade guided Janelle through a long hallway with massively tall windows overlooking the outside world. When she peered through the glass, it was at least four layers thick, causing images of the trees to blur.

Once they reached the end of the hall, Kade unlatched the bolted locks and slowly opened the thick metal door. As Janelle's

Elven vision adjusted to the darkness, she spotted Lincoln and Nola chained to the far back wall, their hands and ankles bound, appearing sound asleep.

Janelle took off running toward them, but Kade reached out, gripped her by the back of the neck, and yanked her back into his chest. He slunk his arms around her waist, pulling her closer.

She felt the heat of his breath tickle her cheek as he whispered, "Easy, Janelle. They're here until they share with us where you're hiding Anaru. Unless you're willing to divulge your little secrets here and now."

"Fuck off!" she said through her teeth. "I don't know where she is, and I guarantee they'll die to keep that secret as much as I would."

"Don't test us, elf. Dorion isn't patient. He won't hesitate to kill every single one of you," Kade said, as a nervous feeling twisted in her gut. "You're depriving him of his *mate*, which makes you our number one enemy right now." A devious smile touched his lips. "However, we're willing to offer you a few options."

As she felt the knot twist in her stomach again, her anxiety surged.

"Remember, we have them inside this cell at our disposal if you don't cooperate. There are plenty of men in our empire, just itching to sink their cocks into a siren cunt. They won't kill her right away, of course. Where's the fun in that?"

"I hate you," she fumed, her voice filled with venom as she struggled to break free from his powerful grip. "Just end me already. Kill me! I'd rather be dead than be around you monsters any longer!"

"Oh, I know that's what you want," he said. "But what we have planned is so much more fun."

# 16

## NOLA

"Wake up, you two!" a deep voice shouted, jolting Nola awake.

Once the men caught her and Lincoln, they injected a needle into their arms with an unknown poison, keeping them drugged and weak for several days. However, that morning they hadn't.

As her eyes adjusted to the dim light in the room, an unfamiliar man stood across the cell door, holding a frightened woman in his arms.

*Janelle!*

He had a firm grip wrapped around her elbow as he dragged the elf deeper into the room. Janelle looked exhausted, and her skin had a pallor that alarmed Nola.

"Lincoln," Nola whispered as the man released Janelle's arm. She gave him a slight nudge to wake him before rising to her feet and rushing to the cell bars.

"You're alive," Nola said as Janelle bolted to the cell to meet her. "Is Elijah with you?"

Janelle discreetly shook her head and pressed her face to the bars. "He's alive," she mouthed, knowing the man behind her was listening.

Nola nodded as Lincoln moved beside her and reached out, gripping Janelle's hand. It was a subtle gesture, but it carried the weight of a promise: they would find him together.

"I'm sorry, Janelle," Lincoln said, gripping the bars and leaning closer. "When the ship landed, we lost the both of you. They caught us before we had enough time to search the land."

Janelle glanced behind her as the shifter leaned back against the wall at the rear of the room, crossing one leg over the other while folding his arms. He fixed his eyes on them, watching.

Listening.

"Have they hurt you?" Nola asked, dreading the answer. There was no mercy inside of those men. She could sense their malice, and Janelle appeared utterly terrified for the first time since she'd met her.

Slowly, she nodded. "Nothing done that will break me," Janelle said.

The brooding man's eyes flickered with curiosity, still fixated on the back of Janelle's head.

"Is Aiden safe?" Janelle asked so quietly that Nola had to read her lips.

She replied with a nod. Nola had no idea if the others were safe, but she didn't want Janelle to worry. "What about you? Are you okay?" Nola went to ask another question when Lincoln grabbed her hand and pulled her away from the bars. The shifter suddenly walked behind Janelle and grabbed her hair, lifting her off the ground while she thrashed and kicked at the man's legs.

"Put me down, Kade. You fucking asshole!"

"Let her go!" Nola shouted. "What do you want from us?"

The man she called Kade lowered Janelle back down, easing his grip on her head. "We have reasonable evidence that you were in the company of Anaru before my brother and his men took you captive. With Janelle here, we can rely on you not to lie, or she'll suffer. Our men have already returned to the cave where they discovered you."

A sudden chill swept through the room.

"We're so close," Kade added, "to finding her. Aren't we? I wonder where she's heading now."

Lincoln stared at Kade with an angry gleam in his eyes. "Anaru is *my* dragon, and I'll *not* let you harm her."

"Lincoln, stop!" Nola cried. "Don't say anything else."

Kade's smile broadened. "I see," he said, turning to look at Nola and raising a brow. "Well, she sure seems to care about you." He flashed his white teeth into something other than a grin. "This might be easier than we thought. Are you and this woman here lovers, then? If I threaten your little siren, can I get you to say anything I want?"

"Lincoln, no!" Janelle said, but Kade yanked her head back, pulled her closer to his chest, and wrapped his arm around her waist. Nola's stomach twisted anxiously as his hand brushed Janelle's hip. Janelle looked even sicker than when she came into the dungeon.

"The fact that you called Anaru *your* dragon won't sit well with Dorion, but I'll try to tame the beast for now. Are you bonded to Anaru?"

Lincoln nodded, but Nola knew it was a lie. Anaru broke that link before they'd left her in the cave.

"Good," he said. "When we torture you, Anaru will feel it, too." Nola's body went stiff. "She'll come running to protect you, and we won't have to look much longer. I wonder, if I cut off your fingers, will you tell me more about you and Anaru?" He clenched his jaw, and a deadly heat shone in his eyes. "The silence ends now."

Nola's face wrinkled in disgust as a shiver of emotion ran through her. She knew that their silence would come at a price. But they couldn't reveal where Anaru was. Nola prayed she had fled the cave and was going to a village to find a healer.

"Time to go, Janelle," Kade said, pulling her across the room. "Oh, and one more thing." He turned to Nola and Lincoln. "Every decision you make from here on out will determine how many fingers we cut off to get you to talk. You may not care about your own life or body parts, but maybe you'll be more cooperative if your friends' lives were at stake as well."

He meant Janelle. He was going to torture Janelle if they didn't cooperate.

"We'll be back for *you*," he said to Lincoln.

Nola shifted her weight and felt a stab of pain as her leg gave out. Seeing Janelle and Kade's promise of torture made her momentarily forget the pain in her ankle caused by fighting the dragon shifter. Lincoln slid his arm under her shoulder to keep her upright. "Nola..." Lincoln said as Kade dragged Janelle out of the room.

"Stop!" Nola shouted, but Kade had already shut the door behind them, leaving her and Lincoln alone again in the dimly lit room. "He's going to hurt her, Lincoln, and you. If they hurt either of you, I will claw that bastard's heart out."

Lincoln raised a brow at her fury while her hands trembled in anger. Nola would be damned if she let those men hurt the people she cared about. When he didn't respond, she hissed, "I mean it. With every fiber of my being, I will kill him."

"Oh, I know. There are so many things I love about you, Nola," he said, running his hand down her long hair. "And this is one of them."

Lincoln wrapped his arms around Nola's waist and pulled her close to him.

"I'm scared, Lincoln," she said, letting out a heavy sob against his chest. She couldn't hide the agony of the possibility of losing him. All Nola wanted to do was pretend they were anywhere else, anywhere that wasn't the hell they had fallen into. Those men were going to take Lincoln and torture him, believing Anaru would come and save him. And Lincoln would gladly shed blood to protect her and Janelle.

"You must promise to stay strong when they take me, Nola. Swear it."

She shook her head as she buried her face against his chest. "I can't promise that, Lincoln. Don't make me promise something I'll likely break."

Nola felt his hand touch her cheek. Even his rough palm gliding against hers felt featherlike and gentle.

"What if this is it?" she said. "They drag you out that door, and I never see you again."

Lincoln's lips crashed against hers, raw and desperate, savoring her taste while his tongue slipped into her mouth. The untamed kiss spoke volumes—a testament to the intensity of their connection and the uncertainty of their future.

Nola wanted to pull back. She wanted to hear words of comfort from him and to listen to Lincoln *promise* he'd come back. But she didn't. Before she knew it, she lost herself in the taste of him.

Neither of them wasted time peeling off their clothes. There was simply no time for it. Lincoln's powerful hands grabbed hold of her hips, propping her up, and her legs wrapped around his waist. A small, muffled moan tore from her lips, mixing with his. The world became a blur. It was a race against time before the Brotherhood ripped them apart.

Perhaps forever.

Lincoln knelt on the hard concrete floor. Nola's hands fidgeted with his pants for a moment before his cock sprung free as he lay her down, moving on top of her.

"Fuck," he murmured under his breath, undoing her pants and yanking her undergarments down. Then, in one harsh thrust, he rammed himself deep inside her. The moan that escaped Nola's lips echoed through the cells as her body trembled at the sensation of him inside her. She quickly bit her lips, trying to subdue any other sounds that could leave her mouth as that tingling wave flooded her.

Lincoln supported his weight with one hand, while the other roamed all over her body like he wanted to memorize her every curve one last time. Nola knotted her hands into his hair, her lips refusing to stray from his.

His hips were now moving at a steady pace, hitting that spot buried deep inside her. She trembled underneath him, grunts rolling off her tongue with each hard thrust. Nola became lost in him. It didn't matter that they were in this new world, locked in a dirty cell. It didn't matter that they didn't know what the future would bring... There was just *them*.

She felt him everywhere, all at once. The electrifying thrill moved through her in intense waves every time he pushed his body against hers. His breathing was heavy against her lips, his hands needy with desire.

"Gods!" Nola cried out, but Lincoln was quick to silence her. Her eyes rolled back into her skull as his palm found her mouth. His lips were now at her jaw, showering it with heavy kisses as he fucked her.

"I need you to be quiet," he panted against her skin, his breath heavy as he slammed his hips against hers. "If I'm going to have you one last time"—another thrust—"I don't want to be interrupted." Nola's entire body was on fire, throbbing, pulsing, and shaking for him.

She couldn't control how her body reacted to his touch, but she nodded to show she had heard him.

"You're the closest thing to the stars I've ever known," he said, his words soft in comparison to the harshness of his body. "My reason to walk through this world and every other."

Pleasure rippled through Nola then, consuming every inch of her. She tensed underneath Lincoln's body, her wetness coating his cock as she came. That tipped him over the edge, too, because it was a mere moment before he came inside her, short of breath. Nola cursed the gods in her mind, fighting the tears threatening to form in her eyes. She didn't want this moment to end, finding it difficult to pull back from him.

A moment later, Lincoln heard steps echo down the long hallway, and he scrambled backward, slipping his cock inside his pants. Nola quickly pulled her pants up, tying the rope around her waist, and stood, even if her legs were still shaky. There was no time to say goodbye. There was no more time for warm embraces and soft kisses.

Not even time for empty promises.

The man named Merrick appeared in front of their cell with a filthy grin on his lips. His stony gaze washed over Nola and then settled on Lincoln. The silence was thick, and Nola's heart picked up its pace.

"I would personally find it more entertaining to torture that little siren of yours," he said at last. Lincoln stood in front of her, shielding her with his body. "But you're the only one connected to Anaru, and we need her to come begging for your wellbeing...right into Dorion's arms."

# 17

## ELIJAH

Arabella rested her back against a fallen tree trunk, sinking into the sand, and looking at the morning sky. "It's been a while since I've seen the sky like this, with each color behind the clouds flowing seamlessly into the next. A beautiful masterpiece, wouldn't you say, Elijah?" She turned to look at him, watching Elijah move his finger around in the sea. "Do they have skies like this on Earth?"

Elijah turned to her, noting the shining innocence on her face. "Yes," he said. "Different colors, but it moves you the same way."

"Moves you," she repeated. "I like that saying, friend."

Elijah gave her a warm smile that didn't meet his eyes. He had been afraid for the first time in years when he awoke in the Ruins. The fear of losing Janelle forever consumed him, but Arabella's friendship and her need to help him on his journey brought a small ray of hope. She wasn't a threat in a strange new world; she became his ally because she didn't know who he actually was. He hid the fact that he used magic for gain or that he had killed countless in his own world.

No, she didn't know the *real* Elijah, and he planned to keep it that way.

"How much longer before we reach the palace?" he asked, already feeling drained from the sun's heat and his legs aching from several days of walking. "Are we looking for a castle?"

She nodded. "Drakentos makes up the entire city, not just where the castle sits. The Lord and the Brotherhood's palace is surrounded by a community of loyal subjects, primarily made up of his guards. Getting too close is not an option; his men will arrest us the second we step on royal ground. The smaller cities on the outer banks should offer a haven of some sort until we come up with an actual plan. We only had a few moments of peace between the Vipers dying out and the Royal Council electing a new emperor. Dorion and his men destroyed everything that had once been beautiful about that place. You're loyal to the Brotherhood, or you're a prisoner."

Elijah blinked. If that were true, Janelle would fight until her last breath, refusing to surrender. He once held her captive in his own castle. Now she was imprisoned again in another fortress. He had failed to protect her.

*She should hate me*, he thought. *I've caused nothing but harm and danger to her.*

"We should keep moving," he said. "But I think we need to search for food."

Arabella nodded. "At least we have water, but we've eaten everything I could fit into my bags. We can hunt, though." She narrowed her gaze down at his hands. "Your hands are kind of soft and pretty. You don't hunt, do you?"

"Pretty?" Elijah bit the inside of his cheek, but then his expression softened. It was clear Arabella didn't mean to offend him, and she was right, anyway. Elijah knew how to strike a sword through his enemy, but he had never hunted with one.

*Kieran was also right,* he thought. *I really am a little rich boy without a crown.*

"And what exactly are we up against out here?" he asked. "What do dragons eat?"

Arabella gazed at the grove of trees, their rustling leaves creating a soothing sound, and her smile widened. "Humans," she said with a wink.

And just like that, the serene moment was over.

"Follow me," she said.

"You're joking, right?" Elijah questioned as his stomach twisted. He knew Arabella was teasing—or at least he hoped, but he was still wary about what dwelled inside that forest. Everything was different in their world, including the predators that roamed their land. "Arabella?"

She didn't respond. Instead, she kept that eager smile and headed toward the tall trees towering over them. An intense warmth pressed onto Elijah's cheeks the moment they stepped into the forest, and the temperature rose several degrees, causing beads of sweat to run down his forehead.

Taking a steadying breath, Elijah followed Arabella through the brush, his eyes scanning the surrounding area. "Why the sudden shift in climate, Arabella?" he asked. "Wouldn't the trees block out the sun?"

Arabella giggled, still focused on the path ahead of them. "That isn't the heat of the sun you're feeling. It's the trees."

"The trees give off heat?"

When she didn't answer, he looked around the forest again, focusing on the branches swaying from the slight wind. They differed significantly from those of Earth, almost smooth on the surface. The bark that covered the trees was so dark that it looked almost black. What caught his eye weren't the trees themselves but the sparkling outcrops of gems peeking through the bark.

*It's beautiful*, he thought.

Arabella knelt on the ground, running her fingers through the dirt. She tilted her head back and took a long breath. Her eyes shifted from dark brown to yellow, illuminating just above the surface of her irises. The dragon within Arabella started chanting as if summoning power. A subtle tremble rippled through the earth, but she kept her feet planted to prevent herself from falling over. Elijah had to hold on to the tree beside him, crumbles of bark and gems slipping between his fingers.

"Arabella, what's going on?" he asked, and she began...undressing. Elijah blinked once to ensure his eyes weren't deceiving him before glancing away. Sure, he had already seen her naked after she transitioned in the Ruins, but the way she disrobed so casually made him suddenly feel awkward for looking at her.

"Get your magic ready," she called out. Elijah hesitantly looked at her again, dozens of questions reeling through his mind. *Still naked.* Arabella glanced over her shoulder at him. "It might get a bit scary."

*Fuck*, he cursed as he withdrew his hand from the tree. He held his arms spreading wide, his palms facing upward while his black, mist-like power dripped from his fingertips. The magic encased them in a dark void as the power moved through the forest.

Arabella lifted her hand, her skin now covered in red scales and looked at Elijah. "It's fast."

"*It?*"

Suddenly, the earth ripped in two, sending debris soaring into the air and hitting him in the face. As he wiped dirt from his eyes, Elijah beheld a sinister creature with eight long legs emerging from the torn ground. It had eight eyes that glittered black and coarse, spindly fur along its crooked spine. The spider-like beast rushed toward Arabella, its mouth dropping to reveal a maw of needle-like teeth. With a hiss, the beast latched onto Arabella's wing as it spread wide mid-transition.

Elijah unleashed a wave of his power, striking the spider and knocking it free, which allowed Arabella to finish shifting. Once in her dragon form, she looked at Elijah and gave him a brief nod of thanks. The creature focused on Elijah and charged, but he cast another pulse of black magic, blasting it away and causing it to curl up defensively. The air suddenly filled with a reverberating hum that pierced his ears, putting immense pressure on his head.

"Fuck!" he cried out, muffling his ears with his hands. He hoped it would block out the noise and pain, but it didn't. He fell to his knees, unable to move away from the spider as it ran, its teeth bared for the kill.

Arabelle roared while using her massive wing to drive the spider back, knocking it to the ground. She exhaled a stream of intense dragon fire onto its back, singeing its body. It let out an ear-shattering shriek, but Arabella didn't stop. She unleashed more of her fire until she consumed the creature. It fell to the earth, its massive body growing still as smoke poured from its flesh.

Once Arabella had reverted to her human form, she ran over to the smoldering remains of the spider and put her hand on its abdomen, sensing for a heartbeat. It took a moment for Elijah to register that she was bare. *Again.* Elijah quickly looked away, clearing his throat. "Let me know when I can turn around," he said, his back still turned to her.

"You can turn around *now*," Arabella stated flatly.

Elijah raised his brow. "You've dressed already?"

He couldn't see her but heard the annoyed sigh that left her lips. "Right, clothes. Of course. I suppose that's a big deal for your kind?" After a few shuffling noises, as if she were putting on her clothes, she said, "You can turn around now. No more bare skin in sight."

"A little warning would have been nice, Arabella," Elijah said as he turned, his heart rate slowly returning to a steady beat. "This is now the second time you've stood naked in front of me."

"Honestly, Elijah, you're quite the prude."

"I just have respect for a woman's privacy. Anyway, why the hell did you decide to lure that monster out? It nearly ripped your wing off."

"These creatures are pretty kind as long as you don't provoke them. But we needed meat, so I antagonized one from its burrow." She placed a hand on the giant body. Elijah swallowed nervously as she dug her sharp nails into the flesh.

"The meat on this will keep us full for days," she continued. "Time to eat."

# 18

## TEGAN

Tegan watched the gentle rhythm of Aiden's chest rise and fall. He appeared peaceful, finding solace in dreams far away from the chaos that reigned in this world. She knew how Aiden would react once he awoke, seeing himself secured with chains at his wrists again, bound to the bedpost and unable to move. They'd allowed him to eat and drink, using the washroom to relieve himself while being tethered to magic so he couldn't leave. Then once again, she'd conjured a spell to pull him back onto the bed and lull him to sleep. The encounters were never pleasant, but between her and Xander's power, they were strong enough to handle him.

*No doubt he'll attack*, she reasoned. *And I'll have to be ready again.*

She watched as his eyes raced underneath his closed lids. *Is he dreaming?* Tegan wondered.

She reached out, placing her hand gingerly on his dark hair, and ran her fingers between his long strands. "Aiden," she whispered.

"If you're in there, I need you to fight. Please fight harder against the darkness that is *killing* you. Your sister needs you. *I* need you."

She felt a single tear escape her eye and quickly brushed it away, and as she stood to walk out of the room, Aiden reached out and took her wrist.

The grip wasn't painful, but its tightness, combined with her surprise, sent a sinking feeling to her stomach.

She turned around slowly, Aiden watching her with hooded eyes. The blue in his irises almost glistened as if he, too, were fighting back tears.

"Hi," she breathed. "Do you feel okay?"

He nodded, his expression unreadable. "The darkness wants to kill Mazie for what she did to put us in here," he said. "But seeing you, Tegan, taking care of me, makes me want to do something *else*."

*Putting 'us' in here*, she repeated those words in her thoughts. He wasn't talking about her. He was talking about the darkness within him.

Tegan arched her brow, but no other words left his lips. Instead, his hand released her wrist and gently glided down to her leg. He caressed her with a slow, ginger touch and traced the curve of her thigh.

She reached down and took his hand, stopping him. The tingling sensation was enough to set her body on fire, but she couldn't do this. Not now.

"We need to talk, Aiden," she said. "There's a war in this world that we've stumbled upon, and if we don't somehow remove that entity from you, there will be no saving any of us."

Aiden turned his head away from her. So, she reached out and gently touched his cheek, trying to get him to meet her gaze.

"Aiden, please," she pleaded. "You must listen to me."

"I have!" he shouted, and she flinched as the sound echoed through the room. Noticing the way she pulled back, his tone softened. "I have," he repeated but closed his eyes, as if talking drew out the most unbearable pain he had ever felt.

"Talk to me, Aiden," she said. "You haven't been the same since Kieran poisoned you with that ominous power. It's feeding on your Elven light, draining your life force. That power is nothing like what runs through my magic. What you carry isn't Newick magic, Aiden. It's something worse, and it's *killing* you."

"I know, Tegan," he said, his voice calming to a whisper. "From the moment I met you, I believed *you* would be my undoing. Your captivating essence made me yearn to worship you in every possible way that I didn't believe I was even capable of. I longed to own your body and mind and give you everything I could in return. I needed you then, and I need you now. But if I am this soulless monster and creature of this world that this darkness wants me to believe that I am, then kill me now. Release me from this pain because I cannot imagine a world where you and I do not exist together. It isn't *you* who will be my undoing, Tegan...I will be yours."

His hand was back at her thigh, but that time, she didn't push it away. That time, she wasn't strong enough to.

"I'm afraid," he admitted. "I want to be able to fight for you and the crew, but I don't even know who I am anymore. I don't care if it destroys me, but I do care if it destroys *you*."

Tegan closed her eyes, a fluttering sensation pulling into her stomach as his hand slid underneath the hem of her trousers. He inched closer between her legs and down to her wet heat. Gods, she had wanted him to touch her like that since before they left Myloria, but she was afraid. Aiden wasn't himself, and although she knew she should stay away until she found a way to free him from that evil, her body's desires ignored all rational thought.

"Aiden, which part of you is touching me right now?" she asked, watching a tiny smile pull at his lips. She genuinely couldn't tell.

"It's me," he said. "The darkness wants me to end you, too, Tegan. It whispers to me to kill you." She allowed her eyes to trail down to his crotch, his hardened cock apparent through his thick pants. "I'm tied up, though," he added, clearing his throat. "You may have to keep me this way, or I'm afraid I'll hurt you."

Tegan swallowed a little, finally daring to study his face. He looked like *her* Aiden, but there was undoubtedly the presence of something sinister...something so dark and twisted that she couldn't fully comprehend it. Still, a part of her held hope.

"I think you're strong enough not to hurt me," she breathed. When she said those words, Aiden yanked hard on the chains, the metal ringing loudly with the movement.

"I want to," Aiden said, his gaze locked on hers. "But Gods, I want to be inside you even more. Let me have you, Tegan."

She was playing with fire, and she knew it, but the magnetic pull that beckoned her toward him was stronger than any logic. Tegan reached out, her fingers slowly gliding over the hem of his pants before unsnapping the button and moving the chains tied to keep him secure. She straddled Aiden, slowly wiggling his pants down and pulling out his hardened cock for him. Tegan's movements were quick and frantic—even rushing before she changed her mind. She quickly pulled her pants and undergarments down her thighs. Just enough for her throbbing core to be bare and revealed to him. Tegan moved on top of his hips, directing his cock inside her in one smooth motion.

They both grunted as a wave of pleasure rippled through them.

Aiden's head fell back, his expression scrunching in sheer bliss. His lips parted as Tegan moved her hips. He instinctively tried to move his hands, but the chains wrapped tightly around his wrists, binding him to the bedposts.

A loud, frustrated growl left his lips. "Let me touch you, Tegan," he demanded, his eyes shining with desire and hunger. "Undo these binds. Now."

Tegan's eyes remained locked on his, but no words left her lips, and she kept her hands still. Her hips moved roughly, sliding him inside her deeper and deeper. She licked her lips, savoring the tingling sensation that washed over her body with each slow breath. Her petite yet powerful hands clutched his shirt, digging into the fabric. Aiden couldn't help but bite his bottom lip as he listened to her steady moans, as if she utterly entranced him.

The sound of their bodies slapping against each other echoed through the room, mixing with breathless gasps and heavy moans. They shared the pleasure that lingered between them, spreading through them with each thrust and each movement of Tegan's hips.

"Fuck," she cried out as he bucked his hips up, going deeper, harder every time she came down. Like he wanted to claim her pussy as his. "Oh, to the fucking stars, Aiden!"

She quickened the pace, taking what she needed from him. When she looked down, darkness swirled in his eyes; a wicked smirk replaced his intense expression. Pleasure radiated from his face. "Tegan, don't you dare stop. Don't you fucking stop! Take my cock. Take all of it."

As waves of pleasure washed over her, she ran her tongue over her lips to moisten them before leaning in to kiss him deeply. His tongue snaked inside, taking her mouth possessively. Aiden tasted different, like something unknown, something foreign, but Tegan couldn't bring herself to pull away.

Tegan rolled her hips as they kissed, moving faster until he let out a groan and spilled his seed into her, filling her up. A mere second later, she was there, too—chasing the ecstasy that exploded through her, filling her body with thousands of tingles.

Aiden tried to move his hands again, but the chains held them to his sides. Tegan took a moment to catch her breath and then realized what she had done.

Once Aiden stopped pulsating inside her, Tegan carefully climbed off of him, looking into his eyes. She saw that his blissful smile had been replaced with a sinister grimace that marred his handsome face.

"Remove these chains, Tegan. Now!" he ordered again, his tone laced with fury. It was clear who was speaking to her, and it wasn't Aiden. "You can't tell me you want me like this. Chained up like a fucking animal."

She ignored him as she pulled his pants up for him, using the blanket to wipe both of them clean.

"That's not going to happen, Aiden," she said calmly, trying not to invoke his anger. She climbed off the bed, the floorboards creaking beneath her weight, and took the dirty bedding with her. The wooden post cracked, and Tegan let out a slight yelp, jumping back and dropping the soiled sheets. He did it again and again, each pull cracking the wood. "It's...it's for the best. I'm sorry it has to be this way."

"Let me fucking go, or I'll rip your beautiful face off with my bare hands!"

The threat caused a sharp sting at the back of her neck, her powers inching toward the surface.

She always knew that once the darkness had entered him, if she had to kill Aiden to protect herself, she would.

She *had* to.

It would hurt deeply, but she'd have no other choice.

"Relax, Aiden, or I'll have Kaeli or Xander return to help me subdue you."

Blackness covered his eyes. The blue that had once shone was now gone.

With one mighty yank on the chains, the links snapped, pulling on the posts and cracking them in half. Aiden moved swiftly, flinging the chains outward with a snap, coiling one around Tegan's neck, and pulling her forward toward him.

"Aiden, stop!" she shouted as she crashed into him. She unleashed her magic, weaving ropes of light and smoke to grab him by the throat. But the darkness leached from his skin, squeezing her body until her bones creaked. There was a tiny gap between them, and it gave Tegan just enough leverage to knee him in the groin. Aiden growled and fell back, the chain loosening around her neck. Tegan shifted to the right, lifted her leg, and kicked him across the room. His body crashed into a dresser and broke it into pieces. As his back hit the floor, Tegan bolted for the door.

"Mazie!" she screamed.

But before she could grab the handle, the dark power slithered across the floor, seizing her by the ankle and throwing her back. Tegan attempted to scream again, but the chain snapped around her neck, and Aiden yanked it tight, cutting out her voice.

With one hand pinned by his thigh, Tegan managed to free the other and press it against Aiden's heart. She poured her smoke magic, laced with Elven light, into his body. She pushed against the dark, trying to find Aiden's essence and bring him back, but the darkness connected with her Newick magic and latched on. Her body grew weaker as power drained from her. Tegan could no longer hold on as it fed. And then, with one final release of power, the connection snapped, and her magic flickered out and died. The evil being had consumed it all, taking it as his own.

*Oh, my Gods*, she panicked. *No.*

The chains tightened until her breath was cut off entirely. Tegan tried in vain to pull the chain away from her throat, but without air, her strength failed her. Her heart slowed as Aiden lifted her head off the ground and began slamming it into the wooden floor repeatedly. As the pain became unbearable, she heard a sickening, wet crack in her ears and *knew*. He had broken her skull open. Hot blood soaked her red hair. Through the haze of unbearable pain, his feral rage and glee were apparent; he was going to kill her.

"There, there, Tegan. Despite my desire to fuck you again and reclaim what belongs to me, your power is too strong." He leaned down, his chest hovering over hers until his lips touched her ear. "I know you know who I am."

His breath was hot on her cheeks, and what feeling she had left in her body went numb.

"The Newick witches were fools to play with power all those years ago. They may pretend I don't exist anymore as they selfishly take my magic...but deep down, they *fear* me. Deep down, I'm their biggest fucking nightmare." Aiden leaned back slightly to look her dead in the eyes. "I'll formally introduce myself to you, though, before I kill you," he said, flashing his teeth in a sinister smile. "My name is Zakari."

Tegan's blood drained from her face upon hearing that name. It was a tale she was told as a child about a creature that the Newick coven had consorted with long ago for incredible power. In exchange, the entity would feed upon their natural-born magic to stay alive and evolve. The coven became selfish but loyal servants of that dark essence.

"I cannot allow you to get in my way, hybrid," he said, leaning back down until their cheeks touched. "You, Tegan, are Aiden's greatest weakness. And weakness must be destroyed. I need his body and mind completely, and I can't have that while you still breathe."

The only part of her body that could move was her eyes as she blinked rapidly, staring back into his. Tegan had always known the Newick witches created her for one purpose: to be a weapon. The hybrids were never meant to fall in love or care for someone, for that matter. Kieran made sure of that, keeping her from men and women she had taken an interest in. Then she met Aiden, and Tegan fell into lust or love...she wasn't sure, but for that, she now had lost everything.

Aiden eased up on the chain, allowing her to breathe. "If you have any last words for me, darling,"—a hint of an amused smile touched his lips—"now would be the time to say them."

"Fight," she rasped. "Your light will always be stronger than the darkness, Aiden. Always. Use your Elven light. Protect your sister. Protect yourself. Embrace your light. I forgive you."

Aiden cocked his head to the right, placing his lips on hers and giving her one last kiss. "Fuck the light." The words felt like poison to her ears. "Now, Tegan, be a good girl and don't scream."

He tightened the chain, twisting it with a powerful force. As Tegan heard her neck snap, a chilling silence fell between them, and darkness consumed her, shutting her eyes forever.

# 19

## MAZIE

Mazie had come running when she heard the scream, but when she approached the door, she froze in horror, hearing chains rattling against the floor on the other side. A chill went down Mazie's spine, and she became paralyzed with fear. She couldn't get herself to open the door to confront Aiden. Silence filled the house, an eerie quiet that left her sick. Something had ended on the other side with horrible, gruesome finality.

*Tegan.*

Taking two more steps back, she shook off her fear, willing her body to move. She broke into a sprint, running out of the house. The sound of crashing wood and racing footsteps soon followed her.

*Fuck. Fuck. Fuck*, Mazie cursed in her mind, sensing the dark entity was right behind her, nipping at her heels. The terror made her run even faster into the colony. She ran until she reached the courtyard and shouted at the top of her lungs, "Kaeli!"

Kaeli and Xander looked up from the trail leading to the sea, Bay fluttering her wings between them. As a chill snaked up Mazie's spine, Kaeli's eyes went wide.

"Xander, transition now," Kaeli called. The two dragon shifters moved swiftly, extending their wings as they ascended to the sky.

Xander let out a roar as Aiden emerged from the shadows of the trees, stepped into the sunlight, and strode down the path toward Mazie. His body was covered in a haze of black smoke, wrapping around him like a cloak. With each step, the smoke trailed further down his arms in the form of long, thin fingers—just as she had seen Elijah do with his magic.

Mazie pulled out her sword as Xander nose-dived toward Aiden, breathing fire upon him. Aiden dropped low to the ground, raising his hand over his head to shield him from the flames. A wall of smoke rose to protect him, but Xander's fire penetrated the barrier, burning intensely into his flesh. He screamed in pain and was forced to drop the magic.

Xander soared upward, while Kaeli extended her long, silvery-blue-colored wings, creating a barrier between Mazie and the elf. Kaeli lowered her massive head and uttered a vicious growl. Aiden froze, his hand covering his burnt, bleeding arm, and his now-black eyes glittered with malice.

Mazie was unsure if the three of them could kill him. The truth was, she held no love for the Elven man, but she cared for those who did. She didn't want Aiden to die, but whoever controlled the magic that now took over his body wasn't Aiden.

It was Death.

The creature inside Aiden looked up, his eyes marking each of them, as if contemplating his next move. Mazie thought the two dragons would outmatch him, given that their flames could burn through his smoke magic. She scanned his face, looking for any trace of the elf behind those eyes.

His irises hadn't changed, though; they remained inky black pools. It was as if the fire and whatever entity possessed him had burned any lingering resistance, snuffing out whatever good Aiden had left inside him.

Slowly, the elf clambered to his feet, straightening his shirt and ignoring the burn wound on his arm.

"I'm going to leave this place, and none of you shall pursue me," he said casually, but Mazie gripped the sword in her hand, stepping forward.

"You will pay for what you've done to her, you son of a bitch," she said. He had done something terrible to Tegan—every fragment of her body was telling her so. Still, there was a tiny part of her that prayed she was, by some miracle, still alive.

"As I said, I'm going to leave, or I will do to you what I've done to her." His features flinched, but his eyes looked void of feeling. "And Aiden *cared* for her, Mazie. Don't think your life means anything to me. It was a quick death, though. Don't you worry." Mazie's stomach dropped at the words—confirming her dark suspicions. "But not with you. You and these dragon beasts will have a slow, painful death if you try to stop me. I'll unleash my power and allow it to move through this colony of yours." His eyes turned to Kaeli. "The little children will all fall at my feet."

Kaeli roared and put her black-clawed foot forward, but Mazie placed her hand on her wing and shook her head. A decision had to be made, and Mazie couldn't allow innocent people to pay the price for a wrong move.

Her eyes held Kaeli's, and in an instant, her body relaxed. The unexpected connection took her aback, as if she could reach Kaeli's mind and beg her not to fight. Mazie wasn't one to turn from a brawl, and it was driving her mad not to be able to do something to protect them both.

Even if she fought with everything she had, could she stop the creature who had killed Janelle's brother—Elijah's best friend?

Aiden was gone.

And they let whoever was inside the elf turn around and walk away.

---

Mazie felt like she was observing herself from a distance, her body and mind disconnected. She was trapped in a haze until the sound of Bay's wings fluttering in her ear broke through, bringing her back to reality. "Mazie?" Kaeli's voice floated into the recesses of her mind, and a rise of awareness flooded her body.

Mazie hurried into the bedroom, only to find blood splattered all over the edge of the bed and most of the floor surrounding it. Bile rose to her throat at the sight, her body going completely numb. She'd had blood on her hands before, seen it countless times in battles. Hell, she had ripped a giant's heart right out of their chest.

But nothing could have prepared her for the gut-wrenching sight inside that room.

Mazie held her stomach when she looked at Tegan's lifeless body lying on the ground, soaking the wood beneath her with crimson liquid. The fucker had cracked her skull open, revealing parts of what she could only guess was brain matter. Her pale face was disfigured with horror, and the chains remained wrapped tight around her crooked neck.

Aiden said her death was quick, but it sure as hell didn't look that way.

Bay gasped behind her as the rest of her group entered the room. Mazie wanted to tell Bay to get out—to not look at Tegan like this, but no words came out. Hesitantly, she approached her lifeless body, placing her fingers on the side of her neck to check for her pulse.

There was none.

Not a single vibration.

Mazie pulled her fingers back, some of Tegan's blood now smeared over her fingertips. It hit her then: Tegan was gone. In the most horrific, painful way, she was *gone*.

The contents of Mazie's stomach rose to her throat, spilling all over the floor before she even realized what was happening. She quickly turned back in a feeble attempt to stop vomiting, but the yellowish substance just continued to pass her lips. No matter how tightly she closed her eyes, Tegan's lifeless body remained imprinted on her mind.

That image would forever be etched into her memory, haunting her for the rest of her life.

A hand found her back, rubbing it in a gentle, circular motion.

"Breathe," Kaeli said softly as Mazie dry heaved. "Xander, wrap Tegan up, please." Mazie heard a rumble behind her as Kaeli's warm hand continued to caress her back.

It took a few moments for the nausea to subdue, just enough so that Mazie could finally speak. "We can't leave her like this," Mazie

said. "We don't leave crew members to rot away in a fucking hut."
She hardly knew Tegan, but she undoubtedly deserved better than
that.

Kaeli's hand stalled on her back. "Then we'll give her a funeral.
A ceremony we hold for our fallen warriors. We would general-
ly hold it in the colony's square, but I'm afraid it would bring
unwanted attention from the Brotherhood." Mazie nodded and
finally turned back to look at Tegan. She was now laid on top of
the mattress, wrapped up in a sheet, though most of it was scarlet
red, drenched with her blood.

With a flick of Kaeli's wrist, the fire spread over the sheet, consuming her body and the bed she now lay on. Kaeli's magic allowed
the fire to remain focused on that area of the room and not spread
any further.

Bay settled by Mazie, too. She couldn't force herself to separate
her eyes from the fire and look at her pixie, but tiny sniffles were
in her ear. The fire consumed Tegan's body, burning any evidence
she had ever existed—aside from the memories that lived in those
who knew her.

Xander started humming. The tune was unusual to Mazie's ears
but soothing, the notes swaying in time with the burning pyre
before them.

"What is that?" Mazie asked.

"It's called 'The Song of the Fallen Dragon,'" Kaeli responded
softly, her hand now lingering on Mazie's lower back. Her heat
radiated against Mazie's spine, and she didn't want Kaeli to pull
away. She was a pirate, used to the sea and the chilly wind, yet the
fire felt like home. "To pay respects to those who leave us...and
comfort them as they arrive in the afterlife."

Mazie clenched her fists.

Whatever darkness lived within Aiden would meet a fate far worse than Tegan's.

And that was a promise.

# 20

## JANELLE

Janelle yelped as Kade flung her onto the bed. "What are you doing?" she asked as a low, feral growl rumbled in his chest. She scrambled backward frantically, watching the intensity in his gaze as he approached the bed.

His eyes were deadly, his body tense.

Kade remained silent as he grabbed her by her ankles, yanking her back on the mattress. She was no match for his physical strength. In a moment, he was on top of her.

She hadn't feared many men besides Kieran.

Kieran, Merrick, and Dorion were the kind of men who carried their wickedness proudly. Men like Kade, however, could easily mask it with their playful charm. It was present when they spoke and in how they held themselves. Right then, when he was silent and on top of her, Janelle was painfully aware of Kade's twisted side.

Right then, Kade was the deadliest creature she had ever known.

Would he kill her? Would he torture her until she shared everything he wanted to know?

"I've told you about Anaru. I cannot help you anymore!" she pleaded, his muscular body caging her in. In any other circumstance, she wouldn't hesitate to fight. She'd scratch, hit, and scream at the top of her lungs—but she didn't dare to do any of that. She couldn't—not with her friends' lives on the line.

Kade gripped her jaw, keeping her face still as he forced her to look at him. "This is something I don't want to fucking do, but Dorion is forcing my hand," Kade said, and she swallowed, not liking the sound of that.

"What...what are you talking about?" she stammered. The look that lingered in Kade's eyes told her he was up to no good, putting the fear of the gods into her. "Please. You don't—you don't need to do anything you don't want—"

"We need to know more," he interrupted her. "Not just about Anaru and her life there, but about Earth and the power that walks your streets and sails your seas. It is crucial to our survival, and we know you'll not willingly give it, seeing how reluctant you were to share that you knew his mate."

With a swift motion, she brought her hand up and slapped him forcefully across the face. A wave of regret washed over her as he snarled back, showing his teeth.

"Are you fucking serious right now?" he growled.

"Please don't touch me," she begged. "Kade, please."

Time seemed to slow as he inched closer, pinning her hips with his knees and releasing her chin. Instead, his hands gripped her wrists and pinned them above her head. Then, slowly, he rested one hand on her bare thigh. Janelle felt the bile rise in her throat as she looked away, willing her mind elsewhere. Was this how he would force her to reveal everything they needed to know?

"I'm going to imprint on you, Janelle, and claim you as my mate," he said. Those words snapped through her ears, making her look back at him in shock. "And then I'll be able to read your thoughts. Everything you know will become mine."

Janelle's hands trembled, and her heart sank into acidic terror from one prison into the next. Her life would never be hers again.

"Don't do this," she said, shaking her head. Her eyes welled up with tears. "I've already been claimed, Kade. You can't have me."

He shrugged, an amused smile crossing his lips. Janelle knew her bond with Elijah would mean nothing to him, even before she said it. "In another world, love. Those celestial laws don't mean shit here. Here...you're mine. *My* mate. And I may do with you whatever I want." He reached up, trailing her bottom lip with his finger and then giving it a tight squeeze. "Don't move."

Immediately, Janelle's eyes tinged with warmth, giving her a comforting sensation rather than pain. Her body tingled like tiny, sharp nails scratching at the surface. When she glanced downward, the black tattoos on his bare chest appeared to sway like branches dancing in the wind. As his hand squeezed tightly around her wrists, that burning sensation returned to her eyes, and she had to close them.

There was a tremendous sensation as she felt energy press into her soul and wrap itself around her—a warm vibration making her head spin. It was like a rope pulling their energies together, stringing them tightly in a knot. The connection felt similar to her bond with Elijah, but this time, it was imposed upon her rather than chosen. She knew Elijah was hers, and she was his, but Kade's presence consumed Janelle's mind. She wanted him, craved him like he was her source of breath.

As he stopped, the magic quieted in her chest, and the room fell silent; Kade climbed off her and walked to the back wall, placing his hand against it and lowering his head, as if the ritual had drained him.

Janelle leapt from the mattress and hurried to the mirror on the wall, looking back at her tattered reflection. Once as blue as the ocean, her eyes had transformed into a mesmerizing yellow shade resembling pure gold.

*No. No. Not this,* her thoughts panicked.

As she turned to face Kade, he straightened up, and his expression softened, like he felt sorry for her.

She didn't give a shit what he felt or what he thought of her now.

Even though her mind surrendered to him just moments ago, she knew it was wrong, and she'd fight against that mating bond, even if it meant destroying every member of the Red Dragon Brotherhood and tearing down their palace walls.

# 21

## NOLA

Each passing minute hung in the air, as if time had come to a halt. Waiting was Nola's kind of torture, powerless to save Lincoln from what was happening. The longer he was away from her, the more panicked she became. To keep herself occupied for a time, Nola took some strips of cloth from her tunic and fashioned a wrap for her injured ankle. It wasn't broken, luckily, but putting weight on it took her breath away. Once she fastened the cloth, Nola sat on the cell floor, her forehead pressing into her knees, and she waited.

Lincoln's only way of stalling was to allow himself to be tortured. Since Anaru had broken their bond, she wouldn't feel his pain and rescue him. Therefore, she remained hidden and safe from those monsters. They didn't know that the connection had been severed, and the thought of Lincoln's suffering terrified Nola.

His love for Anaru would bear the pain of every cut and bruise, ensuring the Brotherhood wouldn't discover where she was hiding. He'd pretend that their cruel tactics were working—that

Anaru felt his pain, and she would reveal herself. Nola wasn't sure how long Lincoln would last before the Brotherhood realized the bond was gone.

Nola looked up as the door swung open with two guards on each side of Lincoln. Her jaw dropped when she saw his beautiful face marred with blood, his right eye swollen shut. He was shirtless, with a large gash over his chest and one right above his left eye. The guards were half-dragging Lincoln across the floor.

"Oh, my Gods. Lincoln!" she cried out and ran to the cell door, but one guard held up his sword and pointed it at her. "Back up, bitch, while I put him back inside."

She nodded, not wanting Lincoln to experience any more pain if she ignored their orders.

Nola quickly returned to the wall until they opened the door and threw Lincoln inside. Then she rushed toward him, kneeling on the ground and wrapping her arms gently around his battered body.

"My love," she said as tears poured down her cheeks. "Are you—"

"I'm okay," he breathed, looking up and placing his hand gingerly on her cheek. "I barely feel a thing."

The guards had now left the dungeon, and she let out a sob. While Lincoln remained brave, she felt her entire world was falling apart. More than anything, she wanted to help him, to ease his pain, but she was limited to what was within their dirty cell.

"Here," she said, rushing to the sink. She grabbed a small towel Merrick had left and felt the cool water run through her fingers as she poured it over the fabric, careful not to soak it all the way through, before returning to him. As gently as she could, she dabbed the blood and cleaned him before he rested his head on her chest, exhausted.

"Now they wait," he whispered. "They wait for a dragon that will never come for me."

Nola swallowed hard, holding him close. "And what happens then, Lincoln? What happens when they realize she's not coming?" The mere thought of it had her mind spiraling. These men were ruthless, and she feared the punishment he'd endure for lying to them.

Lincoln grunted softly. "We'll cross that bridge when we get there, my love. For now, we stall."

Nola drew him in closer. The thought of him enduring more pain and torture shattered her heart, and she vowed silently that they would face the consequences for every moment of hell they had inflicted upon him.

Time continued to drift, and Lincoln shut his eyes, falling into a deep sleep.

As she went to wake him after what felt like hours, she heard footsteps coming down the hall, and Dorion walked in.

"What the fuck do you want?" Nola said through her teeth, watching an amused expression cross his features. Lincoln had been so exhausted from the beating that he was still in a deep sleep, curled up on the hard floor atop a thin blanket. She positioned herself protectively in front of him, shielding Lincoln from Dorion's stony gaze.

"Well, he doesn't look so good, does he?" he said with a wicked smile.

Dorion's words triggered an overwhelming surge of rage to course through her. More than anything, she wanted to get her hands on him and rip him to shreds with her siren claws. "What do you want?" she asked again, not entertaining his provocations. "Lincoln can't take any more."

Dorion glanced at Lincoln sleeping in the corner and then turned to look back at her. "It's you I want, Nola," he said. "Follow me."

---

Dorion closed his hand around the back of Nola's neck and shoved her forward. "Walk," he barked as she purposely dragged her feet the entire way. Despite her frustration, she refrained from reacting, knowing Lincoln's fate depended on how she behaved. Nola had to play the part of the obedient prisoner, or she could lose him.

Once they reached the shoreline, she peered out, watching the tiny ripples of waves crash against the sand. There was a sense of home as she looked onto another world's sea. She didn't have to be from their planet to want to place her feet in the ocean and swim to the bottom, feeling the salty water against her skin.

"Why did you bring me here?" she asked, glancing over her shoulder to see Dorion folding his arms and giving her a barely noticeable smile.

"I need you to get something for me...down there," he said, pointing to the sea. As Nola turned to look back, she caught sight of the sun. It barely set, casting a pink hue over the waves.

"You're sending me out into the sea?" she asked. "I don't know your waters. I don't—"

"But you're so close," he interrupted her. Clearly, *no* wouldn't be something he'd take for an answer. "Straight away and a half

mile down." He took a step toward her. "The previous emperor
of our world stole something from me, hiding it within the reef so
no one can get to it. You're the only creature on our land who can
reach the bottom of the sea without dying. You're quite the lucky
find. We've been waiting for years to retrieve this. So, you'll get it
for me, or your little pirate will meet his death."

Nola swallowed hard. "You touch him again and—"

"And what, Nola? I have no reason to want either of you dead.
You may not be from this world, siren, but surely you understand
how things work. You do as I ask, and I'll let you and Lincoln go.
That's a promise."

Nola's lips parted. She knew without a doubt she couldn't trust
Dorion, but he had given her no choice. She would do anything to
protect Lincoln. "What exactly am I getting for you?" she asked, a
nervous twitch pulling at her stomach.

Dorion took another step forward, brushing a hand down one
of the silver streaks in her hair. "It's called the Eye of Dragão's
Flame. It's completely coated in gold, so you can't miss it. The
closer you get, the brighter it shines, even when buried in the sand.
It wants to be found."

"What does it do?" she asked, fully aware that any object this
significant must possess some supernatural power.

Dorion let out a tiny laugh. "Well, Nola, that would be none
of your business. Your task is merely to retrieve it." He stepped
forward, taking her by the arm and pulling her into the sea with
him. Once they were waist-deep, he squeezed her arm harder. "You
have one hour," he said, twisting her elbow to emphasize his de-
mand. "Swim for a half mile down until you hit an emerald reef.

It's buried beneath it. If you don't return with the Eye, I will cut that pirate's head off and leave it on the shore for you to find."

Nola swallowed and gave him a curt nod before he released her arm, and she dove into the sea, the pressure of her legs morphing together into her tail. The warmth of the water helped her body ease as she moved deeper into the sea. On Earth, the closer to the bottom, the colder the water became, but that wasn't the case here. It appeared warmer, even hot. It even felt lighter, making it easier for her gills to take in oxygen. Once she had traveled in the direction Dorion indicated, she took in her surroundings. The ocean was similar to Earth's, with coral, rocks, sand, and even fish moving quickly, creating bubbles around her. It was beautiful there, under the water's surface. Peaceful. For a moment, Nola felt safe.

Though she didn't want that feeling to disappear, she shook her head, trying to remain focused. Lincoln's life depended on her. As she neared the bottom of the sea, Nola's siren eyes honed in on a bright yellow light filling the entire space the further she ventured. Then she saw an outcropping of unusual rocks before shock ran through her. Those weren't rocks.

It was a city.

*Oh, to the Gods*, she thought. *What is this?*

As Nola swam closer, horror overtook her as she realized what she was truly looking at.

Death and destruction surrounded her.

Skeletons scattered the Undersea, piles upon piles of sea creatures' bones. Some were within the reef, while others were barely covered in sand—thousands and thousands of them.

Her stomach tightened, and her body went rigid. Nola felt like all the oxygen had been pulled from her lungs as she came to a realization about the corpses. They were not wholly human. The bones had skeletal structures that resembled tails.

They were *siren* tails.

Nola gasped, the last of her air expelling in a torrent of bubbles. She put a hand on her pounding heart, willing herself to breathe, to filter air through her gills and into her lungs.

Her eyes darted around, scanning for potential threats. Dorion had sent her to the sea without warning of what to look out for, but it must have been something deadly if it had wiped out her species. As she cast her eyes around the ruined city, she caught sight of the vibrant green reef. Dorion had only given her an hour; every moment that passed could be a moment Lincoln's life was at risk.

When she entered the reef, she spotted the source of the yellow light she had seen before entering the ruins. The light was pouring out from a hole in the reef. Nola slipped her arm in, reaching until her fingers found something round and smooth. She seized it and pulled the object free.

Its gilded, smooth design made it almost slippery to hold, with a dragon eye looking back at her from the center. As she ran her hands over it, it glowed even more, as if it were calling her to steal, use, and run away with. Nola shook her head. Time was running out. Once she trussed it tightly in her satchel, she swam away from the reef and up past what looked to be the remains of a palace. But as she reached the peak of one of their palace's buttresses, she stopped, noticing another body whose bones were strung across the rooftop and half buried in what looked to be an underwater garden. Nola looked closer and saw that behind the corpse's back were smaller piles of bones. She noticed the odd shapes and gasped.

The body had *wings*.

# 22

## NOLA

Water dripped down Nola's clothes as she moved out of the water. She struggled to comprehend what she had just seen, and a ripple of fear and sadness ran through her body. She needed answers, and she needed them now.

"What did I see down there?" she asked as she placed the golden orb into Dorion's waiting hand. "Why are there sirens with wings?"

"You're in a dragon world, after all. Our sea serpents just evolved differently than yours, Nola. Those were the sea creatures of Dragão Terra," Dorion responded. Now that the shining object was in his possession, his posture seemed more relaxed.

*Sea serpent,* Nola repeated in her mind. They were not like a siren. Similar, yet so different.

Nola continued to stare at him, still wondering what damned fate had befallen those creatures below the sea. "How?"

"Our worlds share similar species and creations," he said. "All the realms do. You have Newick witches, and we have mages. Earth has sirens that trace back to humans or fish, ours carry the genes of a dragon. You get the idea, don't you?"

Fear pumped through Nola's veins, but she'd be damned if she showed it. She crossed her arms over her chest. "Tell me everything," she said. When Dorion didn't utter another word, she gestured toward the relic in his hand. "I have just retrieved that for you. I deserve answers."

Dorion's lips tugged upward, as if her words had amused him. "You deserve nothing, but you're lucky. I'm in a good mood today, so I suppose I have some time for small talk."

His gaze drifted toward the ocean in front of them.

"In a world with thousands of parallel universes connected by portals, our mages realized that, at some point, they would have to confront the unknown dangers lurking beyond. They selfishly explored the other realms and saw how much we differed from the populations they encountered, yet how much we were alike," he explained. "Unfortunately, once you open a portal, you cannot shut it. Not completely, anyway. The Vipers, for example. They are a clear demonstration of the negative outcomes that result from the misuse of that power. There was no going back once the mages discovered what they could do with their magic. They had found the secret to traveling forward and backward in time and opening a stream of energy that connects worlds, allowing you to travel through it."

Nola blinked. "Your mages use their *own* power to alter time and space? Not a compass?"

"Here, power comes from within," he replied. "But there are always consequences of a power, no matter what source drives it. A few rebels outside the guild realized they had to create something that could stop what the Ember Guild was doing, just in case. They needed something to fortify our world from the rest, preventing mages from destroying the last remaining beauty of our world. Self-preservation was their priority, and I commend them for that."

He lifted the relic, and the orb glistened beneath the unforgiving sun. The bright golden hue wrapping around it pulsated, becoming brighter as it moved up the two gilded spikes attached to the top, holding four vibrant yellow gems in place.

"As long as two mages harnessing their elemental powers link themselves to it, this relic has the power to close these portals forever, essentially shutting off access between the universes. The first and last time they attempted to use it, several worlds outside ours dissolved into nothing, killing everyone and everything inside...including the mages who used it," he explained gleefully, his smile widening. "Despite the casualties, this right here will keep at least *our* world safe. There will be no more threats from other worlds because there will be none left standing except for our own."

*Oh, my Gods*, Nola thought, nausea rising in her throat. She barely dared to breathe, afraid that the contents of her stomach would spill everywhere.

"You can't..." she stammered, but no other words passed her lips.

"Oh, but I can. I can do *anything* now that I have this," Dorion responded. "Their intention was to seal the portals, preventing people from going through them, but they hadn't realized it would sever the links, causing a complete collapse outside the source. This here can be our salvation, yet it has the power to eradicate everything else. But because of what happened, the emperor of our land at the time ordered it to be thrown into the sea, so that no one could ever reach it. They didn't want Dragão Terra to be responsible for the mass genocide of other realms. But once it hit the bottom of the sea, the power collapsed and killed everything around it. *That* was the destruction you saw below." His gaze darkened. "They tried to protect other worlds, and, in return, they killed an entire species of our own."

Nola's hand shakily covered her mouth. Tears welled in her eyes as she thought of the horrors that took place under the sea, all caused by that relic in Dorion's hand. "Then return the Eye!" she cried out. What had she done? Dorion gave her no choice but to retrieve the item under threat of Lincoln's execution, but the catastrophic consequences weighed heavily on her soul. "If that tiny thing in your hand can destroy realms, why touch it at all?"

"Because your world created something we cannot ignore, and now it walks on our land...the *darkness*."

*Surely there is another way to deal with this*, Nola thought, her mind calculating her next move. She considered fighting and stealing the orb, but given her weakened state from captivity, she didn't stand a chance against him.

"What Kade saw in Janelle's mind was fascinating," he continued. "We took that information and pieced it all together. The Newick witches on Earth have always had the same abilities as our mages do...the power to open time. But when the dark entity that controls Janelle's brother bargained with them centuries ago to exchange a power source, it smothered the power to open portals. The Newick witches had to put that power inside a gem...*and* your Kroneon to make it work," he explained. More pieces of the cosmic puzzle came together in Nola's mind, and things started making sense. "It worked as a conduit to their power. The only way to kill what is inside Aiden and free those witches from their suppressed power is to destroy the realm that created him. We destroy Earth, and the darkness within that elf dies with it."

# 23

## JANELLE

C onfusion clouded Janelle's thoughts as she opened her eyes, her head spinning in circles. "Fuck," she cursed, holding her stomach as bile rose in her throat. As she bent over the mattress, she caught sight of Kade. He was sitting by the small dining table, his gaze fixed on her and watching carefully.

"That feeling will go away," he said. "Don't strain yourself, Janelle."

She wanted to tell him to go fuck himself, but the unpleasant sensation rumbling in her stomach—along with the threat of vomiting—prevented her from doing so.

"Right. I guess it would've been too much to expect you to cooperate in any way." Kade sighed. "How you feel about *me* is the real question."

She blinked. What she felt for Kade was *need*...and hate. She wanted him to hold her while she moved past the sick feeling in her stomach, but she also wished she had a weapon to drive through his heart.

*What the hell is happening to me?* she thought.

She slowly forced herself to sit up, pinching the bridge of her nose between her fingers. Her mind tried to digest the newly found realization, but it only made the bile threaten to rise to her throat again.

Janelle called up an image of Elijah, and all other thoughts and false desires melted away. He was the one who could make her feel whole again—who made her feel safe. Whatever feelings she held for Kade were all illusions and manipulations.

*Elijah is mine, and I am his. There is no one else,* she repeated in her thoughts like a prayer.

"I feel numb," she said. "What the fuck did you do to me, Kade?"

Kade smiled coldly at her. "You don't remember?" he asked, arching his brow.

"It's clear you've invaded my memories, that I know," Janelle responded, blinking once as tears threatened to form in her eyes. *Was there any part of her that these men wouldn't violate?*

Kade stood and walked toward her, sitting on the mattress, so close to her that their shoulders touched. His palm gently cradled her cheek, giving her a kind smile. She fought her body's natural response to his proximity, to the brush of his fingers against her skin. It felt natural, and the realization made her heart race. It was terrifying. "I had to get the information from you, but to do that, I needed to claim you as my mate. When I extracted your memories, it also erased some of them. What *do* you remember?"

"And they say romance is dead," she said blankly. She wanted to put some space between them, but her body refused to move. "It didn't work because I still remember Elijah. My *true* mate."

Kade furrowed his brow. "Interesting," he said. "You're more powerful than we expected."

The thought of losing herself to Kade, losing her sanity as he invaded her thoughts, made her ill. As a child, Aiden had taught her how to defend herself from men, and as an adult, her mentor, Kora, helped harness those skills for combat. Becoming a warrior was ingrained in her since childhood.

But when it came to psychological warfare, Janelle wasn't sure she would survive. If she rebelled against Kade while still bonded to him, he would rip her mind to shreds, destroying her completely. She knew she had to play the part of the dominated female that the Brotherhood wanted her to be. Then Janelle could try to escape before it was too late. Her mind would *never* be theirs.

Kade smiled again, but that time, it wasn't friendly. "You may still have your memories, Janelle, but you cannot break a mated bond. You can try, but it won't end well."

Being in such proximity to Kade made Janelle's stomach tighten. She couldn't ignore the bond's presence in her heart. While Janelle loved Elijah with all her soul, the dragon bond made it hard to ignore Kade. It was pulsing through her veins. The temptation was all-consuming; she had to fortify her willpower to resist the pull. Her body and mind screamed for him to take her against the wall and fuck her repeatedly, her skin aching to feel his hands between her legs.

Even that morning, she awoke with Kade in her thoughts, and she felt sick because of it.

*Elijah.*

Janelle repeated his name in her mind, hoping it would give her clarity in this haze that was the primal need for Kade. She had to fight for Elijah and her to be together again, no matter the dragon planet's cosmic ties and the monster in front of her.

"I didn't want this for you, Janelle," he said, his voice filled with sincerity and regret, as if he genuinely meant it. "I wished there was another way, but we all knew you'd stay silent to keep those secrets hidden in your mind. So, let me be clear. If you deny me, I will force you, and that is not something I take lightly. Dorion won't have any of it and will lock you inside that dungeon with your friends until you die, and now that we're mated, it will tear me to pieces."

Janelle's gaze shot up, her eyes burning with anger as she glared at him. "Excuse me for not feeling terribly sorry for you, Kade," she responded. "After you violated my mind, I *hope* it tears you to pieces. I hope you *suffer*."

Kade sighed, reaching toward her again and brushing a strand of her hair out of her face. "Always so difficult. Why does everything have to be so damn difficult with you?"

She blinked. "I don't understand. You violated my memories already. You have what you need from me. Break the bond, Kade!"

Kade chuckled under his breath and ran his fingers through his messy, dark hair. "It's not that easy. Once you claim someone, that's it. That's your only chance for a mate. The only way out of it is death. So, let me make this very clear." He towered over her. His lips were close to hers. So damn close. It was hard not to get distracted by them. "You're stuck with me. It doesn't matter if you like it or not; it doesn't matter how hard you try to fight it. You're mine. *Mine!*"

Janelle scrunched up her face, glancing away. "Then I'm sorry to say that you're going to get very frustrated with me, Kade. I hope you're fine with a life of celibacy because I'm not opening my legs for you. Ever."

The humorous smile on his lips faded. "Oh, Janelle," he said, reaching out and running his thumb down her jaw, "I may be the kindest of my brothers, but you will end up in my bed, willingly or not."

*Fucking vile piece of shit*, she thought.

Kade's hand slinked up her leg. It was only then that she realized one of his hands was on her thigh all along. The tingling sensation spread through her violently, rushing right to her tortured mind. The electrifying feeling stirred in her belly and then between her legs as his finger found her entrance, hovering there. "Are you honestly telling me you don't want me to touch you even after I marked you?" His fingers inched closer, and he ran a soft caress between the folds. She turned away, disgusted with herself for even feeling slightly turned on by his touch.

*No mating bond can be this fucking strong*, she thought as he slowly ran circles over her clit with his thumb.

But she wouldn't tell him that. She had to fight the sensation she felt at that moment, despite how much her body pleaded for him to drive his finger inside her. "In our world, this is called assault, you sick bastard." She barely got the words out, clutching the sheets and arching her body into his hand.

Kade lifted his thumb from her clit but kept two fingers lingering between her legs. "I think you're a little liar, Janelle. You're so fucking wet for me."

*Elijah is mine, and I am his.* The mantra echoed in her mind as Kade's fingers slowly moved back, resting again on her thigh. Hot, bitter tears of relief ran down her cheeks.

Kade's expression fell before he pulled away completely and stood up. Conflicting emotions radiated from his eyes. "Soon, Dorion will force us to marry to complete the bond," he said. Janelle could only stare at Kade in horror as he stood and smirked down at her. "Get used to this life, *sweetheart,* because there's no going back."

# 24

## ELIJAH

It was clear to Elijah that bringing Arabella along on the journey was wise, but he also feared for her life. She had already gone through so much turmoil in the Ruins and risked everything by saving him, but what would her life be like in the hands of the Red Dragon Brotherhood?

Arabella explained that the Brotherhood spent years deceiving people and keeping them confined behind the walls of broken cities. They spun the lie that they were safe when, in reality, it was to keep the threadbare populace in line. The shifters ensured safety through power. It was the best method to shape society to their desired ideals.

"You know, Arabella, you can still turn back now," Elijah suggested, reclining on the sand with his hands behind his head and using a boulder as a pillow. "It's not too late."

A painful stab pierced his chest then as he imagined the horrors Janelle must have been enduring. As he thought about the men who had taken her, a surge of fury overwhelmed him, unleashing a flood of violent thoughts of what he wanted to do to each one of them. Though he was grateful for Arabella and everything she had done for him, guilt weighed heavily on his shoulders. The same thing could happen to her, and that thought nipped at his sanity, slowly and brutally.

He couldn't allow it.

"Turn back?" Arabella's eyes widened as she looked at him, her tone making it clear she thought he was being ridiculous. "We've spent days traveling, Elijah. Now, why would I do that? Let's be logical; traveling back on my own would significantly increase my chances of dying compared to our travels together," she said stubbornly. "Besides, traveling with you has been the most thrilling experience I've had in years. If I die, I die with a friend. Not alone in my home, living on coffee and stale biscuits. That's more than most of my people could ever ask for."

Elijah looked down and slowly nodded. "My entire life, my father had kept me behind palace walls. I knew the dangers of the world out there, but the palace kept me safe from people knowing the real me. It protected people from *me*."

Arabella shrugged, but her eyes remained soft. "You don't seem so bad, Elijah. You're a bit intense but not *bad*. It may all just be in your head."

*I wish,* Elijah thought to himself. "Do you miss your family, Arabella? Were you close?" he asked, but then he paused, wondering why he would ask such a thing. It wasn't his business, and she might find his questioning insensitive.

Arabella nodded. "More than ever. I thought so many times about doing what you're doing. Leave my home, a place that was a safe cage, and venture to Drakentos to kill the very man who's done nothing for us since he took the throne. But then I had to remind myself that wasn't what my father would have wanted for me. He would have said,"—her voice deepened—"*'Now, Arabella, you keep yourself safe, and if those wicked men come for you...you fight. You fight until you have nothing left. Don't lose your head and do something foolish like confronting the lord.'*" Despite her teasing tone as she mimicked her father's voice, he didn't miss the glint of sadness in her eyes.

Elijah's eyes dimmed, and within seconds, more pain flitted across Arabella's features. The bravery of that woman was unwavering. He wanted to be just like her. Not that he was afraid to die. No, Elijah was ready to die for the woman he loved. It was the fear of losing his family, the people he cared for, that gripped his heart—walking a path utterly alone. He didn't love easily, which frightened him more than the dangerous creatures lurking in this world.

He hadn't realized how much losing Janelle would affect him. Before he met Janelle, he had never thought about spending his life with a woman. Elijah bedded them occasionally, of course, but it was never deeper than that. There were never feelings involved; he never ached for them. But Janelle changed everything in every way possible. He hadn't stopped thinking about her and the torture she had to experience at those monsters' hands.

*I will rip them apart from the inside out*, he promised in his mind.

"What exactly can you do, Elijah?" Arabella asked, pulling him from his thoughts. "As far as your magic goes, anyway."

Elijah sat up and placed his elbows on his knees, slightly leaning forward and deep in thought. At some point, Arabella would witness that magic. What he had used on the spider creature to save Arabella as she transitioned barely scratched the surface.

"I don't want to frighten you," he said.

Arabella raised a brow. "It can't be scarier than dragon fire, and it certainly can't be worse than what I've seen around here," she said. "You know, if I really wanted to, I could burn you to a crisp before you could blink."

Elijah chuckled. "True. But there's a trace of the entity's power inside me that sometimes has a mind of its own. Darkness that—"

"Darkness? I don't..." Arabella's words disappeared into the back of his mind as he zoned out—or at least he thought he did. Something strange was happening to him. There was a slight blur over his eyes as if he were looking through fogged-up glass. He blinked a few times, hoping the blur would disappear, but it didn't. Elijah looked down, watching a tiny bug walk backward and dig itself into the sand, burying its body until it disappeared. His stomach dropped.

*What the fuck?* he cursed in his thoughts and looked up. Something wasn't quite right, but he couldn't figure out *what*. Arabella's eyes widened as she reached out to grab his arm.

"Elijah, what's wrong?" she asked. "You look as if you're about to pass out."

He blinked a few more times until his eyes were clear again. "I did eat a massive spider for the first time," he said, deciding not to mention the blurring vision—at least until he could pinpoint *what* was wrong. "I might be getting sick."

"Hmm, that spider wasn't venomous, but I know the climate here is a bit warm. Here's some water."

Arabella reached into her bag, pulled out a waterskin, and handed it to him. He took a few sips before placing it on the sand.

"Back to what you were saying. What did you mean by darkness?" Arabella leaned forward, her hands propped under her chin.

"It's nothing," he said, sensing he needed to keep that quiet. Arabella was too innocent for a historical discussion about the evil that dwelled inside him. He only knew a part of the story gleaned from his father as a child. It wasn't a secret that the source of his power, the dark entity, had been plaguing Earth since the beginning of time—an accidental creation when life began. The Newick coven was the first to sell themselves to that evil. In return, the entity would bless them with dark powers if they shared their life forces with him, helping him grow and feed on the elements of their world.

Because of that, it suppressed the witches' true magic and replaced it with something sinister.

"It's a long story you don't need to hear right now. Let's just say that magic from our world comes in different forms. My family lineage and their dark history separate us from other witches. Magic that makes me different from you and other creatures out there. It makes me an enemy to most, and I'm certainly not a good man. It's in my blood and something that will never change."

"I'm going to stop you right there," she said, rolling her eyes. "Do you honestly believe I'd let you inside my home if I believed you were evil?"

He didn't answer that question, and she pressed her lips together with disappointment.

Quietly, he released the power from his fingertips, watching as it moved along the sandy ground and danced through the flickering flames of the firepit. The black mist stopped right in front of her and extended its long fingers, hovering so close to Arabella's cheeks that the hairs on her neck stood straight.

Instead of moving back, she carefully stood, holding her hand out to touch it. Elijah felt the connection between them, a comforting feeling he wasn't used to. With that, his power became still, a peaceful change in his magic through her aura.

"See," Arabella said. "Dark power doesn't mean evil, Elijah. It never has." She smiled while their eyes locked. "What you have inside you is *good*. Your soul and your light control even the parts you're ashamed of."

Elijah thought of Janelle and her Elven light and how, together, they created balance. With her, he felt his life finally had a true purpose. And now she wasn't with him, and Elijah didn't *feel* her connection anymore. His heart thudded as he attempted to compose himself, but unwanted thoughts snaked into his mind. What if something had happened to her? What if things were never the same again? How could he ever live with himself without her? The questions that remained unanswered overwhelmed him. He didn't realize its extent until a small tear escaped his eye and trailed down his cheek. He quickly wiped it away, but another one followed, along with a painful grip on his chest.

*Gods, am I dying?* Elijah thought.

It certainly felt so as his chest tightened more, and he allowed himself to weep. A sorrowful sob escaped his lips, filling him with both shame and fear. It was a fear of not getting to Janelle in time. It was a fear that something had happened to Lincoln, and he would lose everyone who ever meant anything to him. He wanted to stop crying, to shut up, but he couldn't. His body *needed* this.

*Is it weakness?* he thought. *Is this me giving up?* Elijah hadn't shed real tears since he traveled back in time to say goodbye to his mother one last time. Time seemed to drown Elijah in his sorrows and worries. It was a while before he could regain his composure and swallow his bitter sobs.

When he looked up, Arabella was already kneeling before him and placed her hand on his shoulder. "Your magic doesn't define you, Elijah. But what you *do* with it does," she breathed. He couldn't force any words to leave his lips, so he merely nodded, rising to his feet. Arabella understood his intention and rose, too.

After smothering the fire and gathering their supplies, they began walking in silence. Arabella didn't question why he cried, nor did she offer many words to comfort him, and that was *exactly* what he needed. As uncomfortable as that was, crying seemed to heal a part of him from which he couldn't free himself. Perhaps he could finally be the man Janelle needed him to be—the man he *wanted* to be for her.

After what felt like a few hours, Elijah's feet began to ache. He had lost track of time, and Arabella had allowed him to exist in silence as she walked beside him. At last, he broke it as he asked, "How much longer?"

Arabella squinted her eyes, looking at the path in front of them. "It will take half a day before we reach the labyrinth."

"A labyrinth?" Elijah asked. "Sounds...great."

Arabella shrugged her shoulders. Her expression didn't reassure Elijah that the labyrinth would be easy to navigate.

"The castle is well-guarded, Elijah," she explained. "It was never going to be easy to reach her."

But he would reach Janelle, he thought, even if it were the last thing he ever did.

# 25

## MAZIE

"Another round of drinks for my mates, please," Mazie told the barkeep behind the counter and raised her mug. She had been sitting there for over an hour after an entire day of traveling through several terrains and forests to reach the tavern; she had no intention of leaving.

Bay flew past her and perched herself on Xander's shoulder instead. Mazie gave her a soft smile. The pixie had grown pretty fond of him over the past few days.

Kaeli and Xander sat beside her, exchanging glances. Kaeli placed her hand over Mazie's and squeezed. "Time to cut you off, Mazie. We still have a half-mile walk to the pier. We can't have you falling over, can we?"

Mazie scoffed, but her face softened as Kaeli gave her a warm smile.

"I know you're hurting, Mazie, and I don't have to know you my whole life to understand what that feels like for you. But you may have forgotten that we're dragons. Even without a bond, we can sense your pain."

The pirate glanced at her empty mug before meeting Kaeli's gaze. "I failed to keep Tegan safe," Mazie said. "The least you can let me do is have one more drink, so the moment I hit that deck, I can pass the fuck out on it and forget any of this happened."

As Mazie went to turn away, Kaeli's fingers brushed up to her cheek and tucked one of her braids behind her ear. "Mazie, when you wake up, the pain will still be—"

The doors swung open, and the sound of heavy boots hit the floor.

"Shit," Kaeli whispered, moving closer to position herself with her back to the door, shielding Mazie.

Mazie tried to look over Xander's shoulder, but Kaeli reached out and wrapped her thin fingers behind her neck, trying to keep her still. "Who are they?" she asked, craning her neck. She spotted two large men standing near the tavern entrance. It was clear that they were members of the Brotherhood's royal guard, their attire identical to that of the men she had killed near the ship. The men scanned the crowd, looking for someone. As their eyes roamed through the tavern, Kaeli quickly turned toward her companions.

"It's too late to leave," Xander spoke in a hushed tone, cupping Bay and helping move her under his cloak to hide. "If we leave, they'll know."

"Stay silent." The look Kaeli gave Mazie made it *very* clear that she was speaking to her. "One wrong move, and they'll kill you here and now or take you to Dorion."

Mazie was itching to take her rage out on someone, but the seriousness in Kaeli's tone told her to listen to someone else for a change. She had been in her fair share of tavern brawls before, but she would never endanger Bay, Kaeli, or Xander's life.

She couldn't save Tegan, but she'd be damned before she allowed something to happen to them.

"I'll distract the guards," Xander murmured as the echo of the men's steps got closer. "You keep Mazie out of their sight."

With those words, he hopped off the stool, approaching what was now about half a dozen guards.

"Gentlemen...how lovely to see you here. May I buy you a drink? In Dorion's name, of course..." Xander's voice trailed off as he led the guards away, venom lacing his kind words.

"Just follow my lead," Kaeli whispered as the men conversed with Xander. Mazie nodded, ready to do whatever she asked.

As Mazie was about to look away to shield her face from a guard who turned toward them, Kaeli's gentle touch guided her chin, making their eyes meet.

"Sorry about this," Kaeli whispered.

And then...Kaeli kissed her.

In a mere moment, Kaeli's lips were warm and soft against Mazie's, and the world blurred around them. Even Tegan completely vanished from her thoughts; all that existed was *her*.

Kaeli.

Instinctively, Mazie reached for her hips, drawing her in closer, while Kaeli's hands cupped her cheeks. In that instant, their tongues entwined, consuming each other. *Fuck,* Mazie cursed in her thoughts.

All Mazie thought about was the passion blooming in her heart, cold embers reigniting throughout her entire body. Everything in her wanted Kaeli closer immediately. A small moan escaped her mouth, muffled against the dragon woman, and that only seemed to prompt her to move closer. With Mazie still seated, Kaeli settled in between her spread thighs, towering over her as they continued to kiss.

Mazie felt like she could barely breathe. Gods, with Kaeli so close to her, she didn't even need air. It didn't feel like she needed *anything*.

Then, from the background, the sound of retreating footsteps snapped them out of the haze of their heated kiss. The guards were leaving the tavern with their drinks, and it was safe again. As she looked into Kaeli's beautiful blue eyes, for once, Mazie didn't know what to say.

---

Mazie leaned over the railing, taking a deep breath as she looked out to the sea, the shimmering waters stretching for miles.

The truth was, all she thought about was Kaeli's lips on hers and how she tasted. The woman had only done it to distract the guards, but the softness and tenderness of that kiss awoke something in Mazie that she hadn't felt in years. That sensation alone seemed to sober her up quite quickly.

"Hey, stranger," Kaeli said softly, walking up from behind her. "Are you okay?"

She wanted to say, *I'm more than okay*, but was distracted by a sparkle in Kaeli's eyes as she smiled, her shimmering blue-white hair gracefully dancing in the wind.

*Gods, she's beautiful*, Mazie thought. "Listen—"

"I'm sorry," Kaeli interrupted her.

Mazie gave her a quizzical look, pinching her brows together. "Sorry for what?"

It could have been a million things, but only one she dreaded.

"The kiss, Mazie," she said.

*Fuck*, Mazie cursed in her thoughts again.

"I shouldn't have kissed you without your permission like that, especially since you had been drinking. It was wrong, but the Brotherhood knows Xander, and I frequent that tavern. If they saw you with us, they would have taken you in for questioning. I had to hide you from them. I had to—"

"It's fine, Kaeli," Mazie said, forcing a small smile. Of course, Mazie didn't care about the kiss. She'd do it again if Kaeli let her.

"I mean..." Kaeli's voice trailed off like something else was on her mind. "Did it bother you?" She fiddled with her dress. "I don't know..." She now seemed flustered, and Mazie's smile became genuine and grew.

"Kaeli, are you trying to ask me if I prefer yours or Xander's lips on mine?"

Kaeli stilled, and Mazie would have sworn she saw a hint of red come to her cheeks. "I don't know what your world is like," she said.

"Our world is complicated, but I've never given a fuck about the opinions of others. Your lips felt divine against mine, Kaeli. I promise you; I wasn't bothered. In fact, I very much enjoyed it."

Kaeli's shoulders relaxed, and she nodded. "Next time, I'll ask, though...and it won't be just to keep you out of the guards' sight."

Mazie met her smile. "I'd like that."

There was a moment of silence before Mazie's gaze swept over the mast. It towered above them with all its sails and then the wooden deck that spread out before them. The ship's long hull was ready to glide through the waves. It differed from the Sybil Curse. The blackened wood was smooth to the touch and polished to an impossible shine. Based on the structure, Mazie estimated it must have taken years to build the ship.

"Where's Xander?" Mazie asked, breaking the silence.

"He should be here shortly," Kaeli said. "At least we aren't traveling by foot anymore, but I'll need to stretch my wings soon. Anyway, he went to go hunt for food before we set sail."

Mazie looked around the deck. "How often do you actually use these ships?" she asked, since Kaeli mentioned before that they mostly carried cargo on their backs.

Kaeli placed her hand on the mast, running her long fingers along the smooth, gilded surface. "Not often. Most of our world's inhabitants are dragon shifters, but years ago, some chose not to shift at all. They'd rather walk or sail, and since water divides so many of the cities, it was the only way. Besides, it's almost impossible to fly with cargo, let alone through portals. It would expose us to the Brotherhood shifters. Using ships is easier; we can load more supplies every three months and transport them over the mountains without being detected."

"Some chose not to shift?" Mazie asked, confused. "If I had wings, I don't think I'd ever let my feet touch the ground again."

Kaeli chuckled, released her hand from the mast, and approached Mazie, tilting her head slightly to the right. "You'd be surprised how much you'll take something for granted once you have it. Xander and I love what we are, but I'd trade all that to be more like my father if I could."

Mazie offered a shrug. She walked past Kaeli to the railing right as Bay flew to her, perching on her shoulder.

"I guess you're speaking about your *other* father...the one who died?" she asked, looking over her shoulder slightly, but her heart wanted to look out into the sea. She already missed the one on Earth.

"I love my dragon, but when I use the magic that my real father gave me, I feel more *alive*," Kaeli said. "Is it also like that for you...when you use *your* magic?"

Mazie let out a hearty laugh. "I don't know who the fuck you've been speaking with, but I'm human."

Kaeli folded her arms and shook her head. "Liar."

Mazie scrunched up her face, but she felt Bay grip the skin on her shoulder with her nails, reminding her to keep calm. For her, magic was a subject best avoided at all costs.

"You can pretend all you'd like, but as you know, a dragon has many gifts, one of them being intuition. You, Mazie, were born with power, whether or not you use it."

"I don't have—"

"I felt it," Kaeli said. "After Tegan died and Aiden came out of that house to find us, there was this primal sense of natural energy. I've never connected with anyone at that level before. Your thoughts became mine briefly—we communicated through our minds somehow, and then it was gone. But even then, I felt this rhythmic pulse surrounding you. Every movement you made felt like a symphony of energy dancing inside you."

Mazie swallowed, feeling a bit violated even though it wasn't Kaeli's fault. She did have magic once upon a time, but she gave it up for the sea when she met Lincoln. She had gone so long without feeling power coursing through her veins that she couldn't even remember what it felt like.

"Well, I wouldn't know, nor do I care," Mazie snapped, instantly regretting it.

Bay's fingernails dug into Mazie's skin again, reminding her not to be cruel.

Mazie looked up as Kaeli's smile fell. "Alright, fine...*pirate*. Would you like to do us the honors and steer us east?"

The energy shifted again, but Mazie couldn't think about that anymore. They had a three-day journey by sea before they reached their destination, and she wasn't about to make the entire trip uncomfortable because she couldn't open up to Kaeli anymore.

Xander stepped onto the deck and tossed several bags and a few blankets on the floor. "The ship already has fresh water below deck. We're ready."

Mazie narrowed her eyes at Kaeli. The dragon woman had challenged her in a way she wasn't used to. Only Lincoln dared to question Mazie's motives and choices that he disagreed with. But with Kaeli, she didn't shy away from pushing back, and Mazie, though she was guarded with some things, respected that. The fire that burned in Kaeli excited her. She felt alive in every sense of the word; she hadn't felt like that in a long time.

Mazie placed her hands on the helm, the smooth wood beneath her fingertips grounding her, and turned the boat east. She looked up as the sail flapped in the wind, providing a gentle push away from the shore.

"I'll prepare dinner below deck," Xander said. "Bay, would you like to accompany me?"

Bay turned to Mazie, and she gave her a nod. She'd rather Bay stay safe below deck as they ventured into new waters.

Kaeli pulled a blanket from her bag and walked to the other side of the ship, sitting on a gray steel bench. Her eyes stayed on Mazie's, though, as if trying to read her. There was a slight flutter in Mazie's stomach, once again confusing her. Kaeli was beautiful. Stunning even. However, she couldn't let her thoughts distract her. She couldn't let the feeling around Kaeli shift her focus from reuniting with her friends.

Kaeli was a dragon shifter. The man who raised her was their enemy. And if Kaeli didn't kill him, she would.

Mazie leaned against the railing near the helm and looked out, trying not to look into the woman's eyes again. "So, what is this place we're going to, anyway?" she asked.

Kaeli stood, walking up behind her, and then rested her elbows on the rail. "Safety," she said. "A place my father and his men, to this day, have never found. We work hard to keep it that way."

Mazie quirked up a smile. "A hidden city within a mountain, huh?"

Kaeli nodded. "They've been there for ten years. They won't be able to find us once we pass by the stone barrier at the peak, even if they fly over. The place is well protected by ancient magic that Dorion doesn't have access to, so it remains undetectable to his Brotherhood."

"How?" Mazie asked, confused. "It's just open waters."

"You underestimate the power of a mage, Mazie."

Mazie understood there was so much to their world she didn't understand, and this was one of them. The fact that she'd been able to hide hundreds of mages within a mountain for the last ten years completely baffled her.

"My father and his brothers are the only ones who know the mages are still alive."

"Wouldn't they follow you to see where you go?"

Kaeli shrugged. "They're too busy building their empire. Mages aren't a threat anymore, but they won't hesitate to kill them if they come out of hiding. With you and your mates coming here, though, it may change things. I don't know if Dorion will let it go until they have someone to blame for opening that portal. And he won't allow it to be me."

"And Dorion controls everything?"

She nodded. "Everything and everyone *but* me. You see, I even had a mate once, but I denied him, and Dorion allowed it to happen."

Mazie's eyes grew wide. "Someone already claimed you?" she asked.

Kaeli nodded. "Dorion gave me a choice. He didn't want me to be trapped in a loveless marriage, so he set me free to choose. And I chose to be alone."

Mazie respected that. She would have begged for the same thing. Hell, she would have rather died than be forced to marry someone she didn't want or choose for herself.

"What happened to the man who claimed you?" Mazie asked.

Kaeli smiled. "The Brotherhood killed him."

Mazie's jaw dropped.

*Well, I didn't expect that answer,* Mazie thought.

"Dorion might be a piece of shit, but I believe he truly loves me in some sick, twisted way of his, at least. Or he did, anyway. He knew that if the Council of Drakentos found out someone marked me and I denied him, they would have forced the union. So, he killed the man to silence him." Kaeli paused for a moment. "Maybe it's mercy because I remind him so much of my mother. I'm not sure."

Mazie turned back to the sea and took in another calming breath.

"Well, I hate that man for what he's done to you and Xander, forcing your hand to protect others from his slaughter," Mazie said. "He did gain... a *little* of my respect for protecting you, at least."

A smile lingered on Kaeli's face as she inched closer to Mazie until their shoulders touched.

"Can I ask you something?" Kaeli started, her words nothing but a whisper.

Mazie answered with a nod.

Kaeli slightly bit her bottom lip before saying, "I would like to kiss you again, Mazie. May I?"

She didn't need to think about it; Mazie's nod was instantaneous. Kaeli leaned in, closing the space between them before her lips found Mazie's again. Their kiss was soft and less urgent than it was at the tavern, like they had all the time in the world, once again blurring everything around them.

But Mazie now knew one thing.

She was damned.

Because Kaeli was all she could think about.

# 26

## JANELLE

Even though she had stopped struggling hours ago, the burns on her wrists still throbbed painfully as the cuffs bit into her flesh.

*What is the point of fighting?* she thought.

Janelle shook her head. It was too early to surrender to despair. Her friends needed her to be strong. She *needed* to hold on to the hope that Elijah would come for her, and together, they'd leave this hell in ruins.

But, even if Janelle could escape from the room, there were dragon shifters throughout the palace who were loyal to that damned Brotherhood. There was little hope for escape, if any.

*I still have to try,* she thought.

Janelle sighed and leaned against the headboard, looking out again. A gentle breeze came through the window, ruffling her tangled white hair, and she closed her eyes. Janelle longed to escape the confines of that room, craving the sensation of fresh air filling her lungs. As the wind moved the curtain to the side, she immediately spotted a couple of beautiful, gold-black dragons soaring above the palace, gracefully gliding through the thick clouds.

Janelle narrowed her eyes as she saw something she hadn't noticed since her capture. Since her arrival, they kept the shades drawn during the day, and she was either locked up in her room or forced to walk through the courtyard. Even if her captors allowed her to peer out the window, everything was swallowed in thick fog.

But not too far past the massive brick barrier that kept the outside world out was a labyrinth.

The labyrinth stretched far beyond what Janelle's elf eyes could comprehend. The maze structure comprised thick green vines that were so tightly wound together that they looked solid. From what Janelle could make out, the beginning of the maze bordered the forest and led to the iron gate in front of the palace.

*If someone wanted to make it here, they'd have to navigate that nightmare,* she thought.

It was almost beautiful.

Almost.

Janelle turned her eyes from the window, feeling the unpleasant ache between her legs, reminding her of what Kade had done...or almost done. But worse, how she felt about him when he touched her.

Once the bond's power simmered down when Kade left the room, she knew it was all a lie. False magic forced them together despite her true heart.

Her heart was Elijah's. *He* was her fated mate.

*Mate.* Yes, the bond with Kade was as natural as the air she breathed; she felt it in her bones, but she cursed the very man who imprinted on her. She'd fight it, even if their planet's gods struck her down.

*No one will decide my fate,* she said in her mind—not even Elijah, and especially not Kade. What she felt for Elijah was real, bonded magic or none. The gods could strip their connection, and she'd still want him.

Still *love* him.

Janelle sat up, adjusting herself on the mattress as the door clicked open. She blinked back tears, determined not to give Kade the satisfaction of her crying. As promised, he had come to retrieve her.

"Let's go for a walk, shall we?" he said, approaching the bed and holding a key to unlock the chains that bound her wrists. "You need some fresh air, and I'd like you to see something."

———— ◦ ————

As they walked through the palace halls and outside the gates, Janelle felt the eyes of the staff and other members of the Brotherhood, watching her with suspicion.

"They've not learned to trust you yet," Kade said. "In time, the people will see you as one of us. Don't worry."

She scrunched up her face. "Why the fuck would I care about that? I won't be their princess or whatever title is forced on me. I'm not one of you, nor will I ever be. So, you can fuck right off."

Kade's playful smile reached his lips again, as if he found her remark amusing. Janelle acknowledged Kade's beauty and charm, which attracted anyone who interacted with him, but they weren't the ones being held captive. She knew a dangerous monster lurked beneath, wanting to destroy her piece by piece. He had created such a glorious façade that no one could see the true him. But she did. She saw Kade's evil heart.

And she wanted to destroy it.

He ran his hand over his black hair and turned to her, his shoulder leaning against the labyrinth entrance. She was so caught up with the fact that he'd let her out of the palace to see the rest of the land that she hadn't even realized how far they had traveled until they reached it.

"Janelle, is this how you always behave?" he asked, his lips curling up. "So filthy and vulgar. Your stubbornness might be cute now, but I promise, at some point, I might snap."

"I'm held here against my will," she said, but when her eyes glimpsed his, she pressed her lips together, refusing to speak anymore. She'd already endured a lot because of him since they took her. Still, the silence grew heavy in her chest.

*I'm done tolerating men like him*, she thought, right as a dragon's roar echoed above them and a great shadow soared through the sky and over the labyrinth.

"Do you want to explore?" he asked, as if he hadn't heard a word of her protest as he pointed down one pathway in the maze. It was split into two parts, allowing you to go right or left, choosing whichever doom it would most likely lead you to.

"You want to get me lost, now?" she asked, raising a brow.

Kade's lip quirked up. "Have you been in one of these?" he asked. "It was designed for the previous royal family." He smiled. "If you can find your way out, you live and can be free to find the rest of your friends. But if you get lost, well, the paths will consume you."

There was nothing playful about those words. Whatever was out there, this was a test of her fortitude. "Alright, Kade. I'll play."

Now Kade was back to his laid-back nature as he bit his bottom lip while his eyes widened, his toothy grin almost bringing a smile to her face.

It irritated the fuck out of her.

*This damned bond of ours. I'd like to strangle him with it,* she thought.

"Here, I'll pick for you. You go right, and I go left. If you can find your way to that forest on the other side without me catching you, I promise I'll let you go."

Janelle's eyes went wide before looking up at the high hedges. She could use this as an opportunity to escape in normal circumstances, but she wasn't a fool. Kade had a plan, so she would have to understand that going in and use that to her advantage.

She would have to be smarter than the dragon, if possible.

"And if I lose? If you catch me?" she asked, waiting nervously for the answer.

"Then I get to fuck you without you resisting me, before or after our wedding night. Depending on my mood." He stepped closer to her and placed his hand on her cheek. "And, as my wedding gift to you, I'll convince my brother to let your friends go."

Now Janelle's stomach pulled into a tight knot. If she were to get through the labyrinth, she could be free. She could search for Elijah, and together, they could rescue Lincoln and Nola. But if she lost, she'd have to betray Elijah by giving herself to another man willingly, and her friends would walk free.

*If* Kade was telling the truth.

In either scenario, she'd lose something.

"Deal," she said. "But can I at least have a weapon or—"

"No," he said sharply.

Janelle rolled her eyes at him and looked into the mouth of the labyrinth.

She had to try. She had to know that if her life wasn't about to be in danger, there was a way out. Janelle wasn't ready to reveal her magic to the dragons, not yet, anyway. Dorion had only seen a small part of what she could do, and it barely grazed him. She hid the rest, never fully showing her strength because she knew they'd use it against her if she did. She needed to rely on her Elven abilities and her training from Kora.

*Be calm, be smart,* she told herself.

Kade folded his arms. "I'm not negotiating anything else, Janelle. I had to sacrifice a lot when I claimed you. What I'm feeling about you and me is the consequence of that. Do you think I want to love and feel bonded to a woman I don't know? Especially an unfamiliar species that came crashing into our world? If and once you're free, I'll have to live the rest of my existence alone or not fully loving another. You get *nothing* out there because I don't trust you won't take any weapon that I give you and kill me with it. I'll wish you luck, though. If you find safe passage through these paths, then you're free. If not, you're mine until we take our last breaths. *In every way there is.*"

She swallowed and inhaled steadily, the reality setting in. Kade truly believed she wouldn't make it through, or he wouldn't have given her that choice.

Janelle turned to the right, looking at where she'd venture alone. She heard Kade shuffling around, and when she looked over, he was pulling his shirt off; his lean body and chiseled chest caused her stomach to flutter.

*Fucking bond*! she shouted in her mind.

"This isn't a race, Janelle. Take your time. I'll see you soon," he said, offering her a wink before sprinting to the left and disappearing down the path.

She was alone again, and a loud clanging sound made her spin around. They had locked the gates behind her, so the only path was straight ahead through the labyrinth.

*Get yourself together, Janelle*, she said in her thoughts. *This might be your only chance.*

The wind picked up, tousling her long hair in her face. Once she stepped onto the path, the atmosphere shifted. It felt warm and cold at the same time.

Her skin was clammy, and her heart pounded in her ears.

As she wandered deeper into the maze, the foundation beneath her began to shake and sway. Janelle had to cling to the hedges to keep herself upright.

It felt like she was standing on the turbulent surface of the Zemiran Sea. Another lurch sent the elf sprawling to the ground.

"What the fuck?" she cried out, her legs buckling, and she fell forward, her palms slamming hard against the pebbled ground. As she picked the little clumps of dirt and sand from her skin, she looked up, and a man stood further along the path in the distance. Her heart stopped beating for a second.

Was it Kade coming to catch her, promises be damned?

He was the same height as Kade and had the same black hair, but his skin was much lighter, and blue eyes glimmered in the sunlight.

"Oh, my Gods," she said, her eyes focusing on his face. "Elijah?"

Elijah sprinted toward her, falling to his knees and scooping her into a tight embrace. Janelle heard a small sob against her neck. She clung to him, hot tears flowing down her cheeks.

*He found me,* she thought. *Oh, my Gods. Elijah found me!*

After a few seconds, Elijah released her and grabbed her hand. "We have to go, love," he said. "Run!"

Elijah kept her flush to his body, his arm around her waist as they hurried through the labyrinth. She had so many questions, especially how he was able to find her, but she couldn't think. She had to run. They had to get out of there.

"I came from that way," he said, pointing a fork in the maze. As they got closer, confusion washed over his face before he pointed to another pathway. "Wait, it was this way. My friend Arabella is waiting on the other side."

*Arabella*, she repeated. He wasn't alone. He came with help.

As more time passed, it became more difficult to find a way out. The further they walked in the maze, the more it seemed they were getting closer to the palace rather than away from it.

"Wait," he said, easing the grip on Janelle's hand. "Do you feel that?"

Suddenly, a loud roaring noise filled the air, and the ground shook again.

She looked up, frantically trying to find the source of the noise. "What is that?" she asked.

"Fuck!" he cursed. "Get your powers ready."

Janelle lifted her hand, drawing her light to the surface of her skin. Right then, the earth cracked open, and a mangled, twisted creature emerged. Its whip-like tentacles lashed out, wrapping around Janelle's ankle and slicing her arm with the thorns covering its flesh.

As it yanked Janelle to the ground, she pivoted and slammed her light magic into the monster's underbelly. The impact threw the beast across the maze, slamming it into the wall of vines. There was an explosion of stone, branches, and leaves as a portion of the wall collapsed.

Elijah summoned his smoke, the mist seizing the creature, and threw his hands apart. The magic ripped the monster in half and dropped the bloody corpse to the ground. When Elijah turned to Janelle, blood was splattered on her face and trickling from her wounded arm.

"Are you okay?" he asked, running to her, but before he could reach her, a red dragon descended from the sky...Kade. The bond yanked at Janelle's soul, nearly knocking her back down.

Kade's sharp claws extended, piercing into Elijah's shoulders while his other paw swooped Janelle up, carrying them both above the maze and back to the castle.

# 27

## ELIJAH

The dragon's claws pulled from Elijah's skin as he was thrown onto a stone floor. As he spun around, the dragon morphed into a naked human male, swiftly grabbing Janelle's hair and yanking her off the ground.

When Elijah lifted his hand to summon magic, only faint wisps of smoke trailed his fingertips before fading into nothingness. "What the fuck?" Elijah cursed as he rose to his feet. But before he could confront the strange man who held Janelle, something slammed into the back of his knees, and he went sprawling face-first onto the dirty floor.

A firm hand gripped his hair, and the sharp point of a sword pressed into his back.

"You move, and this sword goes straight through your spine," a deep voice called behind him. Elijah stilled, not daring to move.

Janelle attempted to break free from the man's grasp, clawing and scratching at his arms that held her. However, the man only chuckled, as he was too strong for her to fight off.

Elijah watched in horror as the shifter dragged Janelle in front of him. His gaze washed over her in panic; she didn't appear to be harmed—at least, not that he could see. But she looked pale, and Elijah noticed a gauntness to her cheeks and jaw. Icy dread coated his heart.

Janelle and Elijah locked eyes, but she said nothing to him, only tears streaming down her cheeks. The man grabbed the front of her shirt and ripped it clean from her body. He then proceeded to tear away the rest of her clothing until Janelle was utterly naked.

Janelle once again tried to fight, slamming her elbow into his ribs, but he barely winced as his arms gripped tightly around her waist, keeping her still.

Elijah growled while the shifter slowly wrapped one hand around her stomach, and another began squeezing and caressing her pale breasts.

Another hard sob escaped her while she tried to wrench free, but it was futile. The shifter was too strong.

*I'm going to fucking kill him*, Elijah thought, feeling the bile rise in his throat. His gaze separated from Janelle's, now staring at the man. Darkness lingered in the shifter's eyes, but that wasn't all; the man almost seemed entertained by the vile act.

"Janelle, my darling, how about we show Elijah exactly what happens when bonded mates fuck for the first time," he said, his hand continuing to fondle her breasts and gently squeezing.

Elijah's eyes grew black with rage.

As the man groped her, though, something shifted in Janelle's eyes, and her head fell back, melting into his arms.

"What the fuck are you doing to her?!" Elijah shouted.

"Easy, witch. She lost a little bet I made with her, and now she is bound to surrender herself to me. Sure, she'll put up a tiny fight now, but once I ram my cock inside her, our mating bond will be complete, and the one you had with her will be severed forever."

*No*, Elijah's mind spiraled in terror, feeling the sword dig more deeply into his back, keeping him from moving.

Janelle kept her head pressed against the crease of the shifter's neck, letting out a slow and steady breath while the man's hand continued to caress her.

And she let him.

"Let her go, or I'll burn you and this entire palace to the ground!" Elijah cried out. "Let her fucking go!"

The shifter's lips pressed against Janelle's tender throat, but Elijah didn't miss his wicked smile. He removed his hand from her breast and gripped her hair, yanking her head farther back before kissing her. There was only a slight resistance then, but she wasn't fighting.

Not anymore.

"Janelle!" Elijah screamed, a shudder running through his body as another man's lips claimed hers.

Lips that were only meant for him.

Kade released the kiss and asked, "Who are you bonded to, elf?"

She opened her eyes and looked straight into Elijah's. "You, Kade," she answered.

Kade smirked at those words. "Don't blame her, Elijah. I claimed her against her will, but her ability to fight me has finally been crushed. Soon, she won't give a shit about you anymore. You'll watch me fuck her right here on the altar." He looked down at Janelle. "And you're going to watch her enjoy it." With his free hand, he pumped his cock, a devilish smile flitting across his lips. His toned legs stood behind Janelle as his cock prodded at her entrance. "Your destiny with your beloved ends now." He leaned in, brushing a strand of her hair behind her ear.

Elijah felt completely and utterly numb as Kade slammed into her in one harsh, deep movement, and Janelle cried out his name, "Kade," right as her eyes turned darker than before, and a subtle smile pulled at her lips.

*No. No. No*, Elijah cried out in his thoughts. *This cannot be happening.*

Elijah felt like his heart was being ripped out. Every second of the filthy sight broke him, yet he couldn't look away. He never understood what bonded mates were until he met her, but magic never forced that need even then. They could choose to walk away if they wanted to, but Elijah was set on the fact Janelle was the only woman for him.

No part of him could understand what was happening.

"Yes," she cried out, a moan escaping her.

The man she called "Kade" wasn't just fucking her, he was claiming her as his, and she was behaving as if she *wanted* it. She didn't care that she was destroying his entire soul. The woman he loved didn't care about anything other than that man taking her.

The shifter grabbed her leg, propping her knee up on the altar and spreading her open for him. Kade's body slapped against hers, again and again, like a war drum in Elijah's ears. Janelle's lips were parted as she gasped every time he buried himself in the depths of her, her face scrunched in pleasure.

*Pleasure*, he said the word in his thoughts. *She cannot want this. Something is wrong. No bonding spell can be this strong.*

Each moan and pant leaving her lips caused a fury inside him he was unfamiliar with. It wasn't sadness that claimed him but anger and pain that overshadowed it all. He let his head hang and stared at his hands. The hands that killed for her, that bled for her.

Janelle was betraying him in the worst possible way. It didn't matter what Kade said. Their bond was stronger than any connection she had with the monster taking her. Why isn't she fighting anymore? Did their love mean nothing to her?

Kade slammed into her again, jolting Elijah to look back up as Janelle screamed.

She cried out again and again, shaking underneath him. She didn't even bother to look at Elijah anymore. It was as if he didn't exist.

Janelle attempted to grip the stone altar, her nails clawing at it as she came. Her whole body was shaking violently as pure bliss hit her. Kade leaned forward, thrusting a few more times while gripping her hips, fucking her until he spilled over, coming inside what belonged to Elijah with one final, heavy grunt.

Kade pulled out with a wry smile, humming a tune that would haunt Elijah for an eternity.

Janelle looked up. "I'm sorry, Elijah, that you had to see that." Her words were so casual and disconnected that it was as if he were a stranger to her.

When she turned away, Kade grabbed her head and forced her to look back at Elijah, and his lips trailed down the soft curve of her cheek.

"A mated bond with a dragon is impossible to resist," Kade said. "She cannot love you anymore because the moment I fucked her, whatever mated bond she had with you became severed, and her heart now only belongs to me."

Elijah tried to resist the person holding him, but the sword dug so deep that blood was tricking down his spine, and he winced. Fury coursed through his entire body, causing his cheeks to burn.

"Janelle does not," Kade taunted, "nor will she ever belong to you again."

# 28

## JANELLE

J anelle's hands clenched into fists, her heart slamming so hard against her chest that she could hardly breathe.

*What the hell is this?* she thought, staring through the cell bars inside their dungeon.

"Elijah!" she shouted as a dark-haired woman placed her fingertips against Elijah's temples. His body lay prone on a black stone dais inside of a prison cell. "Get away from him!" Janelle screamed, her voice growing hoarse from the strain. "Get the fuck away from him!" Kade's powerful hands gripped her shoulders, keeping her in place.

*What is she doing to him?* she wondered, sheer panic clutching her chest. *Is she harming him?*

"Kade, what the fuck is this?" Tears burned behind her eyes.

Kade released her shoulders, went to her side, and looked down at her, his expression unreadable. "That's Arabella," he explained. "She's one of the most powerful mages on our land."

"What is she doing to him?" Janelle asked. "I don't understand. You carried us away from the labyrinth. Then it was as if I blinked, and I was standing here, and he was on that dais. I—" She glanced down at her arm where the vine creature had sliced her skin open, and there was no wound, like the beast had never touched her. Not even a red mark. "What?" she said. "What is happening? Am I—am I losing my mind? Gods."

Kade let out a low chuckle as he moved behind her again, wrapping his arms around her waist this time and pulling her back against him. "No, you're not losing your mind, Janelle." He leaned forward until his lips grazed her ear. "You never left your room," he breathed. "You only woke up moments ago, and then I brought you down here. That little labyrinth adventure was all in your head, conjured by another mage of ours, Arenol. You didn't actually think I'd let you *explore*, did you?"

She swallowed, still not understanding.

"We found Elijah before you even came here over two weeks ago," he said, and Janelle's stomach climbed to her throat. "He's been in this cell the entire time, believing he was on some adventurous quest to rescue you with a friend he met along the way. And just now, our mage made him believe I fucked you in front of him on that altar and that you *enjoyed* it."

"Oh, my Gods!" Janelle cried out, tears flowing down her face now. "You son of a bitch." She whirled around, breaking Kade's embrace, and her hand flew toward his face. But Kade snatched her wrist just before it could make contact. His grip tightened around her wrist, and his eyes darkened.

With his free hand, Kade grabbed her hair from behind and forcefully pulled her closer. His lips trailed along her cheek, kissing her gently and making her skin crawl. The nausea climbed up her throat, and she fought to keep from vomiting.

Kade's lips rested on her ear. "If you cooperate with me and quit fighting, perhaps we won't make him see things that could destroy him further. Or, if you attempt something like trying to slap me again, we alter his emotions so much that he hates you to the point of fucking Arabella to get back at you." Kade chuckled under his breath. "We can do whatever we want with him, maybe even drive a sword through his heart while he sleeps. That is, if you resist me on our wedding night. You'll not fight. You'll not run. You will do exactly as I tell you, or we'll have a funeral that night, too, for your little friend in that cell. Is that understood?"

Janelle's heart shattered into a million pieces, but she nodded a yes.

"Beautiful," he said, gently kissing her forehead. "Now it's time to return to your room."

Within moments, Kade was dragging her across the hall, but she no longer fought. She felt completely numb.

He tossed her back into her room before shutting the door and locking her inside. Once he retreated down the hall, she bolted to the window to look out.

The labyrinth wasn't there. There was nothing but a long, open field that stretched all the way to the forest.

"Demented fucks," she cursed, gripping the windowpane so tightly that one of her fingernails broke from the force.

She was going to kill them. Every single one of them.

Janelle backed up and searched for anything she could use as a weapon, but they had intentionally left her in a bare room—nothing but clothes and a washroom. Even the windows had no glass for her to break to create a knife.

She eyed the bed, a flicker of hope sparking in her mind. It was her last chance: *the Voleric pendant*, she thought. *I can reach Elijah's mind and warn him.*

Janelle rushed over to the mattress where she had hidden the stone and lifted it. A chilling sensation ran down her spine, causing her body to go cold. "Fuck," she cursed aloud. *They found it. Of course, they found it.* Her memories were theirs now. Kade would have seen her hide it.

Janelle sank onto the mattress and buried her head in her hands.

Without the Voleric, Elijah was trapped.

A dark cloak of despair covered her.

They were completely and utterly alone.

# 29

## ELIJAH

Elijah leaned against the prison cell, resting his head back.

He struggled to wrap his mind around what he had just seen. Janelle would never do something like that. She had to have been under a spell she couldn't resist. There was no other explanation. He still felt the bond in his heart and in his magic. It was weakened, but it was still there.

No matter what fated connection remained or what he had witnessed just moments ago, his love for her remained unwavering.

Elijah stood and shouted for help, but no one responded. His voice echoed through the endless hall lined with empty cells, but no guards or dragon shifters came in or out of the dungeon.

There was only silence.

Elijah lifted his hands and tried to summon his power, but once again, there was nothing. No matter how hard he concentrated on his magic, it didn't come. It was as if it had vanished.

"I don't understand," he said, dropping his hands. Desperation threatened to consume him, but Elijah didn't have time to drown in pity. He needed to escape that prison, find Janelle, and rescue her from that man called "Kade." That was why he had come there in the first place. He made Janelle a promise, and he would keep it, no matter the price.

No matter what she'd done to hurt him.

Since he couldn't rely on his powers, Elijah decided to trust his *other* abilities.

Growing up, Elijah had always been a curious child. He became fascinated with picking locks and learned the skills behind his father's back. By the time he reached adulthood, his lock-picking skills were those of a master thief.

Elijah examined the cell door's locking mechanism. There would be no way to discern if they'd laced it with magic, but it looked like the same locks they used in the Zemiran castle dungeons. Perhaps he could work around that.

His eyes roamed through the cell; it was left entirely bare, likely to prevent such attempts from the prisoners. But there had to be something—anything he could use.

He ran his hands over the cracks and surface of every stone on the blood-caked walls. He crouched, dragging his fingers over the dirty stone floor, hoping that one of the prisoners there had somehow left something behind. A pin. Anything.

His hand frantically tapped against the floor, but he could only think about Janelle. The image of her naked on that altar made his heart twist painfully. He thought of the way she arched underneath Kade or the way she moaned in ecstasy. The way she took that man's cock, and the way...she enjoyed it. Once again, Elijah fought the urge to vomit.

Elijah knew her. He *knew* her soul. Something sinister had been done to Janelle, which caused her to act in such a manner. That was the only logical explanation he could come up with.

In his heart, what had happened was a lie.

Though he couldn't erase what that shifter had done, he would make him pay. His body tensed as he considered all the ways he would rip each limb from Kade's body, starting with his most prized part. That man took what was his, and there would be a price to pay.

His mind and chest were heavy as he tried to chase the images of Janelle fucking that man away from his mind. Instead, Elijah focused on the more pleasant memories of her. The way her eyes glittered like jewels when she laughed, the glow of her white hair in the moonlight, or how stubborn she had been when they traveled to Myloria together.

Would he ever have Janelle by his side again?

He didn't know, but he would risk his life to find out.

Elijah stood up, brushing the grime on his pants. He went back to the door when something in the corner of his eye caught his attention. A figure stood before the cell, but its form wasn't solid.

Elijah's vision blurred, and he rubbed the back of his hand over his eyes to clear them. He tried to focus on the figure, but it was difficult to discern any features. He strained to get a glimpse. Suddenly, he saw something—black hair and bright brown eyes flashed before him.

They were familiar...

*There!*

There, he could make out her face—it was Arabella's—the realization of that pumped adrenaline through his body. Arabella was there, and she had come after him. She had breached the walls of the castle to help him save Janelle after they became separated in the labyrinth.

"Arabella?!" he cried out, gripping the metal bars and yanking them wildly, but nothing happened. "Arabella!"

No response. The figure had vanished into thin air.

*Why,* Elijah wondered. He had just seen her there—he was sure of it. He couldn't miss the familiar features of the only friend he had there.

Was he losing his mind?

Perhaps he did, indeed, poison himself somehow along the way. This world was foreign to him, and maybe his body wasn't used to it. Could it be that what was not venomous to Arabella could have been deadly to him?

As Elijah's mind spun with these thoughts, he heard *something*.

He paused, going completely still and holding his breath.

Somewhere beyond the walls of the prison, there was chanting. Slow, melodic sounds that seemed like a holy mantra. Elijah couldn't make out the words, but someone was there, someone who could hear him and maybe help.

"Anyone out there?" he yelled. "Please help me!"

*Help—help—help.*

The word echoed through the cell, followed by crushing silence. Perhaps Elijah was, after all, truly alone.

# 30

## MAZIE

After three long days at sea, the ship finally reached a small port near a massive mountain range. From there, they'd have to travel on foot around the mountain to the other side, where ships couldn't sail.

"We're almost there," Kaeli said. "It's too dangerous to shift, and the ship is too tall to sail through the narrow river pass under the mountain. We are much closer to the palace now. If my father's followers see us, they'll alert him, and he'll know something is happening."

"Walking is fine," Mazie said, as Bay's tiny toes touched her shoulder. "Bay and I will need to eat, though."

Xander emerged from below deck, throwing a bag over his shoulder. "The city we're heading to isn't too far now. You'll be safe there. They're kind but might be a little on edge around Bay."

"On edge around Bay?" Mazie said, looking back at her pixie to confirm that they were talking about the same Bay. "Are you fucking kidding me? Bay's the size of my palm."

Xander chuckled under his breath. "Mazie, it's the fact she holds magic different from theirs. Perhaps you could conceal her wings and the little pixie dust she always sprinkles around. Just until they get to know her better."

Mazie nodded. "Alright, fine," she said. "I'll keep her hidden as best as I can." She glanced over her shoulder as Bay perched right under her hair. "Sorry, Bay. I'm not ashamed of you, okay? They just don't understand."

Bay nodded and sat down, snuggling into the crease of her neck.

Mazie would never put Bay's life in danger, and if there was a possibility that someone could hurt her, she'd do whatever she could to keep her safe. She had lost enough already.

They had only traveled for a half mile before they reached an open cave below the mountain with water flowing beneath it. The sun had set now, making it almost impossible to see right in front of them. Kaeli held a bronze lamp in front of her, a small beam of light piercing through the darkness. Mazie hoped it was enough visibility to navigate through the rivers safely.

Once inside the tiny, wooden boat nestled against the mountain, Xander grabbed a paddle, and Kaeli used her heel to give it a gentle push away from the shore.

The journey on the river was brief, traveling only one hundred yards before they came upon a massive cave within the mountains. The darkness made it difficult for the pirate to see any details about the surroundings. Further into the cave, a few lit torches cut through the oppressive darkness, revealing a makeshift dock of dirt and stone. Xander guided the small boat toward the dock and grabbed onto it to pull them closer.

Once Kaeli climbed out first, she headed toward the back of the cave, hands outstretched. Xander and Mazie departed the boat but hung back, waiting for Kaeli's signal.

Despite Kaeli's claim that it was safe there, her eyes roamed around the cave, searching for danger. Using her senses, she sniffed the air, keeping her eyes and ears open to any shift in the atmosphere, something to alert her to potential hidden threats. Once Kaeli seemed satisfied that all was well, she began to chant.

As Kaeli moved her hands from side to side, a black vortex formed, just like the portals created by the Kroneon. This time, Mazie saw through to the other side. It was a city inside mountains, just like Kaeli had explained.

*My Gods*, Mazie thought, as goosebumps trailed up her arms.

She squinted her eyes, trying to comprehend what she was seeing. Mazie had encountered strange lands when traveling with her family, but this was something completely different.

What lay before Mazie's eyes was unlike anything ever seen in any world before this one.

Stepping forward, she placed her hand on the outer beam of the vortex. A cool breeze brushed against her cheeks, followed by the scent of nature flooding her senses.

As Mazie looked deeper through the window of that world, she spotted more greenery, heavily contrasting with the barren world outside the mountain. There were massive waterfalls and a long, clear river cutting through the city. The sun cast a golden glow over the land, and Mazie wondered how that was even possible. It was a lit-up city inside a bloody mountain, and where she stood was night. It defied logic.

She narrowed her eyes on winding roads. They meandered through the peaks and valleys of the mountains, descending along the rocky slopes. Several wooden homes stretched along those streets, practically blending into the environment, with more lakes and rivers moving around each building. A veil of thick green vines covered each stone building. It looked as if nature and man were one, living in harmony.

Kaeli reached out and took Mazie's hand. "Come on," she said, and together, they stepped through the vortex and into the mountain.

The instant touch of nature brought a smile to her face, and the warmth of the sun made Mazie's body relax completely. She felt as if she had stepped into a dream.

As they walked through the city, Mazie noticed five stone buildings lined atop a hill nearby. The closer they got, the structures seemed to radiate strength and pride. In front of them, a gated archway bore a sign that Kaeli translated as "The Ember Academy."

When they stopped at the gate, Kaeli was still holding her hand, and Mazie didn't want her to let go. Despite the calming ambiance, a nervous flutter settled in her belly.

Mazie looked down as Kaeli squeezed her hand. "Are you okay, Mazie?" she asked.

Mazie answered with a nod and reciprocated, giving Kaeli a tight squeeze back and a gentle smile. The simple act of holding hands alone was enough to send a rush through her body, and her mind instantly drifted to their kiss three days ago. Mazie felt an ache to do it again and questioned if Kaeli had the same desire as she did. During their trip, they had spent nights looking out in the water, holding each other, and even sharing a bed to sleep...but they hadn't kissed again.

Bay's tiny fingers snapped her out of her thoughts as they gripped the collar of her shirt, and together, they walked through the winding roads until they reached a small, grassy field.

"After we joined forces with the Brotherhood to kill off the Vipers, we knew it was only a matter of time before they would seek their version of justice, blaming who they believed was the cause of it all," Kaeli explained as Xander tossed their bags on the grass. Both his and Kaeli's postures relaxed visibly. It was clear that this felt like home to the shifters. "We had to hide the mages before my father took matters into his own hands. The Council of Drakentos elected him to lead, which meant he had the authority to carry out the order to execute innocent lives."

Mazie nodded and turned to drink in the surrounding nature—flowers of all colors and shapes scattered across the grass, dancing in the wind. A stream with clear water wriggled around them, with tiny frogs resting on oddly shaped stones peeking through. Mazie was in awe of the incredible sight before her, but a single worry plagued her mind. "But it's still so close to the palace," Mazie said, still in disbelief that something like this was possible. "Even with the portals being closed and completely hidden, how can no one from the Brotherhood have spotted you out here?"

Kaeli smirked. "Since I didn't have my real father to teach me, the mages at this school stepped in and trained me well in the craft of concealment. I've taken every precaution to protect and shield this place. We won't mess up. No dragon holds this power, and so far, the two mages who work for the Brotherhood refuse to step outside the palace gates. This place allowed us to grow and teach the young how to rebuild a society that was taken from them." She sighed softly. "Hopefully, someday, we will expand the world we're building here outside this mountain, too. Dragons weren't the only victims when the Vipers wreaked havoc in our world, you know. They killed anyone they could sink their teeth into. Mages hid in their temples until my father and his empire passed laws preventing them from using their magic and started executing them. It wasn't until Xander and I became teenagers that we saw what they were doing."

Mazie looked up at the sky created by power and closed her eyes, wondering if Bay felt the life that had been poured into that world, too. It was a moment in time she didn't want to end. Kaeli didn't just protect life, she created it with her own hands.

Mazie's eyes opened when she heard Kaeli's shoes shuffle against the grass, now standing beside her.

"Right here is the family Dorion kept me from my entire childhood because he was too afraid to let the world know I was one of them. It became my duty to protect them and rebuild a society in which they could live and grow. They knew all along I was Anaru's daughter and took me in as their own."

Admiration sparkled in Kaeli's eyes as she stared at the city ahead, as if the mere sight of it were enough to dismiss any worries she carried.

"This right here is my legacy, Mazie."

Mazie stood beside her, her eyes widening as she took in more of the world they risked their lives to protect. The beauty moved her heart. "Was this *all* created by magic?" Mazie asked.

"Most everything that can be created from the elements," Kaeli replied. "That school ahead teaches life lessons that could help businesses flourish again. We're trying to revive some of our long-forgotten craftsmanship." She looked at Mazie, smiling softly. "Shipbuilding is one of them, you know. This place has enormous potential. Outside the mountain, there aren't many towns standing like this anymore."

"Is everyone here a mage?" Mazie asked as Bay flew out from under her hair and looked upon the city as well. Mazie made a low *tsk* noise, and Bay looked back at her, a slight pout forming on her lips. "I know, but I've got to keep you safe here." Bay quickly returned to her shoulder with a huff.

"Yes," Kaeli said. "I promise. You'll be safe. Now, I want to show you the school."

Kaeli radiated such confidence that it was impossible for Mazie not to take her word for it. They gathered their things, and the dragon led them up the hill and through the gate, making a signal with her hands to the guards at the front—a code to let them in.

The gates opened slowly, and two guards on each side waved them in.

"The dormitories will have a few empty rooms. We can stay as long as we need until we sort out a better plan than blindly charging my father's castle."

"This is a school for adult mages, then?"

Kaeli nodded, pointing at another mountain beyond the grounds. "The school for the younger is on the other side of that mountain. We keep the children in a safer, controlled environment."

*A mountain inside a mountain*, she marveled.

Being a pirate and traveler of worlds, she knew she would see and experience things that would shake her. But this, this was entirely different. Zemira had been without magic for over twenty years, its people blind to the horrors that twisted their lives apart. In Dragão Terra, that same fate awaited them if Dorion continued his empire of death.

However, being forced into hiding and unable to practice magic in the open didn't deter the mages. They found a way to live on, in secret, and thrive in a world that hated them.

They were fighting for a better future despite the fear they'd be caught and have it all taken away at any moment.

There was something deep within Mazie's gut, a flame awakening inside her. Perhaps it was the magic blanketing that world or a sense of peace that she felt within, but whatever it was, Mazie wanted to embrace it.

She turned to Kaeli, determination lacing her voice. "How can I help?"

# 31

## AIDEN

Aiden's magic felt like a faded dream slipping through his fingers. Standing with his feet in the water, he gazed upon an empty field, its vibrant yellow flowers swaying gently in the breeze. His body was no longer his own, his thoughts were foreign, and his voice was that of a stranger.

The hollowness in his heart was the only constant. He knew what he had done to Tegan. The images of it were embedded in his mind, haunting him with every breath he took. He had murdered her with his own hands, and that dark mark of power had consumed his soul to make him do it. It was only a matter of time before the remaining shreds of the elf were gone completely.

Aiden wasn't strong enough to fight Zakari anymore. He only prayed that those who crossed his path could escape before the entity made him take more lives.

He stepped out of the ocean, the grainy sand pressing into his bare feet, soothing against his skin. He had been traveling for almost two weeks, and every place he found was either vacant or with only a small family or a single dragon dwelling inside their home. The darkness would take control of Aiden, compelling him to commit atrocities against those innocent people for food and shelter.

Aiden didn't want to do it, but as the darkness grew, he had no choice.

The elf glanced over his shoulder at the grove of trees. For the past hour, an incessant, high-pitched sound had been emanating from that area, grating on his last nerve. Even though Aiden needed to keep moving, something in the forest further down the shoreline needed to be investigated first.

And that was when he heard a woman crying out for help.

It didn't take him long to find the source of the cries. Aiden came upon a familiar figure lying on the ground. Anaru was on her side, her hand pressed against the nasty, painful-looking wound.

It was clear Anaru had been traveling alone for days. Her hair was unkempt, her body caked with dirt, covering purple bruises and bloodied scrapes, and dark circles marred her tired eyes.

"Well, hello there, little dragon," Aiden called out, moving through the brush toward her. He looked down at her and smiled. "You don't look well, Anaru."

"Aiden," she choked out. "Stay back." Her eyes burned into his, and her teeth bared in a snarl.

"You know, I intended to kill whoever was in here. I can't have anyone running back to whatever leaders run this planet and warn them of my presence. But finding their gravely injured, missing empress? Well, that suits me much better."

Anaru blinked. "I understand there's a dark power inside you, but I believe that Elven warrior is still there. You don't want to harm me." Her voice trembled with each word, and her tone dropped before she winced.

Aiden knelt beside her, placing his hand on her stomach. But Anaru hissed and flinched away from his touch.

"Take it easy, Anaru. You don't want to re-open that wound and hurt yourself." The voice from the elf's lips was unrecognizable to his ears. That hungry, intoxicating power was eating away more of himself.

"What are you doing?" she asked as Aiden closed his eyes and hovered his hand over her fevered skin, moving it back and forth.

"You're dying," he said. "You have internal bleeding and a rather serious infection spreading into your blood. It won't be long before death takes you."

Anaru winced and attempted to avert her gaze, but Aiden grabbed her by the throat. He didn't squeeze too hard, but he restricted her breathing enough that panic burned in her eyes.

"I know you want to save your daughter. You even sacrificed all our lives for your own selfish desire to come here." His nostrils flared. "So, I'll tell you what, Anaru. You be my eyes in this land and guide me to where I need to go, and I will heal you." He dropped his hand, and she coughed. "It's a fair deal, is it not?"

Anaru's lips parted. "You cannot heal me, tainted elf. No one has that kind of power but the healers. And even then, an injury like this may be too severe for their power to even work."

Aiden smiled, his mind shuddering at its viciousness. "Not me...but the *thing* inside me has that power. You only have to let *him* in for a second, and he'll do the rest."

"Who...who do you speak of?" she asked, her voice trembling.

Aiden cocked his head. "It might be a bit confusing for you, I know. Newick witches on our Earth were a little more *selfish* than your mages in Dragão Terra. Their natural-born power wasn't enough." He enunciated each word so slowly and steadily that he could tell it made Anaru's skin crawl. The entity wanted to rip her apart for sport but also needed her. *He* needed her to find the mages because the mages were the only ones who carried the power to help him—the same power the Newick coven had who helped Zakari evolve.

On Earth, Zakari was free. He thrived within the Newick coven and fed on their souls, tasting a bit of humanity and growing in its strength. Zakari had been giving away parts of his magic for centuries, and it had exhausted his strength. He had lived a thousand lives within each member of the Newick witches. However, when Kieran decided that the best way to control Aiden was to implant Zakari's entire essence inside him, it had complications—weakening him further. But that time was over. Now, with Zakari having fully consumed Tegan's power yet still feeling a void inside, the darkness realized life could no longer give him what he wanted.

"Get up, Anaru. You're well enough to walk," he said, but she shook her head.

"I need to know what I'm up against before I agree to help you," she said. "I need the promise from whatever that thing is inside you not to touch my daughter once I find her."

Aiden feigned a smile. "You have my word," he said. "And that *thing* is Zakari, and you will address him as such, or he'll not play nice with you, little dragon."

Anaru's eyes grew wide with fear as he put a name to the darkness, and her hands trembled slightly at her sides. She had to have felt the dark power dancing between them.

"What...what does Zakari want?" she asked.

Aiden straightened his shoulders but kept his eyes locked on hers. "Since Zakari has been around since the beginning of time, he has had to adapt to the elements and cultures throughout the ages. He is neither death nor life, neither darkness nor light, regardless of what the Newick witches named him. He simply exists. Each time he shared his magic with a witch, they passed that magic down to their descendants, pieces of him flowing through their veins—a stream of power through time. But then Kieran forced his essence into an elf who carried a power that couldn't quite match with his own. It stripped what was left—no longer helping him grow. No longer making him whole."

"Isn't Zakari becoming weak a good thing, then? You can kill him," she said. "Aiden, you can be free of that darkness."

He slowly shook his head. "Unfortunately, no. That isn't how this power works. For Zakari to die, he must become whole again first." Aiden smiled. "He needs to feed on elemental magic. Tegan's power wasn't enough."

Anaru stiffened. "You killed her, didn't you?" Her expression was full of apprehension and pain. "You killed Tegan and took her power?"

"I had no choice, Anaru. Zakari has grown *tired*," he said. "He doesn't want to exist anymore, but to be released from my vessel, he needs the mages' power. They must be the ones to do it. You and I know that both Earth and Dragão Terra hold the same elemental magic. Your daughter seems to be protecting the mages from this land who can help me."

Aiden fought past Zakari's influence that told him to hurry and take the damned female already. He recalled the moment he left that room he'd been locked in, leaving Tegan's bloody, broken body. Zakari wanted to take Kaeli with him and force her to show him where the mages were. Aiden had used all his strength to run from that place, heading as far east as possible.

After finding an outcropping of stones in a barren field, Aiden grieved deeply for what he had done. He tried to console himself by saying that it was Zakari who took Tegan's life. But the guilt still ate away at his heart. He should have been stronger. Once he shed all the tears that he felt he had left, Zakari forced him to return to Dragon's Cove and take Kaeli...but they were gone, along with Mazie and Bay.

He was relieved they had fled—but also afraid of what Zakari would do next. The monster was determined to find the mages, even if it meant slaughtering everyone in his path until he did.

When Aiden looked back at Anaru, her eyes were wide with shock and eagerness. "Wait, you...you met my daughter?" She winced, pressing her hand to her wound. "Where?"

"A small village, a few day's walk from here. But she and her companions fled. I no longer know where they are."

A small tear fell down her cheek. "What does she look like? What is her name?"

Aiden smiled, even though he felt Zakari speak to him, telling him to stop dawdling. "Her name is Kaeli," he said. "She's beautiful, Anaru. Her eyes and nose are like yours, but her hair is the color of winter, and her eyes sparkle with a vibrant blue like the sea."

Anaru let out another hard sob, and her shoulders relaxed. He was sure she had been waiting her entire life to hear that small amount of information to put her at ease.

"Zakari won't stop until one of those mages helps him. Unfortunately, for one of them to destroy him, he'll have to kill the others first, taking their power. Maybe Kaeli can be the lucky one to help me, and he won't have to strip her of her magic."

Anaru flinched. "So, let me get this straight...You want me to assist you in locating the whereabouts of the mages, potentially leading to their massacre?" Anaru asked, shaking her head with determination. "I won't do it."

"Oh, but you will, Anaru. We are at eternal odds, and he wants to get out. So, Anaru, Zakari would like to thank you for your service in helping me find them." He gripped her arm, giving it a tight squeeze. "Now, stand the fuck up."

# 32

## MAZIE

It had been a few days since Mazie and Bay arrived in the hidden city with the shifters. Most nights, they kept to themselves and explored the land. But that night would be different, livelier.

They were throwing a party to welcome Kaeli and Xander back home.

As Mazie chatted with the mages, she made a conscious effort to remember the names of those who had introduced themselves as part of the Ember Guild that Kaeli had mentioned, but there were too many to remember.

Despite the peaceful atmosphere and sound sense of friendship and family within the guild, Mazie couldn't help but worry about the whereabouts of her own family. She wondered, aside from Janelle, if they had been captured and if the mages in the mountain would truly assist her in rescuing them.

With Bay sleeping under Mazie's hair, she turned toward the firepits, feeling the warmth of the flames on her cheeks. The night planned would be filled with music, wine, and feasting. From what she heard, it had been several months since Kaeli and Xander had visited the mountain.

Mazie searched the crowd and spotted Kaeli standing beside a pale-skinned man with ashy brown hair. He was wearing a black robe and tunic that reached high on his neck, almost touching his chin.

Her stomach clenched as Kaeli reached up and placed her hand on his arm. A question floated to her mind. She looked over and saw that Xander was heading in her direction.

*I'd better ask him,* she thought.

"Xander," Mazie called as he walked by. "Who's that man Kaeli is speaking to?"

Kaeli laughed while the man brushed his hand down her forearm as he inched closer. Mazie was never the jealous type—or at least, she didn't think she was until the man reached out, took Kaeli's hand, and kissed the top of it. Right then, she wanted to cut off the hand that had touched her.

"Mazie, no," Bay's tiny voice broke her thought.

Mazie looked down at her, rolling her eyes.

"He's a friend," Xander said. "I mean, now he is, anyway." Mazie looked at him, no longer wanting to watch Kaeli with someone else. "That ended long ago, though, Mazie. He might still feel something for her, but he never gave her what she needed."

"It's none of my business, anyway," Mazie said before clearing her throat. No, she couldn't just leave it. "What's his name?"

Xander laughed, and Mazie hoped the burning feeling in her veins didn't show. "Quail," he answered.

"Like the fucking bird?" Mazie asked.

"A what?"

"Never mind. Excuse me," she said, strolling over to Kaeli. She was still chatting with the bird man, and Mazie was eager to put some space between them. At least fifty feet, preferably. A tight smile crossed her lips. "Sorry, am I interrupting something?"

It was apparent that she was interrupting something, but she didn't care. Kaeli smiled, gesturing toward Quail.

"Of course not," she said. "Quail was just leaving. Mazie, this is Quail. My...friend. And this is Mazie..." Kaeli paused momentarily, biting her lip like she was trying to decide how to introduce her properly. "She's very important to me."

The shift on Quail's face wasn't exactly subtle, which pleased Mazie. It was apparent he was disappointed.

*Good,* she thought, watching as he quickly excused himself, leaving the women alone.

"So, how do you like the celebration?" Kaeli asked her casually when Quail disappeared into the crowd. "Sorry, I've been absent for the last few days. We had a lot of business to attend to because it's been a while since we were last here."

"It's quite nice," Mazie said, not thinking through her words. "Especially now that there's some room between you and Quail."

"Jealous, Mazie?"

Mazie stepped closer, closing the last bits of free space between them. Kaeli's sweet aroma engulfed her, making it hard to think, especially when her eyes lowered to Kaeli's lips.

"I don't think I have anything to be jealous of," Mazie murmured. Her hand found Kaeli's hip, drawing her closer. She leaned in, brushing her lips against Kaeli's. "Do I?"

Kaeli didn't hesitate as she softly shook her head. Her hand tugged Mazie's shirt, and their lips met in a soft kiss.

*Fuck,* Mazie thought, lost in the taste of her. Kaeli tasted better than any liquor she ever had. She hadn't felt anything like this before...with anyone or anything. Mazie wanted to take her right then and there, but she somehow clung to whatever self-control she had, prying herself away from her.

"So..." she whispered, brushing her thumb against Kaeli's bottom lip. "*Who* is he, then?"

Kaeli let out a low chuckle. "An instructor, I suppose. These people have prepared for a rebellion for the past ten years."

There was a little space between them, but their hands found one another. "So, all their training was in preparation for a fight against your father?"

Kaeli circled her thumb against Mazie's skin, which felt like the most natural thing in the world. "As we mentioned before we had left Dragon's Cove; fighting against my father was always something we knew would happen, but we didn't know *when*. Right now, their safety is the only thing that matters, and Xander and I have kept them from being destroyed by the Brotherhood. They cannot touch them here," she said. "No matter how much hatred I have for him, I couldn't put the others at risk, so we stopped training and just *lived*. I shut down the talks of an uprising, and everyone went about their lives as normal and—"

"The Brotherhood has captured my friends. I don't need to witness their suffering to know the horrors they're experiencing behind the castle walls. But I can't rescue them without your help," Mazie said. "Please don't tell me you're changing your mind."

Kaeli shook her head subtly, and Mazie would have sworn she saw a tear before Kaeli released her hand and glanced away. Even when she turned her back to her, Mazie felt Kaeli's pain. "I'm not changing my mind. But when we confront Dorion and his men, I need to be able to be the one who does it," Kaeli said, turning her head to look at her again. "I have to kill him myself."

Mazie's smile didn't reach her eyes as she nodded. "Until then, how do we protect everyone here?" she asked. "If I go to war with your family, what happens to them?"

Mazie's mind went to the children there. It wasn't just powerful adult mages he'd be slaughtering. The Brotherhood would be killing hundreds of families—children who had barely taken their first steps, their elders who relied on canes to walk, expecting mothers who would never hear their children's laughter.

"The Brotherhood would bring them to trial first, per our laws," she said. "Dorion wouldn't be able to get away with an outright massacre. He would have to go through the Council of Drakentos, the group that was elected to power right before the death of my grandparents. It was the only way they'd let Dorion rule since he wasn't given that title by birthright. They, in return, elected him, so by law, the Council can remove him. Of course, he felt threatened by the mages, not a baby he would instead raise as his own. He'll never admit that to them, not after all these years. He will use the act of war against his Brotherhood as his push to finish his agenda. Bring the mages to 'justice,' and he can finally rest knowing his enemies could never touch him again."

Mazie ran her hand down her face and sighed. Having your crew depend on you was one thing, but hundreds—if not thousands—of people relying on you was entirely different. For once, Mazie worried she might not be up to the task.

"What are you thinking?" Kaeli asked softly.

Mazie shrugged one shoulder. "I think I'm just a woman with a sword who may not be enough."

"Mazie," Kaeli said, placing her hand on her chest and resting it there. Mazie prayed she wouldn't be able to feel how her heart's beat quickened. Then Kaeli gently touched her cheek with her thumb, using her other hand. "I want to try something. Take my hand and close your eyes."

She lowered her gaze as Kaeli extended her fingers, motioning for her to place her hand on her palm. Kaeli curled her fingers around her hand, and they closed their eyes together.

Mazie's breath caught, feeling Kaeli's power seep into her skin. The electric pulse and warmth of fire touched her inner core, causing her entire body to melt into a euphoric daze.

The sensation between them was so intense that it felt like a living, breathing entity was swallowing her whole. Mazie's breaths grew ragged, heavy, and fast as Kaeli's other hand slid down her body and grabbed her hip.

When they opened their eyes, they both panted, and sparks of energy, a mix of black, red, and yellow, danced between them like fire.

Mazie hated the loss of touch when Kaeli lifted her hand from her hip. She didn't want her to let go. She wanted to stay in that warmth forever.

"Your power is incredible, Kaeli," Mazie said, reaching up to cup her cheek. Everything about this woman was exquisite. She couldn't get enough of her. "My Gods, I didn't want you to let go."

Kaeli smiled and placed her hand on hers, leaning into her touch. "That wasn't just my power that you felt, Mazie. It was also yours."

Mazie's lips parted.

"You may no longer remember how to pull that power of yours again after burying it within your heart for so long. But it's there."

Kaeli and Mazie looked up as a swarm of what looked like fireflies moved over them, heading toward the grove of trees within the mountain.

"Even if you don't use that magic, do not underestimate how powerful a woman with a sword is. You, Mazie, are a warrior, and I would be proud to fight by your side."

# 33

## MAZIE

When the festivities were at their liveliest, Mazie quietly slipped away to change into an outfit more suitable for the occasion. She donned a stunning black silk gown Kaeli had lent her, with two slits running up to the top of her long, slender legs. Delicate gold chains crisscrossed over the plunging neckline, adding to the dress's elegant design. She then put two golden bracelets on her left wrist and applied glittering gold dust to her eyelids for a more cheerful look. The gold brought out the beautiful, rich tone of her dark skin. Finally, Mazie strapped two sheathed daggers to her thighs for easy access, hidden under the flowing skirt.

Once dressed, she walked down to where dozens of mages had gathered around roaring bonfires. As she stepped off the path and onto the grass, drums played, encouraging everyone at the party to dance and sing.

Kaeli walked over to Mazie and took her hand. Mazie saw she was wearing a beautiful, almost purple-colored dress with silver and red beads embroidered over the fabric's surface. The outfit made Kaeli's blue-white hair glow like the full moon over the sea. Mazie's heart fluttered, and a bright smile broke across her face. Just for that night, the pirate's worries would be laid to rest.

"You look stunning, Kaeli," Mazie breathed. "Like a true goddess." Kaeli smiled and pulled on Mazie's hand, urging her to walk with her.

"As do you," she replied, leading Mazie to the dancing crowd. Once they were at the center, surrounded by hundreds of mages, Kaeli placed her hand on Mazie's hip. "Do you dance in your world?"

Mazie smiled at her question. "You can't be a Knight if you don't know how to dance."

"A Knight?" Kaeli arched her brow.

"My surname," Mazie explained. "My father taught me to dance when I was just learning to walk, and then my mother took over from there."

"It suits you well, Miss Mazie Knight."

Mazie reached out and tucked a strand of Kaeli's long hair behind her ear. "Did you take Dorion's name or—"

"Kaeli Adara Rylanthion," she replied with her full name, "would very much like to dance with you."

Mazie couldn't suppress her smile as she followed Kaeli's lead, her feet moving with the rhythm instinctively. Once they reached the center of the field, where everyone gathered, the pirate gave Kaeli a bow while taking the dragon's hand and kissing the top of it. When she looked up, she would have sworn she saw Kaeli blush.

A few more musical instruments joined the drums, creating a jaunty melody as the two women danced. The rest of the world slowly faded around them; all Mazie could focus on was the intensity of Kaeli's gaze, her full lips, and the thought of putting her hands all over her body. The sounds she would make—

"You and your friends' arrival has caused a lot of commotion in our realm," Kaeli said, snapping Mazie out of the dirty thoughts that were coming to mind. "But I must admit, I'm happy you're here." She swallowed a little but kept her body pressed close to Mazie. "I suppose...I suppose there is no one I would rather face my father with than you. But I will admit—I'm afraid."

Mazie didn't even think before she placed her hands on Kaeli's cheeks and pulled her closer. Their bodies were flush against each other, lips impossibly close. "He'll not touch you," she said, running her thumbs along Kaeli's jaw. "I swear it."

Mazie felt a pull in her stomach, one she hadn't felt in years. The kind that she had when she first fell for Veronika. Just being so close to another woman again, like *her*, stirred a desire she had long forgotten about.

When Kaeli placed her hand on hers, she stilled. "You're willing to die for someone you barely know?" Kaeli asked.

Mazie's fingertips traced the shape of Kaeli's face. "It's the right thing to do."

There was a sudden ache in Mazie's chest. She knew once the war was fought and won, she'd have to leave Kaeli.

She'd have to go home.

Slowly, Mazie ran her thumb over Kaeli's bottom lip, but before she leaned in to kiss her, the music slowly faded, and boisterous laughter and cheering erupted around them, causing Mazie to release their touch and step back. "I think..." she started when the next song began, but the words stuck in her throat. "I think it's been a long day, and I should sleep."

Kaeli nodded and pressed her lips together, and a million things crossed Mazie's thoughts. *Why the bloody fuck did I pull back?*

"Alright," Kaeli said with what looked like hurt in her eyes, gesturing with her head to the dormitories. "I'll walk you to your room, then."

———◦———

As the women entered the building, several lamps flickered off, one by one, like their fuel was depleted. The shadows grew deeper as most of the city slowly closed its eyes and fell asleep. "I'll bring you some food once you're settled," Kaeli said, turning to the door. "Are you alright, Mazie?"

Mazie dropped her bag on the bed and turned to the door. "I think I'm afraid for the first time in my life," she confessed. "This is the longest I've been away from Lincoln. And Bay, she...wait, Bay—"

"She's safe," Kaeli interrupted. "Since Xander and I are cousins, our dragon bond can let us see through each other's eyes as need be. He's showing her the garden lights right now. She's delighted and finds it beautiful and relaxing. The fireflies are playing with her."

"So, those *were* fireflies we saw earlier?" Mazie asked.

Kaeli nodded. "You see, our world and yours have much more in common than we think." Kaeli stood at her door, eyes locked on Mazie's, almost like she was waiting for something. When Mazie didn't speak up, she gave her one subtle nod before shutting the door.

Mazie looked over at the bed and let out an exhausted breath. It had felt like one of the longest days of her life, and it had nothing to do with fighting and mayhem, but the weight of everything she had learned was getting to her and what she felt for Kaeli.

She wasn't just Anaru's daughter, she was also a mage. Kaeli was the only one who could help her rescue her friends, and she was the key to possibly getting them out of that world altogether. But as Mazie thought about leaving their world to head home, her heart ached.

*Did* she want to leave Kaeli? Could she bear the thought of never seeing her again?

Mazie dropped her clothes to the floor and tucked herself into bed, relishing the warmth of the covers over her naked body. Kaeli's beautiful face came to her mind, the memory of the warm press of her mouth and her kind smile lingering there.

Mazie ran a hand down her stomach until she felt her entrance, slowly entering a finger in her already wet heat. Her thumb ran circles over her clit, stimulating herself even further. Her mind wandered elsewhere, wholly consumed by the dragon with the ice-colored eyes. It was she who was in between her thighs in Mazie's mind, moving her finger in and out of her as her tongue eagerly circled that sweet spot.

Mazie moved her hips up and down, feeling the pressure already climbing in her belly. Her legs tingled with every sensation. She bit her lower lip, fighting the urge to moan Kaeli's name—Gods, what she would give to have Kaeli there with her right then.

No one had touched her like that in years. Over the last twelve years, she and Lincoln had occasionally visited brothels in every port they came across, seeking temporary satisfaction for their physical desires. Of course, that all stopped when Nola joined the crew.

Her heart always wanted more, even if she never admitted it out loud.

Mazie's thoughts of Kaeli drove a wild thrill of physical need throughout her body.

As she gripped the sheets with her other hand, she heard a light tap on the door.

*Fuck*, she screamed silently. Just like that, her peak was gone, and she wanted to strangle whoever was on the other side of that door. "Coming!"

Mazie hastily wrapped the blanket around her body before rushing to the door. As she pulled it open, she saw Kaeli standing there, holding a leather sack in her left hand. Mazie's frustration dissipated instantly when Kaeli looked at her.

"I forgot to give you this. It's a clean headwrap, soap, and a sponge. Something to help you bathe with tomorrow," she said, holding the bag out to her. "I would suggest getting up early if you can. They shut the water off a few times a week to preserve it. So, most of the town will bathe in the lake."

"The lake?"

"Trust me, it's more exciting than it sounds," Kaeli said with a smile, "and the water that comes through our rusty pipes is less clean."

Mazie considered her implication and squinted her eyes. "How early is early?"

"*Early.*"

Mazie took a breath and looked down at the bag. "Then can I go now?" she asked. "I'd like to sleep in."

Kaeli nodded, still smiling. "Sure, if you get dressed, I can lead you there."

Once dressed, she trailed behind Kaeli as they walked through a gazebo onto a wide forest trail behind the academy. The moon was bright that night, coming through the openings of the trees and lighting up the environment around them. The fireflies fluttered in and out of the trees, creating a tranquil atmosphere that left Mazie breathless. "This place reminds me of the Eastland Forest," she said.

"Is that the city you're from?" Kaeli asked, looking over her shoulder as they stepped off the trail and their feet touched the sand.

Mazie shook her head. "I moved around a lot, but the Eastland Forest is where the Fae and Elven people found solace after one of the rulers of Zemira tried to destroy magic. It's actually where Anaru and Dergis lived."

Kaeli smiled. "I wish I knew her," she said. "But I feel like I do in some way."

"You will know her," Mazie said with certainty. "You'll see." As they approached the lake, Mazie scanned the water. She couldn't help but gasp at the ethereal silver light of the moon reflected from the lake's surface.

"Beautiful, right?" Kaeli said, holding out her hand. "Come on."

Mazie took her hand, and Kaeli led her to the water.

"Wet the sponge with the water, lather your body with the soap, and then step inside the lake to wash it off."

She did as Kaeli said and took out the blue sponge, dipping it into the water. After lathering it up, she ran it over her arms and legs—as much as the fabric of her clothes allowed.

Mazie looked up, watching Kaeli pull the straps of her dress over her shoulders and let it fall to her feet. Her breath froze in her throat.

Kaeli didn't seem remotely modest, but Mazie was hesitant to undress.

"Mazie," Kaeli said, not bothering to look at her, "perhaps instead of staring at me, you take your clothes off, too, and get in the water."

Mazie blinked, coming back to the present.

*Fuck...me,* Mazie silently cursed in her mind, unable to break her gaze from Kaeli, who took another sponge, wet it, and proceeded to lather herself.

Mazie swallowed and looked away and back at the lake, a thrill jumping in her stomach at how stunning Kaeli was.

Kaeli dropped the sponge on the sand, stepped into the water, and turned around to face Mazie. "It feels nice. It's a little cold, but you'll get used to it."

Mazie recognized the absurdity of her behavior, so she stripped off the rest of her clothes and quickly soaped up her body before dropping the sponge, walking to the shoreline, and stepping into the water. There was a tiny sting of cold once the water hit her stomach, but her body adjusted to the temperature as she submerged deeper into the lake.

As she swam toward Kaeli, she felt the soap running off her skin and took her hand to wipe the rest from between her legs.

Her feet could touch, but once they moved past the rocks near the edge of the cliffside, she used her hands to keep her afloat, swimming further into the water.

"Tell me about where you're from," Kaeli asked. "You said you moved around a lot."

Mazie felt the warmth of the tide coming through the rocks. It felt nice not to be shivering anymore. "My family and I were part of a nomadic coven, so we moved quite often when I was a child, and I left my home, Westin, when I was nineteen. Then I sailed the seas with my captain, Lincoln, until we came here."

Kaeli's crystal-blue eyes lit up under the bright moonlight. "That sounds exciting."

Mazie laughed. "Which part? The one where my father died, my sister took her own life, and my mom became a murderous ghost, or the moving around part?"

Kaeli swam closer to Mazie. "The sea," she said. "And the murderous ghost."

Both women laughed that time, and Mazie finally felt herself letting go of her worries for just a moment. She spent the next few minutes telling Kaeli about her parents and what had happened to her sister, Bay. She ended the story with her and the crew confronting her mother's apparition along with the rest of the coven, slain by Matthias and forced to relive their last days in perpetual torment.

"That's quite the tale, Mazie. I'm so sorry about your family."

"Yeah, well, magic is a fucking curse, always has been."

Kaeli shrugged. "The magic I wield is exhilarating."

"Maybe," Mazie added. "I grew up with magic, but it never served me any purpose, so I let it go."

"You can't let go of magic, Mazie. You will always carry it within you, even if you bury it."

Mazie thought about that. It was true; she could harness green magic as a child, but as she grew older, she vowed to let it go. What was the point of elemental power if she couldn't use it to bring her sister back from the dead?

In the end, her mother and her entire coven used their powers to keep their souls alive, tethering them to the land, but all that did was destroy who they were. It took away the last bit of kindness and humanity they all once had, leaving monstrous ghosts instead.

"Remind me. Your father was also a—"

"Witch?" Mazie finished. "He was the best at elemental magic. Honestly, my father's magic was so pure and unapologetic. He could walk into any dried, dead land and transform it into a garden full of life. Father kept our families thriving for many years and taught my sister and me everything he knew. He was my best friend until his power of nature turned on him and stole his life."

"He conjured a poisonous plant?" she guessed.

Mazie nodded. "I was at least able to say goodbye. It took him quickly, so I know he didn't suffer much. But it was long enough that he could hold me before he slipped away. Everything changed after that, and once my sister, Bay, died, I swore never to use magic again."

Kaeli's expression fell. "I'm so sorry, Mazie," she said sympathetically. "I never had a relationship like that with Dorion. He was always so cold and distant that his servants and my uncles raised me instead. I'm glad you had that, but I'm also sorry you lost him so young."

It was quiet after that, with only the sound of their hands splashing in the water. Mazie expected Kaeli to ask about her mother, but she didn't. She was relieved by that because, despite her natural ability to love her mother unconditionally, the last memories of them together stung. She didn't want to relive it.

"Let's swim to the rocks. My arms are getting tired," Kaeli said, moving to the cliffside.

Mazie grabbed the edge of the rock to keep her afloat while Kaeli pulled herself up to sit on it. The moon reflected off her lightly tanned skin, and she squeezed out some of the water from her moon-kissed hair.

Mazie thought she looked like a goddess on her throne, Kaeli's eyes turning back to her.

"You're staring, you know," Kaeli said.

"I like the sight." Mazie let go of the rock and wrapped her fingers over the edge of the stone with her other hand on Kaeli's knee. It was a bold gesture that she didn't think she'd mind. "But I like the feeling of you underneath my fingertips even more," Mazie said boldly, testing the waters while slowly stroking her thighs with her nails, climbing higher, and watching goosebumps trail up Kaeli's legs. "If you don't mind..."

"I don't mind," Kaeli said, placing her hand over Mazie's as a soft sigh left her lips. "But I would like you to come closer."

A tingling sensation pulled between Mazie's legs at the sound of her voice. She let go of the rock and moved further in front of Kaeli, settling between her legs. One hand brushed up her left thigh. "What about this?" she asked. "Do you not mind this, either?"

Kaeli nodded, her smile almost vanishing, but it was replaced by a look Mazie understood. The look told her that not only did she not mind it, but she wanted to be touched just as much as Mazie did.

Mazie moved her hands up again, slow and steady, until her thumbs touched the crease of her hips. Her eyes looked at her breasts and then down to Kaeli's exposed pussy.

*Fuck*, she wanted to taste and devour her.

"I wasn't sure," Mazie admitted, looking up.

"Mazie, I would've guessed that the kisses we shared had been a giveaway," Kaeli said with a tiny smile that didn't meet her eyes. "I've been with mostly men and a few women. You?"

Mazie swallowed, moving her hands away from Kaeli's hips and running them again up and down her thighs in a gliding motion. Her breath hitched in the back of her throat at the softness of Kaeli's skin under her fingertips. "Only women."

Kaeli moved forward, taking Mazie's hands that now rested on her knees, and ran her thumb over Mazie's knuckles. "Lucky me, then," Kaeli said. She bent forward until their faces aligned and took her hand, cupping Mazie's chin. She then pulled her forward until their lips collided. Mazie deepened the kiss, taking Kaeli's mouth into hers and pushing her tongue further inside, tasting the dragon.

Gods, she tasted like the sweetest zest of fruit, and she savored every bit of the goddess before her.

Mazie was the one who released the kiss, even though she didn't want that moment to end.

"Lie down," Mazie said, lust consuming her body.

Kaeli scooted back on the flat rock and laid down, her breasts flattening out as she arched her back. She instantly opened her legs as Mazie climbed on the rock and moved toward her. Then she spread Kaeli's legs further apart with her hands and exposed her pussy.

"Fuck," Mazie said, drinking in the sight of Kaeli like this—spread open just for her. "I want to bury myself in between your thighs and never leave them."

Mazie glided her thumbs along Kaeli's inner thighs as she inched closer, settling between her legs. Kaeli was trembling underneath her already, pussy glistening with water and arousal. Mazie took one of her fingers, running it gently over her skin while her thumb found Kaeli's clit and began slow, tender circles. She wanted to take her time and savor every moment she spent touching Kaeli like this. Kaeli moaned, her head falling back on the rock and hips arched with each gentle touch. Mazie moved her finger closer to the woman's entrance. "Yes. More. Mazie, I need more of you."

Her voice came out in a purr, and Mazie could do nothing but obey, as if she were lost in some trance. She pushed her finger inside while moving her own body closer. Her hips now aligned with Kaeli's as she pumped her finger in and out. She then added a second finger, and Kaeli shivered beneath her. Kaeli's expression was euphoric, but her hands reached for Mazie as she attempted to pull her against her chest.

"I need you close to me. Please," she pleaded. Mazie was unsure how much closer she could get than having her fingers rammed deep inside Kaeli, but in one swift movement, she removed her finger and placed one leg over Kaeli's. Now that she was positioned at the perfect angle, their pussies lined up, rubbing against each other and stimulating each other's clits.

"Fuck, Kaeli," Mazie said, barely able to form her words. "Gods, you feel...unlike anything else. Fuck." She leaned forward, supporting her weight with one hand while the other roamed over the curves of Kaeli's body.

"Mazie, my Gods. Don't stop," Kaeli moaned, tipping her head back. Every moan, every word that left Kaeli's lips sent Mazie into some kind of frenzy that had her yearning for more. She wrapped her arm around Kaeli's back, lifting her from the rocks as they moved together, keeping her upright as the dragon's head dipped down, and she took Kaeli's nipple in her mouth and sucked.

"Fuck!" Kaeli cried out like that was her undoing.

All they heard were the waves splashing against the rocks and their heavy breaths as they both came almost simultaneously, messy, soaked, and entangled in each other. Mazie felt Kaeli's juices drip over her as she trembled and pulsed against her, but she was insatiable.

Kaeli reached for Mazie, wrapping her fingers around her neck loosely to guide her upward. As she did, her lips found Mazie's, kissing her hungrily. The pirate let out a low moan, wanting to savor every second of her presence, especially as Kaeli rolled them over. Now she was on the rock, and Kaeli was on top of her, with one hand already between her thighs.

Despite having just come, Mazie's pussy greeted her fingers with a pulse, eager to have them inside. Slowly, Kaeli allowed two of her fingers to slip past Mazie's folds, still not breaking their kiss. The pirate gave a soft grunt, knowing it wouldn't take her long to reach her peak again. Not with how aroused she was. Not with the way Kaeli was touching her.

"My goddess..." Mazie moaned into the kiss, prompting Kaeli to thrust her fingers in and out of her faster. The pirate tipped her head back, and Kaeli's lips traced down her throat, leaving a trail of hungry kisses.

"You're soaked," the beautiful dragon whispered against her skin. "Throbbing around my fingers. I can feel how much you want me." The sound of Mazie's wetness accompanied Kaeli's thrusts, her fingers now reaching that glorious spot inside her that had Mazie trembling. Before she knew it, her pleasure peaked, rendering her breathless as her loud cry tore through the lake. The world around Mazie swirled. At that moment, all that existed was Kaeli and the burning desire to have more of her.

Now that she had had a taste of the dragon, she *needed* more. "I want to taste you," Mazie said, gently laying her back down on the rock before she moved between her thighs. She gripped Kaeli's hips as she squirmed underneath her, tasting Kaeli's juices as her tongue lapped eagerly against her sensitive spot. Kaeli's legs squeezed against Mazie's head, like she couldn't handle another wave of pleasure building up.

Her core ached to be flush up against her again, but her mouth was greedy. Wanting. Needing. And she could do this all night long.

"Right there," Kaeli moaned as Mazie found that sweet spot again that caused the woman's hips to thrust, riding against Mazie's mouth as she slipped her tongue inside her. "My Gods, Mazie, more."

She ate and tasted her until Kaeli let out a cry of pleasure, finding her release and coming undone against Mazie's eager mouth.

As she gave Kaeli a moment to breathe and recover, she laid down next to her, not caring about the pain she now felt in her knees that had been pressing against the rock. That was the most exhilarating experience she had ever had in her entire life.

And she wanted to have her again.

# 34

## JANELLE

Janelle spent most of the morning staring out her bedroom window, watching dragons glide through the sky. A hard lump formed in her throat. It was the day she was to be wedded to Kade, a man she didn't love and never would. Her body felt numb to the apprehension in her heart. It didn't matter what kind of training she had growing up; she couldn't stop what was going to happen. She could only endure.

As she pulled herself back to the present, the door behind her swung open, and the sound of laughter flooded through the doorway as Kade strode in. Janelle knew it was him; the bond was too strong, sensing his presence, much to her chagrin.

"Good morning, my lovely bride," he said, placing his hands on her shoulders from behind. She flinched slightly but didn't move away from his touch. The last time she did, he left bruises.

"You look stunning in all black," he said, running his hands down the lacy dress they had put her in. It was fitting, indeed, as she mourned the life she once knew. Still, she refused to let him break her spirit.

"If you think I'll return the compliment, you better lower your expectations," Janelle said. She expected a response, but Kade simply smiled in the reflection of the window, seemingly in a good mood.

Swarms of servants had filled the room that morning, attending to her makeup and hair and tightening her corset until Janelle could no longer breathe. All the while, she stared out the window, looking on to freedom that she may never see again.

*No*, she reminded herself. *I can't stop fighting—not just for myself but also for Elijah.*

"They're waiting for us," Kade said. "Come." She turned around, placing her hand in his and keeping her expression in calm indifference.

"After you."

As they entered the ballroom, the ringing of bells filled the air, their echoes bouncing off the elegantly decorated walls. Then a pair of ornate iron doors opened and drew everyone's attention to the entrance, where Dorion walked in. He was wearing what looked like full black armor, with golden dragon scales covering his arms and legs.

On his arm was a red-headed woman in a high-necked, floor-length red dress covering most of her body. Similar gold scales wrapped her arms, and a black jeweled coronet sat on her hair.

Dorion led the woman to the head of the main table, where they sat in embellished chairs. The guards then opened a second set of doors, letting in scores of guests, who went to adjacent tables. Chatter and laughter filled the room in a matter of minutes.

With a simple hand gesture, Dorion summoned a group of musicians from the back corner. They immediately began playing their instruments, filling the air with a symphony of sound.

"It's almost time," Kade said, drawing her attention to him.

"Lucky me," Janelle murmured, though it was more to herself.

Kade's rough hand gripped Janelle's arm and yanked her across the room, leading her to where others were dancing. "You're going to dance with me," Kade said. She allowed him to guide her to the dance floor. "You're not resisting me," he noted. "That's a first."

She sucked in a breath and let out a heavy sigh. "What's the point, Kade? You're stronger than me. I can't fight you," she sneered. "And I'm tired of it."

His lip curved into a wide smile. "True. But it's more fun when you *do* fight me. I like it when you rile me up."

*Sick bastard*, she thought, but she didn't dare to say it out loud. She rolled her eyes instead.

Kade tightened his hold and ran a hand down her hair. "If you embarrass me today, you will surely regret it." He looked down at her, his deadly eyes piercing into hers. "Don't forget that we have your friends locked in a cell. The punishments in your world won't come close to what we do in Dragão Terra."

"You embarrass yourself by being a cold-blooded brute. Don't you fucking threaten me or my friends," she barked. "Fuck you. Fuck your brothers. And fuck this entire empire."

Kade slid his hand under Janelle's hair and dug his fingers painfully into the skin of her neck. The other hand crashed against her back, squeezing her. He then wove his fingers into her scalp and pulled her head back. "Let me remind you that you won't be the one I punish. If you do not say '*I do*' when we wed within the hour, we will throw your friends through a portal back to Earth and destroy the threat to our world. Becoming my wife is the only way to protect you from the destruction...and them."

Janelle's eyes went wide. "What are you talking about? What portal?"

*He will send them back?* she questioned in her thoughts. *What will be destroyed?*

"Exactly what I said. You're a little behind on this, so let me fill you in. We are all the same, you and me. Our world only makes up a fraction of the existence of realms. But because witches or mages, whatever the fuck each world calls them, discovered the ability to open portals between us, we have broken a system that has kept us safe."

Janelle pulled her brows together.

"You and Elijah's bond is much stronger than I think the two of you believe. The moment I looked into your thoughts, I didn't just see *your* memories...I saw *his*."

Janelle's stomach tightened, and her body went rigid. Looking into her memories was a violation of privacy she loathed, but knowing he had seen Elijah's, too...it sent a wave of fury through her body.

"The darkness possessing your brother isn't merely a result of dark magic; he's under the influence of a creature born from the depths of Earth itself. That has been the source of your realm's sorcerers' power for millennia."

Janelle's eyes widened. She knew there was more to the Newick witches' history that had been kept secret regarding Elijah's power. Though she lived in Myloria, she wasn't a Newick witch, so Kieran never went in depth about what that power meant. Even Elijah had never told her the exact details because he thought she'd be too afraid. However, he promised her to do everything he could to help Aiden be free from the dark power that bound him.

"If you release Elijah, he can help you," Janelle said. "No one will have to get hurt. There is enough power within all of us to help drive out that magic within Aiden. You can do this without taking lives."

Kade shook his head. "I think it runs deeper than you think, Janelle. Thousands of years ago, the Newick coven sought to destroy this entity, but they struck a deal with him instead. The witches helped whom they called Zakari, ascend to near omnipotence in exchange for a share of his magic. He's undefeatable. It rendered him immune to being destroyed—rather, he only gained strength. He now walks *our* land and will destroy us all if we do not close the portals and prevent their reopening, effectively cutting off the source. Now a dark power stronger than anyone can fight is here. We cannot allow history to repeat itself. The relic Dorion now holds, called the 'Eye of Dragão's Flame,' will sever the connection, destroy Earth, and take the darkness with it. Unfortunately, this also means the end for every human and creature in that world. Including your friends."

Janelle tried to pull back from Kade as horror struck her. All this time, they had been moving swiftly with the rhythm of the music, but his last words made her feet freeze in place. "Are you mad?"

He reached up and gently touched her cheek. "If you marry me today, Janelle, you will be bound to Dragão Terra and will not perish with them. Our gods will protect you. *I* will protect you. That darkness cannot continue to walk in our world."

"You will destroy *millions*," she said. "Please, Kade. Convince your brother to stop this atrocity. I will help you free that entity from Aiden. We all will. There has to be another way."

Kade spun her around as the music ended. "We don't even know where Aiden is. This is the only way to ensure his demise. By sundown tomorrow night, the two mages who work for us will open that portal. They will then link their powers together to activate the Eye and destroy Earth once and for all."

Janelle jerked back, and he released her, allowing her to create space between them. "If all realms are strung together, *every* world will perish if you break that link. Not just Earth."

Kade's eyes dimmed, and he slowly nodded. There wasn't any joy in his eyes then. He looked genuinely afraid. "Except ours, because we hold the source that will break it. Mages couldn't resist meddling with their power, and now the consequences are here. They threaten Dorion's rule by existing. They are the only ones to blame."

Janelle's mind raced with possible outcomes. Nothing she said would change their mind—she had to kill them. But to kill them...she had to become compliant and get them alone.

*I'll play along,* she thought. *I have no choice.*

Kade stepped forward and wrapped his hand around Janelle's back, holding her close before he pressed his lips lightly against her ear. "Become my wife and truly love me, and I will convince Dorion to order his mages to bind your friends to this world. If they are bound, then they won't perish when the portals close. I swear to you, I will save them...for you."

She leaned back slightly to look him in the eye. He wouldn't save her brother, that was certain, but if they could buy some time to escape, she would do whatever he asked.

She didn't respond, but she didn't pull back either.

"There's a good girl, Janelle. I guess none of it will matter once the binding ritual is fully completed. You'll no longer fight me, and we can finally have a normal relationship." He pulled her even closer, a sudden shift in his demeanor. "That little illusion our mage made Elijah see...she also projected it to me, so I could watch. I saw myself fucking you as if I were doing it in the real world, and my Gods, Janelle, it was beautiful. I cannot wait to take you in my bed tonight and ravish you until you finally submit to me as my mate. Once our bodies unite, there will be no going back. You will despise Elijah and adore me so much that you'll worship the ground I walk on. And then someday, we'll put a little dragon-hybrid baby in that womb of yours to help carry on my legacy with you as my submissive, doting wife."

Janelle wanted to tell him to go fuck himself but somehow refrained from saying the words out loud for one reason and one reason only: *Elijah.*

*I have to help him escape*, she thought.

Janelle felt the world's weight crash around her. All would be lost if she and the others didn't act quickly. Once Kade and she were wed, her very existence would be at risk of destruction, and she didn't believe for a second Dorion would save them. But she'd convince the three brothers that she did.

Willing herself to put on the best fucking show of her life, Janelle nodded and felt a gentle caress along her jaw. The soft hum of music faded away, and another bell chimed in the ballroom.

"It's time," Kade said, guiding her from the dance floor. Dorion rose from his chair and walked over to a golden altar in the shape of a dragon consuming what looked like the sun.

Kade dragged Janelle to the altar as Lord Dorion stepped forward.

She didn't hear a single word Dorion spoke as he recited the marriage rites; she only listened to the hollow sound of her voice when she said, "I will."

———◦———

After the ceremony, the hours seemed to drag by. Every agonizing minute in that ballroom made Janelle's lungs close in. She looked up from her plate of untouched food and saw Dorion nibbling on his female companion's neck.

As Janelle watched, she noticed something wrapped around the woman's throat. A familiar pendant hung from a thin, black metal chain. Janelle's body tensed. It was right in front of her—the Voleric.

Sensing Kade's intense gaze, she hastily masked her emotions, feigning disinterest in hiding her unease. Then she returned her attention to the lewd display before her.

Dorion's hands violently tore at the woman's dress, causing it to fall away and revealing her breasts. Janelle watched as he groped her, the woman's head falling back, and she moaned loudly.

Janelle didn't care anymore about public perversion; she was getting that necklace one way or another. An idea began to take shape in a secret part of her mind.

The men there were monsters. Taking what they wanted, when they wanted it, and in front of everyone else. As they gave in to their shameless carnal desires, they'd force everyone to watch.

"Does that arouse you, little elf?" Kade asked, placing his hand on her leg and dragging his palm across her bare skin and under the hem of her dress. But his hand stilled, resting on her inner thigh. He hadn't touched her intimately since that night in her bedroom, where he'd violated her. Janelle wondered if he felt guilty about that or was trying to lure her into a false sense of security.

*Don't be ridiculous,* she told herself. A man like him never felt guilt about any of his wrongdoings.

Janelle picked up a silver goblet of wine and took a swig.

Right then, the woman wearing the Voleric got up from her chair, leaned down, and unbuttoned Dorion's trousers, pulling his cock free. She then lifted her dress and positioned herself over him. She lowered down on his shaft and began bouncing up and down on his cock, fucking him for everyone to watch. His head fell back against the chair, and he bit his lip as she rode him, the noise of their bodies slapping against each other echoing off the walls.

While the other women's faces were relaxed, their eyes reflected abject disgust and anger at their mates' behavior and their lecherous gazes. It reminded her of Kieran and the coven's parties, with no shame or decency. That was her opening.

That was her chance to get closer to the pendant.

"Yes," she replied. "I'm enjoying it."

Kade raised a brow. "Really?"

She turned to him and nodded. "Yes. In fact, I want to join," Janelle said boldly. "Perhaps you would like to watch *that* instead?"

A smile pulled on his lips. "Is my wife suddenly willing to spread her legs?" he asked, and her stomach recoiled at him calling her *wife*. "I would never permit my brothers to fuck you, though."

She shook her head. "No. Not him...*her*."

Kade's brow rose again in amusement. "Dorion would never let you touch her, either. Sabrina is off limits, even to his own brothers."

"It will help me relax, Kade. I realize now that I can't fight you. I feel something within the bond, and if I'm to be forced here, I might as well enjoy it. However, if you haven't noticed, men like you scare me. Being with a woman *first* might help me relax...help me open up to you more tonight," she purred.

"To be with a woman?"

She shrugged. "I have other appetites. Even Elijah and I..." Her voice trailed off when his eyes immediately turned dark. Those words hung in the air, clearly agitating Kade. Janelle smirked mentally and sent a wave of arousal down the bond to sway his decision.

Kade looked up at Sabrina, watching a servant cover her with a robe since the front of her dress had been destroyed. He looked back and wrapped a hand around Janelle's throat. He didn't squeeze tightly but applied enough pressure to tell her he would if she said the wrong thing.

"Let me be very clear about one thing, Janelle." His voice sounded calm, but she heard the rage crackling beneath the tone. "I may be willing to accept your friends, including Elijah, to be part of our society, bound to our land before Dorion destroys your world, but you're never to mention Elijah's name again. If you do, I'll cut out your fucking tongue. And then I will *shred* him to pieces."

He dropped his hand, and her heart pounded as she quickly nodded.

Janelle needed to be more careful with her words, or the façade could fall apart before Sabrina reached the bedchamber.

Instead, she gave him a small, submissive smile. "I'm sorry," she said. "Sabrina would be the wedding present I'd appreciate, if that is what you want, too."

Kade smirked and slightly bit his lower lip, looking down at her mouth. "Our tradition after wedding ceremonies is that the wife waits in the room for the husband while the Red Dragon Brotherhood hunts. It will be several hours before I can meet you in that room tonight. Even then, we'll have to sneak Sabrina in."

*Gods, he's such an idiot*, she thought, feeling her shoulders finally relax. "Then let's sneak her in."

# 35

## AIDEN

Aiden opened his eyes as the daylight entered through the window.

He had brought Anaru to an empty cabin on the eastern outskirts of the forest where he had found her. The damp smell of mold along the wooden walls made it difficult for him to sleep. A storm had moved through that night, and water had leaked through the roof and soaked the bedsheets.

Aiden turned and saw Anaru staring at the leaky ceiling, her eyes wide open. He had heard her tossing and turning all night, unable to rest. She was still in pain, and her condition was getting worse with each passing hour.

He thought that if only she hadn't been so stubborn and had complied with his requests, everything would've been so much simpler.

There was an itch inside Aiden's chest, a rumbling vibration as Zakari spoke to him. The voice became more precise now, filled with the echoes of haunting deeds and unspeakable acts. Not that

Zakari had a thirst for death and blood, but he felt it was his nature to destroy. He truly believed he was doing the right thing. Aiden wasn't strong enough to fight his intentions, so he let the darkness control him to ease that pain.

Zakari wasn't just controlling him anymore; he was *becoming* him.

"We need food, Aiden," Anaru said, turning over on the mattress to look at him. Color had drained from her skin, and the circles beneath her eyes were darker.

As she spoke, her stomach growled. Zakari found the dragon's needs rather bothersome, but if she was going to play her part in his plan, she needed to be kept alive.

He nodded. "I'll go hunt, but I'll need to tie you up first," Aiden said, sitting up from the bed and casting his eyes around the room. "Don't fucking move."

He didn't miss the way her body tensed at his words. "Look at me, Aiden. Where would I go? I'm too weak. I can barely breathe, let alone move—" Her ramble buzzed in his ears.

"Enough, Anaru!" he said firmly.

She swallowed, her voice small and quiet. "There really is no need." She must have realized there was no point in pleading any further. As he looked away, Anaru attempted to bolt off the bed, but he quickly straddled her, keeping her pinned. Anaru groaned as his weight pressed against the wound.

"My, my...see, this is precisely why you need to be tied up." He leaned in close, his gaze deadly as it held hers. "Make no mistake, Anaru. You are a desirable part of the grand plan, but you're *not* irreplaceable. I will snap your neck if I must." Those words did the trick, and he could practically see whatever fight was left in her evaporate from her body. The desperation to see her daughter was an excellent bargaining chip. "I'm going to have to use magic to do this."

Aiden knew he was crushing her as he put his full weight against her tiny frame, but it was the only way to keep her still, just in case. Aiden allowed Zakari to move power through him. Smoky hands wrapped around her wrists and to the bedposts, keeping her secure.

"That will do for now," Aiden said. "If you try to break free of this power, it's going to tighten its grip, and I won't be able to control how badly that might hurt." He titled his head. "And you do want to meet your daughter, at least, do you not? I mean, it'd be *such* a shame if you came all this way to die before you set your eyes on her."

Anaru nodded quickly, knowing full well to listen. Aiden smiled. Submission suited her well, and it made his job significantly easier.

"I have given you a warning, Anaru...but if I come back and you've somehow broken free of this, understand that not even I can stop what *he* will do to you."

"I'm sorry—I'm sorry about trying to escape," Anaru said while nodding. "I would have died already if you hadn't brought me here, so I'm not going anywhere."

"Good." He smirked and stood. "I'm glad we can agree on that one thing, at least." Aiden looked down at her one last time before exiting the cabin and running into the woods to hunt.

———◦———

Aiden had searched for food, but it was as if all the creatures of their land had fled, hiding from him. Zakari's dark power was a plague that even the animals and insects feared. There was nothing for him to hunt for, not even fish in the nearby streams. Back in his world, Aiden would've excelled at this and had no problem bringing food back to Anaru. But here...here, he was nothing.

*Nothing but a weak, murderous elf,* he thought.

He relished the feelings that he knew would soon die with Zakari.

Pain, guilt, and shame were his only comforts in this place. Aiden had long given up hope of forcing Zakari out. Once, he believed he might have stood a chance, but as Aiden watched the life leave Tegan's eyes, he realized he was wrong.

Trying to fight Zakari was no longer possible. Nothing was left inside him, and the desire for the entity to destroy was all-consuming. The inner peace he once had was now a void inside his soul, and his Elven light was all but a small flicker in eternal darkness.

It was time to let go, once and for all.

Aiden removed his gloves and placed his hands on the soil, digging his fingers into the dirt and closing his eyes. He pondered his decision for a moment. Instinctively, his thoughts drifted to Tegan. *What would she think if she saw me now,* Aiden thought, *soaked in disgust?*

*It doesn't matter,* he realized. *Tegan is nothing but ash now.* He had seen it himself when he traveled back to Dragon's Cove. He fought back the tears, drawing in a sharp breath.

Perhaps by letting Zakari have control, he would no longer feel that pain. Or anything at all.

"Zakari," Aiden called. "I give you what's left of me...Master. It is all at your disposal."

His head snapped back, his eyes turning black as a starless sea. The magic within him dwindled as a sense of rushing water flowed through his veins. The Elven light that once gave him life melted away into that void. Aiden was just a body, an empty vessel—a prison for another that was now about to be released into the world.

Aiden opened his eyes, and it was as if he were seeing through the sight of another, an out-of-body experience that left him numb to everything. He could no longer feel, breathe, or see with his physical body. He was now just a spirit within Zakari.

The pain was finally gone, and relief took over him. But Zakari was now entirely in control, and Aiden had let him.

# 36

## ANARU

After an hour, Aiden walked back into the room. Immediately, Anaru felt something was wrong. The elf's posture no longer carried a warrior's pride, the pride she had seen him hold for years back in the Eastland Forest. His shoulders were slumped, and his long black hair hung in his eyes. When Aiden looked at her, a shock ran down her spine. It was like the abyss was looking into her soul.

"Zakari, what did you do to Aiden?" she asked, but she knew the answer. It was clear Aiden was gone, and the creature that had just reentered the room was more dangerous than anything she had ever imagined. As the energy danced around them, her skin tingled like tiny prickling needles.

"Get dressed," he ordered, throwing a tunic and leather pants to her.

Her heart dropped. Aiden didn't return with food, but that was the least of her worries.

"Zakari," she said, even if deep down she knew there was no point in trying to reason with him. "Don't do this, please. Aiden is a good man."

Calling Aiden by the entity that consumed his body felt wrong. But she saw within his eyes that there was nothing left of the Elven man. Aiden was a shell.

His lip turned up. "I said get dressed."

Zakari flicked his wrist and released the power that bound her. She rubbed her skin like the magical smoke had burned it.

Zakari rolled his eyes, moving around the bed until he reached her, and then he grabbed her wrists and ran his thumb over her swollen skin.

"I'm fine," she said. "I'll heal."

She rose and attempted to move past him, but he stepped in her way. "Anaru," he said, reaching out, taking a strand of her hair, and running it through his fingers as if examining her like a new prize. "There are many creatures I've seen throughout my existence, but never anything like you. Dragon shifters...you are quite the fascinating species."

Anaru ignored his words. "Food, Zakari. You might not need it, but I do. And if I don't have my strength, I will die a lot faster, and I won't be able to help you."

Zakari let out a low chuckle, his laughter causing goosebumps to spread over her body. "I'll give you some of my magic, so you can manage for the next few days. When I entered the wild to hunt, every beast fled from me. It was as if they sensed the darkness and were too afraid. There isn't any food for miles, I'm afraid."

Her instinct was to run, too. But how could she escape with such an injury?

Anaru let out a breath. "Water?"

"Water, yes. But I need you to be able to walk today, and this injury of yours..." Zakari placed his finger where her wound was and pushed against her skin, causing her to wince and cry out.

"Aiden! Stop!"

"Aiden is *dead*," he responded coldly as she whimpered. Anaru tried to move away from him, but the pain made it impossible.

"Zakari, please. That hurts."

"I know, beautiful dragon. Watching you cry out is making me feel all kinds of things." He leaned forward and grabbed the back of Anaru's neck, sliding his palm to the back of her head and yanking her hair at the scalp.

"Stop!" she cried, grabbing his arm to pull him off. "What are you doing?"

He suddenly seized her mouth possessively against his lips, pressing her harder against the wall as he kissed her. But as he claimed her mouth, black smoke seeped into her, her breath suddenly giving out. She slammed her hands against his chest, unable to breathe, but it was no use. The dark power poured down her throat and spread across her body.

She half-expected to succumb to the magic, but something else happened. Her body sparked with light, her pain subsiding where her injury was, and her strength returned.

When Zakari released the kiss, he stepped back.

"Did you...did you heal me?" she asked shakily, lifting her shirt and looking down at where the bruises were. They were gone. "I—"

"Don't get too elated, dragon," he said. "The moment I pull that power back out of you, you'll go right back to dying."

"Will I become like you?" Her voice trembled as she asked, feeling a nervous pull in her belly. The mere idea of Zakari's power consuming her made Anaru feel physically ill.

Zakari shook his head. "Not completely, but you won't be yourself. That's for certain," he said. "So, until we find what I'm looking for, you'll welcome that power as if it's yours. But if you use it against me, Anaru, you will see exactly what I am capable of. What you've seen Aiden do thus far is nothing. I will have no mercy on you because I am incapable of it." He passed her to reach the wall and grabbed Aiden's bag, throwing it over his shoulder.

As Zakari opened the door, she called out, "You had a purpose, Zakari."

He stopped at the doorway and slowly turned. "Did I?"

"The elements of Earth wouldn't have created you if you didn't."

Zakari winced, but he was quick to recover. His eyes shifted to an impossible shade of black. "My entire existence has been to bring forth pain and destruction. I would think you'd want me to perish from this world."

"Oh, believe me, Zakari, I do. After everything you've done...I do."

Zakari gave her a slight smirk. "Then what's the problem?"

She squeezed her eyes shut, stringing her words together so he'd understand.

"Because you'd have to kill my family for that to happen," she said, feeling the weight of everything crash down on her. "They don't deserve that."

Zakari nodded. "I know," he said. "But if I want to be eradicated from the plane of existence, they have to make the impossible decision of sacrificing their power for my death. I promise you, once they see what my plans are for the rest of this planet if they don't, they'll gladly give up their lives to stop it."

# 37

## MAZIE

Kaeli's hair spilled over Mazie's chest as she snuggled against her. Once they finished their "evening bath," the women returned to Kaeli's house, sleeping beside each other for the rest of the night.

As much as she tried to sleep, she couldn't get Kaeli out of her thoughts—her lips, smile, and body against hers. She wanted to have her again and again, but they knew what the next few days meant. They were going to war, and moments like last night would have to wait.

As Kaeli opened her eyes, she moved her arm over Mazie's stomach, giving her a tight squeeze while her head rested on her naked breasts. "Hey, beautiful," Kaeli said, looking up. The blue in her eyes sparkled in the sunlight, and a warm flicker went through Mazie's heart.

Mazie smiled at her and brushed the long white strands away from Kaeli's eyes. "Hey," she said back.

Kaeli yawned and looked up at the window. Then she lifted her hand and moved her fingers in a graceful dance before a second small window opened to the outside world—a tiny portal before them. They both watched the western sun rise above the trees outside the mountain. "It's two in the afternoon, I think," Kaeli said before closing the portal with a swipe of her hand.

"I didn't want to wake you and have to lose your warmth," Mazie whispered, her touch gentle as she traced her fingertips delicately down Kaeli's spine. If she could, she would have stayed there forever.

Kaeli bit her bottom lip. "Unfortunately, we need to get up and prepare. The instructors will be assembling the students in the temples soon. They've become so skilled at the craft since our last time here. I'd like to see their progress."

"Alright," Mazie said, but as Kaeli moved to get up, she wrapped her hand around her waist, pulling her back into her arms.

"Mazie!" Kaeli chuckled, but she allowed herself to fall back into her embrace. Mazie felt drunk on bliss—despite everything that had been happening.

"They can wait for a few more moments," Mazie said, her grip firm but tender on Kaeli's body.

"Mm, you're right," Kaeli hummed softly, leaving a kiss on her shoulder. "I think I have an idea on how to pass the time..." And then she left another kiss a little lower, lingering against Mazie's collarbone. Mazie practically melted into her touch. The beautiful dragon's effect on her was unlike anything else.

"I like this idea," Mazie said. "Perhaps a little lower."

Mazie's breathing grew heavier as she continued to shower her skin with kisses. She wanted Kaeli to savor every inch of her while she surrendered her body completely.

Kaeli looked up at her. "I'll make each moment count," she said, her hand drifting in between Mazie's thighs, which spread open for her eagerly. She was already soaked with arousal for her. "Don't you worry."

"Fuck, Kaeli," Mazie moaned under her breath as Kaeli's fingers slipped lower, prodding at her entrance. "*Yes...*"

———◇———

It had been over two weeks since they had arrived on Dragão Terra.

Mazie was no longer sure her friends were safe or even alive. But she took an oath all those years ago that if anyone were to lay a hand on Lincoln, she would come for blood, and their death would be slow and painful. She would make those who offended her captain cry like a little bitch until the end.

Dorion and his despicable band of murderers would pay for what they had done to Anaru and Kaeli.

"What are you feeling right now, Bay?" she asked. "Are you afraid?"

Bay nodded, flying up to land on Mazie's shoulder. "I'm afraid for you," Bay confessed. "I'm afraid of what will happen when we leave this place and fight the dragons."

Bay was never a talker, often remaining silent for days, but when she did speak, when she expressed her heart...it always hit Mazie to her core. She felt her duty was always to protect the pixie like a little sister.

"You don't need to worry about me, Bay," Mazie assured her, her tone soft. "I can take care of myself. You know that—you've seen it before." Bay's worry didn't seem to lessen. "We have friends here who are helping us, and we'll find the rest of the crew, too. We're not alone."

Mazie tilted her head, allowing her cheek to touch Bay's wing. Then she closed her eyes and felt Bay flutter her wings at rapid speed, tingling her skin.

"I love you," Bay said in her tiny voice, nestling down in the collar of her shirt, and closed her eyes to sleep.

"I love you, too, Bay," Mazie said, but Bay was already slipping into a slumber for her afternoon nap.

"There you are. Do you want to join us?" Kaeli said as she entered the courtyard. "The graduates are sparring near the meadow's creek and practicing their portals. Put Bay to bed, and see who you will be fighting beside you."

Mazie's stomach twisted into a tight knot. They were so close to leaving that place and fighting against the Brotherhood.

Of course, she was ready. It had been sixteen days since she and the captain parted ways in search of his brother and Janelle. She prayed to the gods he was safe, and it wasn't too late, but at the same time, it wasn't familiar territory. She was fighting against something like the Shadow Creature. It was an unknown world and power she wasn't ready for.

Mazie followed Kaeli down to the training grounds, where the students and their families gathered. Their curious gazes followed each step she took. Mazie stalled her gait, feeling like she should address the reason why she was there. She turned to the crowds of mages and raised a hand to quiet the murmurs. "I may not use magic like you all," she said, "but I want you to fight me with everything you have. I can't fight alongside you if I don't understand your magic."

Kaeli turned to her. "Do you want them to hold back?" she teased, a smile lifting at the corner of her mouth.

"Not unless they want me to put them flat on their back," Mazie said, her eyes fixated on the three sacred temples before her. Tall, majestic stone columns surrounded the two enormous dragon statues engulfing the entrance. Some students were already training on the grass field beside them. Mazie counted about three dozen magic wielders, with a few mentors monitoring and guiding them as they opened portals and released surges of their powers.

Magic was so tangible within that world; Mazie could practically feel it. But not only that. Deep inside her was an itch—one she thought she had forgotten a long time ago.

"Come, join us, and show us what you can do," one mentor said. She was a tall, slender woman with dark beige skin and soft ocean eyes. Over the last hour, Mazie noticed that every time one of her students got stuck, she would push them forward with kindness and words of encouragement. It seemed to work wonders.

"I don't—that's not what I'm here for," Mazie said, clearing her throat. "What I mean is, I don't use magic."

The woman—whose name she didn't know—tilted her head. "That's odd," she commented. Mazie felt as if her blue eyes were piercing right through her, and she hated it. "I can...*feel* the magic inside you. It's very powerful, too. It would be a shame not to use it and—"

"I'm not here for that," Mazie interrupted, feeling oddly exposed. "I'm here just to learn about *your* magic."

The woman gave her a sympathetic look. "Of course. I under-stand."

Mazie swallowed, and the itch was gone.

———◇———

After several hours of training, Kaeli walked hand in hand with Mazie down to the water. Xander had put Bay to bed early, allow-ing Kaeli and Mazie to speak alone.

"You're wondering if all of this is enough, right?" Kaeli asked her.

"Of course, I'm worried if it's enough," Mazie confessed, turn-ing to her. "Besides the parents who must watch their young, the entire guild will fight with us. That is a lot of people to be responsible for and to lead into a battle."

Mazie momentarily wondered how many people would rise to the cause. All she knew was the numbers were not on their side, but she tried not to let that discourage her. The numbers were not in their favor in some past situations, too, but Lincoln always made the right calls to keep them safe.

*Lincoln,* she said his name in her thoughts. *Is he even alive?*

"He's alive," Kaeli said.

Mazie furrowed her brow, surprised by her words. "Kaeli, how—"

"Ever since last night on the rock," she explained. Her hand gave Mazie a light, reassuring squeeze. "I've felt a connection with you since we met. I didn't want to say anything because I didn't know what it meant. But I think I do now."

"You read my thoughts?" Mazie asked, taking a small step back and resting her shoulders against a tree. "Like my captain and your mother?"

Kaeli shrugged. "Maybe. I don't know. All I know is that it's not all the time. But after last night, it's so much stronger and distinct. I think subconsciously, you're projecting your thoughts to me...the ones you want me to know."

"This doesn't mean that you and I are..."

"No," Kaeli said. "I mean, not that I understand fated mates, but our gods choose for us if we don't. You're not part of this world, though...even if it feels so natural to have you here. It feels as if you belong here with me and always have." Kaeli's gaze locked on hers. "But you come from another place. I don't think it works that way. But for now, if there's something you don't want me to know, I suggest you try harder to keep your mind quiet."

Mazie was more intrigued than upset that Kaeli could read her mind. But then she instantly felt mortified. Mazie had been fantasizing about Kaeli naked ever since they fucked on the rock. Her cheeks grew hot.

Kaeli smiled and giggled to herself. "You didn't block that one out."

"If you weren't so cute, Kaeli, I might have to punish you for that one."

Kaeli stepped toward her and reached up, running a soft caress over Mazie's lip. "Then punish me."

# 38

## JANELLE

Before Kade left to hunt with the Red Dragon Brotherhood, he locked Janelle inside his room. She hadn't been in Kade's chambers yet. It was much bigger than hers, with several more windows to escape from if she had to. Of course, they left her bare of anything to use as a weapon once again.

After several hours of Janelle meditating on her plan, the door clicked open, and Kade slipped inside, dragging Sabrina behind him.

His clothes appeared ragged, and his hair disheveled. It looked as if he had spent hours rolling around among the trees, collecting small twigs and leaves along the way. Janelle found the sight comical and bit back a bitter laugh. Kade was a ridiculous man who didn't deserve the luxuries he held.

"We'll have quite the feast tomorrow, sweetheart," he said. "But now it's time to relax."

Sabrina didn't fight against his hold, but she still looked reluctant to be there.

"A gift for my bride," he said, shoving Sabrina forward.

Janelle's heart hammered, and then she froze. *Fuck*, she cursed in her thoughts. *This is all too easy.*

Now that her plan was finally in motion, Janelle was unsure how to proceed with the next step. Although she had never pleasured a woman before, she knew she had to be convincing enough to distract Kade and retrieve the Voleric.

"If we're going to do this," Kade started, unbuttoning his shirt and slipping it off, "we need to do it now. Dorion just stepped into the bath to clean off the hunt. He'll be looking for her the moment he gets dressed."

"Do you want to wash up?" Janelle said too quickly. "I mean, you're covered in dirt. I figured—"

"You're worried about a little dirt, Janelle?" Kade said, his lips turning up into a smile. "We're going to get quite filthy here in a moment. I think a bit of mud won't hurt us."

Janelle swallowed her nerves and nodded slowly before Sabrina asked, "Well, where do you want us, Kade?" She gave Janelle a kind smile. Sabrina looked like she was afraid and didn't want to be there any more than Janelle.

"Sabrina, I want you on the bed, and Janelle, sweetheart, I want you to straddle her and undress her in front of me. Very, very slowly."

Sabrina did as he asked and climbed onto the bed, moving her back against the mattress. She spread her legs wide, hiking her long blue dress to her knees. Janelle could see she wasn't wearing any drawers as she bared herself.

"Kade," Sabrina said. "I never realized you had these kinds of *appetites.*"

Kade moved to the chair next to the bed and undid the ties on his pants before taking a seat. "It's true," he confessed, "I've only ever experienced pleasure with one woman at a time, but for my bride, I am willing to explore new territories." He slowly spread his legs as he used one hand to pull out his cock, running his hand up and down his shaft to get it hard, looking right at Janelle and not Sabrina. "Janelle, what did I just tell you to do?"

Janelle felt the push to obey the command through the mating bond and clenched her jaw. She knew they were not fully bonded until she and Kade consecrated the marriage, so whatever she did from there on, she would have to take her time. She and Kade may be wed according to their laws, but it wasn't binding until she spread her legs for him. And she had no intention of doing that.

Ever.

*Elijah is mine, and I am his*, she breathed her prayer.

Slowly, she moved toward the bed and climbed on the mattress, inching closer to Sabrina until she reached her legs. Her heart continued to thud while her hands felt clammy.

As she ran her hands up Sabrina's inner thighs, she heard a low growl come from Kade. Janelle didn't want to look, but she turned toward him anyway, watching him slowly stroke himself with a slight, playful smirk. Lust shone in his eyes; he liked what he saw. "I didn't say stop, love. Touch her for me."

Janelle looked back at Sabrina, who arched her hips and reached out, grabbed Janelle's hand, and positioned her fingers against her pussy. "Here," Sabrina said in a mere whisper. "You don't have to be afraid. Let me help." She inched one of Janelle's fingers, sliding it inside her, moving it in and out for Janelle. Her mind was so panicked she barely noticed how soaked Sabrina was. With her other hand, Janelle delicately untied Sabrina's dress at her chest, allowing it to slip off her shoulders gracefully. Janelle leaned forward, intending to nibble on the woman's neck while she discreetly pulled off the necklace...but she froze.

"Shit," she cursed under her breath, intending to say it only in her mind, but she was too stunned at that moment. Sabrina wasn't wearing the necklace anymore.

"You can leave now, Sabrina," Kade said, his hot breath on Janelle's neck. She was so afraid that she hadn't even heard him climb onto the bed.

"Yes, sir," Sabrina said, rolling off the bed and covering herself before exiting the room.

One of Kade's arms snaked around Janelle's waist, pulling her back until her ass touched his hard cock, his erection pressing into her. "Are you looking for this?" he said, dangling the Voleric before her. "Maybe I'll let you touch it for a few seconds and feel its power if you spread your legs for me without a fight."

Her body tensed as she shook her head, still not daring to look back. It had all come down to this moment, then. She'd have to fight him.

"I'd rather die, Kade, over letting you touch me," she said firmly. If he were going to take her, she wouldn't go down without a fight. "I reject you as a mate. You're not worthy of me, and Elijah is a far better man than you will ever be."

"Well..." Kade pocketed the Voleric. He wrapped his free hand around Janelle's throat, giving it a tight squeeze and restricting her air supply. "This is going to be painful, then."

He was rough as he shoved her down onto the mattress, his weight shifting on top of her. Janelle squirmed beneath him, her body frantically trying to turn over so she could scratch at his face.

One of his hands covered her mouth from behind, so all her screams came out muffled as he positioned himself between her legs. Tears streamed down her cheeks as she closed her eyes, feeling the power her father had gifted her spark to life. She was always afraid to use it because she lacked the control to fight without hurting everyone around her, including herself. The last time she had unleashed that kind of power, long before she met Elijah, she had killed innocents. She had hurt people in the wake of the storm because she never had someone help her learn how to harness Elven powers. But right then, it was worth the risk, even if it killed her. If Kade fucked her, everything would change. She would genuinely lose herself, and there would be no future with Elijah.

*There is no future for freedom either*, she thought.

Kade slowly lifted her dress and pulled down her underdrawers just enough to expose her. She felt Kade's lips touch her neck, caressing his mouth against her skin, and he let out a moan, slowly pushing the tip of his cock between her legs.

Just as his lips left her shoulder to arch back, Janelle bit down hard on his arm and let her Elven magic rise to the surface of her skin. The power scorched her as she released a burst of energy that threw Kade across the room.

More light poured out of her, but Janelle held her hands out and slammed her palms together. The explosion of magic slammed into the walls of the room, knocking large chunks of stone loose and shattering the glass windows. Janelle jumped from the bed right as Kade rose to his feet. He held one arm in front of him to shield himself from the light, his eyes glowing bright yellow. A low, vicious growl vibrated from his chest, and scales emerged from his smooth, tanned skin.

"Oh, shit!" she cursed, bolting toward the door as he quickly transitioned. As soon as she grabbed the handle, Kade's dragon tail collided with her, throwing her onto the wooden floor with a hard smack.

The room shook as he charged forward, his nails scraping against the floor on his way toward her. His clothes, torn to shreds during the transition, lay in a heap by the fireplace in the room.

She swiftly rolled underneath him as he slammed his paws next to her head. Moving to the right, she crawled on her stomach and grabbed his pants. She felt the smooth surface of the Voleric, clutching it tightly and pulling it out of his pocket. Kade's paws wrapped around her neck, his claws digging painfully into her skin. That didn't stop her, though. She closed her eyes and honed in on Elijah's mind, what was left of their connection, binding their souls to each other.

"Elijah!" she called out as the image of dark walls formed before her. The pain of Kade's claws ripped through her, but Janelle pushed that out of her mind. She only had seconds to reach Elijah and pull him out of that illusion. She looked around the space, realizing that she was in that prison cell. Which meant the mage was nearby.

Janelle rushed over to Elijah, who was hunched over against the wall, his head buried between his knees.

"Elijah, it's me."

"Janelle?" Elijah jerked up, and they locked eyes. "How did you get in—"

"It's an illusion, Elijah," she said urgently. "There's a mage who has control of your mind. She has the entire time since we came to Dragão Terra. Everything, and I mean everything you have seen since we arrived, isn't real. We are prisoners inside a palace run by dragon shifters. Fight it, Elijah!"

Elijah jumped up and wrapped her in his arms. "Thank fuck!" he called out, burying his head into the crease of her neck. "I saw—"

"I know what you saw, Elijah. It wasn't real. It could never be real. I love you—"

Janelle screamed as Kade's claws dug into her flesh again, and she fell to the prison cell's floor, her knees hitting the cement.

"Janelle, love, what's happening?"

"Fight it!" she cried out. "Fight the power and kill the mage. Dorion is going to use her to destroy Earth. Kill her, Elijah. Kill her now!"

The prison walls faded into mist, and Janelle was thrown from the gem's power and back into her physical body. The Voleric was knocked free from her hand and rolled across the floor. Janelle flipped onto her back and looked up at the monster above.

Kade let out another dragon roar, the sound coated in flames, and scorched the broken wood. The fire quickly spread until it created an inferno circling around them.

"*You do not want to fight me, love,*" Kade projected to her mind. "*Submit!*" The bond pulled hard on her heart, trying to tear away her resistance.

Janelle didn't answer Kade. Instead, she summoned her light magic again, channeling the power into her right hand. She pushed and pushed until her very bones felt like they were burning. She snarled as she looked up at the dragon who made her life a living hell.

"Here's the thing, dear *husband*. I've been fighting you since the moment you dragged me into this godsforsaken nightmare. You are a despicable, disgusting bastard who doesn't deserve to breathe. You and your brothers have earned nothing but death and pain. I meant what I said, Kade. Fuck you, fuck this empire, and fuck the bond!"

Janelle pulled back her fist and slammed it into Kade's chest, breaking through the skin. Searing hot blood dripped down her arm and onto her chest, but she ignored it.

"This is for violating me, you fucking lizard."

She drove her fist deeper into Kade's chest, smashing through muscle, sinew, and bone until she found his heart. Extending her fingers, she grazed the surface of it. She sensed his evil power and the mating bond there and seized them. Janelle screamed and unleashed every ounce of energy she had, snapping the dragon's power into pieces.

Kade screeched and roared right before his dragon tail slammed against the pillars on the bed, cracking the wood in half.

As her magic burst inside his body, she retracted her arm and quickly scrambled back, taking cover behind a broken chair.

Kade extended his wings before he collapsed, beams of light bursting out of different parts of his body. Finally, Kade exploded, scales and flesh splattering against the walls and onto her.

As shouts echoed down the hallway toward the bedroom, Janelle quickly jumped up. It was the guards.

"Fuck. Fuck. Fuck!" she cursed, looking around for another way out of the burning room, but there wasn't any. She may have killed

Kade, but he was the brother of their lord, and if caught, she was dead.

# 39

## ELIJAH

Unlike his experience in the past, Elijah wasn't pulled out of the Voleric's power after Janelle's image faded. He remained in the subconscious realm, surrounded by darkened mists. Only now he could sense the *other*. The mist soon parted, and Elijah saw he was back in the prison. But his mind immediately felt a change in the atmosphere. Something that had been there all along but cleverly veiled, so not even he could sense it. Now that Janelle had alerted him to the illusion, he knew what to look for.

*Who* to look for...

He was relieved that he wasn't losing his mind after all. Something had been wrong all along.

Elijah also knew that the mage had seen whatever was inside his mind—they saw Janelle breach inside. Which meant the mage would act quickly to suppress Elijah.

As he recounted the last time Janelle was in his subconscious, he was unaware of what was happening. This time, however, he wanted the mage to know he was awake.

And he was going to fight.

The cement felt cool against his palm as he fanned out his fingers and pressed his hand against the floor, feeling a sudden vibration. "Release me," Elijah said, looking around. "I am no stranger to mind control, mage...or is it Arabella? Gods, you sure had me fooled."

There was a level of hurt behind that fury—not just feeling like a fool for not realizing it sooner, but he believed he had a *friend*. He confided in her and shared the deepest parts of himself he usually kept hidden from others.

*What an idiot I had been,* he thought.

The sound of a foot scuff made Elijah look to his right, where he saw the woman he had been conversing and traveling with for what felt like weeks.

A lie. A deception.

Her hair was slightly different, though, with long curls around her face, and her eye color was a deeper shade of brown, with no hint of yellow. No, she wasn't a dragon at all. She was just like him. Arabella wore a long red dress like the color of rich wine, with a V-shape cut at the cleavage. Her necklace drew his attention for a second, eyeing a black pendant wrapped in gold wire.

"Finally, we meet," he said. "At least in the flesh."

She shrugged. "It was as real as we made it, Elijah. I'm surprised, though. No one has ever pulled themselves out of The Void."

"The Void?" he repeated. "I'm baffled by your belief that all this should be applauded. You're a monster just like them."

A slight smile touched her lips. "Monster? I wouldn't say that. They have always protected my sister and me when we could have joined the others who perished long ago. We are not the enemy."

Elijah's nostrils flared. "Your existence is not theirs!" he said through his teeth. "Stop pretending as if your actions deserve some redemption. I don't give a fuck that they protected you. Instead, why don't you help me get out of here, so I can make this right? Stop them from what they're doing." She tilted her head, her expression telling him that what he said had no impact on her, nor was she sympathetic. "Using your magic to trap the mind of another sorcerer so that those vile men could corrupt a kingdom while destroying others like it. Well, I am no stranger to that kind of pathetic control of power."

"Is that what you think this is, Elijah?" Arabella said. "The Red Dragon Brotherhood gave us a second chance at life by binding us to the power of their land. Here, we are more free than those his dear daughter keeps hidden."

Elijah's eyes went wide. "You're a fool if you think this is freedom."

"Oh, Elijah," she said. "The truth will open your eyes to a greater world than Earth ever was for you. The Newick witches were only but a tiny moment in history. Mage power has been around since the beginning of existence. *We* are your ancestors from another parallel realm. Over time, the mages of this land grew, while yours had to succumb to dark magic to find their inner strength. They were cowards. This darkness that has corrupted your magic *must* be destroyed. It was never supposed to exist. Let me help you. The Red Dragon Brotherhood has kept me safe and given me a purpose. You can be a part of that. I can save you, Elijah. If I can keep you in this state just a little longer, then perhaps I can pull out that power that's eating you alive and bring you back to your natural state of elemental magic. I can free you from the mistakes your people made—give you back that which you were born with. Not what your ancestors forced upon you."

Elijah stepped back. "It all sounds so righteous on paper, doesn't it?" he said.

"You can't save her," Arabella said. Her tone was oddly sincere, but Elijah didn't let himself get fooled again. She had seemed genuine in The Void, too. "She is bonded to a dragon of the Brotherhood. You'd do best to walk away and save the others if you must. But I am begging you to stay. Let me contain that power, so you can truly be free. Janelle will not want you this way."

Her words hit him in the chest. It was his greatest fear. Janelle could profess her love for him over and over again, but in the end, he never felt worthy of her.

"Janelle's magic is too good for this world. But yours...your power will be her undoing. You'll destroy her."

Elijah shook his head. "Release me, Arabella. Now. I won't be asking you twice."

"Elijah, I am bound to protect our world from monsters like you. Until I release the darkness within you, you'll be in this state for the rest of your life."

Elijah let out a growl, his magic calling to him. He didn't care if he lost his mind while destroying the mage's power that controlled it. If it meant his freedom, it was a risk he had to take.

"Don't, Elijah. It will kill you," she warned.

Elijah ignored the mage and placed his hand back down on the ground, allowing the power to leave his body. The essence of his magic crept along the walls and blanketed them in a dark smoke.

"Drop the power, Elijah. Now!" she warned again, but all he could do was focus on his magic, releasing wave after wave of power until it latched onto her. He felt Arabella attempting to sever the link, but it was too late. He gripped her throat but felt her presence elsewhere. Of course, he did. She wasn't really in the room.

All the images he had seen since he arrived flashed within the dark cloud—the Ruins, Arabella's fucking coffee, the dragons who attacked him in the alley, even the spider creature they slaughtered for meat. Each image crawled out through the black smoke, trying to reach him, and the buzzing sound of chaos caused him to feel faint. Elijah kept going, pushing against the barrier encasing him in that prison.

As the images disappeared, he heard a scream that was cut short and dropped his power. Elijah blinked a few times, clearing away the grainy haze in his eyes, and looked up at the ceiling. He realized he was lying on an altar. He quickly jumped off and looked down. Arabella lay on the floor, sprawled out with blood coming out of her mouth, eyes, and ears.

He knelt down and gently covered her eyes with his hands, closing them for her. A slight, guilty ache hit him in the chest. It was all a lie, but it felt so real. Losing an illusion shouldn't have hurt as badly as it did.

Frantically, he looked around the cell. They were alone, at least. He placed his hands on the bars and used his powers to pry them apart, breaking through the metal until he could squeeze through them. Then he rushed down the hall and out of the dungeon.

# 40

## JANELLE

The pounding against the door grew louder and fiercer. The repeated blows knocked splinters of wood free and clattered on the floor. Kade had locked the door from the inside, so unless the guards were already in their dragon forms, it would take some time to break through and give Janelle time to think.

Kade emptied his bedroom of anything Janelle could have used as a weapon. Even the wood had been burned to ash. Thankfully, the dragon's inferno had died out quickly, and the smashed windows left an opening for the smoke to flow out, allowing Janelle to breathe.

"Shit, what do I do?" Janelle cried out as she scanned the room. She couldn't jump out the window; the fall would break her legs or worse.

Janelle turned to face the disintegrating door and held up her hands, channeling light into them. "Alright, assholes. Come at me!"

When the door cracked again and the hinges snapped, it crashed to the ground with a loud bang, sending thick clouds of ash and dust into the air. There, emerging from that choking fog, with his hands outstretched and smoky power radiating beautifully from his fingers...was Elijah.

Janelle dropped her magic and sprinted toward him, leaping into his arms. He wrapped her in his warm embrace, running his hands over her body. "Is this real?" he asked, his voice filled with disbelief. "Are *you* real?"

She nodded quickly, placing her hands on each side of his cheeks. "It's real. I am real." Janelle pressed her lips against his, savoring the taste of him she had missed so much.

"I love you," she cried out. "I'm so sorry for what they've done to you. For what they made you see. I would have never—I could have never—" She let out a heavy sob, cutting off her words.

Elijah shook his head, gripping her cheeks and forcing her to look at him. His eyes were filled with sincerity. "I didn't want to believe it. But even then, it didn't change how I felt about you."

Right then, Elijah looked over her shoulder, seeing bits of dragon body parts scattered around the room, walls covered in dark, dripping blood and gore. Elijah realized she was also covered in blood and let out a shocked laugh. "Fuck," he said. "You did that?"

She nodded. "When Dorion and Merrick find out what I've done, they'll kill me to avenge Kade. We need to go. Now."

Elijah took her hand and ran out of the room. He paused for a moment, his head cocked as he listened for more guards to enter the hallway. Looking down, she noticed at least six of Dorion's men with broken necks.

"You did that?" she asked, raising a brow playfully.

Elijah gave her hand a tight squeeze. "Anything for you, love. Come on."

As Elijah pulled her around the corner down the hall, two more guards rushed past, but they stayed hidden within a shadowed alcove, holding their breath so they remained quiet.

"Who else is here?" he asked.

Once they were out of sight, Janelle replied, "Lincoln and Nola. They're being held on the east side of the palace." She stopped as a slight panic hit her. "The mage. Is she?"

"Also dead," he said, placing his hand on her cheek. "We're almost free."

She gave him a quick nod. "Okay, we'll have to sneak through the main grand hall to get to the other side. There are too many guards near the tunnels."

"Alright, lead the way. I'll kill anything trailing us."

As they ran toward the grand hall, the ground beneath their feet began to tremble.

"What was that?" Janelle asked.

Elijah shook his head. "I haven't got a fucking clue."

Before they could press on, the ground lurched again, and the walls alongside them cracked, sending dust and stone tumbling down.

"I think the castle's falling apart," Janelle said. "We need to hurry."

They entered the hall leading to the cell, and Nola and Lincoln immediately jumped up. Another wave of relief flooded Janelle as she saw her friends. They were covered in cuts and bruises, but they were alive.

"Elijah!" Lincoln shouted as Elijah's powers wrapped around the metal bars, breaking off the door's hinges.

"Let's go, brother," Elijah said as Lincoln gripped Nola's hand, and the four moved toward the eastern tunnel.

"Lincoln, watch out!" Nola shouted as a guard leapt in front of them, brandishing a long sword.

Lincoln skillfully dodged the blade, the razor edge barely grazing his left cheek. It left a faint mark without drawing blood. Elijah released a surge of power, the black smoke slamming into the man's back. The impact caused him to fall forward, his sword clattering to the ground. Lincoln lunged at the guard, dropping to his knees on the hallway floor and letting the smooth tile propel him toward the sword. As the hilt tapped his knee, he picked it up and swung it at the guard, severing his neck in one swift motion.

The guard's head rolled to Janelle's feet, and she stepped back.

"Shh, wait a moment," Lincoln whispered as two more guards ran toward the hallway. However, they diverted away from the entrance and toward the ballroom instead. The group sighed collectively and took a moment to get their bearings.

"We can't be too far from the front gate," Janelle said, keeping her voice to a whisper. "I know we have to get past that doorway and head north." She pointed down the hallway to a narrow iron door.

Nola moved closer to get a better look, but the sound of approaching footsteps made Lincoln quickly press her against the wall. Using his other hand, Lincoln signaled for Elijah and Janelle to go to the other side. "We're going to need a distraction. There are too many dragons for us to escape unnoticed," Lincoln said.

Elijah nodded and released Janelle's hand. He summoned the dark smoke to flow down his hands and arms, covering most of his upper torso.

"I know what you're thinking, Lincoln," Nola said sharply, but she kept her voice low. "They'll kill you both. If the castle is already falling, they'll be too occupied to stop us. We're not leaving you two."

Lincoln turned and placed both hands on her cheeks. "I would never leave you, love. But if you don't go out through that door with Janelle, all four of us will die. We can't take on dragons."

"Nola," Janelle said. "Listen to him."

Janelle knew what those men were capable of, and as much as she wanted to stay back and fight, she had to trust Elijah and Lincoln had a plan.

"They'll be right behind us. Let's go," Janelle continued as she reached out to take Nola's hand, pleading for her to listen. The protest was visible on every inch of Nola's face, but she knew now was not the time to argue. "Now, Nola."

Nola quickly turned to Lincoln and touched his lips with hers, pulling him deep into a kiss. She stepped back and said, "We'll see you right outside on the field. Make it out alive, Lincoln. Or I swear—"

Lincoln cupped her cheeks. "My little siren. Whatever adventure you go on, I will follow you to the ends of the world."

She smiled warmly and placed her hand on his cheek. "Which world?"

With those last words, Janelle gave her another tug and pulled them away from the men.

Lincoln and Elijah sprinted down the hall, their footsteps echoing loudly and catching the attention of more guards, creating a diversion that allowed the women to escape.

As Janelle and Nola ran through the palace gates, they came upon absolute mayhem. Flames stretched out in a massive ring around the forest, forming a formidable barrier to keep them trapped inside. The dragon shifters had fanned out, searching for them along the tree line and the crumbling palace. The warmth of dragon fire touched their cheeks, and thick smoke filled the air, nearly choking them.

"Come on," Janelle said, gripping Nola's hand tighter as they ran across the field to the tree line.

Before they reached the rocks, the ground shook again, more violently, throwing the women into the dirt. They looked back and saw that the castle was breaking into pieces, and large cracks were forming in the earth beneath it.

"What's happening?" Nola shouted.

Suddenly, an ear-splitting roar cut through the air, causing the women to slam their hands over their ears.

Janelle looked behind her and saw something jutting out of the left side of the castle, deep below the ground. Red light poured through the cracks. She narrowed her eyes and realized that the cracks were, in fact, the bars of a gigantic cage.

Something was thrashing inside, trying to break free and shaking the earth below it, including the castle.

"What is that?" Nola asked, stepping in line with Janelle to look.

The cage rattled and groaned as something massive strained against it. The bars snapped free, and a side of the cage collapsed.

There, a wing, black as pitch, rose to the sky. Nola covered her mouth in horror. The wing was as tall as the palace itself.

Razor-sharp claws stepped onto the grass, followed by the rest. Both women gaped, their bodies growing numb as the massive dragon freed itself, extending its wings and standing tall.

"Oh, to the Gods," Nola said.

"If I had to guess..." Janelle swallowed. "I'd say that the empire has just learned that I killed Kade."

"You *what*?" Fear was present in Nola's voice, but their attention quickly shifted back to the dragon.

The sight of such a horrible beast defied all logic in Janelle's mind.

"Is that a shifter?" Janelle asked. "How is it so massive?"

Nola closed her eyes and focused on the beast. "When I tried to use my siren call to lull Dorion's men to sleep when they first attacked us, it didn't work," she said. "I don't know if I can do this."

"Keep trying," Janelle said.

As Nola drew in her powers, it looked like, for a moment, she connected with the dragon's mind. Her body went still, and she cocked her head slightly to the right. "He can sense me," she said.

The dragon's eyes moved quickly, locking with Nola's when she opened hers, and her throat constricted, panic overtaking her. "The dragon isn't a shifter, Janelle. He...he's being controlled by one, though."

"Fuck," Janelle cried, the both of them stepping back as Dorion exited the castle and made eye contact with the beast, giving him a nod.

"Run!" Nola cried as the creature rocketed high into the sky before nosediving toward them.

Nola grabbed Janelle's hand and pulled her away as a burst of dragon fire scorched the ground. As they ran toward the forest, Janelle lifted her hands, creating a bright beam of light that shot out along the grass. As her magic hit the barrier, a wisp of air pushed through the flames to create an opening for them to jump through. Once they were clear of the inferno, they ran into the forest, the searing heat at their backs.

Sprinting through the trees, they hoped the thick canopy would block them from the beast's line of sight, and it wouldn't be able to follow them.

They were mistaken.

As the dragon soared overhead, it released another wave of fire over the treetops and surrounding brush, creating another blazing inferno.

The fire was so enormous that the women were driven to the edge of a cliff, their feet knocking rocks into a roaring river below. The surrounding smoke was so thick that it now blocked the trees, making the forest even more challenging to see.

"What do we do, Nola?" Janelle asked. "We have to jump, but...I...it's too high. I can't swim like you. They'll catch me and drag me back. I—"

Janelle was panicking, her heart pounding in her ears. Nola gently took her hand and brushed a thumb over her skin soothingly. "Shh, it's okay," she said. "Hold on to me as tight as you can. When I shift into my tail, I'll carry you. I'll protect you."

Janelle nodded, and they both looked up as the dragon roared above them, ready to make its next strike.

"On the count of three," Nola said as Janelle took three slow breaths to calm her nerves. "One. Two. Three!"

As they leapt, another roar echoed below in the darkness. Right before they hit the water, Janelle felt her body slam into something hard and warm.

She placed her hands on the surface, running her fingers over rough silvery dragon scales. Janelle blinked a few times, and fear took her breath.

*Oh no!*

When she looked up, her gaze connected with Mazie's. "Well, hello there, lassies," Mazie said, tipping her hat with one hand while the other remained wrapped around the dragon's neck. "Meet my friend, Kaeli."

# 41

## ZAKARI

A smile played across Zakari's now-physical lips. He was enjoying the elf's body immensely. It moved with a grace and fluidity that no other body he possessed in the past had. However, he knew that this wouldn't last. To consume the entire life force of a vessel meant death would come soon. Soon, Aiden's soul and power would dwindle into nothing, and Zakari would be the puppet master of a corpse. There was a misconception around eating and using a vessel's power. Though Aiden's light had become a powerful tool, Zakari possessed the ability to harness that same essence, warping it into something else. How he used that power determined its alignment between good and evil. It was just magic being used. Unfortunately for those who got in his way, he didn't know what that difference was.

He was not born with a conscience, guilt, or shame. He had to rely on the moral code of human interaction through each person who used his power. Given his time with Kieran and the sorcerers who came before him, the morality of his actions was questionable at best.

Aiden's magic, that Elven light, could destroy thousands, and he hadn't even realized it. Zakari could feel it, in any case. The ominous power ran through his magic, latching onto Aiden's surrendered soul and feeding upon that terrible raw light.

*Soon*, Zakari told himself. *It will all be over soon.*

"Zakari," Anaru said, sliding a drink his way. "We aren't far from the city."

Zakari smiled. Having Anaru be more compliant than she had been made the journey much more enjoyable. If his time was ending, he wanted to have as many human experiences as possible, not fight a dying dragon woman at every turn.

His power now, just a tiny portion of that magic, supported her, but it wouldn't last. Once Zakari was gone, Anaru would die.

The tavern they entered that morning was only a few miles from the Graeten, the city of the Ember Guild.

"One more drink," he said, tossing back the last of his whiskey. "I need to relax. Not only has Aiden given up, but his body is succumbing to my power. It's weak."

"Isn't that what you wanted?" she asked. "To destroy him so that you could have utter control before you died?"

Irritation ran through him. "Succumbing to my power to the point of being completely worthless doesn't benefit me. Aiden is slowing me down."

"Perhaps you live with the consequences of those actions, *Zakari*."

She tried to stand up to walk away, but he reached out and gripped her wrist, yanking her back.

"Wait," he said. "Perhaps something else could help. I'm feeling a different kind of itch."

She narrowed her eyes at him as he looked over her shoulder, watching a woman who had just finished servicing a man on the upper level walk back to the bar, still adjusting the straps of her thin dress.

He leaned forward, pressing his lips near Anaru's ear. "I'm getting a craving to experience everything *he* did."

Anaru's face hardened as she realized what he was implying. "I may be willing to assist you in finding the mages, but that doesn't mean I like you, Zakari. And it certainly doesn't mean I will open my legs for you." Her face scrunched up in disgust. "Find it somewhere else."

He moved back, looking over his shoulder at the tavern entrance, where the twisting staircase led to the brothel. "Let's go." Zakari reached out and gripped her hair, and she winced while he dragged her. With each step, she resisted the control until they reached the bottom of the stairs, and he looked up. "Go."

"Fuck you, Zakari. Fuck. You!"

He gave her a wicked smile. While he usually had no patience for her brief outbursts and disobedience, he found her resistance amusing. Zakari lifted a hand and summoned a rope of smoke, wrapping around her wrists to keep her from pulling free and running. Zakari then tightened that power until Anaru hissed in pain, the bones in her wrists creaking under the strain. "Walk upstairs. Now."

Anaru tried to pry the smoky fingers away, but it was no use. She growled and dropped her hands in surrender. Once he released the magic, she turned and walked up the stairs, Zakari following her.

Loud moans echoed against the walls and into the hallway, and Zakari felt Aiden's body react to the sound, his cock getting harder with just the thought of experiencing fucking again like he had with Tegan. He wasn't fully connected then, only as if he were experiencing the thrill of it all in his head. But it was Aiden who truly felt her—cherished her.

If he was going to die soon, he wanted to have that moment for himself. Just once. Only once.

In an open room, they found a woman with dark brown hair and peachy skin lying on her back. "Place your money on the dresser," she said. "I'm Neva." Her eyes looked over at Anaru. "Mmm, it's been a while since I've had two at the same time."

"No," Zakari said, walking toward her. "I just need to make sure she stays put." He turned to Anaru. "You don't have to watch, but you're to stay in the room. Understand?"

It was apparent then that Zakari had never intended to take Anaru against her will, and he could see the relief wash over her. He might not have a conscience, but he had lived long enough to understand what actions would give him pleasure, and taking an unwilling woman wasn't one of them.

Anaru let out a sigh, which only made his smile grow wider.

"Sit over there," Zakari said, pointing to a chair in the corner, and Anaru obliged.

"What kink are you into, handsome?" she said. "It might be a bit more, depending on—"

"Keep your mouth shut," he said, and the woman smiled.

"Okay, I'll run with that," she said. "Clothes on or off?"

Zakari walked to the dresser, placed a stack of stolen coins on top, and then turned to her. "On."

Zakari climbed onto the bed and immediately straddled her, putting all his weight on her hips before pulling up her dress until it bunched at her waist, then flipped her over, lining his cock against her.

"Alright," she said, already panting. Zakari felt the warmth of her body underneath his, the way she eagerly rolled her hips upward like she was inviting him to give her more.

He licked his lips, having every intention of doing so.

"Stay still. Don't move. Don't speak," he said. "I want to feel everything." With those words, he spat on his cock, pumping his fist around it for a few seconds and spreading the saliva all over his shaft. It was already throbbing and itching to slide inside her.

"Just not too rough—"

"Shhh," Zakari murmured, prodding his wet cock between her legs. His tip hooked against her entrance, and he fought the urge to ram himself inside her. If he were to do this, he wanted to do it slowly and savor every second. "I won't hurt you."

And with those words, he slipped his tip inside her.

Pleasure struck him in a wave of tingling sensation all at once. She was so warm, so wet, and throbbing around the head of his cock. His eyes rolled back into his skull, and he let out a low, throaty grunt. He pushed himself deeper inside until she winced, but it wasn't from the pain. Neva's body relaxed beneath him, as if savoring their connection just as much as he did.

*Perhaps this world isn't all that bad*, he thought. It felt good—so fucking good.

Neva let out a small, muffled moan, and Zakari's entire body reacted to the sound. Despite wanting to remain buried deep inside her, he pulled his hips back and then slammed himself right back in again. More pleasure tingled through him, making his hands shake as he clutched her hip.

His other hand found her ass cheek, spreading her open. With her curvy bottom, he barely saw his cock pump into her. And he wanted to. Zakari wanted to enjoy every sight, every sound, and every sensation.

After all, it was the first and last time he'd ever get to do this.

His pace picked up, and the sound of his body slapping against hers echoed through the room, mixing with the sound of Neva's wetness.

"Oh fuck...fuck," Zakari moaned. His entire body was shaking, and he was short of breath. The pleasure was so overwhelming that it made his head spin. He had the weirdest urge to caress his hands all over her body, to feel every curve, to enjoy the softness of her skin.

"I take it back," Neva grunted underneath him. "I want you to go harder." She rolled her hips back into him desperately, like she wanted him deeper inside him, so much deeper. "Oh, Gods, harder!"

Suddenly, Zakari no longer minded the words leaving her mouth, nor could he fight the urge to be closer. His free hand explored her hips as he continued to thrust harder, just as she requested.

Looking back at him over her shoulder, her expression was euphoric. Zakari wasn't one to appreciate mortals, but her beauty was undeniable—at that moment, at least. Her lips slightly parted, her expression scrunching in pleasure, and her pussy taking all of his cock.

The pleasant sensation inside him intensified with each thrust, making it hard for him to keep his composure. He wanted this to last forever, but he felt himself near a grand peak he couldn't fight.

He was shaking and panting, and his cock pulsed violently, threatening to explode at any point now.

The moment Neva's pleasure rippled through her was the moment Zakari tipped over the edge. Her pussy clenched around him so tightly, stimulating him in a way he didn't even think was possible, and he buckled over her in the all-consuming pleasure of his own.

It took him a fair amount of time to pull himself together before he finally pulled back. Neva was still a sweaty, shaky mess when he looked at her and said, "So, how much more is that going to cost?"

# 42

## MAZIE

"I've always known Dorion was a twisted monster," Kaeli said, her forehead pressed into her palms. "But I never, in my life, imagined he would go to such lengths such as this." She raised her head and looked at Nola, who had explained the events of the last three weeks, including her exploration of the destroyed undersea city.

"Are you sure it was the Eye of Dragão's Flame? That's what he called it?"

Nola nodded grimly. "I held it with my own hands," she said. "He told me that the relic wouldn't work without—"

"An anchor," Kaeli finished, blowing out a breath. "The Eye was created to be used by *two* mages, with the purpose that two must connect their powers to amplify the relic. This was a measure to prevent a rogue mage from taking the relic's power for their own whims. With Arabella dead, Dorion will be more motivated to find the Ember Guild. Unless..."

"Don't you dare!" Mazie said, knowing exactly what Kaeli was thinking.

"If it buys us time, I don't have a choice," she said. "He will come for my family to find one to replace Arabella, but if I can bargain with my father to bind you all to this world, you'll not perish if we cannot get the relic back."

"It's not a matter of 'if', Kaeli," Nola said. "My family...our friends, and innocent lives are at stake. We have to get that relic back."

Kaeli nodded and turned to Mazie, giving her a hopeful look, but Mazie couldn't share the same feeling. All she thought about was her captain and what he and his brother might be going through at that very moment.

"What about Elijah?" Janelle asked. "Could Newick power be enough, or does it have to come from this world?"

Kaeli shook her head. "I don't know. But pieces of Zakari's magic thrive within Elijah. It most likely would only feed that entity rather than destroy it. My guess is that the mage controlling his mind was trying to help him for that very purpose."

Mazie felt a level of relief, but she didn't see it in Janelle's eyes. She had just gotten him back, only to have them ripped apart again.

"Then we strike tonight. We barge into that fucking castle, rescue my captain and Elijah, and find the relic," Mazie said. "We go now, or we risk everything!"

Mazie wasn't thinking rationally, and she knew it. Their plans had changed because of the new information they received, but her urgency to rescue Lincoln was clouding her judgment.

"It's the middle of the night, Mazie," Kaeli said. "I might be able to see in the dark, but humans can't. The only reason we even left the city was due to the ground shaking and the sentries' report of fire rising from the forest. We were lucky to find them when we did. We need to come up with a better plan than marching through that forest and provoking a fight. And do you honestly want to send your friends out there after everything they've gone through? They've been assaulted and separated from their mates, and Janelle just learned that her brother killed Tegan. Nola and Janelle are finally safe, Mazie. They are in no condition to fight."

"Safe? They won't be safe if our world is fucking gone because of your father!" Mazie snapped.

Kaeli's face fell. "Mazie, are you listening to me? Dorion won't be able to harness enough magic to use that relic without another mage's power. For now, we're safe. The mage who works for him, Arenol, will not be enough, especially now that Arabella is dead. I understand your desperation to march over there, take your revenge, and save your captain, but unless you all have your heads on straight and we create a better plan than we had yesterday, we will get ourselves killed—"

"I don't want to hear those words," Mazie interrupted. "Lincoln is my captain. My *friend*. He took me in when I had no one. I don't need anyone's help here. I'll do it myself."

Kaeli's eyes dimmed. "Don't be ridiculous, Mazie. I'm not letting you go into that castle, only to be slaughtered before you reach the gates. We're talking about entire planets being destroyed. If he gets his hands on our power, that's it. It's over."

"Then get them somewhere safer if you don't think this place is enough," Mazie snapped. "But I'm leaving."

"Mazie!" Nola snapped. "I think you should listen to her. We're not about to lose you, too!"

A lone tear fell down Mazie's cheek. "Lincoln and I fought many battles without an army of magical witches behind us, so I can do it again." Mazie lifted her chin. "Then, after it's over, you'll take your portal-opening power and send us home."

"There won't be a home for you to go back to if we fuck this up," Kaeli reminded her, and Mazie flared her nostrils in anger. Kaeli's words had struck her like a dagger to the chest. This was the first time they had argued about anything.

She hated it.

"Lincoln is most likely dead, Mazie, and all my father needs is one more of us with elemental power to turn on that relic and destroy millions...if not billions."

Mazie felt the anger drop out of her, and grief replaced it with cruel swiftness. She dropped back down in the chair and ran a hand over her face.

Kaeli reached out and placed the gentle touch of her palm on Mazie's cheek. "But I think I may know what to do."

---

That next morning was considerably colder, sending an icy chill across Mazie's skin and leaving goosebumps. She rubbed her arms to keep warm as Kaeli cleared her throat and approached her.

Mazie felt her eyes burn with exhaustion. Her mind was filled with so much anxiety the previous night that when she finally went to bed, all she did was toss and turn.

"Were you able to reach him?" Mazie asked Kaeli as she stepped beside her.

Kaeli nodded. "I had to teleport close enough to the palace to link the dragon bond, but yes. Dorion is willing to meet with me, but *only* me."

After their fight, Mazie regretted her actions and sought out Kaeli to apologize. The two made amends and spent the rest of the night developing a plan, the only one with a chance of success.

Of course, Mazie didn't like the idea one bit, but it was the only option they had.

"He knows I'm lying about wanting to help him," Kaeli said, "so I expect him to have his men ready. I have the members of the Ember Guild who are willing to stand by me as bait when that happens."

"And Nomryd?" Mazie asked. "Are you sure it will work?"

Kaeli shook her head. "No, Mazie. I'm not sure about anything, but using my father's dragon beast is the only choice we have." She reached out and laced her fingers with Mazie's. "Nomryd is the last of the pure bloodline of dragons before men played with the Gods' power and created the shifters. He is bound to Dorion for now, but if we can reach his mind, we can break that link."

Mazie gave Kaeli a tight squeeze, nodded, and then headed into the dorm where Janelle and Nola were waiting.

Nola had just bathed and dressed, while Janelle held the Voleric in the center of her palm. They both still looked exhausted, but the worry was most prominent on their faces.

"You still have it?" Mazie asked, her eyes going wide.

Janelle swallowed and ran her hand down its smooth surface. "I'm afraid to use it now," she said.

"Because if you feel nothing...?" Mazie asked.

"Then she'll know he's really gone," Nola added, sliding her foot into her boot. There was a heaviness in the air all three of them shared.

"I can do it for you," Mazie said, breaking the uncomfortable silence. "From what Elijah explained to us, you don't have to possess magic to activate its power. The power comes from within the stone. If I can't reach Elijah and Lincoln's mind, I'll pretend it didn't work."

Janelle looked up and nodded. It was a ridiculous idea, and Mazie knew it, because either way, she'd know.

Mazie took the Voleric in her palm and instantly felt a nervous twitch in her stomach. She hadn't used the strange stone before. "Alright, tell me how to use this thing?"

A tap at the door drew Mazie to look over. Nola answered, and Xander walked in with Bay sitting on his shoulder. "She missed you," he said, and Mazie's eyes lit up. They had left her home last night to protect her, but being away from Bay that long was almost unbearable. She was used to the little pixie always being around her, and last night, she didn't want to wake her.

Bay flew over and sat on Mazie's shoulder. Mazie lifted a hand to her, and Bay ran her tiny fingers along her skin. "You're scared?" Bay asked.

Mazie nodded. "Kind of."

Bay's wings fluttered, and she flew over to Janelle, sitting on her lap, and looked up. Then Bay reached out her hand for Janelle.

"What is she doing?" Janelle asked, making eye contact with Mazie.

"She can sense your fear," Mazie said. "Go on, take her hand."

Janelle lowered her brow and reached out, touching Bay's tiny hand with her pinky finger. Then Janelle shut her eyes and took a slow, steady breath. The pirate had seen this before, and she knew what the elf was feeling: the euphoria of peace brought by a pixie—a rare pixie, that is.

It wouldn't shut off Janelle's thoughts of the worst, but she knew it made her feel a sense of peace for a moment—a moment to breathe.

Mazie followed and closed her eyes, holding onto the stone.

"Let's start with Lincoln; it might be easier because of your relationship as his first mate," Nola said, stepping in her direction and placing her hand on Mazie's hip. "Picture his face. When you fall, I'm here to catch you."

Nola walked her through the steps to connect, and slowly, she felt her body fall. Mazie became weightless in the siren's arms, so she cradled Nola's chest as a white cloud covered Mazie's eyes.

There wasn't a sense of foreboding like she expected. It was peaceful. The room was dark, filled with stacks of books in the far-right corner—a pillar with a golden gem at the center.

"Well," Mazie said, "This is interesting, Captain. Missed searching for treasure, have you?"

Lincoln smiled and stepped toward her, reaching out his hand. "Gods, I'm happy to see you," he said. "Where are you? Are you safe? How's my girl?"

"We're safe. We found Nola and Janelle uninjured." Mazie smiled. Lincoln's posture visibly relaxed, as if that news alleviated so much worry in his heart. "Nola's afraid," she continued. "We all are, but given how I can connect to your mind, you're alive?"

Lincoln nodded.

"And Elijah?" Mazie asked. "Are either of you injured?"

A brief pause hung between them before he said, "The dungeons collapsed when that massive dragon's tail hit the castle. They're keeping me locked inside a cage around the outside perimeter." Lincoln folded his arms and looked away.

She blinked, the words slipping from her lips. "What the fuck, Captain? So, they did catch you?" she asked. "You're not okay?"

"Mazie, you have to go on without me," Lincoln said, still refusing to look at her.

"Bullshit." She shook her head. They never left one of their own behind, and she wasn't about to start now. "Is Elijah in that cage with you?"

"I made him escape without me," Lincoln said. "It was the only way to save at least one of us. He's gone looking for you all. He's using his connection to Janelle's power. So, she needs to extend her light out for him to find her."

Mazie's breathing picked up. She knew enough about Lincoln to know he was planning something utterly reckless.

Tears of anger burned in her eyes, and panic formed in her belly. "Dammit, Lincoln! Damn you!" He was family to her, but she wanted to punch him in the face right then. "You are the captain of the fucking Sybil Curse; you are not some dumb stooge who goes into a situation this blind!"

Lincoln stepped forward and placed his hand on Mazie's shoulder. "Mazie, please, will you deliver a message to Nola for me?"

Mazie shook her head. "Fuck no! Deliver it yourself. I'm not a fucking pigeon."

Without hesitation, Mazie dropped the Voleric and quickly jumped to her feet, moving away from Nola. She couldn't look at her; she couldn't.

But when her eyes glanced up, Nola knew.

"Janelle, Elijah got away," Mazie said. "You need to get to the field beyond the trees outside the mountain right now."

Janelle nodded and stepped up, giving Nola a pained look.

"Is Lincoln alive, Mazie?" Nola asked.

Mazie nodded, and Nola released a heavy breath, but it didn't ease her pain. She placed her hand on her chest and took a few breaths to calm herself.

"Tomorrow morning," Nola growled, her eyes glowing with a siren's anger. "Tomorrow morning, we will unleash hell on these monsters until every one of those motherfuckers is dead."

# 43

## ANARU

It was early afternoon before Anaru and Zakari reached the Graeten temple. They had spent most of their trip there in silence. Anaru found it difficult to chase the images and sounds of Zakari fucking that woman away from her mind, which only made it more challenging to focus on everything else.

*At least he didn't hurt Neva*, she thought. *Or me.*

"Listen, Zakari," Anaru said as his gaze turned to look at her. Her tone was pleading. "The mages' magic is powerful. Stronger than you. Stronger than Elijah. Stronger than *anyone*. If you threaten them, they'll—"

"Kill me?" Zakari interrupted her with a smile of amusement. "Anaru, I do not quarrel with the people on this land. I've been around for billions of years. I wasn't always like this, though—once a tiny atom floating in the sea of infinity, feeding off the elements. Then, when the witches found me during a spell, their magic gave me life and a purpose. I have seen things that would haunt even me. After all this time, my purpose has come to an end. I do not care what wrath comes upon me as long as I perish in the end."

Anaru didn't know what to say. "How do you know they can even do what you want them to do?" she asked, trying to reason with him. "Even after you take their power, the remaining mage may not even understand the spell. It wasn't the mages here who helped you grow. Our worlds are similar, but the magic may not be the same."

"And if I don't try, then I remain in your world with no promise of peace."

*Peace*, she thought. *When has our world ever had peace?*

Whatever Zakari decided, she couldn't stop it from happening. She knew that now. She could only hope the mages would know what to do when they arrived.

———✦———

Graeten was far too quiet, and it put Anaru on edge. She sniffed the air but found no scents beyond the foliage. When she had been there years ago, the city was lively, with the laughter of children and the elders' songs echoing from the temple. It was a place of life and joy. Now it was gone.

The walls of the temples were crumbling, and withered vines crept along the pillars. Anaru smelt the stale scent of incense and something else inside the temple.

Anaru's stomach dropped, and she backed away from the decrepit building.

"This isn't the same place," she said, fighting back tears. "They would have never done this. It was a place of peace, spiritual guidance, and life." She looked around. The city had been completely abandoned. "Where are they?"

She took a deep breath and entered the temple, following the scent she was afraid to identify. The sight before her left her numb, and Anaru fell to her knees, burying her face in her hands. The room was filled with the bones of mages, some floating in a greenish pool beneath the bloodstained altar. A thick layer of dust, ash, and dried blood covered every surface.

It was clear that no one had stepped foot in the temple for decades.

Dead.

They were all dead.

"Oh, to the Gods. No," Anaru wept as the heartbreaking truth set in. She could barely breathe as sob after sob escaped her lips; the image of what must have taken place raced through her mind. Children screaming, parents weeping. Dragons burning innocents in the streets.

Chaos. It would've been chaos.

The Red Dragon Brotherhood had slaughtered every single one of them.

Zakari walked past her and bent to the ground, placing his hand over a pile of bones. "This was a massacre."

"I can see that, Zakari," she said sharply, her hands shaking. The sight shattered her heart into a million pieces, urging her to look away, yet she couldn't. "Some of them look as if they were holding each other. This temple has always been a place of peace but also protection." She closed her eyes, clutching her chest as she thought about the day she came to the temple over thirty years ago for safety.

The pain was not only for an entire city wiped out by hatred, but this was Julian's family—the ones who treated her as their own. The ones who had taken her in and offered nothing but kindness and love. And what did she give them back?

Death.

Anaru looked down at her hands. The reality of what all that death meant settled.

While Zakari moved to the altar on the other end of the pool, Anaru leaned back against the wall, settling on the cool marble floor. She felt defeated. Not only that, but she also felt enormous guilt that she'd carry with her for the rest of her life.

*I should have been here to help them*, she thought. *This was revenge because I left Dorion.*

"I need to know what happened to them, Zakari. Please," she begged. "Grant me this one request. Magic created you. Allow the elements that stay within them the ability to replay the past beyond their death. Their bodies will tell you everything."

He gathered several piles of bones and placed them on the altar behind the pool, hesitating as he looked at her. Anaru expected him to deny her request. After all, he didn't answer to anyone's desires but his own.

For whatever reason, he didn't. He didn't say a word, but he used a piece of broken glass from the shattered window and sliced his finger, dripping Aiden's blood at the center. He hovered his hands over the altar and began to chant. The mist-like magic turned from black to red, swirling around and mixing with the decayed bodies.

Anaru knew that the magic of death was evil, but she needed to know the truth. She took the pain of this action and added it to her crushingly guilty soul. The red mist rose to Zakari, touching his chest, and he stepped back, letting the glowing power dissipate into his body.

"What is it?" she asked, watching Zakari's eyes shift from blue to jet black to a luminous white so bright that they glowed. After chanting, he dropped his hands and glanced back up, his eyes returning to Aiden's natural blue. "Please—I need to know."

"You won't like what I tell you, Anaru," he said coldly. "Are you certain you want to know?"

Deep inside, Anaru already knew the answer. She only needed confirmation. "Yes."

"The Red Dragon Brotherhood invaded the temple a decade ago, resulting in the deaths of all those who practiced magic within the Ember Guild. They blamed them after snake-like creatures slipped through the portal twenty-eight years ago. Once Dorion took power, they set out to bring those who caused it to justice."

Anaru's lips parted, and she gasped. She never would have imagined the aftermath of her departure into the Earth realm.

"The Vipers, they called them, killed thousands, nearly wiping Dragão Terra's populus out," he continued. "Once they killed the Vipers off, Kaeli, who had barely turned eighteen, came into the temple and warned the mages to flee."

"Kaeli did that?" Anaru said through tears as pride consumed her. Despite the massacre that happened at this place, there was still something for her to hold on to—a glimmer of hope.

"It was too late, though," he said. "Kaeli had little time, only being able to save the children and their parents, along with a few teachers, to train them. Those who stayed behind to protect their home are the ones you see here. They sacrificed themselves to buy time for the children. The new emperor of this world had to blame someone for what the Vipers had done, and mages became their pariahs."

*Did Dorion really kill these people because he was jealous that I loved Julian more than him?* she wondered. *Or did he really believe he was administering justice? Or both?*

The Ember Guild, aware of her pregnancy with Julian's child, speculated that the baby would inherit Julian's abilities. Once she fell into the Earth realm, Anaru knew. Anaru knew that it was Kaeli who unintentionally opened that portal that day—a secret she had planned to take to her grave.

Though Anaru had no control over what had happened that day when the portal opened into another world, the heaviness of guilt ate away at her. Either way, the Ember Guild's elders made the ultimate sacrifice.

For her and for Kaeli.

"Kaeli and her cousin, Xander, told the elders they were heading north to a hidden city within the Mountain of Hera," Zakari said. "They were going to build another home to keep them safe." His steps echoed as he circled the temple, unfazed by the gruesome knowledge. That was how she knew there were no feelings inside him. That place was enough to make even the coldest of men weep.

"The Mountain of Hera?" she repeated, looking up in surprise.

She couldn't quite understand why they'd be hiding so close to their enemy, but she had to trust that Kaeli had her reasons to do so. However, it was the only mountain on their planet where fresh water flowed beneath it, stretching over a mile. Their survival there might have been the only option.

"What now?" she asked. "I did what you wanted. I brought you to the mages, and no one is left to help you."

"Then we shall travel to the mountain," he said, returning to her. "If Kaeli is with them and she sees you, I promise, she will give me whatever I want."

Anaru resisted as Zakari grabbed her arm and pulled her with him. "And then what?" she seethed. "Kaeli will not sacrifice hundreds of mages for one person—not even her mother—and I don't even have the magic to open up a mountain when she doesn't."

Zakari slowly turned, and his lip quirked up. "I don't doubt she'll keep them safe, but let's remember one thing. I require the magic of several to become whole, but I only need *one* of them to end me." He reached out, touching Anaru's cheek with his other hand. "And Kaeli will do just fine."

# 44

## JANELLE

Janelle quickly changed clothes and ran out the door of the dormitories. She made her way to the mountain portal before a guard stopped her, but she gave him a pleading expression.

"It's all right, open the portal," Kaeli said to him. Janelle nodded in gratitude and stepped through the dark vortex. She came upon their small boat and quickly rowed down the river and out of the cave.

Once she reached the shore, she hurried down the long path leading to the fields Mazie had described.

She reached the grass and stopped, looking around for any sign of Elijah. When she saw nothing, she held her hands outstretched and began channeling her light, the veins of power searching for its shadow counterpart.

But there was nothing. Not even a whisper of their connection.

Janelle pushed more of her power into the channel where Elijah's magic had once been, trying to find him.

"Elijah, please, where are you?" she cried out, tears of panic burning down her cheeks. Janelle searched the fields and forest of the mountain again.

She wondered if their connection was strong enough for him to feel her light, even from when she was on the other side of that mountain.

"Elijah!" Her voice strained her throat as her cry echoed through the trees.

Janelle fell to her knees, the sharp rocks and stiff grasses digging into her skin.

There, she wept, overwhelmed by the possibility that their bond had indeed been broken and that, instead, he had been traveling in the opposite direction. She didn't want to face the idea that it was the end for them, but she couldn't bear the weight of it on her heart.

Clouds passed overhead as she pressed her face into her hands. Her light magic had spilled from her fingers and swirled around her like a cloud caught in a storm. Janelle knew that the Brotherhood would succeed if she broke now, and Elijah would be lost forever. She had to stand, move forward, and run until she found him. Even if she ran to the end of the world.

"Do not cry, little elf," a deep voice said from above while dark magic surged like a river breaking free from its dam, rushing down her spine.

When she looked up, the sun shone through the trees against Elijah's jet-black hair like a beautiful halo. He knelt before her, placing his warm palm on her cheek. For a moment, he looked like a god, but she feared he was some hallucination.

She parted her lips and let out the breath she held. "Y-you found us," she stammered. The next moment, she threw herself at him, embracing Elijah tightly around the waist and causing him to topple over.

"I found *you*," he said, wrapping his muscular arms around her and pulling her closer. The rest of the world vanished around them. Every single worry and heavy thought she ever had was gone. Janelle felt her magic trickle out of her, searching for Elijah's and intertwining with it. Their powers slid together perfectly, and the connection was renewed, stronger than before. It spread around them, forming a protective shield as they got lost in each other. No one could hear them. No one could see them.

Janelle straddled Elijah and pressed her mouth firmly against his, kissing him with an intense passion that consumed them both. Their tongues danced with each other while one of his hands cupped her ass, giving it a tight squeeze.

"Fuck, woman," Elijah said, breaking the kiss. The look in his eyes was pure worship as he caressed her body. "May I curse the gods that kept us apart?"

"Curse them until the stars crash around us. Never again," Janelle said, burning with desire to have him closer. It clouded any rational thought—anything other than him. She reached out and untied his pants, and Elijah helped her get them down just enough so his cock would pull out, free and ready for her. His breath was heavy against her lips as Janelle slid her leather pants down, exposing her already wet pussy.

There was no time to disrobe or find a secluded place. She'd have him right there and then, in the middle of a forest. And she didn't care about the consequences that may follow.

Elijah lifted his back slightly from the ground, ripping her shirt down the center, bringing her pert nipple into his mouth, and sucking and tasting her. Janelle's head fell back as she lowered herself onto his cock, letting it slide inside her with ease. It had been far too long since the last time they had been this close to each other, and she ached for him to consume her.

"Gods, I missed you," she moaned breathlessly, her eyes rolling back as she felt him push deeper. "I missed you inside me and your lips all over my body." His hands tightened their grip around her at those words, drawing her closer. Elijah's tongue moved around her nipple, circling and toying with it.

He was driving her mad.

"I missed you, too. So much it hurt." He panted as she bounced up and down, feeling the entirety of his length hit her inner core. One of his hands snuck in between her thighs, reaching for her clit and stimulating it softly. It sent another tingle of pleasure through her, making her shudder in sheer bliss. "I swear to the gods, Janelle, I will never let you go again."

He lifted his hips then, ramming himself into her with more intensity. Each thrust had her shaking. Her hands entangled in his dark hair, noticeably longer than before, as she dragged his lips to hers. She ached to kiss him.

She ached to have him everywhere, all at once.

"Elijah!" she cried out, but he silenced her words with another rough kiss. Then his free hand gripped her hip, rolling them over. Now that her back met the ground and he was on top of her, he was in complete control of his movements.

The way he moved was hard and rough, but Janelle could practically taste the need and love laced in it. It made her head swirl.

One of his hands grabbed her thigh, spreading her open for him, while the other continued to work its way around her clit, only heightening the pleasure that flooded her.

"Elijah," she moaned against his lips desperately, "Elijah, I'm so close. You're going to make me—"

"Come all over my cock," he told her, planting a few kisses on her lips. It made it harder for her to breathe. "I need to feel you come for me, my love."

Having him close like this erased all the pain and suffering they had gone through for the last month—at least in that moment. All that existed was bliss—undeniable, indescribable bliss. A few more harsh thrusts of his hips, and she was there, screaming against his lips as she trembled underneath him, coming all over his cock.

"Fuck, Janelle, you feel..." Elijah's own words were interrupted as he reached his own peak with a heavy grunt, and his lips remained pressed against hers, refusing to pull back.

Janelle didn't mind. She wanted to bask in his presence forever.

At last, he broke the kiss, but their bodies remained intimately intertwined. He shifted onto his back, bringing her on top of him as his hands secured her in place. Janelle laid her head on his chest and listened to his heart's dancing beat as he spoke.

"I can stay like this forever," he whispered. His fingers were all over her, caressing and ensuring she remained close to him. Their breathing was heavy, and Janelle's body was still shivering from her release.

Janelle placed a gentle touch against his cheek. "Don't leave my side again, please."

Elijah nodded. "I will burn this world down if anyone tries to take you away from me again. I'm not going anywhere, love."

# 45

## MAZIE

Kaeli placed her sword back in the sheath and tore off her blouse to change into a new one. Tension still lingered between them, and Mazie knew she needed to address it, the part they *didn't* discuss when they laid out their plan of attack against the Brotherhood.

As Kaeli stepped by Mazie to head into the washroom, Mazie reached out. "Can we talk?" she asked. "About what happens *after* we defeat your father?"

Kaeli stood there, still shirtless, and turned around. "Mazie, you came here to banish a creature into our world and then got stuck. I get it. Your situation is not ideal, and I understand your goal is to return to your realm. But I'm not ready for you to leave yet."

Mazie's body visibly tensed at her words. "I don't know what I'm doing," she admitted.

"Neither do I," Kaeli said. "But I'm willing to try. Are you?"

Mazie didn't know the answer to that question. She didn't expect to fall for someone in another world, but she also couldn't fight the attraction. There was that magnetic pull that beckoned her toward Kaeli, and it felt like the gods themselves had crafted fate to bring them together.

"Not after meeting you, I don't know," Mazie admitted as her heart ached to touch her. It wasn't just because it was difficult to focus when Kaeli's naked breasts were right in front of her; she meant every word. "But it feels right. Gods, nothing has ever felt more right to me."

Kaeli's expression softened. She stepped forward and placed a hand on Mazie's shoulder, gingerly running her fingers down her arm.

Immediate goosebumps prickled her skin.

*She really needs to put her shirt back on*, Mazie thought. Her mind felt tangled in a web of a thousand thoughts, making it impossible for her to think straight. Not that it was ever an option around Kaeli.

"Mazie," she said, placing her other hand on her cheek and stepping even closer until her bare breasts pressed against her. "I will say it again. I don't want you to leave."

"Why?" Mazie asked, swallowing hard. "What would this world offer me that mine won't?"

"Me," Kaeli whispered, and Mazie's entire body burned at the thought. She was right. She could return to her world and even meet other women, but none would ever be her. "I know you'll be happy wherever you go. So, maybe I'm being selfish. But being around you, for the first time in my life, I have butterflies in my stomach."

Mazie's lips parted. *That cannot possibly be true*, she thought.

"You have butterflies in this world, too?" Mazie asked, but she couldn't suppress her smile.

Kaeli mirrored her features, but then she bit her bottom lip, shivering as she spoke, while her lips curled into a playful smile. "I'm getting cold now," she said. Mazie spotted the way her nipples hardened and the prickles that rose all over her skin. She wasn't lying.

Mazie trailed her hand down Kaeli's bare chest, causing her to shudder more. "I better do something about that, then," she murmured softly. "Would you like me to warm you up a little?"

Kaeli nodded eagerly as Mazie slid her back against the wall, pressing her against it. Then she snaked her hand down between Kaeli's legs, slowly prodding at her entrance. She was already aroused, and Mazie throbbed at the wetness that greeted her fingers.

"So ready for me," Mazie said as Kaeli spread her thighs further apart to give Mazie better access. "You're a needy little dragon, aren't you?" Her fingers dipped inside, still merely teasing, but it was enough for Kaeli to twitch around her fingers.

"Only for a certain pirate," Kaeli whispered, her words mixing with a gasp.

One more of Mazie's fingers slipped inside while Kaeli moved against it, rolling her hips into the fingers.

*Gods,* Mazie said in her thoughts. *This woman will drive me insane.*

Mazie leaned forward, meeting Kaeli's lips with a passionate kiss that caused Kaeli to let out small, muffled sounds. It was like Mazie fed off them; they prompted her to slide her fingers inside Kaeli deeper, resting a thumb on her clit as she fucked her.

Kaeli whimpered against her lips, and her hands roamed all over Mazie, drawing her closer. The way Mazie's hand moved showed just how desperate she was for the woman. Back and forth, back and forth, harder this time, again and again.

"Mazie!" Kaeli cried out in bliss as they broke the kiss.

She wanted to lose herself in Kaeli until the end of time or, at least, until she felt the dragon come all over her fingers, throbbing and squirming as she rode the pleasure. In Mazie's eyes, Kaeli was always beautiful, but right then, as pleasure painted her face, she looked like fucking perfection. Once Kaeli managed to catch her breath and recover from her blissful peak, Mazie dragged her fingers out.

Kaeli bit her bottom lip, adjusting her underdrawers. "Don't leave me, Mazie. Stay."

Mazie wanted to say yes, but she couldn't find the words. All she wanted was to lie with Kaeli until morning, feeling the warmth of her embrace and never letting go. "How about for right now," Mazie said, "I join you in the bath?"

# 46

## KAELI

Kaeli assisted Mazie in securing her chest armor and adjusting the back strap. "Is that tight enough?" she asked as Mazie turned around to smile at her.

"It's perfect. Thank you."

Bay's wings fluttered as she hovered over Mazie's shoulder, her tiny pink light glowing in the early morning hue.

Mornings usually symbolized a new beginning and hope that life would be better, at least amongst her people in Dragão Terra. That day, however, the morning felt particularly heavy. The stakes were much higher now because they had more to lose.

*So much more,* Kaeli thought to herself as she turned to Mazie.

Xander looked up at the sky. "The sun is over the trees now." He turned to Kaeli. "Dorion should be waiting for you."

They stood, hidden within the forest, only two hundred yards from the treeline before the field leading to the castle. This distance was far enough for Kaeli to connect to Dorion but not enough for any dragons flying overhead to see them.

Kaeli closed her eyes and felt Dorion's presence. He didn't seem furious then, almost oddly calm, but there was also a lingering sense of hurt and grief inside him. She felt it as if it were her own. Somehow, that was even worse than his anger.

"Dorion wants me to come alone," Kaeli said. "He promised not to attack unless we threaten him first."

"And you believe him?" Mazie asked, shaking her head. "Forget it. There's no way I'm letting you go there and face that asshole alone. I'd sooner—"

"I can tell through the dragon bond if he's lying," Kaeli interrupted her. "He's telling the truth."

Mazie looked at Xander like she was asking for confirmation that this was a terrible idea, but her cousin nodded. "You better get going, then," he said.

Kaeli stepped forward, but Mazie reached out, wrapping her fingers lightly over her wrist to stop her. Concern shone in Mazie's eyes. Despite Kaeli's ability to feel Dorion's potential deceit through the bond, Mazie still asked, "Are you sure you don't want me to go with you?"

Kaeli squeezed her hand. "I know we initially agreed for you to go to the meeting with me, but you're safer here with Xander until the mages file through," she said, brushing her thumb against Mazie's cheek. "I'll signal when to come. My hope is that we can come to a peaceful agreement with no one dying. But knowing my father..." Kaeli stepped forward outside of the forest, her blue eyes shifting to amber-gold. The urge to kiss Mazie was there, but instead, she gave her one more nod. "Nola?" she called, and the siren stepped forward. "Be ready."

Once she connected with Nomryd the night they escaped, she realized the beast was their only hope of surviving any battle with the shifters, and any mistake she made from that point on could determine whether they were left standing by the end.

Within a moment, Kaeli's wings emerged from her back, and she dropped to her hands and knees, which quickly morphed into claws and scales. Xander hurriedly attached a leather satchel with spare clothes and armor to her foreleg. Then the mage-born dragon launched into the sky, away from the rising sun and toward the palace.

———◇———

Kaeli soon arrived at the smoldering, broken remains of the palace. She landed just outside the palace gates to return to her human form and quickly dressed in armor, securing her white hair in a ponytail. She headed for the gates, where her father and Merrick waited.

Dorion and Merrick were clad in armor that blazed like the color of flames. It was a symbol of mourning for the fallen dragons.

When Kaeli approached the two men, it was she who spoke first.

"From the looks of things, your empire seems to be shaken. I'm sorry about the loss of Kade. I once cared for him, too." She lifted her chin. "However, I am not sorry that he's dead. You let him roam unchecked for too long, and after what he did to Janelle, his punishment was justly administered."

After all the cruelty Dorion and his brothers had done to *her* people for nearly thirty years, she held no love for that false family.

Xander and the mages were her only family now until she could find her mother.

Dorion and Merrick looked at her with disgust, but she only bared her teeth at them, showing that she no longer cared.

"My child, I can't stop what's going to happen," Dorion said, taking a step forward. "If you're with the enemy, I can't protect you. Kaeli, please understand that I'm doing what is right for this empire."

"What's right? You can stop lying," Kaeli said. "You're going to kill innocent lives. If you truly believe there's no hope of saving the other realms from collapse, we can find another way to draw the darkness from the male elf and send the others back to their world. I will work with Arenol to create a spell and then use their Voleric pendant to tap into the elf's mind and find out where he is. I swear to you. If you consider this option, I will return to the palace and do whatever you want. I'll even take responsibility for what happened twenty-eight years ago. I'll confess to the Council of Drakentos while you beg them to show mercy to me. If they do, I'll even agree to marry whomever you choose. I can replace Arabella, and you can use my magic however you wish." She bit the inside of her cheek, hating her next words. "I will even call you *Father*."

Dorion's forehead furrowed like he was considering her offer, but Merrick snorted.

Kaeli shot him a stern glance. "What's so funny, Uncle? You know this is what he's always wanted."

She looked back at Dorion, and he arched a brow. "As much as I want you home, my daughter, there is a much bigger picture here. It isn't just pulling that darkness from the elf. If we do not seal those portals, we risk more lives lost if another deadly creature wreaks havoc on us. The only way to be safe is by closing the portals forever." When she said nothing, his lip curled up. "Then the decision has been made. Besides, there really isn't much you're offering. We slaughtered the Council of Drakentos years ago, Kaeli. They don't care who let those Vipers in...now that they're ash."

Kaeli's stomach dropped as she stared at him in disbelief. She must have heard him wrong. Killing the Council of Drakentos meant there were no laws that could halt his madness. He was free to commit genocide. "There are millions of people on Earth alone. How can you sleep at night, knowing they'll all perish by your hand?"

"Oh, I'll sleep very well, trust me," Dorion said. Kaeli realized his plan was far more sinister than anything she could have ever imagined. Even if they could release the darkness from Aiden without destroying the other realms, he would destroy them anyway. The only one he cared about was himself and his illusion of ultimate control.

Dorion stepped forward and tried to reach out, but she flinched away. "You cannot undo what you have already done," she added. "But you and I can still repair what we have let destroy us all these years." She lowered her brow and looked at him with desperation. "Throw the Eye of Dragão's Flame back into that sea, Father. We will find a way to help Janelle's brother without anyone dying. Do it now, or you will lose me forever."

A barely noticeable smirk reached Dorion's lips. "I think I've already lost you, Kaeli. It happened a long time ago when you chose those filthy mages over us."

Dorion took one step back before swiftly turning into a dragon. His massive tail cracked against the castle's stone gates, sending more rubble tumbling down. He let out an earth-shaking roar and slammed his enormous body down. However, the trembling ground didn't cease, and Kaeli realized it was not her father's doing.

Nomryd emerged from behind the castle, and an icy fear skittered down Kaeli's spine. Keeping her mind calm, she conjured fire in one of her hands, its warmth radiating against her skin. "You can use Nomryd to *try* to attack me all you want, *Dorion*. But you know that once you two are dead, his power and will are mine. This is your last chance. Merrick, stop your dragon now."

Merrick only chuckled at her, his cold eyes glowing bright yellow. He would shift soon, and she'd face two shifters and one full-blooded dragon alone.

With a deep breath, Kaeli made her proclamation, using her dragon power to amplify her voice. "As the true heir to the Rylanthion Empire and mage of the Ember Guild, I decree that the Amulius brothers and the Red Dragon Brotherhood are traitors and murderers to Dragão Terra. I sentence you to death!"

She turned around and threw her hand out to the side, opening two giant portals a hundred feet from behind her.

"Harakaei!" she shouted.

Mazie had asked her that morning what the signal to attack would be, and Kaeli grinned. *"It is the ancient word for 'battle,' and it's like a warrior's cry before going to fight."*

Hundreds of men and women charged through the portals, their powers blazing as they headed to the castle across the field.

Kaeli shifted into her dragon and let out an ear-splitting roar before launching into the sky.

To death and war.

# 47

## MAZIE

After jumping through the portal, Mazie unsheathed her sword, its sharp edge glinting in the sunlight. She took up the cry and ran toward the palace, leading a group of mages behind her.

Xander shifted and soared into the sky to confront the Brotherhood's army that had taken to the air. Janelle, Nola, and Elijah raced across the field, flanking Mazie on both sides.

Bay was no longer in sight, but Mazie had to trust that the little pixie was safe. Mazie had insisted that Bay stay behind with the children, but she refused to leave the pirate's side. So, reluctantly, Mazie allowed her to come.

As she ran, she felt a deep, heavy feeling in her chest. Her mind went to Kaeli and her safety.

*I shouldn't have let her go alone,* Mazie chided, trying to ignore that weight in her mind. She looked upward as she and the mages cleared the field and entered the castle grounds. Dozens of dragons flew above, shooting streams of fire down on their heads.

Mazie dodged an attack as the fire scorched the grass right beside her and looked around frantically. She felt slightly relieved when she spotted Kaeli in the sky, heading back toward them.

Kaeli was fine—*for now.*

Mazie looked ahead in time to see a bare-chested man charging at her, a broadsword swinging high above his head. She sidestepped the man's blow and parried it with her own. Effortlessly, she slashed her blade up, drawing a spray of blood that splattered her sword. The man staggered back, his eyes blazing red.

*Oh, shit!* she frantically cursed in her thoughts.

"Mazie, down!" Elijah shouted, throwing his power out. The man's attempt to shift ended when Elijah's smoke grabbed his throat and decapitated him.

In the corner of her eye, Mazie spotted Nola charging toward the castle, a bow and quiver strapped to her back. Most of Dorion's men were so focused on their attack that she remained undetected. She had only one goal: to find Lincoln.

Xander joined Kaeli in the air, extending his wings and flying so high he almost reached the clouds before they whirled back to the ground, flames spewing from his jaws.

Each swipe of Mazie's sword as she slashed through Dorion's men gave her power, strength, courage, and might. There was so much happening all at once, but Mazie was hyperaware of her surroundings. A pirate was always dancing with the possibility of death, so being keenly aware was part of her instincts.

A burst of Elven light in Mazie's peripheral had Mazie looking at Janelle. She had never seen Elven light used in combat before, and the elf woman was wielding it with admirable proficiency. As three guards advanced toward her, she extended her hands and spun around, summoning an immense power that struck them in the chest, reducing the men to mere ash and bones.

A male ran up to Mazie, throwing a punch at her face. Mazie luckily caught the fist before it could break her nose. She yanked the wrist down and twisted hard, feeling bones crack. She took her sword and drove it through the man's chest, dropping his corpse to the ground.

When she wrenched the sword free, the massive palace dragon Kaeli had told her about soared over her head.

It was time.

The beast swiftly flew toward Kaeli, razor-sharp teeth ready to rip into her flesh.

"Oh, fuck, Kaeli!" Mazie shouted. She looked around and saw Bay flying toward her.

"Bay! Bay, I need your dust," she begged, her voice sounding desperate in her ears. "Send me up there. Now!" Mazie never once ordered Bay to use her power; she had always *requested* it and never argued when the pixie said no.

Bay shook her head frantically, protest evident in her eyes. "You'll die," her tiny voice croaked. "No, Mazie."

"Fuck! Bay, give me the damn pixie dust. I have to help her!" Mazie screeched, feeling like she was about to lose her damn mind. She was moments away from a catastrophe; she didn't have the time to fight with her pixie.

But Bay shook her head again, fluttering her wings and pointing up.

"Bay!" Mazie yelled again, even more desperate now, as another one of Dorion's men lunged at her. Her blade sliced right through his throat mercilessly, his head rolling on the blood-soaked ground.

As Mazie looked back to the battlefield, a woman in mid-transition charged toward her, her fingers morphing into sharp talons. Mazie couldn't defend herself before the woman knocked Mazie back with her strong, red-violet wing. She flew backward, her head colliding against a hard surface that had her surroundings fade to blackness momentarily. Mazie groaned in pain, reaching for the injured spot, where she felt a warm liquid oozing out.

Looking back at the sky, she saw Kaeli move through the clouds with Xander flying beside her, attempting to fend off Nomryd, who obeyed Dorion's will.

Mazie felt disoriented, her head filled with a thick fog that clouded her thoughts. As everything around her swayed, she felt an overwhelming need to close her eyes and disappear.

# 48

## NOLA

Nola approached the castle, scanning the area and looking for the cages Lincoln said he was in when he spoke to Mazie through the Voleric.

She looked around again and spotted the twisted metal of a gate leading to the gardens jutting up from the dirt. As she crept closer, she heard the muffled shouts of a man straight down the alley flushed to the castle wall.

*Lincoln!*

She bolted in that direction but quickly ducked behind some brush as she watched Lincoln being dragged out of the cage, now flanked by two guards covered with vine-like tattoos prominent in the sunlight.

"Shit," she cursed quietly.

They had Lincoln bound in chains that wrapped around his wrists and neck, and he was being dragged across the dirt like livestock.

Nola knew all she had in her arsenal was precision with the bow. Her siren call wasn't effective against the dragon shifters. They weren't entirely creatures, nor were they weak-willed men. Only a well-placed arrow would do, but she needed a distraction.

*It's time to summon the beast,* she said. It was the one piece of the plan they all believed would help them win. They needed the dragon to submit to Nola.

She looked back to where the mages and dragons were locked in battle, blood and fire staining the dry grass in shades of crimson and black. The palace dragon, the one called Nomryd, was wrestling with Kaeli, attempting to pin her down. However, Kaeli was able to outmaneuver the beast, shooting fire at his belly and tail.

It was now her time to act. That brief connection with Nomryd the other night gave her hope.

Nola had never tried her siren call on a *real* dragon before, but if there were any truth about the gifts of her people, the Shelei Sirens, the dragon would submit to her power. Kaeli just wasn't sure if it would work in a different realm.

Nola took a deep breath and tried to concentrate on the dragon. Her heart was beating frantically, so Nola practiced some deep breathing to calm her mind. If she was too agitated, the call's power wouldn't work, and it *had* to work.

The siren closed her eyes, willing her mind to settle as she tapped into her power. She released a haunting sound of a lullaby that vibrated in her chest. The beautiful notes echoed through the sky, its energy wrapping around the dragon to keep it in place. Immediately Nomryd resisted, using its wings to pull back and fly higher into the sky, but she held on.

Her eyes glowed as Nomryd bellowed, swinging his massive head to look straight at her. Yellow beams of light emanated from the dragon's eyes, as if piercing straight into her soul. Dorion's influence over the dragon was frayed at best while he fought the others, so it was easy for Nola's magic to replace his power with hers. With only one more shift of resistance, Nomryd's eyes softened, while wings flapped wildly in the sky, keeping his attention on the siren. As she sang, the dragon stilled, and the connection sprang to life again, snapping into place.

She had him.

"Come to me, beast," she whispered into the wind. Nomryd stretched out his wings, soaring down to her, and crashed to the ground, creating large craters in the grass with his paws. The dragon lowered his head to her and let out what sounded like an eager whine. Nola reached up and stroked his snout, her call now a subtle hum.

"Nomryd, I command you to kill your oppressors. Kill the enemies who kept you in a cage for so long. Kill them all!"

The dragon lifted his head and roared again, launching into the sky and unleashing a vicious attack on Dorion's men.

Now that the dragon had thoroughly distracted guards and the Brotherhood army alike, Nola sprinted back to where those two were dragging Lincoln. She came upon them staring at the sky, clearly baffled as to why Nomryd was killing their comrades. Nola pulled out an arrow, nocked it, and fired on the first man before he turned his head to see her.

He fell without making a sound. The second shouted and shoved Lincoln to the ground. Nola ran toward him, pulling her sword free and swinging it at his neck. The man blocked the charge with his sword and kicked Nola hard in the chest. She flew back, barely able to keep her feet under her and not topple over. The guard raised his blade again to strike when chains whipped around his neck, yanking him off-balance. Lincoln had taken the slack of his bindings and used them to lash around the guard.

Nola flung the blade forward, releasing her grip on the hilt. The sword flew with immaculate accuracy and pierced the man right at the center of his forehead.

Lincoln and Nola's eyes met, and the world around them stilled for a moment; the screams, the torment, and the sound of swords clanging against each other all tuned out as they looked at each other.

As the guard went slack against the chain, Lincoln dropped the body to the ground. Nola pulled the sword from the shifter's head and then threw herself into Lincoln's arms. He wrapped a tight embrace around her as he stumbled backward, letting out a loud sigh of relief.

"To the stars, Nola," he said, his lips close to her ear. "That was bloody sexy." Nola pulled back slightly, pressing an eager kiss to his lips. Now that he was beside her, there wasn't anything she couldn't face. As she forced herself to separate her lips from his, she jammed her sword into the links of the chain, breaking them apart.

Nola winked. "Now, let's get the hell out of here."

As Nola and Lincoln rushed to the field, she spotted the crew fighting for their lives. Just as they were almost within reach of Janelle and Elijah, she felt her legs stiffen. A tingling sensation moved through her ankles and up to her knees until her body could no longer move.

It wasn't just happening to her. Everyone on the battlefield stopped moving as a violet-colored power crept along the grass, freezing everyone in place.

"What's happening?" Nola cried out, turning to Lincoln and gasping in horror. The light had left his green eyes as if in a void. His arm was outstretched, his fingertips barely grazing the fabric of her shirt before becoming paralyzed.

Nola tried to move, but it was no use. Something had rooted them all to the ground, and they had become living statues.

# 49

## ANARU

Once they reached the cliffs, Anaru stepped onto the path leading to the docks. "The ships are this way, Zakari. We have to travel ten miles east to reach the Mountain of Hera."

"There," he said. "We're changing course to head northwest instead."

"Zakari, that's the palace. If you want to reach the mages, it wouldn't be in the heart of enemy territory."

He shook his head. "They aren't inside the mountain anymore. I can sense their power." Zakari closed his eyes, and a trickle of smoke dripped from his fingers, flowing over the path leading to the palace. "I'm sure of it," he said, opening his eyes slowly. "The mages are already there." He pulled the power back into himself.

Anaru turned to face the palace. "Are you sure?" she asked. Not that she wanted Zakari to reach her family and take their power, but the magic he poured into her struggled in the fight against him. As Zakari stepped forward, she willed herself to step back, not wanting him to touch her. "Let's think this through—"

As she pulled back, he reached out and grabbed her arm, yanking her forward until she slammed into his chest. "Is my power giving up on you now?" She frantically shook her head right before Zakari's lips crashed against hers and pushed more of his power inside her. Anaru felt its dark presence consume her. It left a bitter aftertaste inside her body, stripping her of her free will again.

When Zakari released the kiss, he smiled. His fingers brushed against her cheek. "I need you to cooperate, Anaru. Now, walk."

He held out his hand for her. Anaru looked at it momentarily before she reached out and took it. As they shifted course toward the palace, she no longer had the strength to fight him.

———◇———

Once they crossed the border of the palace's territory and passed the river feeding into the land, Anaru paused, her stomach aching. An uncomfortable familiarity overwhelmed her as she took in the surroundings. It had been years since she stepped foot on her family's land, the place that used to be her home.

The breeze that brushed by her brought a bitter smell to her senses, and she sniffed. "Do you smell that?" Anaru asked, afraid of the answer she knew deep down.

Zakari smiled and nodded. "It smells like a battle is being waged. The air is thick with smoke," he sniffed. "And burnt flesh."

Anaru's chest tightened, her mind reeling with different scenarios. Was Kaeli there? Could she have been hurt? "Something is wrong. We need to move...." Her words trailed off as she hurried closer to the castle, entering the field bordering the gates.

Anaru dropped her hand from Zakari's grasp and ran to where the great iron gates lay in ruin. She couldn't believe the level of destruction that was before her.

When she drew closer, she saw that the Brotherhood's army was out in full force, seemingly locked in battle with the mages.

*The mages! How?* she thought. *What are they doing here?*

Fear choked her breath as she scanned the grounds. Dragons and humans alike lay dead, their mingled blood and flesh soaking the grass. Some bodies were so severely burnt that Anaru couldn't distinguish any features. Those who were standing seemed to be frozen in place.

"What is this?" she asked.

Zakari brushed past her but stayed flush with the trees; his gaze was fixated on something further ahead. Anaru started after him, trying not to look at the bodies littering the field in front of them.

When she caught up with Zakari at the edge of the forest, he gestured to a woman with long blue-white hair dancing in the wind.

Zakari turned to her. "Go find what you've been looking for, Anaru. I'll watch from the forest until you call for me."

Just a few feet in front of the woman stood Dorion, the man she rejected all those years ago.

Her stomach lurched at just the sight of his face.

Another woman stood next to Dorion. Anaru recognized her as Arenol, one of the mage twins, who had been a mere child when she last saw her. She looked for Arenol's twin sister, Arabella, but saw no sign of the second mage on the field.

The wind shifted, and Anaru caught the scent of the white-haired woman, making her heart stutter. Even without seeing her face, Anaru knew who that precious girl was. Her body tingled with warmth. It didn't matter that death lay between them, for in that moment, Anaru was truly happy.

The bond she felt with her daughter glowed, having been there since Anaru felt that flutter of life in her belly all those years ago. Her daughter was there, standing on the field in front of the palace, and a realization struck her.

"It all makes sense now, doesn't it?" Zakari said. "Go on, Anaru. Look her in the eyes, and say what you need to say before it's too late."

The oracle's vision was coming true.

Anaru had spent countless hours contemplating Borenna's words from the day Kaeli was born twenty-eight years ago. The weight of the oracle's prophecy had always haunted her. She would bring *darkness* into their world...and she did: Zakari—leading her to that other vision that she received in Myloria.

Darkness led her to her daughter. Her *light*.

And she was in danger.

# 50

## KAELI

Kaeli's eyes widened in horror as the world around her suddenly came to a standstill. They were all frozen to the ground—rendered vulnerable. The one hope they had to defeat her father—Nomryd—had been killed.

She raised her hands as her father's mage moved closer. "Stop, Arenol. Please don't do this." Anger burned through her. They were so close to victory, but Arenol appeared on the battlefield and cast a paralysis spell that the other mages and Kaeli couldn't counter in time.

She had been battling Nomryd high above the clashing armies when Nola subdued the dragon with her call. Once in control of Nomryd, Nola sent the dragon to attack Dorion's men on the ground. When Kaeli descended, she spotted Mazie lying prone against an outcropping of rocks. Terror and dread twisted her insides at the thought of Mazie dead. Kaeli reached out with her magic, touching that faint link she had felt in Dragon's Cove. An answering flicker broke the dread. Mazie was alive, but she was unconscious. By the time Kaeli had landed and shifted back to her human form, that damned paralyzing spell had seized everyone except for her. Meanwhile, Arenol used another spell to seize Nomryd and drive the beast to the ground, killing him.

They were doomed. Her father had turned the tides.

Kaeli quickly slipped on her clothes and armor, which were left on the grass where she transitioned, and rushed to her father with one of the mage's swords tightly in her grip. But she stopped twenty feet from him. "It's a little ironic using a mage's power to win, isn't it, Dorion?" she asked. "And kill the dragon who you fought for years to claim as your own." When he didn't answer, Kaeli pressed on. "Do you believe their value matters less than your own?"

Dorion pulled a golden orb from his pocket, and Kaeli stilled as he handed off the Eye of Dragāo's Flame to Arenol. It glowed the moment it touched her palm, the gold shimmering so brightly that she had to shield her eyes briefly before the light settled.

Kaeli had never seen the relic with her own eyes. It was a story told to her as a child, the magical weapon the Ember Guild created centuries ago to seal the portals if it ever became too dangerous. The relic that, for years, had been kept safe beneath the sea.

She watched as Arenol began to murmur, moving her hands around the orb, which began to glow again. Suddenly, there was a flash of light, and something slammed into Kaeli's body, seizing her magic. But rather than drain it, Arenol used the light to tether Kaeli's power to the Eye before reconnecting her own. "Dorion, stop!" Kaeli shouted, falling to her knees. She pushed into her magic to fight off the Eye's power that latched onto her.

"I wish I could," Dorion said. "If we don't do this, the last remaining lives in Dragão Terra will be doomed. We don't know where that darkness is, but it's out there, and it's only a matter of time before it corrupts our own mages like it had the witches on Earth. Then we're all fucked."

"You don't know that! Do you want to go down this path of unhinged evil?" Kaeli asked. "There has to be another solution. It is not up to us—not up to *you*—to destroy other worlds." Her eyes turned to Arenol, remembering what her uncles had told her years ago. "The Eye will kill us if you summon that sleeping power while we're connected with it."

Arenol's lips formed a soft smile. "And I'm willing to make that sacrifice, Kaeli, to sever our world from theirs. Arabella would have done the same thing. Just as you will. That darkness killed my sister, and I will gladly join her in death if it means destroying the entity."

"You see?" Dorion said. "There isn't another way. We knew it, and the mages knew it. It all came down to this moment in time. There is no joy or satisfaction to be found in any of this. But we are about to face more extinction if we don't act now! These ruthless pirates and their allies took the lives of both my brothers...your own family. I'm not saving any of them."

Kaeli blinked. She had been fighting in the sky with Nomryd, so she hadn't even noticed who had fallen.

"I'm sorry about Merrick," Kaeli said, looking around. She didn't see his body anywhere, so she looked back at Dorion. "It didn't have to be like this. No one had to die." There was an ache in her chest. "Kade and Merrick didn't have to die. You had plenty of time to stop all of this. Instead of talking to the people from

Earth, you decided to torture and assault—" Her nose wrinkled in disgust at the thought of him hurting those women. "This delusion of invasion has corrupted you completely. You've caused enough death."

"*Everyone* dies," he said. "Your new friends have disrupted our lives and caused losses that can never be brought back. It's time they face the consequences of entering my empire and spilling *their* evil onto this land."

Arenol waved her hand back and forth, magic spilling and circling until a portal opened beside her and Dorion. Kaeli saw a bright-blue sky and, far below, its watery twin, with tiny, white-cresting waves.

"They call it the Sea of Zemira," Dorion said. "Their final resting place."

A sudden cry came from behind her as Kaeli strained to stand up and stop her father.

"Kaeli!"

She froze.

As Kaeli turned toward the voice, a storm of emotions came to her. The power tethering her to the Eye made it difficult for her to move.

A tall woman emerged from the forest with light-brown skin and shining black hair that reached the middle of her back. The woman looked as though she hadn't slept in weeks. Her hands were tightly clenched, and deep purple circles shone under her eyes. But she was still beautiful. The woman smiled at Kaeli, and tears streamed down her cheeks. Kaeli felt the bond tug at her chest, and her heart warmed. *Home*.

"M-mother?" she stammered.

She was there.

Her mother was *truly* there...and she had found her.

Anaru stepped forward, her hands up. "Dorion, close the portal. Now! Order Arenol to release her."

Kaeli took one step toward her mother, finally shaking off the shock that locked her up before she felt a whip of power latch onto her throat and pull her back, where she landed at Dorion's feet.

"No!" Anaru shouted, running toward Kaeli, but Arenol flicked her free hand, and a wave of magic snaked the ground and seized Anaru's legs, locking her mid-stride. Kaeli struggled to move, but Arenol's ropes held firm. She attempted to probe Arenol for any weakness, but her powers weren't strong enough—she was trapped.

"Enough," Anaru pleaded. "Let her go!"

Dorion wrapped a hand around Kaeli's throat, lifting her to stand. She felt the breath in her lungs cut off, burning as she struggled for air. While Kaeli hated the man she had called "Father" all her life, she had never imagined he would lay a hand on her like this. He had always been unloving toward her, but this was a new level of cruelty. Kaeli tried to pry his fingers off her throat, but he only gripped harder, sending waves of pain into her head.

Dorion was not bluffing; he would kill her without remorse. He would claim her life and a million others without batting an eye.

When Anaru summoned her dragon fire, Dorion tightened his grip on Kaeli's throat. "Ah. Ah. Ah," he said. "Make a move, and I will toss your bastard child into that portal, right into monster-infested waters. At the same time, I will use her magic against her to destroy the very world she'll fall into. If the impact doesn't kill her first, I had Arenol suppress her shifting abilities."

Anaru dropped her magic instantly and fell to her knees. "Punish *me*," she pleaded, tapping her chest. "That's what you wanted all along, isn't it? Then punish me. Not her."

Dorion threw his head back and howled with laughter. "This *is* your punishment, Anaru. You came all this way to find Kaeli just to have me kill her in front of you. It's fucking beautiful." He cocked his head. "She's only been good for one thing, helping me close these portals once and for all. Once I break the link that ties the realms, my reign as emperor of Dragão Terra will be absolute."

Kaeli's mother tightened her fists again and snarled, her tired eyes burning bright gold.

"Gods, Anaru," he said. "You know, for many years, I mourned your loss. Then there would be brief moments of delusion where I would—somehow—convince myself that you were still alive. I never lied to Kaeli that you died, just how, because you falling through that portal felt like I'd watched you die, even though there was a glimmer of hope burning inside me occasionally that you landed somewhere safe. And then, when this crew of creatures came to our world and shared that you were, indeed, still alive...Oh, what relief I felt. Do you want to know why?" His words were laced with venom. "It's because I *knew* you would return someday and find Kaeli. I *knew* you would find yourself here just to watch what I was about to do. Of course, I had other ways I had planned to kill her. This seemed much more brutal."

"You bastard." Kaeli winced in his tight grip, but Dorion ignored her. His focus remained on her mother.

"If it weren't for you, Anaru," he continued, "our world would have taken a different path. You fucked a mage when you were destined to be mine and had this abomination, who was the reason our world was left in shambles." Dorion's eyes, rife with hatred, locked on Kaeli's, but there was a hint of hurt there as well.

Kaeli expected nothing from Dorion, especially unconditional love, but right then, hearing those words come from his lips made her stomach twist in disgust, and her heart broke into a thousand pieces.

Kaeli sniffled, letting her emotions break free. "You never loved me, did you?" Kaeli asked. "All the times you tried to convince me I was your daughter and that you were just trying to protect me..." Her words trailed off as she turned to him while he eased up slightly on her throat. "It was all a lie to control me."

Dorion shrugged. "How could I love you?" he said with a scoff. "You're just like your mother. A rebellious little bitch who should have stayed quiet and let the real leaders do what was right."

Arenol began to chant, raising the relic over her head. The golden light poured out in pulses that nearly blinded everyone. Her chanting became louder as the magic swelled, infusing with the swirling vortex of the portal. Kaeli's blood chilled as the power of the orb vibrated in her chest, using her magic to amplify it. They only had minutes before everyone died.

*Mazie* would die.

"It's that simple, Anaru," Dorion said. "Once the portal is sealed, everyone from Earth will disappear into nothing. Doing so will pull out the darkness within the Elven warrior who's out there somewhere, doing who knows what to my people. You brought that darkness here; now you must pay for your crimes. We won't have to worry about more creatures coming from other realms, and we can finally be at peace. Then you can live with the fact that I killed your daughter while being tied up to my bed for the rest of your fucking existence, giving me the only thing that matters anymore: a male heir that can carry on my legacy."

Kaeli's heart pounded as Dorion pulled her back against his body and turned to the howling vortex. As a strong wind tore through the portal, Kaeli looked through it, seeing the vast ocean far below her feet.

"Goodbye, Kaeli. I'm sorry it had to come to this." Dorion released her throat and lifted his leg as a black ring formed around the vortex. The link was severing. Kaeli struggled to disconnect her mage power right as Dorion kicked her in her back and sent her flying toward the portal.

A scream filled her ears as Kaeli flew through the opening, the smell of sea and wind filling her nose. As she fell, Kaeli accepted the death looming before her, but a black mist slammed into her back and wrapped itself around her waist. With a sudden jolt, she was forcefully thrown back onto the soft grass, and her magic snapped free from the orb.

Kaeli looked up to see a second strand of mist shaped like black claws swoop past her and slam into Arenol. The mage barely had a breath to scream before the mist gripped her neck, and her power seeped out through her skin, latching onto the mist and trailing through it like water down a stream. Her magic was draining from her body.

*Oh, my Gods*, Kaeli thought. Right as the last of the power left Arenol, the black mist wrapped around her throat and snapped her neck, her body hitting the grass.

Dorion roared in fury and lunged toward the offending magic, fire curling around his mouth and elongating his teeth. A low, rumbling laugh filled the air as a wall of black smoke crashed into him, knocking him back. As he rose to attack, the blackness slammed through his chest. Dorion looked up, a trickle of blood coming from his mouth. Kaeli heard the wet snap of his spine and watched him collapse, red blood pooling beneath his head.

Kaeli grimaced at her father's body and let out a sigh. Once the portal closed, everyone whom the mage's power had frozen collapsed to the ground and looked up at them.

"Zakari, no!" Anaru cried out as Kaeli felt a fist grip her hair and pull her off the ground. "You promised me. Please! Don't! No!"

Kaeli's heart raced as Mazie staggered upright, brandishing her sword and lunging in her direction. Kaeli held up her hand.

*"No, Mazie. Don't save me! Wait."* She pushed the thought to Mazie. The pirate blinked slowly and lowered her sword, nodding slightly.

"I promised you I would take you to see your daughter. And I did. Now she's my only hope without destroying Earth." The man who had introduced himself as Aiden now held her in place—or at least he looked like Aiden. Kaeli felt the dark presence inside him—the same uneasiness she'd sensed before. Only now, it had taken over Aiden's body entirely.

"Don't hurt her, please," Anaru continued to plead, her eyes welling up. Stepping forward, her face contorted with sheer desperation, her mouth trembling. "She's all I have left. Zakari..."

"Shhh," he hushed. "She might survive. She might not." Zakari brushed Kaeli's hair away from her face and ran his hand gingerly over her cheek. "Kaeli, my name is Zakari. In a few short moments, I'm going to unleash my power on the guild. They will give me what I need to become whole again, and once I'm restored to my true essence, you will take your magic and strip me from this elf and then destroy me."

Zakari smiled as Nola, Janelle, Elijah, and Lincoln shouted simultaneously, pleading for him to release her. Xander moved forward as Bay fluttered around him in a frenzy, while he held up his hands, begging Zakari to stop.

But he wouldn't listen; he only held on tighter.

"You should thank me, honestly," Zakari said. "I don't want Earth to be destroyed. I never have. I saved everyone just now. In the end, you're alive. Now, *you* might not survive this, Kaeli, but your friends will have a home to return to. That's a better outcome than what Dorion had planned out, right?"

*It is,* Kaeli thought to herself. She nodded, and Zakari released her. She fell to the ground and looked at Zakari. "I'll do it," she said immediately.

"Kaeli, no!" Anaru shouted. "I swear to the gods, Zakari!" She stepped toward him. But he raised his hand, and her body froze, silencing her pleas.

"Aiden!" Janelle cried out, moving closer. "Please—"

"Ah, the sister," Zakari interrupted her, flicking his wrists and causing everyone to fall to their knees, the power keeping them back. Kaeli's gaze drifted toward Janelle, who had shock painted all over her face as she stared at her brother's eyes. Then there were Mazie and the others—all bound by his magic—all people who would likely get hurt if she didn't agree to his terms.

Kaeli felt her chest tighten as she wondered who he'd hurt first if she didn't do what he asked.

"Tell me what to do," Kaeli said. "I'll do..." Her words trailed off as a faint movement drew her attention to her left. Bay flew off Xander's shoulder, whipping past Mazie to fly toward Zakari.

"Bay, no!" Mazie screamed. "Stop!"

Bay rushed forward to save Kaeli, but Zakari's hand shot out with lightning speed, seizing the pixie tightly around her waist. In a swift motion, his fingers squeezed around her, cracking her spine, then dropped her lifeless body to the ground.

# 51

## MAZIE

It took a moment for Mazie to comprehend what had just happened. Bay's body was on the grass, broken, and her wings were utterly still. Mazie's tears streamed down her face, but she couldn't make a sound. Her body felt disconnected, like her brain could neither comprehend the sight nor force her limbs to move. Bay.

Her pixie.

She was dead.

*She was dead.*

The more that realization sunk into her mind, the more everything around her felt distorted. She looked up at Zakari with no emotion on his face.

He killed her friend.

Her family.

Her sister.

There was so much death. Why the hell was she always surrounded by death?

Mazie's shaky fingers gripped her sword. She suddenly felt her legs and moved, pushing back the power he held over them. Elijah reached out to stop her as she charged forward.

Zakari shot out a band of smoke, but she brought her sword down, knocking the magic to the side with the blade. The magic struck the ground, burning the grass into ash. Mazie didn't care. She didn't care about anything else but driving her sword into his evil heart.

As Zakari bared his teeth, Mazie sprinted forward, kicking off a tree into a powerful leap, descending upon Zakari, and driving the gleaming blade deep into his chest.

It contained all her pent-up feelings. Pain. Anger. Grief.

A broken heart.

As Aiden's body fell to the ground, the black smoke that held everyone back cleared, allowing the crew to run toward them. Though her friends and what mages were left alive now stood around her, the sound of their hushed voices faded into the background, her eyes fixated on Aiden's shirt. She watched the slow, steady spread of blood staining the fabric across his chest. It should have given her some sense of revenge for Bay, but it didn't, not even the slightest bit. The pain just tore away at her as she placed her hand on Bay's tiny chest, her little body no longer moving.

"Kaeli!" Anaru cried out, grabbing her wrist and pointing. Kaeli sprang to her feet as utter blackness poured from Aiden's mouth and eyes. It thickened and bubbled like tar, spreading slowly across the field.

Mazie looked around numbly. Mages started to flee from the entity, making their way into the forest so they could teleport. But the black sludge moved with deadly swiftness, seizing mages one by one. With each kill, their bodies crumpled and twisted, their magic being forcefully pulled and absorbed by Zakari's. Other mages tried to ward off the darkness with their powers, but all that did was help him feed and grow from them.

Kaeli rushed to the field and held up her hands.

"Kaeli," Mazie said, finally looking up, "what are you doing?"

"He's killing them, Mazie," she said. "I'm ending this."

Mazie touched her hand, taking in those blue eyes. "You can't." She let out a hard sob. "I don't want to lose you, too. Bay…" Mazie's voice failed her.

Kaeli pressed her lips against Mazie's, claiming her mouth and tongue in a wave of passion and grief. "It'll be okay."

Kaeli turned back and kept her powers hovering at her fingertips. "Zakari!" she shouted. "You wanted to perish from existence. Now, take your fucking death with you!"

She quickly channeled her mage powers into a thick black ball. With a scream, she released a blast of energy that surrounded Zakari's magic and pulled him toward her.

He was much stronger now from sucking out the power of those who fled. Mazie felt the energy vibrate around them.

But as the power pulled from Kaeli's hands, she fell to her knees, gasping for air.

Using that amount of power was killing her.

Mazie stood and sprinted toward Kaeli, trying to stop her, but a great force of energy threw her back. Zakari's power now circled around Kaeli like a storm.

Mazie hit the ground hard, and before she could scramble upright, Elijah was already running past her, his magic flowing down his hands and arms. He crossed over the energy barrier and slammed his hand onto the earth, using his power to encircle Zakari and hold him.

The entity roared but held out his arms, finally surrendering to his fate. He had taken what he needed from the mages, and he was ready to die.

Elijah rushed to Kaeli's side and grabbed her hand. Together, they unleashed all their power.

Their magic flowed through his darkness and broke it into fragments of shadows. With a final burst of black light, Zakari vanished into thin air, leaving nothing behind but a scattering of ashes that swiftly disappeared with the wind.

Mazie pressed a hand to her chest and fell to one knee. She turned to look at Bay's body again, lying on the grass. Kaeli had survived, but...

*Bay.*

She needed to get back to Bay.

Mazie stumbled back to where Bay lay on the grass. She knelt next to Xander, who had covered his eyes. He wept softly, the tears leaking through his pressed palm. Mazie gently picked the pixie up and pressed her to her cheek. Loud, heart-wrenching sobs escaped her.

The pain in her heart was so immense that Mazie wished for death. To join Bay in oblivion so the torment would stop.

A hand gripped her shoulder, and Kaeli knelt beside her.

"Mazie, I'm so sorry. All of this is my fault," Kaeli whispered. "But there might be a way for *you* to bring her back."

Mazie shook her head, barely able to breathe. As she sobbed, she felt everyone's eyes on her while clutching her friend's body.

Everyone was there: Lincoln, Nola, Janelle, and Elijah. But it felt like she was alone with Bay in an endless void, just the two of them.

Her mind returned to the battle, when she begged Bay to sprinkle pixie dust on her. She had yelled at her because Bay refused to do it. Gods, how would she ever live with that? "I can't bring her back, Kaeli. I don't have magic." She choked on every word. "My pixie is dead. My *friend* is dead."

Kaeli reached out and cupped Mazie's cheek, forcing her to look at her. Mazie could barely see through her tears. "But you do. It's within you. You're just afraid."

She *was* afraid. Mazie couldn't bring back her sister, so how could Kaeli be sure she could do it with Bay? Her heart dropped to her stomach as she looked down at Bay's body. The pixie's tiny eyes were closed, her little wings broken, and her pixie dust was gone.

With desperation burning in her chest, Mazie gently placed her back on the grass. In the corner of her eye, she saw Janelle rush to Aiden's body. She clutched his bloodstained shirt, shaking him relentlessly as if that would make him open his eyes.

"What do I do?" Janelle wept, looking up at Kaeli. "Help me." Janelle placed her hand on Aiden's chest, letting Elven light flow inside him. "I can't do this. Gods! What do I do?"

Mazie carefully picked up Bay and carried her next to Aiden's body, placing them beside each other. She took a deep, shaky breath, forcing her body to calm down. With certainty in her voice, Mazie looked at Janelle. "Then we do this together."

The women took each other's hands while pressing their palms flush against Bay's and Aiden's bodies.

"I don't feel shit," Mazie said, fighting the disappointment. She was *meant* to know what to do—how to bring Bay back, but she felt nothing. No instincts, no natural knowledge. "What the fuck am I supposed to do?"

Janelle released her hand and looked over at her. "Your family were green witches, yes?"

Mazie nodded.

"Then use the earth," she said. "Put your hand on the ground and focus there."

Hesitantly, Mazie touched the grass, feeling the lush green brush against her skin. She hadn't used that kind of power since she was a child. Centering herself, she allowed the grass to move over her skin to reach for the gifts her father had given her.

As she placed her fingertips on Bay's chest again, she felt a delicate electric sensation tingling through her hand that touched the earth. It slowly traveled up her arm and grazed the nape of her neck. Looking down, she noticed a cluster of tiny mushrooms sprouting around everyone, while colorful flowers bloomed on the grass between their knees and feet.

"Mazie, look," Janelle said, using her head to gesture to Mazie's arms. Mushrooms grew through her skin, sprouting from her pores, and grass prickled at the surface of her body.

Mazie released the earth, placed her full hand on Bay's body again, and centered that power until she released it into her. While she did that, Janelle rested her hands on Aiden and moved her Elven light to retrieve his from the depths of darkness.

Power circled as foliage and greenery grew thick and tall all around them.

"Here," Elijah said, sitting beside Janelle and placing his hand on Aiden's chest with her.

Janelle nodded. Together, they weaved their power and pushed it into Aiden's body, washing him in black and white light.

As the last ounce of power left Mazie's fingers, she opened her eyes. While the pirate knelt there, everything around her seemed to fade into silence, except for the rise and fall of Bay's chest.

Mazie stared in shock. She didn't dare to hope for anything just yet, needing another moment for the sight to sink into her mind. Tears flowed down her cheeks as she let out a breath, overwhelmed by the rapid flutter of Bay's wings and watching her eyes open.

Aiden groaned as his eyes peered up at the sky right before turning to his sister and gripping her hand. "Nelle," he whispered, and she let out a hard sob before burying her face in his chest.

Bay flew up from the grass, and Mazie gently took her into her arms and cradled her to her chest. It was as if nothing had happened to her.

"You scared the shit out of me," Mazie sobbed, embracing the pixie gently. "Don't you ever do that again. You hear me?"

"I'm sorry, Mazie," Bay said, her tiny voice barely audible. "I wanted to save Kaeli."

"You're not supposed to save us. Just...don't ever leave me again, okay?" Mazie looked down at Bay, who nodded. As Mazie released her from the embrace, Bay settled on her usual spot—by her shoulder, just slightly under her hair.

When Mazie looked over, Kaeli was kneeling on the ground, pulling her mother into her arms.

Not everyone was healed.

Anaru was dying.

# 52

## KAELI

Anaru wiped her daughter's tears, trickling down her cheeks. "What's happening to you?" Kaeli asked.

Ever since she was a little girl, she imagined what her mother was like, and now that she was finally beside her, Kaeli couldn't comprehend the possibility of losing her.

"You were fine a moment ago. Did Zakari's power touch you? I don't...I don't understand." Her eyes quickly swept over her mother's body, looking for any wounds that could be responsible for her rapid decline.

"I was already dying, Kaeli," Anaru said softly. She reached for the hem of her tunic and pulled the fabric up. Kaeli heard a collective gasp behind her as she stared at a large, bloody wound. There were signs of cauterization, but it did nothing to conceal the deep, black veins that traveled along her stomach. Kaeli realized that her mother's skin was now fiery-hot with fever. "Now that Zakari is dead, the power he granted me to keep me alive and subservient is gone. It was just enough power to see your face and tell you I love you since I never had the chance to do it when you were born." Her mother reached for a stray strand of her hair, tucking it behind her ear.

Kaeli shook her head, feeling panic rumble from her chest. "No," she said. "No. *No.* This isn't right. Look, if you die, then we can bring you back. There is enough magic here to bring you back. I'll...I'll get help. People will help me bring you back."

*This can't be the end,* she thought, looking at the severity of the wounds.

She and Anaru had so much to catch up on...so many memories yet to be made. Kaeli wanted to hear everything about her life and real father. This short period granted to them was not enough.

"We can't, Kaeli," Janelle said gently, rubbing her shoulders soothingly. "My magic only worked on my brother because his Elven light is tied to mine. Elijah's magic acted as an amplifier to his fated mate, and it's apparent that he couldn't harness such power himself."

Kaeli turned to Mazie and pleaded with her eyes. No words were spoken. Mazie looked torn as she stared at her, silent.

"I'll try," Mazie said finally. "Bay is so small, and that drained me. I don't know if I have the strength. But I'll try for you." Her exhaustion showed clearly on her face and how her hands trembled.

"No," Anaru said, bringing Kaeli's attention back to her. "No, you won't let her do that. I can feel your heart right now, Kaeli. You're falling in love with her, and I'll not be responsible for ending Mazie's life, so I can be resurrected. I won't allow it." Anaru's hand found Kaeli's. "I have lived a long life, my sweet daughter. I have experienced love, true friendships, childbirth, pain, heartbreak, and everything in between. My only wish was to meet you before I died, and Zakari granted me that wish. I can't ask for anything more than that."

Kaeli wiped her tears and looked over at Mazie, nodding. She didn't want to hurt Mazie, but watching her mother die after just getting her back felt like the world was falling apart. How could the gods be so cruel?

She dreamt of her mother for as long as she could remember. Why did it have to be like this? Why did it have to be cut so painfully short?

Kaeli reached out and brushed her mother's dark hair away. She held back sobs, not wanting to make the moment harder.

Lincoln moved beside them, placed his hand on Anaru's chest, and closed his eyes. "Thank you," he said. "Thank you for everything you taught me. Being your rider for these past two years was an honor."

Kaeli looked around as everyone else gathered around them, and they all knelt in silence and solidarity. Even the mages came to say their goodbyes before the fallen dragon. She loved each one of them despite all the prejudice and mistrust between the two groups. Anaru had loved them and united their people with Kaeli's birth.

"Lincoln," Anaru said, her voice growing steadily weaker as she reached up to cup his cheek. "It wasn't just your courage and strength that made me choose you as my rider. I knew you had the Kroneon; it was my only possible way to get home if needed. My need for revenge against the man who stole everything from me was too great. It was selfish and something I cannot take back."

"Anaru, it's okay," he said.

"No, it's not. Please let me finish. I grew to love you all, and through that, you gave me a family after I was robbed of that all those years before." She coughed, and a tiny bit of blood seeped out of her mouth. "Thank you. Thank you for loving me when I didn't deserve it."

While tears streamed down his cheeks, Lincoln clutched his chest, looking into Anaru's eyes. "We are but imperfect beings in an imperfect world. You may have broken our bond, but this love will forever be in our hearts."

Kaeli turned to her mother as Lincoln moved back to kneel beside Nola. "I love you," she said. "I didn't have to be raised by you to know that. Deep down, I felt you were alive out there, even though Dorion said you were dead. I just felt it, you know? A part of me knew it in my heart and never gave up hope. I love you, Mother."

"My sweet child," Anaru said gently, smiling as the color drained from her face. "You're everything I ever imagined. You remind me so much of your father and everything he stood for."

Kaeli's heart thudded at the mention of her father. She knew little about him except what the mages shared...only his name. Julian.

"Julian loved you long before you were born," Anaru said.

Kaeli sniffled as more tears streamed down her face. She could barely see her mother now as her eyes glistened, but she wanted to hear more of her voice. She needed to memorize it for the rest of her life. "He had a beautiful name. Will you tell me about him?"

Anaru smiled. "His hair was the color of snow, similar to yours, without the hints of blue." Her hand attempted to reach Kaeli's hair, but her strength had failed. "His eyes were like frozen glass that shimmered in the sunlight when he laughed. I fell in love the moment I saw him. He had such a pure, beautiful soul. He was my *true* mate until the end." Anaru paused, her tone quieter as she continued, "He knew I was fated to another and risked his life to save me...to save *you*. In the last minutes before his death, he made a sacrifice that I have had to live with my entire life, but it was to protect you. Julian could feel your power before you were born, and he was ready to do anything for you, even at the cost of his life. That was the kind of man he was," she whispered. "He loved us both, Kaeli. He would have been so proud of you, just as I am. I am so, so proud of you...."

Kaeli gave her a soft smile as Anaru's chest rose once more before her body sank into her daughter's arms, and a fire flickered out.

# 53

## MAZIE

After helping Mazie and Xander bury the bodies of the fallen, the crew gathered in the courtyard of what was left of the castle, waiting to go home.

Kaeli didn't just have to bury mages she had protected over the last ten years but also her mother. She stayed behind at the funeral pyre, singing the same warrior song from when they said goodbye to Tegan. After the ceremony, Kaeli would take her mother's ashes and inter them in the royal crypt, next to her grandparents and ancestors.

Although Kaeli said little, her face showed her heartbreak. Mazie knew the feeling all too well; she remembered what she needed when her sister died—time alone with her to say her last goodbyes. In the meantime, Mazie and the crew gathered what they needed to head home.

"Where is Kaeli now?" Nola asked as Elijah, Janelle, and Lincoln walked to the field beside the courtyard to wait. Lincoln's expression was grim as he grieved over the loss of Anaru, too.

"She left the tomb just a short moment ago to head back into the palace," Mazie said softly. She didn't want to rush Kaeli as she said goodbye.

"And how is she holding up?" Nola asked.

"As well as you can imagine," Mazie responded, crossing her arms. Bay rested on her shoulder. "She's heartbroken. She only had a few minutes to spend with her mother. It wasn't the reunion she hoped for." Mazie wished she could ease Kaeli's grief and take some of that pain away. But for now, she could only be there to comfort.

Nola raised her brow. "Are you not going to say goodbye, then?" she asked. "Elijah is itching to open that portal and take us back home. It should happen soon."

Mazie shook her head. "It's incredible that Elijah held that kind of magic this whole time. Zakari's power was snuffing it out. Once the darkness lifted, his magic could breathe again. I wonder if the Newick sorcerers will notice anything?"

Nola smiled softly, sympathy shining in her eyes. "Elijah plans to visit Myloria upon our return and see what sorcerers stayed after Kieran died. If there is peace within that power now, they might need someone to lead them."

Mazie nodded and looked up at the castle, sighing heavily.

"Go on, Mazie. She's waiting for you. We'll see you in fifteen minutes. Go say your goodbye."

*Goodbye.* Mazie's stomach churned at the word, and a weird, chest-tightening feeling overcame her. Could she truly leave Kaeli behind?

Because Kaeli was right, Mazie could travel to wherever she wanted to, but Mazie knew she'd never find another like her.

She turned to the castle and headed inside the west wing, where the grand hall remained intact. As she walked up the staircase, she contemplated what she would say to Kaeli. Once she reached the entrance to the hall, her breath hitched as she took in the sight before her.

Kaeli was seated on a large throne made of black glass, flanked by two golden dragons holding the sun. She was in the middle of a conversation with a couple of mages and shifters who had sworn allegiance to her. Atop her shining white hair was a silver crown with red and blue gemstones that glittered in the sunlight.

*She really is a goddess,* Mazie thought as she cleared her throat. *She will do wonderful things for Dragão Terra and her people.*

Kaeli's smile tore at her heart a little before the dragon dismissed the group and made her way toward Mazie.

"Hail, the Empress of Fire, Kaeli Rylanthion," Mazie teased.

A quiet chuckle escaped Kaeli's lips. "You know, I never thought I'd ever see myself leading anyone in this world. Now...now I'm leading everyone."

Mazie closed the space between them and took Kaeli's hand in hers. The warmth trickled through her fingers like a campfire on a starry night.

"You were the leader of hundreds of mages, Kaeli, inside a hidden mountain you all built together. Don't be silly."

"Not like this," Kaeli said, shaking her head as her hand squeezed Mazie's. "This was meant for my mother, not me. Even if she were still alive, I don't think I could do this."

"Of course, you can," she said. "My Gods, Kaeli, you were born for this. Those people out there have endured a lifetime of torment because of Dorion and his cruel laws. It's now up to you to change that and save them. And you *will* do it right. Your people trust you, and you care about them. That's all you need to be a good ruler."

"Do you truly think so?" Kaeli questioned her, regardless. "You think I was made for this?"

"You created an entire city where life blossomed, and mages could seek refuge from the terrors of the outside world," Mazie said. "You defeated Zakari."

Kaeli let out a soft laugh and stood. After what she just endured, the sound of her laughter made Mazie's heart flutter. "I couldn't have done it without you," she said.

"I'm just a pirate at your service, my empress," Mazie joked before Kaeli surprised her by planting a kiss on her lips.

Mazie relished the taste of her lips. Her hands found Kaeli's hips, drawing her closer. It was so easy for Mazie to lose herself in that beautiful woman, even when she knew she'd have to say goodbye in a few brief minutes.

Kaeli broke the kiss, but her lips still hovered over hers. Her tone was pleading as she said, "Don't leave."

Mazie didn't know how to take Kaeli's words. *Don't leave*? How could she not? This wasn't her home, even if Kaeli made her feel like it was. Mazie's hand remained on Kaeli's hips, but her expression was torn.

"Kaeli, I can't leave my captain," she said. "I'm sorry. I have...I have an obligation—a duty. And to leave it—it would be selfish. It would be ungrateful and against everything I stand for. Even if it's for a woman that I lo—" Her words cut off as she realized what she was about to say. It was so natural and effortless that she had barely noticed until she nearly said it. "I just can't leave."

Mazie hadn't felt that kind of pain in a while. This pain felt like her own soul was being ripped from her. Like she would never be herself again. She wanted to stay and get to know Kaeli better, but she just...couldn't.

"I'll walk you to the field, then," Kaeli said, her eyes shimmering with unshed tears. "It's the least I can do."

Mazie felt like she would choke if she said anything else, so she nodded. Kaeli took Mazie's hand, and they left the castle together. The walk to the field was brief, but in Mazie's head, it lasted an eternity. And she wanted it to last even longer. She didn't want it to end at all.

But it did. Kaeli and Mazie walked over to where the crew was waiting. Elijah nodded and lifted his hands, drawing energy to create a portal to Zemira. Slowly, a vortex of swirling mists formed, opening into their world.

*Home.* Mazie forced down her burning tears.

Lincoln stepped up and bowed to Kaeli when she gripped Mazie's hand, the portal still vibrant and strong. "Thank you, Kaeli, for everything you've done," he said, straightening up and turning to Xander, who stepped by his cousin's side. "Xander, to you, too. You saved our lives. We can never repay you for everything you've done."

Mazie released Kaeli's hand as she stepped forward and hugged Xander, while Bay flew over and gently kissed him on the cheek.

She then turned to see Janelle wrap her arms around Elijah. Knowing they had separated the last time they had ventured through a portal, it was no surprise that they refused to stray away from each other. Bay flew back to Aiden and perched on his shoulder.

The look in Aiden's eyes was clear. He carried a lot of guilt, which only proved that he was, indeed, Aiden again. Zakari's mark on his soul would likely never heal, but he could one day learn to bear it. And Janelle and the others would help him.

"Are you ready, Mazie?" Lincoln asked. "Or do you need a minute?"

Mazie was far from ready. She should have been happy that she was heading home, but she wasn't. The pirate could barely comprehend the thought of leaving Kaeli behind. She tried to—she honestly did—but Mazie concluded that life without Kaeli would be one massive...shithole. She looked back at Bay, who only smiled at her and gave her a nod, like she already knew her decision had been made.

"No," Mazie said at last. "No, I'm not ready yet. And I think I'm going to need a lot longer than a minute."

Kaeli's face broke into a wide, elated grin, and Bay fluttered from Aiden, landing on Mazie's shoulder. Her proclamation had been spoken, and Mazie's heart glowed with joy and relief.

As Mazie reached out and took Kaeli's hand in hers, the emotions carried her away at the mere touch of her hand.

"You're going to stay?" Kaeli whispered.

Mazie stepped forward and gently cupped her cheek as she nodded. "If this place turns out to be shit, you can just open that portal and send me back. Right?"

They all laughed behind them, and Kaeli nodded with a wide grin. "So, does that also mean you'll court me?" she asked teasingly.

"Court you?" Mazie repeated. "Oh, Kaeli. I don't want to just court you." She tucked a strand of hair behind Kaeli's ear. "I want to spend the rest of my life by your side."

Kaeli leaned in, gently kissing Mazie's lips. She then rested her forehead on Mazie's. "Then we rule this planet together. Forever."

# 54

## JANELLE

Everything seemed different when they returned to Earth, as if she were seeing it through fresh eyes.

King Liam had left Myloria with his soldiers and had taken control of the palace in Terth, Zemira's capital city. It was finally peaceful, with no wars or creatures ripping through their towns. The land flourished, and so did the people. A good ruler had done wonders for his kingdom in a few short weeks.

Before their departure to Myloria, Nola and Lincoln traveled to Baylin, where her parents, Duncan and Val, lived. They helped her parents pack their belongings and moved them into the castle. Liam made the arrangements with Elijah right before the former king had abdicated the throne and passed the crown to him.

Nola spotted her parents waiting for them at the castle gates and rushed to them, leaping into her father's arms. She had been gone for almost a month, but it felt like a lifetime. "We are here to stay," Nola promised.

Back at the port, Elijah gently grasped Janelle's hand and led her to the end of the dock, carefully setting their bags down beside him.

"Lincoln bought you a ship?" she asked, turning to him. "A ship? For you?"

"Stop looking so surprised, my love." Elijah looked slightly offended, narrowing his eyes. "Well...he bought *us* a ship. At least, until he steals it back because he misses sailing too much."

Janelle let out a laugh. "You're a pirate now?" she said, a teasing smile lingering on her lips.

Elijah chuckled and gripped her hip, pulling her toward him. "Fuck no," he said. "But with a ship, we can see the world now. We can do whatever the hell we want. I like the idea of not knowing where we'll be tomorrow or next week, as long as we do it together."

Aiden moved past them, grabbing the bags on the ground. "Let's go," he said flatly. Janelle sighed at the sight of her brother. He tried to act like everything was fine, like he was holding up alright, but deep down, she knew he wasn't okay.

"I need a moment with him," Janelle said to Elijah. "Please give us ten minutes alone before you head up."

"Alright," Elijah said. "The sun sets in an hour. We can be in the next town up the coast by then." He kissed her on the cheek, and she turned to follow Aiden onto the ship.

Janelle followed closely behind Aiden as she stepped onto the gangplank. When they reached the deck, they sat on a bench against the railing and looked at the sea. The soft movement of the waves was soothing, almost hypnotic, as it licked the side of the ship.

"Forgive yourself for what happened," she said. "It wasn't your fault."

Aiden glanced at her before turning back to the sea, but his eyes lacked any forgiveness he could give himself. They just seemed...empty. "The image of her face as Zakari killed her is still etched in my mind. I can still smell her blood. I didn't fight hard enough. It *was* my fault, Janelle, and I must live with it for the rest of my life."

"No one knew the extent of his strength, and I can understand why you couldn't handle such an evil weight. None of us could have." She reached for his hand, giving it a slight squeeze. "We all do the best we can at every given moment. You fought the best you could."

"But it wasn't enough."

"Yet it was all anyone could have asked from you." Janelle looked at him. "You have to find forgiveness within yourself. You can't live the rest of your life like this." She paused. "Tegan wouldn't want you to. If you can't do it for yourself...do it for *her*."

Aiden looked at her once more and gave her a nod. "I promise I'll try."

There was a sincerity in his tone that Janelle hoped would come to fruition. After a moment of the two of them leaning onto each other and taking in the salty air, Elijah came back on the deck. "Aiden?" he called. "How about you steer us east?"

Aiden turned and kissed Janelle on the top of his head. "Thank you, Nelle," he said before standing up. "For everything. Father and Mother would be proud of the woman you've become."

As Aiden turned on his heel and headed toward the helm, Elijah reached out to help Janelle to her feet.

"I don't know what the fuck I'm doing," Elijah said.

"Well, then, I suppose Lincoln giving you a ship wasn't the best idea. I figured you'd know how to run one," Janelle teased him softly. Elijah rolled his eyes, but his arm wrapped around her.

"You're impossible," Elijah murmured against her ear. "And I'll definitely remember this later when we're in the cabin...."

Janelle let out a soft giggle. "Do any of us know what we're doing, though?"

"You're the only thing in my life I'm certain about," he said, lifting his hand as deep purple power hovered over his palm. "The only thing that makes me feel like...me."

Janelle felt her stomach tingle with adoration, but her eyes focused on the power that danced on his palm. "How does that new power feel?" she asked.

"The absence of Zakari's influence makes me feel liberated, like a weight has been lifted. More alive." He leaned forward. "But it doesn't mean I won't use it to kill any fucker who tries to hurt you."

Janelle's smile grew. "Why do I love the sound of that so much?" Elijah gripped her chin and pulled her close, his lips touching hers.

"Here's to finally being free from monsters," he said. "And to finally finding the love of my life."

# EPILOGUE

## NOLA

TWO YEARS LATER

ZEMIRA

Nola's leg nervously tapped against the wooden floor as she stared at her reflection in a massive, gold-adorned mirror. Janelle stood behind her, delicately weaving the strands of Nola's long hair into a beautiful braid.

Nola held the bandana that Lincoln had gifted her long ago, rubbing her fingers over the stitching that bore her pirate name, "Finola, Queen D'Sea."

*Former pirate, I suppose,* she mused, tucking the cloth back into her bodice.

"Gods, Nola. You're going to give yourself a leg cramp if you keep doing that," Kitten said as she clasped a necklace around

Nola's delicate throat. The pendant was a beautiful sapphire that reminded her of the Zemiran Sea, crowned with silver—a gift from King Liam himself for the special occasion.

"I can't help myself," Nola admitted. Lincoln was her other half. The past two years had been good to them, deepening their love for each other. Even so, the thought of walking down the aisle there at the Terth Palace had her every nerve tingling with anxiety.

"I understand," Kitten said, nodding. "It's not every day that King Liam officiates someone's wedding."

She was right. It was unheard of, but with how close the king and Lincoln had grown, King Liam insisted on it. It had been a year and a half since Lincoln had hung up his pirate sword and instead worked at the palace as the king's naval advisor. He didn't *have* to work per se, since King Liam's wealth was technically Lincoln's and his brother's, allowing them to have whatever they needed. However, it gave Lincoln a new purpose in life, and there was no need for pirates in the Sea of Zemira.

"There," Janelle said as she finished braiding her hair. A few delicate flowers peeked between the carefully woven strands, matching Nola's dress. Its snow-white fabric, embellished with exquisite lace and intricate beadwork, gleamed in the sunlight streaming through the window. "Now, stand up. I need to tighten your corset."

Nola smiled as she stood. It was nice to have everyone back together, even if it was just for a day.

Janelle and Elijah now lived in Myloria, so she and Lincoln rarely got to see them anymore. It was okay, though, because they were finally living the ordinary life they ached for all along. Now that Zakari's power was out of the Newick witches, he was helping them learn how to use their magic for good, and the world was a much better place. Even Borenna remained with the witches, lending her power to steer them toward peace with her insightful guidance. Magic was thriving the way it was always meant to, giving the Earth the life and vitality it had been starved of for too long.

Kitten and Boots were now proud parents of two little girls. They had abandoned life on the sea for good and settled in a tiny home overlooking the shore a day's ride from the capital. Neither complained; they were made to be parents and have a family together.

"I can't even find the words to tell you how much you two being here means to me," Nola said as Janelle moved behind her. She clutched the silk laces of her corset and momentarily pushed the air out of Nola's lungs as she tightened them.

"Like we'd ever miss this," Janelle said, entirely focused on getting control of the corset laces. "Elijah and I have seen everything we wanted over the past two years. Now that we're settled in the Newick mansion, teaching the coven how to open portals, there is nowhere we would rather be than here. Newick will be fine without us for a few days. We're family, Nola, and nothing could make us miss this."

"Family is right," Kitten added with a smile. "And like Hill would ever miss a chance to get sloshed and pass out on the fine marble floor of the grand hall."

Nola couldn't help but laugh. "It doesn't surprise me he and Ardley opened a tavern together."

"And it's doing well, too," Kitten said, leaning against the wall. "Ardley barely made it in time to our home to deliver my little

Arcelia." Her words sent another wave of laughter overflowing the room. It was almost easy to forget that some people dear to Nola's heart were missing. *Almost.*

Nola's eyebrows furrowed as a whooshing sound suddenly filled the air, intensifying with each passing second. All three women turned to look at the spot the sound seemed to originate from, but there was only silence. At last, a tiny, fiery circle formed, and Janelle took a protective stance in front of Nola and Kitten as it grew more expansive.

*Not on my wedding day,* Nola said in her thoughts. Her instincts had her ready for danger. The past two years had been peaceful, but it sounded like her wedding day would be anything but.

And then a familiar voice echoed through the portal.

"I hope we're not late."

Nola's mouth dropped open at the sound of Mazie's voice, tears instantaneously forming in her eyes.

*It couldn't be,* she thought.

As soon as Mazie and Kaeli emerged from the portal, with Bay floating above, Nola rushed over and embraced them both. Nola's cheeks hurt from a broad smile that stretched from ear to ear.

Mazie was dressed in an ankle-length deep-purple gown with long sleeves and a swooped neckline, revealing a hint of cleavage. Resting on her head was a tiara glittering with a combination of purple and black gems. Its spikes resembled twisted vines. On the other hand, Kaeli's black dress stopped at her knees, revealing her smooth legs. Her crown perfectly complemented her dress, adorned with vibrant red rubies on its peak.

Floating between the women, Bay wore a simpler ensemble—a sunny yellow dress paired with sparkling silver shoes. Her blonde hair was pulled neatly into a tight ponytail, and she had tucked a tiny pink blossom into the tail, giving her a lovely, springlike presence.

"Gods! I didn't think I'd see the three of you here!" Nola beamed, taking a step back. "I thought you were too busy reforming Dragão Terra."

"True," Kaeli said. "Busy or not, though, we'd never miss this. Dorion has done a lot of damage that still needs to be taken care of, but..." She looked at Mazie, smiling. "We're making it work. When Elijah contacted Mazie to remind us about the wedding...we knew we had to be here."

Mazie nodded. "We left everything in Xander's hands, so technically, things should be fine while we're gone." She gave Nola's arm a light rub. "I only hope you have two extra seats at the wedding....And that there will be some rum afterward."

"Sorry, all the seats are full," Nola said, her hand resting on her chest. "So, I'd like you both to stand beside me with Kitten and Janelle."

Mazie smiled. "Not yet. Something's missing." Mazie reached out her hand and flicked her wrist, allowing a golden power to shimmer against her skin while a purple flower bloomed at her fingertips. "Your *hair* is missing something." The pirate placed the flower through Nola's strands, intertwining it within her braid. "My sister, Bay, loved purple daisies."

Nola smiled at the joy on Mazie's face as she used magic freely and unapologetically.

Her true self.

Everyone she held dear to her heart was now at her wedding. Janelle had even managed to talk Aiden into coming. He was doing better now. From the brief update that Janelle gave her, Nola learned he was slowly learning to forgive himself for what had happened with Tegan. Not only that, but he also allowed himself to fall in love again. With an Elven warrior named Helena, nonetheless. Nola had yet to meet her, but there would be plenty of time after the ceremony.

A soft knock on the door interrupted the women's conversation, and the door creaked open.

Nola's father, Duncan, stepped inside, smiling. His glassy eyes proved he had shed some tears, even if Nola knew he'd try to assure her he didn't.

"They're waiting for you, Nola," he said softly, extending his hand toward her. To her left, Kitten grabbed a bouquet that she handpicked alongside the Zemiran coastline and handed it to Nola. She took the flowers in one hand and linked arms with her father in the other.

"We'll meet you at the ceremony," Janelle said, giving her shoulder a light squeeze as she passed by them. As the rest of the women left, it was just Nola and Duncan.

"You look stunning, Nola," her father told her, his hand squeezing hers. "There are three days I consider the happiest ones of my life. The first was when I met your mother, and the second was when we found you in the sea, and our lives changed for the better...forever." His other hand wrapped around her, pulling her in close. "And the third is happening right now. Though I know Lincoln takes good care of you, I have difficulty letting you go."

"Father...I'll always be with you," Nola said softly. "I'll continue to visit you frequently until we're done traveling, and then I'll settle back at the palace with you. Nothing is really changing."

"I know, I know." Her father made a small, waving gesture with his hand. "It's just a father's nonsense. You'll understand someday *if* you choose to have children."

Hand in hand, they headed to the grand hall of the Terth Palace. The hall echoed with laughter and joy as the guests awaited Nola's arrival. With each movement she made, the floral fragrance became increasingly noticeable in the air. It was as if flowers had sprouted over every surface in the hall. Elegant crystal chandeliers crowned with dozens of candles hung on the high ceiling, casting a soft glimmer over the entrance—several guards lined against the walls, monitoring about two hundred guests.

Nola drew in a shaky breath, trying to ease her nerves, but it was hard to do so when she knew everyone's eyes were about to be on her.

Right then, at the other end of the long aisle, she saw Lincoln, and the world stilled as their gazes met. All the noise faded into the back of her mind. No one else existed but him.

Nola's life didn't truly begin until she met him, and now she would get to spend the rest of it with him by her side.

Until the very end.

# ABOUT THE AUTHOR

D.L. Blade has always been passionate about creative writing, focusing on poetry during her younger years. One night, after having a vivid dream, she was inspired to pick up her pen and write her debut novel, *The Dark Awakening.*

Initially, Blade had focused on writing young adult fiction, but she has since shifted her focus to adult fantasy, paranormal, and dark romance. Through her stories, she takes readers on a journey into a world of unconventional love, morally gray men, and deliciously handsome villains.

When she's not writing, Blade enjoys reading, spending time with her husband and two children, attending rock concerts, and exploring new restaurants in Denver. She dreams of continuing to create exciting novels for her readers and taking them on a journey through the magical realms that spill from the pages of her books.